Ben Kane was born in Kenya and raised there and in Ireland. He studied veterinary medicine at University College Dublin but after that he travelled the world extensively, indulging his passion for ancient history. He now lives in North Somerset with his family. For more information visit www.benkane.net.

Also By Ben Kane:

The Forgotten Legion
The Silver Eagle
The Road to Rome

Spartacus
Spartacus: The Gladiator
Spartacus: Rebellion

Hannibal
Hannibal: Enemy of Rome
Hannibal: Fields of Blood

Hannibal: Clouds of War

BEN KANE

preface

Published by Preface 2014

10 9 8 7 6 5 4 3 2 1

Copyright © Ben Kane 2014

First published in Great Britain in 2014 by Preface Publishing
20 Vauxhall Bridge Road
London, SW1V 2SA

An imprint of The Random House Group Limited

www.randomhouse.co.uk
www.prefacepublishing.co.uk

Addresses for companies within The Random House Group Limited
can be found at www.randomhouse.co.uk

The Random House Group Limited Reg. No. 954009

A CIP catalogue record for this book is
available from the British Library

ISBN 978 1 84809 408 6

The Random House Group Limited supports the Forest Stewardship
Council® (FSC®), the leading international forest-certification organisation.
Our books carrying the FSC label are printed on FSC®-certified paper.
FSC is the only forest-certification scheme supported by the leading
environmental organisations, including Greenpeace.
Our paper procurement policy can be found at:
www.randomhouse.co.uk/environment

Typeset in Fournier MT by SX Composing DTP, Rayleigh, Essex

Printed and bound in Great Britain by Clays Ltd, St Ives plc

For Camilla and Euan, comrades in Northumberland during a dark time. More than a decade later, you're friends still. Enough said.

Republican Italy in the late third century BC

N

A l p s

Placentia CISALPINE
GAUL
Trebia   Padus

Genua   LIGURIA   ITALY

Pisae   A p e n n i n e s   Ariminum

ETRURIA   Lake
Trasimene

CORSICA

Rome   LATIUM
Ostia   Gerunium

SAMNIUM   Cannae
Capua   APULIA
CAMPANIA   Aufidius

SARDINIA

ILLYRICUM

A d r i a t i c   S e a

Brundisium

Tarentum

T y r r h e n i a n
S e a

B R U T T I U M

I o n i a n
S e a

M a r e   Messana
Rhegium

SICILY
Enna

Akragas
Syracuse

I n t e r n u m

Carthage

CARTHAGE

0	50	100	150	200 miles
0	100	200	300 km	

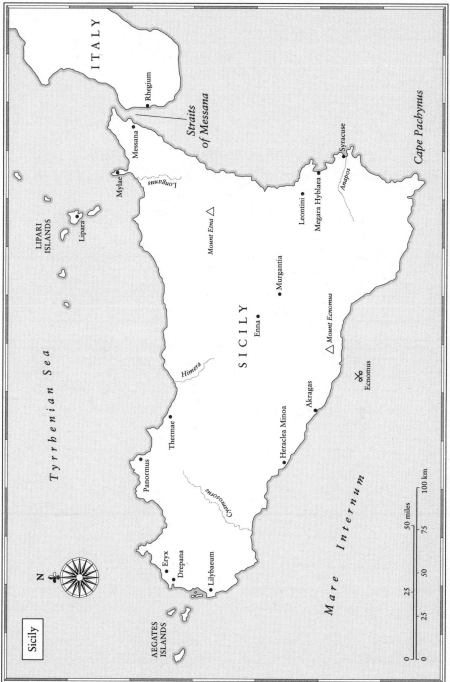

Sicily

ITALY

Rhegium

Straits
of Messana

Messana

Mylae

Longanus

LIPARI
ISLANDS

Lipara

Tyrrhenian Sea

Mount Etna △

Leontini

Megara Hyblaea

Syracuse

Anapos

Cape Pachynus

SICILY

Enna

Murgantia

△ *Mount Ecnomus*

Himera

Akragas

Ecnomus

Heraclea Minoa

Thermae

Panormus

Cynosotus

Eryx

Drepana

Lilybaeum

AEGATES
ISLANDS

Mare Internum

N

0   25   50   75   100 km

0   25   50 miles

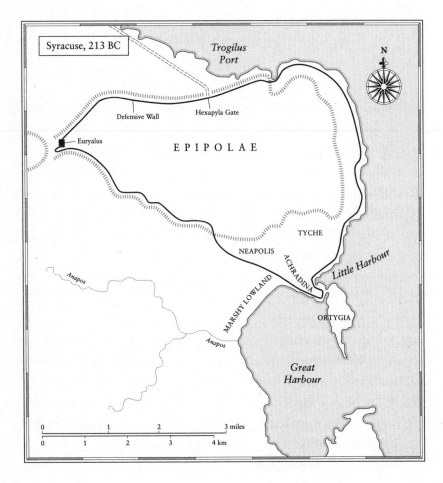

Syracuse, 213 BC

Trogilus Port

Defensive Wall   Hexapyla Gate

Euryalus

E P I P O L A E

N

TYCHE

NEAPOLIS

ACHRADINA

Little Harbour

Anapos

MARSHY LOWLAND

Anapos

ORTYGIA

Great Harbour

0   1   2   3 miles

0   1   2   3   4 km

Prologue

Apulia, southern Italy, summer 216 BC

After their stunning victory over more than eighty thousand Romans, Hannibal had let his soldiers rest for a night and a day and another night. It was as well, thought Hanno, studying the faces of the assembled officers and chieftains, some fifty-odd men. They were Carthaginians, Numidians, Iberians and Gauls. Their faces and arms had been cleansed of blood, and they might have caught up on some sleep, yet to a man they looked shattered. Exhausted. Drained.

Hanno, a lean young soldier with black hair, felt the same way. How could he not? The fighting at Cannae had lasted all day under a burning summer sun. Even when the tide had turned against the Romans, the killing had gone on, because the legionaries had been surrounded. The unrelenting slaughter had finished only when darkness fell, when the Carthaginian soldiers were covered in gore from head to foot, when their horses had been crimson from the bottoms of their necks to their hooves. Gone were the fields of stubble that had been there at dawn; in their place, the fighting had left fields of blood.

The toll on the survivors had been more than physical. More than fifty thousand Romans lay dead twenty stadia hence, but eight thousand of Hannibal's men would never see another dawn either. Hanno's father Malchus had died that day. Hanno stifled the grief that rose within him.

Most of those nearby had suffered the loss of a loved one too; if they had not, it was certain that they had seen close friends and comrades die. Yet it had been worth it. Rome had been dealt a hammer blow the likes of which it had never felt. Its standing army had been reduced by more than two-thirds; one of its consuls had been slain, so too had many hundreds of its ruling class. The devastating news would already be sending tremors through every town and city in Italy. Against all the odds, Hannibal had beaten the largest army ever assembled by the Roman Republic. What would he do next? Since Hannibal had ordered them here, to the open ground before his tent, the same question had been on everyone's lips.

Hanno caught his older brother Bostar's eye. 'Any idea of what he'll say?' he whispered.

'Your guess is as good as mine.'

'Let's hope that he orders us to march on Rome,' interjected Sapho, the oldest of the three siblings. 'I want to burn the damn place to the ground.'

For all that his relationship with Sapho was fractious, Hanno longed to do that too. If the army that had just defeated them so decisively turned up at its gates, surely Rome would surrender?

'First, we need to move our camp further from the battlefield,' said Sapho, wrinkling his nose. 'I'm sick of the stench.'

Hanno grimaced in agreement. The summer's heat would only intensify the ever-present odour of rotting flesh. Nonetheless, Bostar let out a *phhhh* of contempt. 'Hannibal has more on his mind than your offended nostrils!'

'I was making a joke, something you wouldn't understand,' growled Sapho.

Hanno scowled at them both. 'Enough! He's here.' The black-cloaked *scutarii* who served as their general's bodyguard had snapped upright.

A moment's pause, and Hannibal emerged from his tent into the early-morning sunlight. The tired officers raised a rousing cheer. Hanno bellowed for all he was worth; so too did his brothers. Here was a man worth following. A man who had led his army thousands of stadia from Iberia, across Gaul and into Italy, there to heap humiliations upon Rome.

Hannibal was dressed as if for battle. Over his purple tunic, he wore a burnished bronze cuirass; layered linen *pteryges* protected his groin and shoulders and a simple Hellenistic helmet covered his head. A strip of purple fabric covered the space where his right eye should have been. He carried no shield, but was armed with a simple sheathed *falcata*. Hannibal also looked tired, but the pleasure on his broad, bearded face as he met his officers' acclaim seemed genuine. His remaining eye sparkled. Planting his feet a stride apart, he raised his hands.

Silence fell at once.

'Has it sunk in yet?' asked Hannibal.

'What, sir?' Sapho enquired with a wicked grin.

There were loud chuckles, and Hannibal inclined his head with a smile. 'I think you know what, son of Malchus.'

'It's beginning to, sir,' answered Sapho.

Murmurs of agreement; satisfied looks shared. Before the battle, thought Hanno, no one had doubted Hannibal's tactical expertise, but now his abilities seemed to verge on the godlike. Their fifty thousand soldiers had faced twice that number of Romans and come away not just victorious, but all conquering.

'Any time I forget, sir,' added Sapho, 'the smell reminds me of how many of the enemy we killed.'

More laughter.

'We'll be moving camp soon enough, never fear,' said Hannibal. He paused, and the amusement died away.

'Where to, sir? The plain of Mars, outside Rome?' shouted Hanno. He was pleased that many officers nodded in approval, including Maharbal, Hannibal's cavalry commander.

'I know that is what most of you want,' Hannibal answered. 'But that is not my plan. It's nearly two and a half thousand stadia to Rome. The men are exhausted. Our grain mightn't last the journey, let alone feed us once we got there. Rome's walls are high, and we have no siege engines. While we sat outside building them – with empty bellies – the Republic's other legions would be marching to attack us in the rear. By the time that they arrived, we would have to fall back or be caught between them and the city's garrison.'

Hannibal's words fell like lead shot. Hanno's enthusiasm waned before his general's certainty. The same unhappiness was clear in many faces around him, in the muttered words between neighbours.

'It may not come to that, sir,' challenged Maharbal.

A surprised hush fell.

'We've beaten the Romans three times, sir,' Maharbal went on. 'Trounced them at the Trebia, Lake Trasimene and here, at Cannae. They must have lost a hundred thousand men by now. Only the gods know how many equestrians and senators have died, but it's a large portion of the total. We're free to wander their land, burning and pillaging. If we march on Rome, they will sue for peace – I know it!'

'Damn right,' said Sapho.

There were loud rumbles of agreement.

Maharbal's words appealed, but Hanno was remembering how his friend Quintus, aged just sixteen, had faced up to three armed bandits – on his own. He had to be one of the most stubborn, courageous people Hanno ever met. These were not unusual characteristics for a Roman. During the battle two days before, many of the legionaries had continued to fight on even when it was clear that they had been defeated.

Hannibal rubbed a contemplative finger along his lips. 'You're so sure,' he said at last, eyeing first Maharbal, and then Sapho.

'Yes, sir. Who can take such a beating as we delivered two days ago and continue to fight on? No one!' declared Sapho.

'He speaks true,' said an officer. 'Aye,' rumbled another.

If Quintus lives, he will not give up while there is a breath still in his body, thought Hanno grimly. He would struggle to the death rather than submit.

Hannibal's bright eye fixed on Sapho. 'Maharbal knows the entire story of our first war against the Republic, but do you?'

'Of course, sir. I grew up on my father's tales of it.'

'Did he ever tell you of the occasions when the Roman fleets had been sunk, and their treasuries were empty?'

Sapho flushed a little, remembering. 'Yes, sir.'

Hanno could recall the story too.

'Any normal people would have recognised defeat after such major disasters. Instead, the Roman nobles sold their own properties to raise money for the construction of new ships. The war went on, because the stubborn bastards would not admit that they had been beaten. And we all know what happened at the end of that conflict.'

Angry murmurs, mention of reparations and territories lost.

'The Romans have never been vanquished as they were here, though, sir,' said Sapho.

'True,' admitted Hannibal. 'And therefore my hope and expectation is that they will sue for peace. With that in mind, Carthalo' – here he pointed to one of his senior cavalry officers – 'will tomorrow lead an embassy to Rome, there to deliver terms to the Senate.'

This might work. 'What terms, sir?' asked Hanno.

'Rome will recognise the honour and power of Carthage. It will return to us Sicily, Sardinia and Corsica, and acknowledge our pre-eminence in the seas west of those islands. If the Republic does not accept these terms, then, as the gods are my witness, it will see enough death and destruction visited upon its citizens to make the battle here look like a skirmish. This, while the non-Roman peoples who come over to us shall live under our protection.'

Maharbal shook his head, but many officers exchanged pleased looks. 'Those demands are reasonable enough,' said Bostar. 'Rome will see that, surely?'

They had been releasing captured non-Romans for a good while, but Hanno hadn't fully appreciated Hannibal's purpose before. 'You want to break up the Republic, sir?'

'I do. It isn't that long since peoples such as the Samnites, Oscans and

Bruttians were conquered or came under Roman influence. I want them to seize their liberty with both hands. Allied to Carthage, they will be free to determine their own futures. Few of you will know, but there have already been approaches from leaders of cities such as Capua about severing their links with Rome.'

That went down well with the officers.

Sapho looked disappointed, but Hanno didn't notice. Defeating Rome was what he had always craved, but he had another reason for wanting the war to be over. Quintus' sister, Aurelia, had flashed into his mind. If the fighting ended, he would be able to seek her out. A burning hope lit in Hanno's heart. Let Rome see that it is beaten, he prayed. Let there be peace.

'Would it not be better, sir, to be more aggressive? Why not let me ride ahead with our cavalry?' asked Maharbal, his expression eager. 'The dogs will only hear of our approach after we have arrived. I could deliver your message with thousands of horsemen at my back. You and the rest of the army can follow on behind. If the Romans have not agreed to the terms by then, your appearance would make up their minds.'

'I agree, sir,' said Sapho. 'We should march on Rome.'

'*Should?*' Hannibal studied Sapho for a moment, and his lips thinned. Sapho met his stare at first, but he couldn't keep it up. Hannibal's face softened as he cast his gaze at Maharbal. 'My mind is made up. Carthalo and his companions will carry my words to Rome. The troops need rest, and so do your riders. I am going to give it to them.'

'Truly the gods do not grant everything to the same man,' said Maharbal sombrely. 'You know how to win a victory, Hannibal, but you do not how to use one.'

PART ONE

Chapter I

Two and a half years later . . .
Apulia, late winter

I
t was a fresh morning. A light, cool breeze carried in from the east, where the sea lay, one hundred stadia away. The worst of the winter weather had gone, for which Hanno was grateful. Over the previous few months, the temperatures had not often been harsh, but he still missed the warmth of Carthage, his home. The sun's heat on his face, and signs that the plants were beginning to grow again, would be welcome.

As usual, he found Muttumbaal among the Libyans of his phalanx. If his second-in-command wasn't sleeping, he was with their men. They were his entire world, for he had neither wife nor family, and he was assiduous in their care. No one had ever called Mutt by his full cumbersome name, except perhaps his mother, thought Hanno wryly. To the world, his dour subordinate was just known as Mutt. He was a damn fine officer, and had covered for Hanno on innumerable occasions. Saved his life more than once too.

Mutt was drilling the men on the open ground beyond the camp perimeter. It was a habit that Hanno continued to find amusing. They were some of Hannibal's most hard-bitten veterans, who knew their craft inside out. Career soldiers, they had travelled from Carthage to Iberia, from there to Gaul, over the Alps and into Italy. They had fought – and won – more battles for Hannibal than anyone could remember. Yet that didn't stop Mutt from insisting on regular drill and marching sessions. 'Let them sit on their arses for too long, sir, and they'll get rusty,' he'd said when Hanno had questioned the tactic. Over time, Hanno had had to admit that Mutt's reasoning was sound, given the existence that they had all lived since Cannae. There was still occasional fighting, but much of their routine was to stay in camp. Yes, there were marches to defend a pro-Carthaginian town or city from a Roman army that was threatening it, but their fearsome reputation meant that this tactic usually made the legions withdraw without a fight. Large swathes of southern Italy were now on their side, which meant that combat had become less common. Frustratingly, that didn't mean that the war had been won. Far from it, Hanno thought bitterly. Plenty of Rome's allies remained loyal, even when their territory was surrounded by those friendly with Carthage.

Capua was allied to Hannibal, but nearby towns were not. He pictured Quintus' sister Aurelia, how she'd been when he had last seen her near Capua, and his heart squeezed. There had been no chance to find her since, and there probably never would be. He swallowed down his feelings. It was as well, for she would have forgotten him by now.

Spotting a dust-covered rider urging his horse towards the camp, his mood soured a little more. 'Who'll be begging for help this time?' he said to no one in particular.

Mutt heard him, and wandered over. 'It'll be the same old story, sir. "A Roman army is at our gates. We need your assistance. Come with all haste."'

Hanno laughed, before saying something that he would admit to few others. 'Sometimes it seems as if Cannae wasn't enough. If only their new legions would take us on. We'd kick their arses.'

Mutt hawked and spat. 'I'd be surprised if they're that stupid again, sir.'

Mutt was right, thought Hanno angrily. Since Cannae, their enemies had recruited and trained more than ten new legions. They operated in consular-sized forces of two legions throughout the peninsula – substantial enough to be militarily potent without losing the ability to be manoeuvrable and fast-moving – concentrating on the defeat of cities and peoples who had deserted the Republic.

'Cannae taught them a real lesson, sir.'

'They're scheming dogs.' Hanno knew all too well how it worked. If Hannibal tried to face these legions, or to draw them into pursuit, they backed away or retreated into the mountains where the huge Carthaginian superiority in cavalry was negated. Not for the first time, Hanno remembered Maharbal's warning just after Cannae. Had their general made the wrong decision when he decided not to march on Rome? Hanno wasn't sure, nor would he mention it to a soul other than Mutt or Bostar. As well as feeling disloyal by discussing it, no one really knew the answer. It was impossible to predict what might have happened. Obsessing about the past did nobody any good, he decided. They had to deal with the present. 'We're hardly doing badly. Hannibal is undefeated; at no time since Cannae has it looked any other way.'

''Scuse me, sir.' Mutt had noticed something untoward. He strode towards the men, shouting orders.

Hanno fell back to brooding. In Iberia, the situation was not as good as it had been. A number of Carthaginian defeats had seen many tribes changing sides to support Rome. Happily, Sicily was another story. There Carthage had new, powerful supporters. Hippocrates and Epicydes, two Syracusan nobles who had fought with Hannibal, and been subsequently sent by him to the island to foment unrest, had of recent days seized control of the great fortress of Syracuse. This advance – upsetting the city's fifty-year status as an ally of Rome – increased the likelihood of further help from Carthage on the island. Hanno prayed that the Syracusan and Carthaginian troops on Sicily would be victorious. That outcome would see Hannibal receive reinforcements, which would be warmly received.

The war has taken us from one end of Italy to the other, thought Hanno. His right hand strayed to his neck, the fingers slipping under the cloth that hid his scar from the world. He'd received it as a prisoner in Victumulae, thousands of stadia to the north. Pera, the Roman officer who had given it to him, had been a sadistic bastard. No doubt the sewer rat had been killed in the sack of the town, but Hanno wished that he could have personally seen him on his way to the underworld. Bomilcar, the Carthaginian who had saved Hanno's life, had been assigned to a different Libyan phalanx afterwards. He had survived Trasimene and Cannae, and the campaigning since. Hanno felt a stab of guilt that he hadn't been better at keeping in touch. I'll seek him out tonight, he decided. Bring along a jug of decent wine.

Hanno tramped over to join Mutt. The pair spent the next couple of hours sweating, shouting at the men and getting involved in the more complicated manoeuvres. By the time that they had finished, Hanno had forgotten all about Aurelia and his concerns with the campaign. 'Mutt, come with me this evening,' he said as they led the soldiers back to the camp.

'Where, sir?'

After this long, the honorific still jarred. Hanno had told his second-in-command on numerous occasions not to bother with it, but Mutt was intransigent. 'The men need to know that there's a difference between you and me, sir, just as there is between me and them,' he had replied. Mutt was as stubborn as a mule, so Hanno said nothing.

'I want to find Bomilcar. The man who got me out of the cell in Victumulae,' he explained when Mutt's face remained blank. 'I haven't seen him in months. It'd be good to have a few cups of wine with him. I would appreciate your company. He would too.'

'Aye, sir, that sounds—' Mutt broke off as a troop of chattering Numidians cantered past, as ever clad in nothing but their sleeveless tunics. '—good,' he finished.

'Excellent.' Hanno clapped him on the shoulder. He could feel a fine session looming. On the rare occasions that he'd persuaded Mutt to drink with him, things had got very messy indeed. It didn't matter if that happened, though. Life was quiet at the moment. No one more senior would care if he spent the following day in his blankets, recovering.

It was then that he caught sight of Sapho walking towards them. Hanno's mood dampened. No one more senior would disapprove perhaps, but his oldest brother, who was of equivalent rank, undoubtedly would. Since their youth, Sapho had liked to act as if he were Hanno's moral guardian. 'Not a word about tonight,' he hissed.

Mutt knew Hanno well enough. 'My lips are sealed, sir.'

'Ho, brother!' Sapho called out. 'Well met.'

'Well met indeed.' Hanno pulled a smile that was only half fake. Some of the time, he got on with Sapho. To his endless annoyance, he could never quite predict which brother would greet him: the snide, ruthless Sapho who had – probably, although Hanno had no proof – considered letting him drown in a mud pool in Etruria, or the jovial, considerate Sapho who brought wine and told him what Hannibal was planning, as had happened before Trasimene.

'Training your men?' Sapho fell into step beside him.

'Indeed.'

'Mine are on a hundred stadia run with my second-in-command.'

Hanno heard his soldiers' dismayed mutters as Sapho's words carried over his shoulder. 'Any special reason for that?'

'They're getting wine bellies from lying about, doing nothing but drink. It's time that they got back into shape.'

A devilment took Hanno, and he poked at his brother's stomach, which wasn't as flat as it had been. 'Shouldn't you be with them?' He heard Mutt's snort quickly converted to a cough.

Sapho shoved back at him, annoyed. 'I'm as fit as I ever was, you cheeky pup!'

'Of course you are,' said Hanno. I shouldn't have said a word, he thought. It's not worth the aggravation. To his relief, Sapho let it drop.

They made idle chitchat on the walk back, passing through the large gateway that granted access through the tall earthen fortifications. Relieved that Sapho appeared not to have sought him out for any particular reason, Hanno began to relax. He was beginning to consider the idea of inviting Sapho along that night – surprising himself – when he spotted Bostar with a couple of other officers, coming their way. His heart sank. Any time his two older brothers got together, there was potential for trouble.

To his surprise, a convivial air reigned as the groups converged. Bostar introduced his companions, two phalanx commanders whom Hanno vaguely knew but whom Sapho hailed like long-lost comrades. The five men chatted about the usual sort of things: the weather, the state of their men's fitness, how bad their rations were, whether there had been any reliable sightings of Roman forces, where the next enemy attack would be and so on. Everything was fine until Sapho mentioned, as he just had to Hanno, that his men needed to improve their fitness because of the amounts that they'd been drinking. At this point, Bostar pointed at Sapho's belly and commented, 'There's a bit of extra flesh there, or my eyes are mistaken, brother.'

Sapho flared up like a bush fire. 'What are you saying?'

Bostar, who was still lean as a hunting dog, shrugged. 'You have a slight gut. Some exercise would do you some good too.'

Sapho's eyes filled with suspicion. He swung from Bostar to Hanno and back. 'You two have been talking behind my back, haven't you? Laughing at me!'

'No!' protested Hanno truthfully.

'We haven't said a word,' said Bostar with a trace of a smirk. Hanno cursed him for it. Now was not the time to rile Sapho further, over something so inconsequential. The two other officers already looked embarrassed – and less than impressed.

Of course Sapho homed in on Bostar's expression like a fly to shit. 'Then why the little smile, eh?'

'We haven't said a word to one another, Sapho, I swear it,' said Hanno, annoyed at the way this was degenerating.

'Really?' Sapho's mistrustful expression eased, but his face was full of rage as he turned on Bostar. 'Just had to get a joke in in front of your friends, was that it?'

'As if you wouldn't do the same, if I were overweight!' retorted Bostar.

'Screw you!' snarled Sapho. Before anyone could react, he'd stepped in and thrown a powerful punch to Bostar's chin, snapping his head and body backwards. *Thump*. He went down on to the flat of his back. Sapho waded in, throwing kicks and stamping on Bostar with his studded sandals. 'Always think you know better than me, don't you?' he shouted, spittle flying from his lips. 'Well, you don't!'

Hanno shoved himself between Sapho and the groaning Bostar. 'Get off him!'

Sapho didn't seem to hear. With superhuman strength, he pushed Hanno out of the way. The tiny delay had given Bostar a chance to get up, however. Roaring with anger, he flung himself at Sapho, arms outstretched, and caught him around the middle. The pair went sprawling on to the dirt, each raining punches upon the other. Hanno looked on in dismay. From the corner of his eye, he could see Bostar's two companions and Mutt doing the same. His inaction lasted only a moment. This had to be stopped. As much as anything, it was a terrible example for the men to see officers brawling.

'Help me separate them,' he ordered Mutt. 'You grab Bostar. I'll go for Sapho.' Hanno leaped in and grabbed one of Sapho's flailing arms. With that grip he was able to heave his brother back, managing at the same time to seize his other arm from underneath. Hanno bent his elbows, securing his purchase on Sapho's upper body. Sapho spat and cursed, but was unable to break free. That didn't stop him aiming another kick at Bostar, who was lying helpless underneath Mutt. There was a groan from Bostar as the blow landed, and Sapho chuckled. 'How do you like that, you filth?'

Hanno wrenched Sapho back several steps. There was a yelp of pain.

'Gods, my shoulders!'

'Good.' Tightening his grip, Hanno dragged him back another pace or two. Sapho began to speak, but Hanno had had enough. 'Shut your trap!' He peered over Sapho's shoulder. 'Mutt?'

'Sir?'

'Have you got Bostar under control?'

'Yes, sir.'

'Good. He's to promise not to start fighting again. Then you can let him go. If he won't, hold him down.' Hanno moved his lips to Sapho's ear. 'This has to end. Do you hear me?'

'I—' Sapho began to growl.

'No, Sapho, I won't have it! You're a grown man, and an officer, not a ten-year-old boy!' There was no response, so Hanno squeezed with all his might, forcing Sapho's arms upwards and back even further. Another hiss of pain from his brother. 'Understand?' demanded Hanno.

'Fine. Yes,' came the surly reply.

'Bostar has agreed,' said Mutt.

'Release him.' Hanno slackened his grip on Sapho, allowing him to step away. He moved to stand between his two brothers, still furious. Bostar was regarding him with surprise, and Sapho with smouldering anger. Hanno was so incensed that he didn't care what either of them thought. 'You're both a disgrace to your rank and station! Senior officers, fighting like two drunks, and in front of common soldiers. Hannibal would have the pair of you flogged for this. I've a good mind to do the same myself.' Their mouths opened in shock, but Hanno wasn't finished. 'Father might be gone, but that doesn't mean he's not looking down on you in disgust, the last of our family. He would have told you that our war is with the damn Romans, not each other. Isn't it?' He eyeballed them.

'It is,' mumbled Bostar after a moment.

'Sapho?'

'Yes, I suppose.'

'Then start acting like a man, instead of a child!'

Sapho flushed, but did not answer back.

'I want you both to take an oath that this quarrelling will end here and now,' commanded Hanno.

His brothers looked unhappy. 'And if I don't agree?' demanded Sapho.

'As the gods are my witness, I will tell Hannibal,' replied Hanno from between clenched teeth.

Bostar sighed. 'I will swear.'

'My little brother has all grown up,' murmured Sapho.

'What's your answer to be?' barked Hanno.

'I will also swear,' said Sapho mildly.

Hanno didn't trust the look in Sapho's eyes, but he had backed down. Hanno moved his fingers away from his sword hilt, where they had begun to stray. 'Speak your oaths,' he ordered.

One after the other, his brothers swore to all the Carthaginian gods that they would bury their feud forever. When they were done, both glanced at Hanno. They're waiting to see if I am satisfied, he realised, shocked by the sea change in their relationship. A few moments before, he had been the youngest brother, lowest in the pecking order. Now he had acted as their father might have, and they had accepted it. 'Fine.' He glanced at Mutt. 'We've wasted enough time here. Have the men form up again, ready to march.'

Mutt roared out a command. Sapho, Bostar and the two others quickly moved out of the way. Hanno began to feel proud of what he'd done. Whether the two would honour their promise remained to be seen, but the strength of their vow would prevent them from fighting, for the time being at least. He wondered if Sapho would seek revenge on him for the humiliation. If he does, I'll be ready, he decided. As I have been for some time. 'Forward march!' he cried.

'Hold!' shouted a voice.

Thinking it was one of his brothers, Hanno continued to advance. Mutt and the rest followed.

'HOLD, I SAY!' repeated the voice.

Realising it was someone else altogether, Hanno ground to a halt.

A short distance away, a nondescript soldier threw back the hood of his cloak. He was one-eyed, broad-faced, bearded.

There was a universal gasp of amazement.

Hanno was first to react. 'Attention!' he cried, snapping upright. 'Your general is here.'

His men stiffened to attention. His brothers and their companions did the same. Hannibal stalked over, his face a blank. Hanno began to feel nervous. It had always been their general's habit to wander among his soldiers incognito, his purpose to assess their morale, their mood. Since Cannae, this practice appeared to have lapsed. Until now, thought Hanno. His certainty that he had acted in the correct manner wavered. Hannibal was liable to punish lapses of discipline severely. *Gods, what will he do?*

Neither Bostar nor Sapho could meet Hannibal's eye as he spoke. 'I've been aware of the animosity between you for a long while, but I had no idea that it was this bad.'

'Sir, I—' began Sapho.

'Quiet!' Hannibal's voice cracked like a whip.

Sapho subsided.

'Sapho, the wild but courageous one. Bostar, also brave as a lion, but more dutiful.' Hannibal's gaze moved to Hanno, who squirmed beneath it. 'The cub, usually the one to do as he pleased. The one who needed disciplining the most, or so I thought.' He paced to and fro, letting the brothers sweat.

'Under normal circumstances, this incident would have passed me by,' Hannibal said at last. 'But I was here, and I saw it.'

Hanno's eyes flickered to his brothers' faces. He wasn't alone in holding his breath.

'It's a poor sign when two of my phalanx commanders brawl with each other like a pair of drunks outside a whorehouse.'

Hanno stared at the ground, acutely aware that he would have to accept whatever punishment was meted out to them – and him.

'It seems to me that the vow Hanno forced you to take should be enough to keep the peace.'

Relief – and a little disbelief – all round, although none of the brothers dared to relax.

'If we were not at war, I would strip you both to the ranks, *at the very least*.' He glared at Sapho and Bostar, who both looked ashamed. 'However, we *are* at war, and in a foreign land. Officers of your calibre are impossible to replace.' He raised a warning finger. 'Yet the matter cannot go unaddressed. Therefore, despite your oath, I am going to separate you. Permanently.'

All three exchanged worried glances, and Hannibal laughed. It was not an altogether pleasant sound. 'I've had word that my brother Hasdrubal in Iberia needs experienced officers. Despite the shortage in my own forces, I am going to send him a few men. Bostar, you will be one of them. You will have to go by sea, because it would take too long to travel by land. The voyage will be dangerous in the extreme – I expect you know that. Two of the last three ships sent from Iberia have been sunk or taken by the Romans. Gods willing, *you* will make it. Once there you will do all in your power to help Hasdrubal and our other generals defeat the enemy.'

'I will do my best, sir,' said Bostar with a resolute nod.

'Good.' Hannibal rounded on Sapho, who flinched a little. 'You, I will keep by my side. Don't think that that means life will be easy. For a start, you and your phalanx will be on extended patrols for the next three months.'

'Thank you, sir,' said Sapho stolidly. 'We will do all that is asked of us.'

Why did it have to be Bostar who was sent away? thought Hanno furiously. He might never see his favourite brother again. That idea was terrible to contemplate. Hannibal's attention fell on him then, and Hanno forgot about his brothers. Where was he to be sent?

'And so to you, youngest son of Malchus,' said Hannibal.

A pulse hammered at the base of Hanno's throat. Punishment would be forthcoming, of that he had no doubt.

'Your father was ever a valiant servant of Carthage. His loss was a personal sorrow for you and your brothers, of course, but I too grieve for him still,' said Hannibal.

'Thank you, sir,' Hanno replied. It helped to have his father's sacrifice acknowledged. Bostar and Sapho also seemed pleased.

'Malchus would be proud of you today. What age are you now?'

'Twenty-three, sir.'

'Young still. Your actions were impressive.'

Uneasy with the praise, Hanno shifted to and fro. 'Th-thank you, sir.'

'I have need of a trustworthy officer to undertake a dangerous mission. I had thought to send someone else, but what I have just seen has changed my mind. You will go instead.'

Hanno's heart began to thump even faster. 'Where, sir?'

Hannibal lowered his voice. 'To Sicily.'

'Sicily, sir?' Hanno repeated, like a fool. Glancing at Mutt, his heart-strings tugged painfully. Mutt and his men felt like family. Besides, what use could he be without his soldiers? 'Who will command my unit in my absence?' he asked, stalling.

'Why, Mutt here. Not as if he hasn't done it before, is it?'

Panic flared in Hanno's belly. Did his general know about his unauthorised leave of absence, before Cannae, when he had sought out Aurelia? His eyes went from Hannibal to Mutt, whose expression was as innocent as a babe's, and back again.

'The original officer who led your phalanx died in the crossing of the Alps. Mutt looked after them until I appointed you,' said Hannibal.

'Of course, sir.' How could he have doubted Mutt? Hanno smiled as if he'd understood Hannibal's meaning all along.

'Come by my tent as soon as you've finished with your men.'

'Very good, sir!' Proud yet sad at what this meant, Hanno threw off a parade-ground salute.

'As you were.' Hannibal waved a hand in dismissal. Slipping up his hood, he walked off, just another ordinary soldier again.

'So you two get special treatment while I have to stay in Italy.' Sapho's voice was sour.

'You're *staying* with the most important general in Carthage,' retorted Hanno.

'It's as honourable to remain with Hannibal as it is to be sent overseas,' added Bostar in a surprisingly conciliatory tone. 'Hannibal values you. He's said as much before.'

'True,' Sapho conceded, but the jealousy in his eyes gave the lie to his answer.

Sapho wouldn't be happy whatever the outcome, thought Hanno. He felt a whisper of relief that he would soon be far away from his oldest brother, yet that emotion was mixed with a contradictory sadness that he would be parted from not just Bostar, Mutt and his men, but Sapho too. There was every chance that they would never see each other again.

'We'll have to get together before any of us leave. Offer a sacrifice to Father's memory.' He paused. 'And then get royally pissed.'

Chapter II

The light was fading as Hanno arrived at Hannibal's pavilion, his head full of thoughts of Sicily. Since losing the huge island in the first war with Rome, every Carthaginian had wanted it back. After all, much of it had been colonised by Carthage for nigh on two hundred years.

Half a dozen scutarii were on duty outside his general's tent. Hanno gave his name, which saw him ushered inside. A massive *scutarius* led the way.

The rich interior made Hanno feel as if he were stepping inside the house of one of his father's wealthy friends in Carthage. Fabric partitions divided the space up into rooms. Thick carpets covered the floors. In the larger chambers, bronze candelabras had been suspended from the rods that held up the roof. The hardwood furniture – chests, chairs and even couches – was heavy, and of good quality. They passed straight through the spacious meeting area where he and other officers sometimes received orders from Hannibal, and Hanno's stomach twisted a little. The fact that he was being guided to his general's private quarters was more proof that his mission was important.

The scutarius halted at a final partition, before which stood a similarly large specimen, notable for the massive scar across his nose. This hulk eyed Hanno with open suspicion. 'He's here to see the boss. Hanno, commander of a Libyan phalanx,' said the first soldier.

Scarface gave Hanno a salute that did what it was supposed to but still managed to convey a level of contempt. Hanno just stared back.

Everyone but the inner circle – men such as Maharbal – received the same treatment from Hannibal's bodyguards. Scarface turned his head. 'Sir?' he called.

From within came a familiar voice. 'Yes?'

'Hanno, phalanx commander, is here, sir.'

'Send him in.'

'After you, sir,' said Scarface to Hanno, with a trace more civility. He pulled aside the drape and waved him in. The first scutarius vanished back to the entrance.

Self-conscious, for all that he had shaved, washed his hair and was wearing his finest tunic, Hanno stepped inside. Hannibal was sitting at a desk, with his back towards him. He half turned, smiled. 'Come. Sit.' He waved a hand at the chair that stood to one side of his table.

'Thank you, sir.' Nervously, Hanno obeyed.

Hannibal's one eye regarded him kindly. 'Welcome. Wine?'

'Please, sir.'

'Sosian, do the necessary, will you?'

Hanno took not a little pleasure from the way that Sosian – Scarface – hurried to obey, becoming the servant rather than the threatening bodyguard. When both of them had a full cup, Hannibal raised his towards Hanno. 'To your father, Malchus. A brave heart and a loyal servant to Carthage.'

Hanno swallowed the sudden lump that had formed in his throat. 'To my father,' he said.

They drank. Hanno offered up a prayer to the gods, asking that they look after both of his parents.

'To victory against the Romans,' said Hannibal.

'I'll drink to that, sir,' said Hanno eagerly.

'May it come sooner rather than later.'

Hanno studied Hannibal's face, trying to read his thoughts on that matter. He couldn't discern a thing, and didn't dare to ask. They drained their cups. Scarface moved in, refilled them both.

'It's to your taste?' asked Hannibal.

'Yes, sir. It's delicious.'

'It comes from a little estate near Cannae, funnily enough. There's not much of it left now. I keep it for special occasions.'

Hanno's nerves gnawed at him afresh. 'I see, sir.'

Hannibal chuckled. 'Relax. I won't bite you.'

Hanno had felt the edge of Hannibal's temper before. That's not why he was here tonight, though. He nodded. 'Very well, sir.'

'Tell me what you know of Sicily.'

'It's a rich island, sir. My father used to tell me that it was littered with large farms and prosperous towns.'

Hannibal's eye twinkled. 'So did mine. The bread basket of Italy, he called it. What else?'

'It is the stepping stone between Africa and Italy, sir. Supremacy there would make our task immeasurably easier. Reinforcements and supplies could be moved from Carthage to Italy with few problems. Our army could be fed with the island's produce, meaning that we wouldn't need to change camp so often. The problem is that Rome controls most of Sicily, and the rest belongs to Syracuse, which has been no friend of Carthage for many years. Syracuse's ruler allied himself to the Republic before the first war between our states.' Here Hanno faltered a little. He knew that Hiero, the tyrant of Syracuse for more than half a century, had died soon after Cannae, but not the exact details of the deals and counter-deals that had happened since. 'Since Hiero's death, I know that his grandson was briefly in power. I've heard in recent days that Hippocrates and Epicydes may be ruling the city, and that they favour Carthage. More than that I don't know, sir.'

'It's not surprising that you're unaware of the very latest news. I'll explain. Hiero's grandson Hieronymus was a youth of fifteen when he ascended the throne. I had high hopes for him, because he initially spurned Rome. Before long, though, it became clear he was both rash and impetuous. Having sought alliance first with me, he began communicating directly with the authorities in Carthage.' Hannibal frowned. 'Cheeky pup.'

'You were quick to respond to his overture, sir. I remember the departure for Sicily of Hippocrates and Epicydes. So their efforts have finally borne fruit?'

'Indeed. The rumour you heard is true. At first, it seemed that they wouldn't achieve anything, and for more than a year, Syracuse's ties with Rome remained unsevered despite Hieronymus' overtures to us. Their chance came some months ago when Hieronymus was murdered by a faction of disaffected nobles; soon after that his successor, an uncle, was assassinated along with much of the royal family. The bloodshed left a power vacuum. Hippocrates and Epicydes lobbied hard for two of the most powerful magistracies in the city – positions that had been left vacant by the wave of killings – and managed to secure them. When I heard that, I hoped that they would take control of Syracuse. But many still regarded them as outsiders, and they couldn't rally enough support. So, instead, they seized Leontini, a town some two hundred stadia north of Syracuse. Bit of an unwise move, because it attracted the immediate attention of Marcus Claudius Marcellus.'

'That's the commander of the Roman forces on the island, sir?'

'Yes. Within weeks, Hippocrates and Epicydes were driven from their new fiefdom. Humiliation – and then, on the road back to Syracuse, the two of them ran into a strong force of local troops marching to Leontini's aid. Things looked dire, but instead the pair's fortunes completely reversed. It's funny how, for no apparent reason, disasters can turn into triumph,' Hannibal said, chuckling. 'Truly the gods can be generous.'

'I don't understand, sir,' said Hanno.

'The soldiers leading the force were Cretan mercenary archers, who as fortune had it, were well disposed towards Hippocrates and Epicydes. Even that wouldn't have been enough to take over the entire Syracusan force, however. So, undeterred, the brothers told the rest of the soldiers that Marcellus had massacred the population of Leontini – which was a downright lie. Yet it was believed. They succeeded in persuading the eight thousand men to drive off their Syracusan officers and to accept them as commanders. With this small army at their backs, Hippocrates and Epicydes marched on Syracuse where, against the odds once more, they managed to seize power.' Hannibal banged his cup on the table. 'So there you have it! A city of huge importance to Sicily, and therefore the whole war, is in the hands of two men who are no friends to Rome.'

Hanno felt rising confusion. 'I don't understand how I can help, sir.'

'I've picked you because you are loyal to me, heart and soul.'

Hanno's heart swelled at this unexpected recognition. 'Aye, sir,' he muttered thickly.

'That's more than I can say of Hippocrates and Epicydes. They only ever fought for me in the hope that I could one day help them to become the twin tyrants of Syracuse. They'll side with Carthage while it suits them, but either one would slit my throat – or yours – if the price was right.'

Hanno saw some of Hannibal's intent now. 'I am no spy, sir. I'm a simple soldier. Fighting is what I do. There must be other men you could send in my stead.'

'Maybe so, but I have need of them here. That's not to say that I don't require you also,' Hannibal added reassuringly, 'but your second-in-command can fill your place for the moment. You're an experienced officer, used to leading men and making decisions in a crisis. Hippocrates and Epicydes had the same opportunities as you, but neither ever made a particularly good leader. They have done well to achieve so much, but I worry for their future. You can help them. You're intelligent and, even better, you are decisive. You showed that today.'

The praise made Hanno's cheeks flush with renewed pride. 'Thank you, sir. So you want me to assist them, militarily?'

'Something like that, yes.' Hannibal saw his indecision. 'I won't order you to go if you don't want to. I'm asking you because I think you will do well.' His eye burned with an intensity that held Hanno's gaze.

Hanno forgot Bostar and Sapho. Forgot Mutt and his men. 'I'd be honoured to do it, sir.'

A pleased nod. 'I want you to be my eyes and ears in Syracuse. You will gather intelligence – about everything you can – and send word of it to me when possible. Hippocrates and Epicydes will be told that you're to act as a military aide to their cause. You're to win their trust if you can, and to help them carry the fight to Marcellus and his legions with all of your ability. When reinforcements arrive from Carthage – and within twelve months, they will – you are to try and ensure that relations between the two sets of leaders are cordial from the start. When the Romans are beaten on Sicily' – here a wolfish smile – 'you are to keep Hippocrates and Epicydes sweet. Once that happens, all Carthaginian forces on the island will need to be transferred to Italy, but I'll want Hippocrates and Epicydes to provide us with soldiers and supplies as well.' Hannibal finished and studied him in silence.

Hanno's heart thudded in his chest. Gods, he thought. This is massively important to our cause. To the war. Far more important than leading a phalanx. 'I will do my best, sir, or die in the attempt.'

'Good man!' Hannibal clapped him on the shoulder. 'Let us hope that you succeed, and that you also survive to appreciate the fruits of your labours.' He slipped a heavy ring off the index finger of his right hand and held it out. 'I will give you letters of introduction of course, but this will act as proof that you are my man.'

Awestruck, Hanno took the gold ring, the top of which was embossed with a lion: one of the symbols used by the Barcid family. He would never be able to show this to Sapho. 'I . . .' he began, '. . . thank you, sir.'

'May the gods go with you to Sicily. We'll talk again before you leave.' Hannibal turned back to the parchment he'd been studying when Hanno entered.

He was being dismissed. Gripping the ring tightly in his right fist, Hanno stood. 'Thank you, sir.'

Wrapped up in his thoughts, with the ring burning a hole in his hand, Hanno wasn't watching where he was going. *Thump*. His head collided with someone. 'I'm sorry. That was my fault.' Even as the words left his mouth, he was stunned and delighted to recognise Bomilcar.

'Of all the men in the army to walk into!' cried Bomilcar, rubbing his forehead and beaming at the same time. 'It's good to see you, Hanno. How long has it been – six months?'

'That and more,' replied Hanno ruefully. 'The funny thing is, I was planning to seek you out this very evening.'

'That's what they all say!' Bomilcar winked to show that he meant no offence. 'Time just passes us by, eh? How are you keeping?'

Hanno moved the hand holding the ring to his side. 'I'm well. And you?'

'Fine. Been to see the chief?' Bomilcar jerked his head in the direction of Hannibal's tent.

'How did you guess?'

'You had that look that men have after talking to him. Pensive,' came the shrewd reply.

'He's sending me to Sicily,' Hanno confided.

Bomilcar's eyebrows rose. 'You're moving up in the world.'

'It seems so.' Hanno felt a little disappointed that Bomilcar did not ask more. 'Have you also been summoned?'

A nod, then a whisper. 'I'm to travel to Rome.'

How the world changed, thought Hanno. All he'd known since joining Hannibal's army was fighting and battles. Now everything seemed to be about espionage and subterfuge. 'As a spy, I take it?'

Bomilcar winked again. 'I'm fair-skinned. Thanks to my years in captivity, I speak Latin like a native. Who better to venture into the wolf's lair? There have been rumours of the enemy trying to force us down into the heel, or perhaps the toe of the peninsula. Hannibal wants me to find out if they're true.' Bomilcar cast a look at the sun. 'Here, I'm late. Let's share that cup of wine tonight. I'll tell you more, and you can fill me in on your mission.'

'I look forward to it,' said Hanno, grinning.

By the time that he, Mutt and Bomilcar had consumed the contents of two small amphorae of wine, the moon had risen high in the night sky and

Hanno was feeling decidedly the worse for wear. A warm, fuzzy feeling encased him, and he felt goodwill towards all men. Well, not towards the Romans, he thought blearily, but even they weren't as bad as some made them out to be. He had spent more than a year living with Quintus and his family, had he not? They hadn't been any different to him and his own family. Not evil. Not perfect, but decent, hard-working people. It wasn't possible that they were different from the rest of their race. No, Hanno decided, many Romans were all right. Pera, the officer who had tortured him at Victumulae was an exception, clearly. The rest, however, just happened to be the enemy. A damn stubborn enemy too. 'Why couldn't the fools have admitted that they were beaten after Cannae?' he muttered.

'We should have marched on Rome then,' said Bomilcar. 'They would have surrendered.'

'Would they?' asked Mutt, letting out a contemptuous fart. He waited until the chuckles had died down before continuing. 'I don't think so. The only thing that will make them surrender is when every city, every ally they have, deserts them. When they're on their own, with their backs to the wall, they will sue for peace.'

'For that to happen, we need to defeat the enemy in both Iberia and Sicily,' said Hanno grimly, already feeling the pressure of his mission. 'That would free up two armies of ours to travel to Italy. Once they arrived, Rome's allies would desert them like rats escaping a sinking ship.'

'Aye, that's about right,' replied Mutt, taking a big mouthful from his cup.

When it hadn't happened after Cannae, Hanno had begun to suspect that the path to total victory would be long and tortuous. Articulated now, the prospect of winning a war on three fronts sounded close to impossible. Stop thinking like that, he ordered himself. 'We have to succeed, damn it!'

'We will pray to the gods and do our best. A man can do no more, eh?' Bomilcar held out his cup to Mutt for a refill.

That did not sit well with Hanno. Failure – or, at best, satisfaction with one's efforts – was not something that he ever wanted to feel comfortable with. It smacked of mediocrity. An image of Aurelia came into his mind then, as she had been that night outside her home near Capua. His groin throbbed and for a moment, he forgot about Sicily, and duty. Shame at not having tried to contact her after their last meeting scourged him. Yet there had seemed no point. She was to be married, and they were from opposite sides in the war. The most practical thing would have been to try and forget her, yet Hanno hadn't. Couldn't. A wave of memories surged back. Gods, but how good it had been to kiss her. Why had he not sent her messages? They would never have got through, but he should have tried. Impulse seized him. He nudged Bomilcar. 'Will you pass through Capua on your way north?'

'It's the last friendly city before Rome, so yes, probably. Why?'

Hanno didn't answer immediately. He was being foolish, he thought sadly. Capua had come over to Hannibal some time since. Those who remained loyal to the Republic would have fled the city after that. He could not imagine Aurelia's mother and father, and by extension, her husband, ever changing sides. She would not be in Capua. He let out a heavy sigh. 'It doesn't matter.'

Bomilcar threw him a quizzical look, but said nothing. Mutt, on the other hand, chuckled knowingly. 'It'll be a woman. Mark my words.'

'What makes you think that?' Hanno demanded, worried that Mutt was about to mention his illegal forays before Cannae. Despite Bomilcar being a friend, the fewer who knew, the better.

Mutt gave him a glance as if to say, 'You don't need to worry.' He winked at Bomilcar, and then regarded Hanno. 'It's the look in your eyes, sir. You're like a moonstruck calf.'

Is it that obvious? wondered Hanno, grateful the darkness didn't reveal the colour of his cheeks.

'Who is she?' asked Bomilcar.

Damn it, thought Hanno, what did it matter if Bomilcar knew? It wasn't the act of a traitor to have feelings for a woman who happened to be one of the enemy. 'She's the sister of the Roman who bought me. Aurelia is her name.'

'Is she pretty?' Mutt's face was eager.

'Very.' He pictured her as she'd been the night they had met at her family's estate. Grown up – a woman, with woman's curves. His erection stiffened, and he shifted position to hide it.

The others chuckled. 'She must be good-looking, for you to remember her after this long,' said Bomilcar.

Hanno was glad that Mutt didn't say a word. He brooded on the fact that Aurelia would now have been married for some time. For all he knew, she had a child or two. It was all too possible that she had died in child-birth— Stop it. She's alive, he told himself.

'You want me to seek her out in Capua?' asked Bomilcar in a low voice. 'Give her a message?'

'That's good of you, but she won't be there.' Quickly, Hanno explained, before poking a stick into the fire in frustration.

'Forget about her, sir. You'll never see her again,' advised Mutt. He raised his cup and gave it an appreciative caress. 'Best give your love to this. You'll never find a place where you can't find some. Might be vinegary, or off, but it will still do the job.'

Hanno glared at Mutt. That's what I thought when I escaped with Quintus, but then I *did* meet her once more. To extinguish the dream that he might do so again seemed too brutal. Everything else in his life was about war and death, and duty to Hannibal and Carthage. This one thing was his alone. 'This is different,' he muttered.

'First love!' said Mutt. 'Oh, to be young again.'

Hanno threw the dregs from his cup over him.

Mutt shut up.

'Tell me what you would say to Aurelia,' urged Bomilcar. 'I will try to find her in Capua. Even if I fail, I might hear word of where she has gone.'

Hanno sensed that Bomilcar was just humouring him, but he didn't care. Was it not better that he carry a message of some kind – any kind – than nothing at all? His heart ached at the idea that Bomilcar might actually meet Aurelia. 'Tell her . . . that I think of her often. Often. Tell her that with the gods' help, we will see each other again one day . . .' His voice died away.

No one spoke. Hanno glanced at Mutt, saw sympathy in his eyes. Bomilcar's expression was also understanding. Even in the midst of a war, we don't have to be unfeeling, Hanno thought. He took a swig of wine and stared out into the blackness.

'If I find her, rest assured that I will tell her,' said Bomilcar.

'Thank you,' replied Hanno gruffly.

The knowledge would make his journey to Sicily that little bit easier.

Chapter III

North of Syracuse, Sicily

Lifting a hand against the rising sun's rays, a Roman legionary squinted into the distance.

A tall man with black hair, Quintus Fabricius was in a clearing, halfway up a small, tree-covered hill. Below his position, a road led south, to Leontini and, beyond that, Syracuse. It was empty of traffic. So it had been since he and his comrade Urceus had taken over from the previous sentries in the pre-dawn chill, several hours before. Satisfied, Quintus glanced casually around him. There was no great need to worry about attack from anywhere other than the south, but it paid to be vigilant. To his back, about a mile away, loomed the mass that was Mount Etna, its lower slopes covered in farms and vineyards. Northwards, the road ran up towards Messana, into Roman-held, secure territory. To the east, the sea was a deep, inviting blue. The mainland was only a mile or so across the strait; the mountains that ran down to the point of the 'boot' were clearly visible. There were no sails on the water yet – it was too early. Yawning, Quintus stood; he leaned his *pilum* and shield against the rock that had been his seat and walked up and down a few paces, stretching his muscles to get the blood flowing again.

'Cold?' asked Urceus. Short, brave, funny, he'd been nicknamed Urceus, which meant 'jug', because of his prominent, handle-like ears.

No one, even Quintus, knew what his real name was. It was a source of endless interest to the maniple. Corax, their centurion, might have known – he'd been the one to take Urceus' oath when he joined up – but he never let on.

'Two tunics and a heavy cloak and I'm still chilled to the bone,' Quintus grumbled.

'You shouldn't sit on your arse so much then.'

'Piss off!' retorted Quintus, his grey eyes dancing.

'At least there's been sod all to look out for,' said Urceus. 'For the moment anyway.'

'It's peaceful around here,' agreed Quintus. 'It makes me think of home.' His mind turned to his family, and sadness took him. In Rome, the sun was rising on his mother Atia, his beloved sister Aurelia, and her little son Publius. The gods keep you safe, he prayed. One day, I'll see you again. Lucius, Aurelia's husband, might be with them, but according to Aurelia's most recent letter, it was more likely he'd be in Rhegium, on business. Quintus saluted in the direction of the port, which kept supplies flowing to the Roman troops on the island. He had met Lucius once, just after Cannae; he'd seemed a decent man, and Aurelia made no complaints.

Urceus threw him a quizzical look. 'What's that for?'

'My brother-in-law. The one I told you about, who has business in Rhegium.'

'Loved ones. It's hard not to think of them when we're stuck here, eh?'

'It is.' The familiar bitterness rolled in, and Quintus spat. 'We fought until we could fight no more at Cannae. We retreated when the battle was lost, so that we could fight another day. And our reward?'

'To be exiled to Sicily – for life,' snarled Urceus. 'Fuck the Senate and everyone in it.'

Once, Quintus would have been shocked by such sentiments. Now, he nodded in agreement.

'May Fortuna be smiling on my brothers,' muttered Urceus. 'They'll be seeing more action than we are.' His two brothers had joined the army after Cannae, and had been assigned to a different legion. Roman soldiers in Italy saw more frequent action, the troops of many areas having gone over to Hannibal.

'Still no word?' asked Quintus. He knew the answer, but it showed solidarity to enquire.

'Course not. Paying a scribe to write a letter would seem like a waste of money to my brothers, same as me! We can but pray to the gods and hope that all of us make it.' He threw Quintus a sympathetic look. 'It's the same even if you can write, isn't it? Sicily is far enough from the mainland that it might as well be the damn moon.'

Quintus nodded in agreement. Not for the first time, he remembered the messages he'd sent to Gaius, his oldest friend from Capua. There had been no replies. Was Gaius dead, or had he and his father Martialis gone over to Hannibal? The latter notion wasn't unlikely, Quintus had reluctantly concluded. Gaius and his father held Roman citizenship, but they were Oscan nobility through and through. Their people had only been conquered by Rome two generations before. When Capua had changed sides after Cannae, severing its ties with Rome, the majority of its leaders and ruling class had done so too. Quintus couldn't think of a reason that Gaius wouldn't have done the same. He didn't have it in himself to hate his friend if that was the case. They'd known each other since they were babies, had shared almost every experience of life from early childhood to the date that they had taken the toga. Wherever you are, Gaius, he thought, I hope you are well. If you fight for Hannibal, I pray that we never meet.

'To my brothers. To old friends and comrades!' said Urceus. He poured a small measure of wine from his skin on the ground as a libation before taking a swig. He handed the bag to Quintus, who echoed his salutation. To Gaius, he said silently. Out loud, he added, 'To Calatinus.' Then he took a mouthful. The wine was vinegary, but Quintus enjoyed the warming feeling as it went down his neck. He slugged another.

'Calatinus was your cavalry comrade from the battle of the Trebia.'

'Good memory,' said Quintus. 'I've hardly seen him since joining the infantry.' Until Urceus came along, Calatinus had been the comrade he'd missed the most. Fortunately, they had bumped into one another before Cannae, and afterwards too. The mere fact that they'd both survived the bloodiest defeat in the Republic's history had been enough excuse to get drunk together. That was the last time they had met. Quintus had no idea where on the Italian mainland Calatinus was serving now, so he saluted from northeast to southeast, encompassing the entire peninsula. 'May Mars keep his shield over you, my friend. May we meet again, in happier times.'

Urceus was watching. 'You made it happen. Not seeing him again, I mean. Ordinary foot soldiers don't mix with equestrians, Crespo.'

Quintus smiled. Crespo was the name he'd taken when he had enlisted in the infantry. It had taken him a long time to reveal his true name, and identity — that of an equestrian — to Urceus. Finally, though, he'd mentioned it one night when they'd had plenty to drink. His friend had made little of it, which had been a relief, but even now, more than a year later, Quintus was wary of talking frankly about the life he'd led before joining the infantry.

'You were mad to leave the cavalry,' opined Urceus, not for the first time. 'You wouldn't be stuck here, on fucking Sicily, if you'd stayed.'

Quintus had thought about this countless times, yet he still wouldn't have changed the way he'd done things. Humble citizens they might be, but Urceus and his comrades were as dear to him — dearer — than anyone but his family. 'If I wasn't here, you wouldn't have anyone to keep you out of trouble,' he shot back.

Urceus chuckled. 'Listen to you! It's the other way round, you know that! If not for me, you'd be dead a dozen times over.'

The truth of it was that they had both saved each other's lives more than once, but the banter was part of their routine. 'Enlisting in the *velites* was the only way that I could continue to fight Hannibal. My father, gods rest his soul, was so angry with me that he'd ordered me back to Capua.'

'I remember. But the lowliest class of infantry?' Urceus tapped his head with a finger. 'Choosing that, when you could have been sunning yourself on the family farm?'

'You know as well as I do that I wasn't going to sit at home, not with Hannibal roaming the land. Becoming a *veles* was the best choice I had.'

'Bloody fool,' said Urceus, but the affection in his voice took all the sting from the insult.

'Besides, I've risen in the world since.'

'A fine *hastatus* you may be, but I'd wager your mother still doesn't approve.'

'She will have come to accept it by now,' Quintus said. Once she had recovered from the shock and relief of seeing him alive after Cannae, Atia had been quick to express her displeasure that he was a foot soldier. Until that point in his life, Quintus had always obeyed his mother. Not that day. He'd listened to her outburst and then told her that he would be remaining in the infantry. To his surprise, she had backed down. 'Just stay alive,' she had whispered.

'Mothers are good at accepting what their sons do. It's part of their job. Least that's what mine used to say.' Urceus jabbed a thumb at the trees. 'I'm going for a piss.'

Quintus grunted. He was thinking about his former friend Hanno. Was he dead? Four and a half years had passed since their last meeting. In that time, there had been scores of battles between the legions and Hannibal's army. Hanno could easily have been slain. If he had survived, he would be on the mainland, for none of Hannibal's troop had yet landed on Sicily. That knowledge made Quintus grateful. Hanno was one of the enemy, and it would be preferable if they never met again. He couldn't prevent a sneaky thought that wished Hanno still alive. There were worse men in the Roman ranks than he. Quintus couldn't quite bring himself to pray for Hanno, but he did not wish him dead. Enough good men had lost their lives, including his father, at Cannae.

'Gods, but I needed that,' said Urceus, returning. 'There was enough in my bladder to put out a burning house.'

'It's the wine you drank last night. If Corax caught you tipsy on sentry duty, he'd fucking kill you.'

'But he won't, because we're two of his best men, so he leaves us be,' Urceus said, grinning. 'Besides, I wasn't tipsy. Just happy.'

Quintus snorted, but Urceus was probably right. He could hold wine the way a barrel of sawdust soaked up water. Quintus' tolerance was far lower, which annoyed and pleased him in equal measure. He could do without the ribbing he got from his comrades for holding back, but it was good to feel normal the morning after a piss-up when the rest of them were grey-faced, sweating and vomiting. His eyes roved the landscape again. Far off to the south, a flash of light on the road drew his attention like a vulture to a corpse. 'Look!'

Urceus shot to his side, the banter forgotten. 'What?'

Quintus pointed. 'I saw sun glinting off metal. There it is again. And again. That's more than a couple of travellers.'

'It isn't going to be a merchant caravan. They're rare nowadays.'

'A Syracusan patrol then.' They watched as the group drew nearer. Corax would want details, and the newcomers were far enough away to risk waiting. That didn't stop them both gripping the hilts of their swords. Eventually, they could see the force was made up of horsemen and foot soldiers.

'How many?' asked Urceus.

'I'd say upwards of fifty riders, and four or five times that number of infantry. You?'

'About that. What in Hades' name are they up to?'

'Scouting around Leontini, perhaps? They won't be happy that we took it a while back.'

'You could be right. Maybe Hippocrates and Epicydes want to prove that they've got balls. This lot could be scouts for a larger force that will attack Leontini.' Urceus gave him a huge nudge. 'Either way, Corax will want to know. You keep an eye on them. I'll go.'

'Fine.' Quintus was already preparing himself for the fight. Since Hippocrates and Epicydes had taken control of the city, all Syracusans had become enemies. Corax wouldn't let this force by. His duty was to defend the road that led north. It wouldn't matter that the Syracusans outnumbered his men. He would want to give the enemy troops a bloody nose at the very least.

It was a pity that the approaching soldiers weren't Carthaginians. They were the ones who had started this damn war, who had killed his father. The Syracusans had reneged on a time-honoured treaty with Rome, though. They were the foe here. If we kill enough of the whoresons, Quintus decided, if we slay so many of them that we can build a bridge to the mainland with their skulls, the Senate will *have* to reinstate us. Frustration stung him, because even if they displayed such extreme savagery there was no certainty that it would convince the Senate of their loyalty. It seemed more likely that he would end his days on Sicily. That he would never see his mother or Aurelia again.

'What have we got to look forward to?'

The familiar voice dragged Quintus back to reality. He spun, saluted. 'A strong enemy patrol, sir.'

Corax, a middle-aged man with a narrow face and deep-set eyes, returned his salute casually. His eyes scanned the road to the south. 'I see the miserable dogs – moving along as bold as brass, eh? Like they own the damn place.'

'They must think we have no forces in the area, sir,' said Quintus.

'A stupid mistake to make,' replied Corax with a nasty leer. 'We'll have to teach them the error of their ways, eh?'

Quintus and Urceus exchanged a look. Corax had always been a tough taskmaster, but since he'd saved all of their lives at Cannae, his status had risen close to that of a god. Despite the familiar nervous feeling that pres- aged combat, they both grinned. 'Yes, sir,' they said in unison.

'Best get a move on. We want to be in position long before they reach us.'

Corax had picked a spot for their camp close to a massive old holm oak that had been torn down in a winter storm some months prior; its fall had entirely blocked the road. In peacetime, local landowners would have removed the obstruction. These days, travellers had simply hacked away enough of the smaller branches to be able to pass single file along one side of the carriageway.

'Marcellus will want the trunk shifted when he leads the legions to Syracuse,' Corax had declared when they'd arrived, 'but until then we'll leave it be.'

'Good idea not to move the tree, wasn't it?' Quintus whispered now. 'It's a perfect place for an ambush.'

'Damn right,' Urceus replied, chuckling.

Quintus didn't voice the concern that kept twisting in his guts. What if the Syracusans saw them?

Corax, who was pacing up and down behind them, whacked Urceus across the calves with his vine cane, and they fell silent.

Quintus, Urceus and the rest of the eighty men in Corax's century were hidden in the thick scrub nearest the 'passage' through the branches of the fallen tree. Sections of juniper bushes had been cut and laid in great heaps to conceal them. Every fifteen paces or so, there was a 'gateway' in the roughly made 'wall', covered over by a wedge of branches; a hastatus had been assigned to each, his job to pull the vegetation out of the way when Corax gave the word. Half of Corax's *hastati* had been placed some way beyond the blockage, and half before it. Quintus and Urceus were with Corax in the latter group; Ammianus, the century's second-in-command, led the former. Vitruvius, the maniple's junior centurion, lay on the other side of the road with his eighty soldiers, his force similarly divided.

Their hiding places would pass a casual glance, but Corax's tactic was risky. If the Syracusans were being vigilant, they would be exposed before the trap was sprung. Corax had said that if things went against them, they were to retreat towards their camp. At least the enemy cavalry wouldn't be able to follow them there. But Quintus didn't fancy being pursued by a superior number of infantry either. They won't see us, he told himself. Mars has his shield over us.

Through carefully cut gaps in the vegetation, they had glimpses of the road for about two hundred paces towards Syracuse. There was still no sign of the enemy troops — a final sighting from the sentry point had confirmed them as that — but it couldn't be long until they appeared. Quintus' mouth was bone-dry. He wiped his sweaty palms on his tunic, one by one, uncaring who saw. There was no shame in feeling scared. Any man who didn't was a fool, his father had said once, and he'd been right. Courage was about standing and fighting despite one's fear. Great Mars, he prayed, guide my sword into enemy flesh, and keep my shield arm strong. Bring me through this. Help my comrades in the same way, and I will honour you afterwards, as I always do.

An elbow in the ribs, and his attention shot back to the present.

'They're here,' hissed Urceus, who was squatting alongside.

Quintus peered again at the road. A file of riders, perhaps five abreast, had come into view. Sunlight glinted off their bronze cuirasses and Boeotian helmets. Their horses were also equipped in the old-fashioned Greek style, with chest plates and face guards — so they were definitely Syracusan. They looked unconcerned, which was promising. One man was whistling. Two others were arguing good-naturedly about something, shoving at each other and oblivious to their surroundings. Don't worry about them, Quintus thought. Unless there's a balls-up, we won't have to face the cavalry. That'll be up to Ammianus and his lot.

'See them, lads?' Corax whispered, stooping over the friends. 'Remember, not a fucking sound. We attack on my signal — when the horsemen have gone by. Javelins first, then a charge. Kill plenty, but not them all. I want prisoners. Marcellus needs to know what's going on inside Syracuse.'

'Yes, sir,' they muttered back.

But he was already gone, repeating his words to the rest of the hastati.

On the Syracusans came. The tension among the Romans was palpable. Men shifted from foot to foot; they gripped their javelin shafts until their knuckles went white. Lips moved in silent prayer; eyes were cast skyward. A man close to Quintus grabbed his nose in an effort not to sneeze. It didn't work, and he buried his face in the crook of one arm to deaden the sound. Veins bulged in Corax's neck, but he could do nothing to stop it. Close up, the choked sneeze seemed incredibly loud, and Quintus readied himself to charge forward. The ambush would be ruined, but they could still give the Syracusans something to remember them by.

His spirits rose as the enemy troops continued to advance. The noise of fifty horses and riders had concealed the sound of the sneeze.

No more than a hundred paces now separated the Syracusans from the holm oak.

A chorus of complaints rose as the obstacle became fully apparent. The patrol ground to a halt. Shouts carried to and fro as the situation was relayed to the commander. Eventually, two riders urged their horses right up to the fallen tree. Men were always aware of being looked at, so Quintus stared at the ground, his heart thumping in his chest. There was nothing stopping his ears, however. Greek. Of course they were speaking Greek, he thought. Syracuse had been founded by Greeks. Like any equestrian, Quintus had had to learn the language as a boy. For the first time since his childhood, he was glad of the fact.

'This damn tree wasn't here the last time we rode by,' said a deep voice. 'It's probably a trap.'

There was a derisive laugh. 'A trap? Who's going to cut down a thing this size, Eumenes? It'd take Herakles himself to push the damn thing over. Look at its roots – pointing to the sky. It fell over in a storm, most likely that one that lifted all the roof tiles in the city two months back.'

'Maybe it was blown over, but this is a perfect place for an ambush,' Eumenes grumbled. 'Thick bush on both sides. Most of the road blocked. We'll have to lead the horses through, break up the infantry's formation.'

'There hasn't been hair nor hide of a Roman patrol since we left Syracuse. They're all further north, I tell you. Here, take my reins. I'm going to take a look past the tree.'

Quintus glanced at Urceus, saw the tension in his face, realised that he had no idea what was being said. 'It's all right,' he mouthed. He risked a slow, careful look at the road, and his heart nearly stopped. Eumenes, a big, bearded man, appeared to be staring right at him – from twenty paces away. Two horses were visible right behind him. Shit! thought Quintus, dropping his gaze. For long moments, he remained frozen to the spot, uncomfortably aware of the rapid breathing of the men to either side, the little clicks from knee joints that had been bent for too long. To his intense relief, there was no cry of alarm from the road.

'Ho, Eumenes! Stop scratching your balls.'

'Piss off, Merops. Well, did you see anything?'

'Not so much as a Roman sandal print. I walked round the corner, had a good look to either side. The coast is clear.'

'Sure?'

'I'd stake my life on it.'

That's what you've just done, you fool, thought Quintus, beginning to hope that Corax's plan might work.

'C'mon. The boss will want to know what's going on.'

Next, the sound of men mounting up, horses walking away.

Quintus breathed again.

'What the fuck were they saying?' Urceus' lips were against his ear.

Quintus explained. Seeing the fear on the face of the hastatus to Urceus' right, he muttered, 'Tell your neighbour. I'll do the same on my side.'

Corax evidently spoke some Greek too, because he came along the line, telling men to be calm, that the enemy had no idea they were there. Reassured, the hastati settled down to wait. A message was sent to Ammianus to inform him of what was going on.

It wasn't long before the Syracusan horsemen dismounted. Quintus could hear them grumbling as they walked in single file towards the tree. Someone's horse was lame. Another rider's arse was sore. Who cared about that, complained a different man: he was starving! More than one said that their commander was a pain in the neck, or asked how much further they would have to ride that day? Quintus' lips tugged upwards. Soldiers everywhere were the same, whatever their allegiances. Be that as it may, they were the enemy, he reminded himself. They were no different to the Carthaginians who had slain his father. They were here to be killed, taken prisoner or driven from the field.

Stealthy looks told him how many of the cavalrymen had gone by. Progress was slow, and the tension unbearable, but the Syracusans remained focused on negotiating their way around the fallen holm oak. Five riders led their horses by, then ten, and twenty. Few men even glanced at the bushes skirting the roadside. It was as well, thought Quintus nervously, more conscious than ever of the stacked branches that served to hide him and his comrades.

Perhaps thirty of the horsemen had reached the other side when the hastatus who'd sneezed earlier convulsed in a new effort not to do so again. Corax was on his feet in a flash; darting over, he shoved a fold of the bottom of his tunic into the man's face.

Despite the danger, Quintus felt a smile creep on to his face. He saw the same amusement in Urceus' eyes. The idea of blowing snot on to Corax's clothing defied belief. Quintus had no doubt that the unfortunate soldier would pay for his mistake later. If he survived the fight, that was. *Gods willing, we both will.*

Chooo! Corax's attempt to kill the sound of the sneeze failed. The hastatus threw a terrified look at Corax, but the centurion was staring at the road, his jaw clenched.

Quintus' heart hammered out a new, frantic rhythm. His eyes shot to the enemy troops. So did everyone else's.

A short rider with a tidy-looking roan was next in line to work his way past the tree. Instead of moving forward, however, he was peering in their direction.

Shit, thought Quintus, he heard it. His gaze moved to Corax, who was as still as a statue.

The short rider glanced again, scowled. He turned to the man behind him. 'Look over to our left,' he said in Greek. 'The branches about twenty paces in, do they seem stacked to you?'

Fuck it! Quintus' mouth opened to warn Corax—

'Ready javelins! Aim high! LOOSE!' roared the centurion.

Quintus stood, flexed his right arm and lobbed his pilum in one smooth motion. He didn't try for a particular target. With the enemy soldiers filling the road, there was no need. Forty javelins flashed up into the air with his, a beautiful and deadly sight. Orders rang out from the far side of the fallen tree, and from the bushes over the road. Another shower of *pila* shot up, landing a couple of heartbeats after the first one. The screams from men and horses were just reaching their ears when Corax ordered a second volley. Quintus hurled his javelin skywards, praying that it too found a target. His next moves were reflex: drawing his sword, hefting his shield, muttering yet another prayer. Everyone was doing the same.

'Open the gaps,' Corax bawled. 'Men to the left, move first, then those to the right. Spread out. Hit the bastards, hard. GO!'

Quintus and Urceus were among the first hastati to advance. They had to move single file to the 'gateway', which felt slow, too slow. The instant that they were out the other side, however, they fanned out and formed a ragged line. Everyone broke into a loping run. Branches ripped at their faces, and the uneven ground made the footing treacherous, but there was no stopping the charge. The thrill and fear of combat had seized control.

'ROMA!' shouted Quintus. Urceus repeated the cry. So did his companions.

'ROMA! ROMA! ROMA!' the hastati opposite yelled in reply.

They covered the twenty paces at speed. Quintus' heart lifted at the scene that greeted them. Everything on the road was chaos. The javelin volleys had had maximum impact on the horses. Riderless mounts barged about, some wounded, some not, but nearly all out of control. A few horses were down, neighing in pain and lashing out with their hooves. A number of riders were still mounted, but there was no space for them to manoeuvre. To their front loomed the holm oak, and to their rear, the mass of infantry.

The cavalrymen were finished as a fighting force. Best to panic the rest of the Syracusans, thought Quintus. If they realised that they outnumbered the hastati, things could go bad, fast. 'That way!' He pointed at the enemy foot soldiers.

He led the way; Urceus and half a dozen of their comrades followed.

A pair of cavalrymen jumped into their path, brandishing *kopis* swords. Only one had a shield. Raising his *scutum*, Quintus made to slam it into the shieldless man's chest. He hadn't counted on his opponent's curved kopis blade coming in over the metal rim of his shield. Quintus jerked his left arm up, partly taking the blow on the metal rim of his scutum, but the tip of the kopis still struck the top of his helmet. The force of it buckled his knees. A heartbeat later, the pain arrived, a great wave of it that rushed from the side of his skull, filling his brain with stabbing needles. Reflex, training, the bitter knowledge that if he didn't keep moving, he'd be dead, kept Quintus from collapsing.

Straightening his legs, he drove forward, hoping that the cavalryman wouldn't react in time. A metallic clang as his scutum hit the man's cuirass told him that he hadn't. The weight of the kopis vanished from his shield, and he was staring down at the cavalryman, who had fallen on to the flat of his back. Naked fear filled the man's eyes. It's you or me, thought Quintus harshly, ramming his sword into his enemy's mouth. In. Twist. Feel the flesh open, the muscles part, the bone grate. Out. Gouts of blood chased his retreating blade. Quintus felt, but didn't see, the red tide that showered his lower legs and feet. He looked left, right. The other cavalryman was down, savage hacks in his neck and arms evidence of Urceus' efficiency. A horse with a javelin in one haunch came backing towards them, snorting with fear, but one of the other hastati smacked it with the flat of his sword and it bolted forward again. Then, a moment of calm in the madness.

Quintus touched his helmet where the kopis had hit. He felt a massive dent, but no break.

'You were fucking lucky there,' said Urceus. 'Head sore?'

'Worse than after a night on the piss,' replied Quintus ruefully.

'Can you fight?'

Fury replaced Quintus' embarrassment. He had to make amends for such a basic mistake, even if he wasn't quite ready. Had to stick with his comrades. 'Aye.'

Urceus knew him well enough not to argue. He nodded at the Syracusan infantry. 'They're scared, see? Not formed up tight yet. None of our lads have hit them at the front either. Let's take them. Four wide, two deep. Now!'

Their companions growled in agreement. They formed up, Quintus grateful that his friend had taken charge. He and Urceus stood side by side, each flanked by another man. The remaining four shoved in behind them, where they would provide momentum to their advance and be ready to step into the front rank if needs be.

'Move,' ordered Urceus. 'At the double!'

Skirting the bodies of the cavalrymen and that of a dead horse, they advanced towards the Syracusans. Had every enemy officer been injured or killed? Quintus wondered. Or were they that ill disciplined? None of the infantry were facing them. Instead they had wheeled to meet the attacks of the hastati from both sides of the road. Seeing the opportunity this granted, a swelling roar left his throat. If it went well, this had the potential to rout them in one fell swoop.

It was too good to be true.

A figure in a magnificent Attic helmet turned and saw them. He spat an obscenity, bawled orders. Men began to react, to face Quintus and the other hastati. Within a few heartbeats, a wall of shields had formed. Only ten or so of them, but they were the massive Greek ones, which protected the men behind from eyes to toes, and which locked in with their partners on either side.

'Nothing for it. We've got to charge,' said Urceus, baring his teeth. 'If we don't break the mangy sheep-humpers now, we'll never do it.'

Quintus' temples felt as if they were about to burst; he could taste bile at the back of his mouth, but there was no going back. He could not desert his comrades, could not run. Could not betray his father, who had died for Rome. 'Let's go.'

'With us, lads?' shouted Urceus.

'Aye!' came the response.

For all Quintus' fear, he loved the comradeship in such moments. Loved the feeling of men standing shoulder to shoulder with him, and at his back. They would stay by him because he would do the same for them. If he was to die, this was a better place than any.

Fifteen paces separated them from the Syracusans. It was close enough to see the designs on their shields, the deadly tips on their thrusting spears. As the eight hastati charged, the enemy line wavered, but it did not break. The officer behind continued to roar encouragement. Quintus hated him in that moment. A leader like that made the difference between men standing and running. This one was far beyond their reach, though. He'd be the death of them. Spears had a greater reach than *gladii*.

Thirteen paces. Ten.

Astonishment overcame Quintus as a javelin arced down from nowhere. It took the Syracusan officer in the face. His hands reached up to grab at the shaft, but his strength had already gone. He was a dead man, standing. With a horrible choking noise, he fell from sight. A wail of dismay rose from the soldiers around him. The heads of the men in the front rank turned to see what was happening. They moved back an involuntary step.

'Hit them – NOW!' It was Corax's voice.

In the blink of an eye, the balance of power changed. The confidence ebbed from the Syracusans and flowed back into the hastati. It had been Corax who had thrown the javelin, somehow Quintus knew it. The Syracusans would break when they struck them; he knew that too.

As they'd been trained, the hastati slowed down just before meeting the Syracusans. Hit an enemy too fast and you risked losing your footing. All the same, an almighty *crack* went up as they met. For a heartbeat, Quintus was back at another battle, when the sound had been as loud as thunder, when the very ground had trembled. That had been on the fields of blood. Today won't be like that, he thought fiercely. Break the shield wall, and they'll run. A spear scythed forward at him, but he ducked

48

behind his shield and it shot over his head. He repeated the move that he'd used on the cavalryman, using the power of his thighs to drive up and at the Syracusan. His opponent rocked back on his heels, but the shields to either side held his one in place. The Syracusan wasn't ready for Quintus' sword, however, which Quintus thrust over the top to take him in the neck. Instead of pulling back his right arm, Quintus shoved it forward again, at the same time pushing with his scutum. As the Syracusan died, he could do nothing to stop Quintus from forcing his shield from its position in the wall.

His headache forgotten, Quintus roared a battle cry and drove into the gap. It was an incredibly dangerous thing to do – he'd seen more than one man die by hurling himself at the enemy like this – but the opportunity could not be ignored. To his relief, there were no Syracusans in front of him. All he could see was the backs of two shield walls, the formations that were trying to contain the Roman attacks from each side of the road. In between stood another officer, shouting orders first at one group and then at the other. He hadn't seen what Quintus had done.

Quintus spun and stabbed an enemy soldier in the back, ramming his blade through the man's linen cuirass and doubling the size of the hole in the enemy line. Urceus came storming into it as Quintus half turned and cut down the Syracusan who'd been standing on the other side of the man he'd first killed. He had a chance to scan the scene. 'They're holding their own against the rest of our lads, but only just.'

'Whichever lot we hit from behind will break,' replied Urceus, panting.

'If that happens, the other group will shatter as well.'

'Aye.'

A moment later, five of their six comrades arrived, having killed or put to flight the remaining Syracusans. Two were bleeding from minor wounds, but all had fierce grins plastered across their faces.

Quintus laughed. It wasn't amusement; escaping Death's grasp did odd things to a man. 'Ready? One more effort and we'll nail the bastards' hides to the wall.'

The hastati roared their bloodlust back at him. Quickly, they formed up again, four wide with the three remaining men behind.

Quintus roared, 'ROMA!' and they charged.

Peeeeeeep! Peeeeeeep! Peeeeeeep!

Even with the battle fury running through him, Quintus heard Corax's whistle. He spat in the direction of the fleeing Syracusans whom he was pursuing, a mob of perhaps thirty men. They were in full flight to the south. Shieldless, weaponless, many not even wearing their helmets, the enemy soldiers did not look back as they ran. Their injured comrades who had fallen were forgotten. Everything was forgotten in their overwhelming desire to get away.

Peeeeeeep! Peeeeeeep! Peeeeeeep!

Quintus' training kicked in, and he came to a gradual halt. Sanity returned with each heaving breath. Soon he was glad to have been called back. Cutting down the Syracusans had been easy when they'd broken, and for the first few hundred paces of their headlong retreat. Yet a stage had come, as it always did, when chasing men who were no longer encumbered by weapons and armour became a real test of one's endurance. Quintus was grateful for the extra protection of his mail shirt, but it weighed ten times more than the bronze chest- and backplates that he'd worn as a newly promoted hastatus.

He shouted after his companions who appeared not to have heard the summons. Nearby, Urceus was doing the same. Only a handful of men who needed recalling. They had all been through enough war to know when to call it a day. Everyone knew of soldiers who had pursued so eagerly that they had become isolated and turned on by their prey. And that, Corax had drummed into them, was yet another stupid way to die.

They wandered back up the road, twenty-odd hastati, stripping the dead of water skins and dispatching the badly wounded Syracusans as they went. It was hard to be sure how many enemy infantry lay scattered around, but it was easily a hundred. The cavalrymen had fared even worse. Quintus had seen two or three riders galloping away from the slaughter, but that was it. Despite the sneezing hastatus, the ambush had been a resounding success. Those of the enemy who could walk were herded towards the main ambush site, some distance to the north.

Corax was interrogating a prisoner. He broke off from his questioning with their arrival. The side of his mouth lifted a fraction: it was his excuse for a smile. 'You heard my whistle?'

'Yes, sir,' answered Quintus.

'Any fools still chasing the Syracusans?'

'No, sir.'

'Good. Any officers among those you've got there?'

'Not a one, sir.'

'Kill them then. I've got the second-in-command here. One way or another, he'll sing like a canary.'

'Sir.' Quintus wasn't surprised. Corax wanted information, and if they couldn't provide that, captives were of no use. They had scant rations for themselves as it was; they could spare neither food nor men to guard even a few prisoners. He took no joy in killing men in cold blood, but the order had to be obeyed. He eyed his companions, readied his sword arm. 'You heard the centurion, brothers.'

'Not you, Crespo.'

Quintus stared at Corax in surprise. 'Sir?'

'Speak any Greek?'

The mere fact that the centurion had asked spoke volumes. Quintus had long wondered if Corax suspected that his origins were not what he'd said when enlisting. Quintus didn't know why; it was just the way that Corax looked at him sometimes. He hesitated for a heartbeat, aware that the longer he left it before replying, the more it appeared as if he were lying. 'A little, sir, yes.' Feeling awkward, he began to lie, 'I learned it when—'

'Save the explanation. Mine is as rusty as hell. Come here and translate.'

'Yes, sir.' Doubly relieved – that he'd escaped further questioning, and that he wouldn't have to help execute the prisoners – Quintus turned his back on the sobbing Syracusans, who were bunching together as Urceus and the rest closed in on them.

The well-built officer, who was bearded and a few years older than Quintus, had a shallow cut on his right arm but was otherwise unharmed. He regarded Quintus proudly. 'Are all of my men to be slain?'

Corax understood. 'Yes. Each one dead is a sword arm less on the walls of Syracuse,' he said.

Quintus looked at the officer. 'Did you understand that?'

A lip curl. 'Not really.'

Quintus translated.

'Is the same going to happen to me?'

Quintus didn't answer at once, and the officer said, 'Your commander's Greek is shit.'

Quintus glanced at Corax, who laughed. 'He's a confident prick, I'll give him that,' Corax said. 'He's right too. I've gathered that his name is Kleitos, and that he's second-in-command of a phalanx, half of which was on patrol. The commander was one of the cavalrymen. He's lying over there, missing half of his head. I can't make out any more of what he says.'

'What do you want me to ask him, sir?'

'The purpose of their patrol. Are there more of their forces in the area? Start with that.'

Quintus regarded Kleitos. 'Do you speak any Latin?'

'A few words, that's all.' This with a disdainful shrug. 'Decent Syracusans don't have much use for your tongue. Why would we?' He jerked his chin at the captives taken by Quintus and Urceus, many of whom had already been slain. 'You're fucking savages.'

'As if your soldiers aren't capable of the same,' Quintus replied, unmoved. 'I'm surprised by your lack of interest in Latin. Hiero was a faithful ally to the Republic for half a century.'

Another scornful look. 'He was a damn tyrant! Not everyone supported him, you know. There are plenty of nobles who are happy to see power now resting in the hands of Hippocrates and Epicydes.'

'I see.' Quickly, Quintus translated for Corax before regarding Kleitos again. 'What were you doing here?'

'Taking the air. Around Mount Etna, it's meant to be especially good for the health.'

'Don't be stupid,' said Quintus, his temper flaring. 'We'll get the information from you, the easy way or the hard. Those men being executed are only the start. Trust me, you don't want to piss off my centurion.'

Kleitos looked a little less certain, but then his chin jutted again. 'Why would I tell you anything? You'll kill me anyway.'

'Are there more Syracusan troops in the area?'

Kleitos stared balefully at him.

'What's going on?' demanded Corax.

'He thinks that we're going to get rid of him when we're done, sir,' replied Quintus. In an undertone, he added, 'Are we?'

'That depends,' rumbled Corax. 'If the dog tells me something worth knowing, I could release him. If he doesn't, well—'

Quintus felt uneasy at the idea of pushing his centurion, but he didn't want to lead Kleitos on under false pretences. 'Have I your word on that, sir?'

'You've got some balls, boy.' Corax's gimlet eyes pinned Quintus, but he didn't back down. After what seemed a long time, the centurion nodded. 'As long as his information is useful, he can go free. Tell the sewer rat that I'll be watching him, though. If I suspect the slightest treachery, the smallest lie, I will cut his damn throat myself.'

'Yes, sir.' Quintus turned to Kleitos. 'Tell us what you know. If it's of use to us, my centurion guarantees that you will be set free.'

'How can I trust you?'

'You have his word, and mine,' said Quintus. There was silence for a moment. He could see Kleitos was warring with himself. 'There's no glory in dying just because your men have to,' he urged.

'What would you know?'

'I was at Cannae,' replied Quintus soberly. 'You must have heard of the slaughter that day. By the time the sun was going down, there was barely a Roman alive. Those of us still living had given up hope, but not my centurion. He led us out, and we fought our way to safety. Our reward for that was to be sent in disgrace to Sicily. For all that, I'd rather be here, breathing, than for my bleached bones to be lying in the mud in Italy.'

Kleitos threw him a look of grudging respect. 'Very well. We were sent out to scout the area; to see if there were any Roman forces moving south yet. Hippocrates and Epicydes know that Marcellus will advance on the city; they want to know when.'

Quintus explained to Corax, who said in poor Greek, 'That sounds reasonable. Go on.'

'Are there more of your troops nearby?' demanded Quintus.

'Nowhere close.'

This pleased Corax. 'What is the current strength of the garrison in Syracuse?'

Quintus translated.

Kleitos scowled; then, oddly, he smiled. 'What does it matter if you know? You will never take the city. Upwards of thirty thousand men are under arms within the walls.'

'Thirty thousand?' repeated Corax, who had understood the number. 'How many of those are professional soldiers?'

Quintus asked the same in Greek.

'More than two-thirds. There will be time to train the rest when the siege begins,' replied Kleitos proudly. 'In addition, the slaves freed by Hippocrates and Epicydes number perhaps five thousand. Those are being armed and trained as well.'

Corax took a moment to digest that, but he didn't comment further.

That many defenders would mean fierce resistance to any attack. Quintus had never thought it was going to be easy, but this was bad news.

'What about catapults and the like? How many of those are there?' asked Corax.

'Catapults?' Kleitos had recognised the word. 'I don't know exactly, but it's a lot. Scores and scores of them, from small ones up to the beasts that can throw a stone the size of a temple altar.' He winked. 'We have no shortage of ammunition.'

Corax frowned when Quintus told him that. 'It's to be expected, I suppose,' he growled. 'A city like Syracuse isn't going to have stood there for hundreds of years without strong defences. It will have its own wells, and enough food to last many months. That's without supplies coming in from the sea, which will be difficult for us to prevent. It might be a long siege.' He eyed Kleitos. 'But Rome will prevail in the end.'

'We'll see about that,' answered Kleitos when Quintus had interpreted. 'Carthage will soon come to our aid.'

The word 'Carthage' and the tone of Kleitos' reply needed no explanation, although Quintus did so. Corax grinned when he was done, which made him look even more fearsome. 'One day, we'll see who was right, and I wager my left bollock that it won't be him. Tell the dog that. Then he can go.'

'I've no wish to take just one of your centurion's balls,' said Kleitos. He smiled but the gesture didn't reach his eyes, which promised something else altogether.

Quintus didn't bother translating. 'You're free.'

Kleitos inclined his head at Corax, who returned the gesture. 'Can I have my blade?' he asked, indicating a fine kopis on the ground nearby.

Quintus had to admire his bravery. 'He wants his sword, sir.'

'He must swear not to attack any of my men for a day and a night,' said Corax.

Quintus went and picked it up. Its blade was covered in blood. Roman blood, he thought angrily. Warily, he approached Kleitos. He had never returned a weapon to an enemy. 'You must take an oath not to harm any of us for a day and a night.'

'I swear before Zeus Soter not to do so,' said Kleitos, reaching out for the kopis.

Quintus hesitated for a heartbeat. They stared at each other over the sword.

'May he strike me down if I break my oath,' said Kleitos in a firm tone.

Quintus handed it over.

Kleitos' eyes smouldered. 'If we meet again, I will kill you. And your centurion.'

'You can do your best. We'll be ready for you,' retorted Quintus angrily. 'Now, go.'

Without another word, Kleitos strode past, over the bodies of his men, towards Syracuse.

'A courageous man,' observed Corax. 'If all the defenders of Syracuse are like him, the siege might take longer than Marcellus thinks.'

Chapter IV

'We see G-anny?'

Aurelia smiled. As ever, Publius' reedy voice mangled the word 'Granny'. Her mother hated it. No matter how many times Aurelia told her that he would eventually learn to say it, Atia had to correct him. She gazed down at him fondly, squeezing his hand. 'Yes, dear. We'll see Granny soon. It's not far now.'

It was mid-morning, one of the safest times of day to be out in Rome, and this part of the Palatine was a respectable area. That didn't stop Aurelia's grey eyes from roving the crowded street, searching for trouble. The brutal attack she'd suffered in Capua before Publius' birth, two and a half years prior, had left a lasting scar. Elira, her Illyrian slave, padded at her back – company and a buffer to criminals at the same time. Agesandros was walking a step or two ahead of her. Aurelia had been mistrustful, even fearful, of her father's Sicilian overseer since the death of Hanno's friend Suni, but on the capital's filthy streets, she was glad of his presence.

It wasn't that odd that he was also here. When they had first had to abandon their farm, and then to leave Capua itself, Agesandros had been left with no real role. He'd been with the family for many years, however. Almost by default, he had become a servant cum bodyguard for Aurelia's mother, Atia. During the chaotic, terrible weeks after Cannae, when it became clear that Fabricius would not be coming home, he had become indispensable to Atia. Nowadays, with mother and daughter living in Rome, he barely left Atia's side. Aurelia, who resided at her husband Lucius' house nearby, could not protest to her still-grieving mother about that. It wasn't as if she had to see him every day, and at times like this, he provided security.

Aurelia studied Agesandros as he walked. He was as bandy-legged and wiry as he had been all her life. The only discernible sign of ageing was the patch of silver hair above each ear. The cudgel in his right hand dangled nonchalantly, but Aurelia knew how fast Agesandros could spin it through the air. There would be a dagger secreted about his person too, of that she had no doubt. Nearing fifty, he was still an intimidating, ruthless presence. Men tended to get out of his way, which made their journey much easier. It struck her again that he was moving faster than he would usually, yet her son was growing heavy in her arms. 'Agesandros, stop. I need to rest for a moment.'

His head turned. Aurelia thought she caught a twitch of impatience in his lips, but it had gone so fast she couldn't be sure. 'Of course. Over here.' He gestured to their left. A few steps away, customers were sitting on stools at the counter of an open-fronted restaurant.

The smell of frying sausages and garlic hit Aurelia's nostrils as she set down Publius with a relieved sigh. She wasn't the only one to notice. 'Sau-sage?' her son piped. 'Sau-sage?'

'Not now, dear,' said Aurelia. Spotting Agesandros' foot tapping, irritation took her. 'What is it?' she demanded.

'Eh?' His face was a blank.

'You seem impatient. Are we in any danger?'

His eyes flickered over the passers-by, came back to her. 'No.'

Since he had slain Suni before her very eyes, Aurelia had feared Agesandros. She was still capable of interrogating him. 'Something's going on. What is it?'

His mask dropped for an instant; Aurelia saw the fear in his eyes.

She didn't like it one little bit. Since Cannae, their life had achieved some kind of stability. True, she didn't see her husband much, and Quintus and his best friend Gaius not at all, but Publius kept her busy. Life trundled by without daily trauma. No one dear to her had been hurt, or died. 'Agesandros. Tell me what's going on.'

'It's your mother,' he said reluctantly. 'She's not well.'

'I saw her a week ago,' protested Aurelia. There had been mention of a few nights' poor sleep, and that she had lost a little weight, but what woman complained about that? The first was the norm, and the second was always to be desired. 'She was fine then.'

'Sau-sage, Mama,' said Publius, scuttling away from her towards the counter. 'Sau-sage!'

Darting in pursuit of her son, Aurelia missed Agesandros' reply. She retrieved a grinning Publius, who had been handed half a sausage by the jovial woman serving at the counter, and returned. 'Well?'

He wouldn't look at her. 'She's been vomiting a lot. Complaining of a pain in her belly.'

'Something she ate, surely?'

'I doubt it. I've eaten everything she has, and I am fine.' He glanced up the street. 'Can we go?'

Aurelia scooped up Publius and followed Agesandros. She'd seen the look in Elira's eyes when he'd mentioned eating Atia's food, so it wasn't just her who had imagined the worst. 'Is Mother worried about being poisoned?' People's heads turned at the mention of the word 'poison', but she didn't care.

'Not at all. It's a coincidence that we had shared the same dishes.'

Not the food then. Her mother only ever drank water from a spring, so it wasn't that either, Aurelia decided. 'Has a surgeon attended her?'

'This morning. His visit is the reason that I came to fetch you.'

Real worry began to gnaw at her. 'Why? What did he discover?' Agesandros didn't answer, and Aurelia increased her stride to catch up with him. Publius bounced up and down, gurgling with delight at what he thought was a race. 'Agesandros. What did he say?'

He regarded her dispassionately. 'Your mother ordered me not to talk about it. She wants to tell you herself.'

'I see.' Aurelia's lips set in a thin line, but inside she had begun to panic. This kind of behaviour from her mother was unheard of. She took a deep breath, bestowed a warm smile on Publius. 'We'll see Granny soon, my darling!' To Agesandros, she said, 'Let us get there quickly.'

Apart from Publius, they made the rest of the journey in grim silence.

Atia sat up in the bed as Aurelia opened the door and made an effort to smooth down the rumpled bedclothes. 'Aurelia. Publius! How's my little soldier?'

'G-anny! G-anny!' Publius hurled himself on to the bed and into Atia's embrace.

Aurelia gazed approvingly at the reunion, but she was struggling to conceal her shock. To find her mother abed at this hour was unusual enough, but in a darkened room, and looking like this? In the seven days since Aurelia had last seen her, Atia had aged a decade or more. The poor light could not conceal her grey complexion, nor the fact that her sharply delineated cheekbones were bare of their usual dusting of ochre. Her black hair, normally held up and behind her head, hung in limp tresses on either side of her haggard face. 'How are you, Mother?' she said, hating the stupidity of the question.

A wan smile. 'I've been better, but I've also been worse. It will pass, with the help of the gods.' Atia stroked Publius' head. 'Would you like a sweet pastry, my little soldier?'

'Yes! Yes!'

'Run along to the kitchen then. Ask the cook if he has anything for you.'

Aurelia let a beaming Publius push past her before moving entirely into her mother's bedchamber. Her nose twitched with distaste. 'It's so stuffy. When was the last time you aired the place? It can't be healthy for you to be stuck in here all hours of the day. Come out to the courtyard. It's a lovely morning. Fresh air will do you good.'

Without a word, Atia lifted the blanket and swung her legs towards the floor. They too had become thin.

Suddenly, Aurelia felt old. Whether her mother realised it or not, their relationship had changed. She had become the carer, and Atia the patient. Whatever the outcome of her mother's illness, their roles would never fully be reversed. It was a natural evolvement in the parent-child relationship, she realised, but not one she welcomed at this particular moment. She held out her hand to Atia and together they walked outside. The daylight did her mother no favours. Aurelia fought her rising concern. The bags under Atia's eyes were as deep as craters; she stooped now rather than walked upright. It won't be anything serious, Aurelia told herself. Mother is as strong as an ox; she's never ill. She guided Atia carefully to the wooden bench by the step that led from the colonnaded walkway into the courtyard. The spot caught the sunshine; it was her mother's favourite place in the house. Aurelia suspected that she thought about Fabricius here. 'Look – the sun is still shining. It must be for you.'

'Ah,' whispered Atia, her eyes lighting up. 'I have missed sitting here.'

Aesculapius be with her, prayed Aurelia. She must be as weak as a kitten not to be able to make her way this short distance alone. They sat down side by side, Atia with a sigh of relief. Publius' shrieks of happiness could be heard from the kitchen. Overhead, a small bird trilled its optimism that winter was ending. The shouts of a mobile food vendor carried in from the street. Agesandros lingered in the courtyard, making a pretence of tending the vines, but more often than not, his gaze strayed to mother and daughter.

'Agesandros tells me that you haven't been feeling well.'

'Not for a number of weeks.'

'Why didn't you say?' Aurelia's guilt that she hadn't noticed and fear for her mother came out as anger. 'When I last saw you, you seemed fine! You mentioned losing a little weight, not sleeping that well, but it didn't seem to be anything of concern.'

'I didn't think so either. I've had such illnesses before, when I was younger. They passed, however. This hasn't.'

'So you called for a surgeon.'

A weary nod.

'Who was it?'

'A Greek, of course. One recommended to me by Lucius some time ago.'

Aurelia felt a little relief. If the surgeon came with her husband's approval, he wouldn't be one of the many charlatans who preyed upon the unwell. 'You should have had him attend you sooner,' she scolded.

'That's water under the bridge. He has seen me now.'

Would she have to prise the information out with a pair of pliers? 'So? Did he discover what ails you?'

'He thinks so.' A pause.

Aurelia's impatience grew, but when her mother's eyes lifted to hers and she saw the sadness there, utter panic took its place. 'W-what? What did he find?'

It was as if Atia hadn't heard her. 'I've been feeling bloated much of the time, even when I haven't eaten for many hours. Nauseous too. My skin itches for no apparent reason. Even on cold nights, I've been too hot; sweating as if I were in a *caldarium*.'

Aurelia was baffled, frustrated, scared. She wanted to shake her mother, but she reined in her fear. 'What did the surgeon find, mother?'

Atia placed a hand on her belly. 'During his examination, he felt something in here.'

Time stood still. Although Atia was right beside her, she seemed far away – almost as if Aurelia was at one end of a tunnel and her mother was at the other. '*Something.*'

'Yes. A growth of some kind.'

'A growth,' repeated Aurelia stupidly. 'Where?'

'He wasn't sure, but possibly on my liver.'

Aurelia felt sick. If the surgeon was correct . . . 'Can he treat you?'

'There are some herbs, some preparations he wants to make up for me.' Atia's hands, all skin and bone, fluttered in the air. 'He says they might help.'

The only way that Aurelia could make this horror real was to say the harsh words. 'Help, not cure.'

'Yes.'

'Is there no surgery that could be performed?'

A trace of Atia's old self returned; her eyebrows rose in disbelief. 'You know the answer to that question, child.'

Tears filled Aurelia's eyes. She felt utterly helpless. 'So you're going to die?' she whispered.

Atia's lips crooked. 'We all die.'

'Don't joke about it!' cried Aurelia. From the corner of her eye, she saw Agesandros' head whip around to watch them. Curse him, she thought. It's none of his business. She's *my* mother. 'You know what I mean.'

Atia took her hand and stroked it. 'The growth will kill me, yes. The surgeon was regretful, but sure of his diagnosis.'

'He could be wrong!' Aurelia said. Lucius' confidence in the Greek might be misplaced. 'We can get another surgeon to examine you.'

'I already have. One of the neighbours called in a few days ago; when she saw how ill I looked, she had her husband, a surgeon, come by when he returned home. He found the same lump in my belly.' Atia's gaze was calm. 'They won't both be wrong.'

There was no point arguing. The divine powers had done what they wished – as they had at Cannae, when her father had been among the slain. Damn them all! Aurelia's grief and fury threatened to overwhelm her, but then she remembered her reaction – raging, shouting, cursing the gods – when she'd heard the news of her father's probable death. Was this punishment for that outburst? It was hard not to think so. Aurelia longed to utter the same curses again, but she dared not. In the time since Cannae, she had curried favour with every deity in the pantheon, spending a fortune on sacrifices and offerings in temples, asking that her loved ones be looked after. Now, despite her devotion, this calamity had befallen her mother.

The gods were so fickle, so faithless, she thought bitterly. But fear sealed her lips. Publius and her brother were one reason to keep silent, Gaius and Hanno another. It was a long time until her son was five, and beyond the age that saw at least half of all children die from illness. On Sicily, Quintus risked being killed on a regular basis. The same would be true – if they were alive – of his friend Gaius, and Hanno, for whom she still had strong feelings. Aurelia couldn't bear to think about her loved ones dying. The gods had to be kept happy at all costs. I must be strong, she thought. For Mother's sake. She will need me in the days and weeks to come. Aurelia managed a confident but false smile. 'That doesn't mean that a third opinion won't be useful.'

'Very well,' Atia replied, closing her eyes and lifting her face to the sun. 'Do as you wish.'

This demonstration of her mother's weakness made Aurelia's grief resurge but, at that moment, Publius came hurtling into the courtyard. 'Mama! Mama!'

Reality hit home yet again. She *had* to go on, for her child's sake as well as her mother's. She hoped that Lucius returned home from his business trip soon. Although they were not that close, their relationship was serviceable. His presence at home would give her strength, but until that point, she was on her own. 'Here I am, my darling,' Aurelia said, opening her arms.

Aurelia had been frustrated and disappointed when the third surgeon, who had been suggested by her husband's business partner Julius Tempsanus, came to the same diagnosis as the previous two. She'd had no knowledge of the second surgeon – her mother's neighbour – so could therefore not make a judgement upon him. She respected the first, however, the Greek recommended by Lucius. He had attended her and Publius more than once; he was a sober, professional individual whose treatments had been effective. The last man had seemed no less skilled. He had also been the most sympathetic, telling Aurelia that her mother might live for months. 'The progress of these diseases cannot be predicted,' he'd said. 'Look on each day as if it might be her last, but tell yourself that she will still be here at Saturnalia.'

. Aurelia had seized on his advice, using it to give her strength in the trying time that followed. She had immediately written a letter to Quintus, telling him of their mother's illness; it had been truly bittersweet that a short message from him had arrived the day after she'd sent hers. Life was hard on Sicily, Quintus had said, but he was healthy and fit. Other than asking the gods to grant the same to his family, there was little he needed. He sent his fond regards to them all. When Aurelia had read that, she had broken down in tears. Lucius' news from Rhegium, that he would be detained by business for at least another two weeks, made her life even harder to bear.

She'd had no time to wallow in her grief. Publius had come down with a bout of vomiting and diarrhoea that confined him to bed for a week. Terrified that it was cholera or a similar disease, Aurelia had had the surgeon attend him twice a day. Despite her distrust of the gods, she had sacrificed at the temples of Aesculapius and Fortuna. To her intense relief, Publius had made a slow but steady recovery. The moment he was better – that very morning – Aurelia had hurried to Atia's house. During Publius' illness, she had refrained from visiting for fear of giving the disease to her mother. She'd had to rely on Agesandros, who had acted as a messenger daily.

The week might as well have been a month, or even two, she thought bitterly. Her mother, who was sitting on the same bench where Aurelia had first heard of her illness, had lost even more weight. She resembled the victim of a famine, with her skin stretched tight over her bones. Aurelia's heart bled to see her like it. 'Mother,' she said brightly. 'There you are.'

Atia turned, and Aurelia saw with horror that the whites of her eyes had turned yellow; there was even a tinge of the same colour to her complexion. At this rate, Aurelia decided, she wouldn't last until spring.

'Daughter.' Her voice was husky and weak. 'Where is Publius?'

'I left him at home with Elira. He's still not fully recovered.'

'The poor little mite. I have been looking forward to seeing him again.'

'I'll bring him tomorrow, Mother.' She held up the covered pot in her hands. 'I've made you some soup. It's vegetable, your favourite. You should have some – it will give you strength.' She twisted her head, looking for a slave to fetch a bowl and spoon.

'I'll have some later,' interrupted Atia. 'Not right now.'

Aurelia noted the beads of sweat on her mother's forehead. 'Very well,' she said sadly.

'Come. Sit by me.' Atia patted the bench.

Fighting tears, Aurelia sat, placing the soup between her feet. They clasped hands.

'You're the image of your brother,' said her mother out of the blue. 'You have the same black hair, the same eyes, the same chin.' There was a sigh. 'How I wish he was here.'

The longing in Atia's voice brought a tear to Aurelia's eyes. 'You'll see him again,' she lied.

'I won't.'

Aurelia pretended that she hadn't heard. 'How are you feeling?'

'I've never been one for subterfuge, child, you know that. I'm dying.'

For all that the evidence was before her, Aurelia was still shocked. 'Don't say that, Mother!'

Atia took her hand and placed it on her belly. 'Tap it.'

Horrified yet fascinated, Aurelia obeyed. The feeling of fluid thrilling beneath her touch was unmistakeable. 'What does it mean?' she whispered.

'My liver has failed. The growth has doubled in size, the surgeon says, or more. I'm not surprised. I'm constantly nauseous now. Even drinking water makes me want to vomit. There are worse signs too, things I wouldn't want you to know.'

Aurelia stroked her mother's fingers in an effort to stay composed. 'Did he say how long?'

A tired laugh. 'At this stage, I think I know better than he does what will happen. A few more days, that's all.'

An odd feeling of calm settled over Aurelia. 'You're sure?' she heard herself saying.

'Yes.' Atia's yellowed eyes were serene. 'I will be reunited with Fabricius sooner than I imagined. How I have missed him!'

But you're leaving me behind! I have no friends in Rome, and only Publius for company, Aurelia wanted to scream. Instead she said, 'He will be overjoyed to see you, Mother.'

They sat in silence for a little while, Atia lost in her own thoughts and Aurelia trying to divert her grief by thinking of the arrangements that would soon need to be made. Not for the first time, she cursed the war, which meant that there was no chance of Quintus attending the funeral, or of holding it at their home near Capua. Capua and the area around it now followed Hannibal. 'Have you decided where you might like to be . . .' Her voice cracked and broke. '. . . buried?'

Atia's touch on her cheek was more welcome than she could remember. 'Child, you must be strong. Publius needs you. Your husband relies on you. Quintus will need your letters as well. You are the centre point of the family.'

Aurelia swallowed, nodded. 'Yes, Mother. What I was going to say is that the family mausoleum is too far away, and too dangerous for us to use.'

'I've made some enquiries. It's not expensive to have a simple structure erected on the Via Appia. Agesandros can give you the details of the stonemason with whom I spoke. My ashes can be placed in the tomb after my cremation, to remain there until the war is over. After that, you can take them back to Capua. I'd like it if you could put a vase with your father's name beside mine.'

Aurelia felt as if a scab had been picked off an old wound. Her father's bones would never be retrieved. With countless thousands of others, they still lay unnamed on the fields of blood, at Cannae. 'Of course, Mother.'

'That's settled then.' Atia smiled. 'I drew up my will some time since. Naturally, Quintus will receive the farm and the remaining slaves. He will also get what money remains. Despite what I've had to spend running this household, there's a little left. The sale of the agricultural slaves raised quite an amount. To you, I bequeath my jewellery and personal possessions.'

Aurelia bowed her head. 'Thank you, Mother.'

'There's not much left now. Much of what I had was sold to pay that vulture Phanes.' A brittle laugh. 'If there's one good thing to be said for the war, it's that he sided with the Capuans when they turned traitor. I haven't had to pay him since Cannae. We can't go near the farm at this moment, but one day, when Hannibal has been beaten, Quintus will be able to return there. It will be ours once more.'

Aurelia thought it possible that the conflict with Carthage would eventually be won, but there was no certainty that her brother would come back. She closed her mind to that grim prospect. There was only so much grief that she could cope with. 'I shall visit the farm too. It will be wonderful to see it again,' she said, thinking not of the family tomb but of the last time she had been there, and kissed Hanno. Guilt washed over her that she could think of herself at a time like this.

'There is one more thing.'

Aurelia gave her mother a questioning look.

'Agesandros is to be manumitted, and discharged of his duties to the family once I am gone. He has spent more than half of his life in loyal service to us. Since your father's death, he has been invaluable to me. I know that he desires to return to Sicily before his own death, and as it is in my power to grant this wish, I will do so.' She glanced at Aurelia. 'I imagine that you will not be displeased by this?'

'No. It shall be as you wish, Mother.' I'll be so glad to see the back of him, thought Aurelia.

'That's enough talk of death,' her mother pronounced. 'I want to hear about Publius.'

Aurelia was more than relieved to talk about her son.

*

Atia lapsed into unconsciousness the day after, at which point Aurelia moved herself, Publius and Elira into the house. She was not going to miss her mother's passing. Trusting her son to Elira's care, Aurelia spent every hour of the day and night by Atia's side. On occasion, she tried to get her to swallow some liquids. There was little point. In the brief moments when Atia was conscious, she refused all food or drink. Apart from wiping her mother's forehead with damp cloths and changing the bedclothes, Aurelia's only role was to provide company as Atia slipped away. She tried to accept this bittersweet situation, but it was hard. Aurelia was not alone: she saw Elira and Publius each day, but she couldn't confide in the former – because she wanted to maintain a distance between them – or the latter. When Agesandros looked in on Atia, Aurelia avoided him. Two more days passed in this lonely fashion.

On the fourth day, Atia woke again, appearing a little stronger. It was stupid to feel encouraged, yet Aurelia couldn't help herself. They had a short conversation – about, of all things, Atia's own childhood in Capua – before her mother asked to see Publius. 'I want to talk to him one last time,' she said. Aurelia trembled with emotion while her son was in the room, but the gravity of the situation was lost on him. Like any very small child, Publius had no real concept of death. After he'd kissed Atia farewell, he was happy enough to be led from the room by Elira with the promise of a honey cake. 'Bye, G-anny,' he said over his shoulder.

'Bless him,' whispered Atia, closing her eyes. 'He's a good boy. I will miss him. And you.'

'You will be sorely missed.' Aurelia kissed her mother on the forehead.

Atia didn't really speak again. It was as if her mother had saved up the last of her energy to say goodbye, thought Aurelia as the tears rolled down her cheeks.

Not long after sunset, Atia stirred a little under her blankets. Aurelia, who had been dozing on a stool alongside the bed, woke at once. She caressed away the straggles of wispy hair that had moved over her mother's face, and murmured what she hoped were reassuring words.

Atia muttered 'Fabricius' twice. She took a deep breath.

Aurelia's heart caught in her chest. Even after the last few days, she wasn't ready for the end.

Her mother let out a long, slow exhalation.

Aurelia had no idea if it was the last breath, but she bent and touched her lips to her mother's anyway. If at all possible, the soul had to be caught as it left the body. She sat, her back rigid, watching Atia's chest to see if it moved again. It didn't. *She's gone.* Aurelia placed a hand on her mother's ribs, under her left breast. The heartbeat she felt was irregular, and slowing fast. When she wet a finger and placed it beneath Atia's nostrils, she felt no movement of air.

Aurelia placed her hands in her lap and regarded the body that had been her mother. It was done. Just like that, Atia was gone. It didn't seem real. The sound of Publius' voice, carrying in from the courtyard, and Elira's tones, replying: they were real. But this wasn't. It was a horrible dream, from which she would wake at any moment.

Except she didn't. The harsh reality sank home some time later when Elira came in to let her know that Publius had gone for his nap. Aurelia looked again. Her mother still lay unmoving on the bed before her. The waxen sheen of death had begun to appear on her skin. There was no denying it now.

Elira came a little further into the room and saw Atia. She gasped. 'Is she – is she gone?'

'Yes,' murmured Aurelia, leaning forward to close her mother's eyelids.

Elira let out a little sob. 'She was a good mistress. Always fair. May the gods look after her.'

'I'll need help to lay her on the floor, and to anoint her. She must be cremated in her finest dress,' Aurelia heard herself saying in a monotone. Elira threw her a concerned look, but she didn't acknowledge it. The only way that she was going to get through this was to remain completely matter of fact. She could grieve later, when it was all done. 'Then we must lay her on a table in the *atrium*, and place a coin in her mouth. Word must be sent to the family's friends in Rome, and arrangements made for the funeral.'

'Yes, mistress,' replied Elira, respect filling her eyes.

'Fetch Agesandros to me. Bring oils, and clean cloths, and the dress my mother used to wear to banquets.'

Elira scuttled from the room.

When she had gone, leaving Aurelia with her mother's corpse, her mask slipped a little. The tears began to flow again. Her marriage to Lucius had separated her from Atia, but the space between them had never been more than the distance between their two houses. In its place there loomed a chasm that could never be bridged. Why did it have to be now, with the war keeping Quintus away? Aurelia railed silently. Her mother had been fit and well for her entire life. She could have expected to live for another five to ten years.

The quiet knock helped Aurelia to regain control. She wiped the tears from her face. 'Come.'

Agesandros slipped inside. His dark eyes drank in Atia's body, and his lips thinned. 'She is dead then. Although it was a release for her, I am sorry for your loss.'

Aurelia inclined her head in recognition. 'I want you to go to the Forum and the markets. Find the stonemason whom she spoke with first. A tomb needs to be built.'

'And the plot that it will be built on?'

'I will see to that. There are lawyers who act for the vendors of such land. You must also find musicians and actors for the funeral. Some of the household slaves can be pallbearers.'

'They will be honoured. I will act as one too, should you permit it.'

How could she deny him that? 'Very well.'

'My thanks.'

'Mother spoke highly of you before the end.'

Agesandros looked pleased. 'I have always done my best, first for your father, and afterwards, your mother.'

It felt bizarre to be having this conversation over Atia's body, but Aurelia felt he should know. 'You are to be rewarded for that service with manumission, and not only that, but discharge from any duties to this family. It was one of my mother's last commands.'

Wonder, and then joy, flared in his eyes. He approached the bed, lifted Atia's hand and kissed it with great respect before replacing it on the covers. When he straightened, he was very close to Aurelia. It took all of her self-control not to retreat. 'You will be glad to see me gone,' he said.

Despite her fear, she met his gaze. 'I will. We both know why. Suni was no threat to our family.'

'I disagreed, and so did your mother,' he said emotionlessly. Then, 'If the paperwork can be drawn up in time, I will depart after the funeral.'

You're not free yet, she thought angrily, but she didn't possess the energy for an argument. 'That can be arranged. You'll travel to Sicily?'

'If I can find a ship to take me, yes.'

'It will be dangerous there, with the war.'

'Good. I intend to take service with the legions, in whatever role they will have me.'

Her temper flared up. 'The Carthaginians whom you encounter will be innocent of the murder of your family.'

His anger rose to meet hers. 'I don't care! They're all gugga dogs, who need killing.'

Aurelia recoiled from his fury. She thought of Hanno, whom Agesandros had hated, and tried not to feel scared for him. He was serving on the mainland. Even if he ever came to Sicily, there was no chance of him and Agesandros meeting. That didn't stop her from toying with the idea – for a guilty moment – of refusing to grant the Sicilian his freedom. Yet her mother's wish, made on her deathbed, could not be denied. Aurelia had no desire to court more divine misfortune. Rallying her courage, she said,

'That is your opinion, and that of a slave. To me, they are just our enemies. They need to be defeated, but not annihilated.'

The walk from the city behind the slaves carrying her mother had taken an age. Aurelia had hated every dragging moment of it. The slow pace. The actors wailing at the front; the musicians playing solemn dirges. Atia's body, rocked gently from side to side by the motion of the litter. The disinterested, even annoyed looks from pedestrians on the packed streets. Once out on the Via Appia, it had been only a little easier. They had had to negotiate their way past hordes of travellers and files of carts and wagons bound for the capital. Their arrival at the newly constructed brick tomb, some two miles from the city walls, had been a welcome relief, but the screams of the pig, as it was sacrificed in honour of the goddess Ceres, had not. Nor had the falsely eulogistic words of the priest she'd hired for the occasion. In a daze, Aurelia had watched the placing of her mother's body on the pyre that sat alongside the vault. Her grief had come bubbling up then and she'd been grateful for Tempsanus' fleshy hand on her arm, and for his support when she'd had to step forward with the burning torch and set the timbers alight. It had been the right decision to leave Publius behind. The protest had been there in Elira's eyes when Aurelia had ordered her to look after him, but she hadn't argued. Regardless of what others might say about children attending funerals, thought Aurelia, seeing a human body burn was not something that a two-and-a-half-year-old should witness.

Thank all the gods that the wind was blowing away from them. Despite that, the stench of burning human flesh hung in the air, trapped perhaps by the towering cypresses that stood around. Even when the pig had been butchered and set to cook on another fire, the normally welcoming smell of roasting pork had not helped. Nonetheless, she had eaten some of the meat. It was part of the ritual. Somehow, she had prevented herself from bringing it back up again, had accepted the condolences of the dozen or so mourners, who had mostly been aged relations. A number of hours had passed since then. Few people remained. Tempsanus, bless him, had stayed by her the entire time. She was grateful for that. He hadn't tried to talk to her; his mere presence had helped. At last the smell from the pyre was waning. There would be little left now of her mother but bones and ash. Aurelia stirred; offered up a last prayer. The slaves would tend the fire until her mother's remains could be removed and placed in a funerary urn. She could return the following day to oversee their interment in the plain tomb alongside. That would be difficult, she knew, but for the moment her ordeal was almost over.

Or so she thought.

Initially, she paid no attention to the clatter of hooves from the nearby road. The Via Appia was the busiest thoroughfare in the land; scores of horsemen had ridden past them that day. It was when a horse and rider cantered off the road, towards the pyre, that she felt the first stirrings of alarm in her belly. All eyes focused on the newcomer, a young man in a dusty tunic. He looked exhausted, but there was nothing wrong with his voice. 'I seek Aurelia, wife of Lucius Vibius Melito,' he called out. 'I was told to seek her here, among the tombs.'

The attention reverted to Aurelia. She took a deep breath and stepped forward. 'I am she.'

The rider dismounted and threw the reins to a slave. He approached Aurelia, delving into the leather satchel that hung from a cord over one shoulder. 'I beg your pardon for disturbing you at this time, my lady.'

She waved a hand in dismissal. The fashion of his arrival had driven all thoughts of her mother from her mind. 'What is it?' she asked, fighting real anxiety.

'I bring news, from Rhegium.'

Instead of the normal elation she would have felt at this news, Aurelia felt dread. What was going on?

'Have you ought for me?' Tempsanus interrupted. 'I am Melito's business partner.'

Relief blossomed on the rider's face. 'Yes, sir. I have a note for you as well.'

Aurelia advanced a couple of steps. 'Could you not find our house – Melito's house?'

'I found it, mistress, but I was charged with delivering the note into your hands and no one else's.'

So the messenger had ridden past them, into the city, and back out again to where they stood now. From the corner of her eye, she could see Tempsanus frowning. Despite the pyre's heat, cold sweat began running down Aurelia's back. 'Is everything all right? Is my husband well?'

The messenger would not meet her gaze. Silently, he proffered the letter.

Aurelia closed her eyes. Let me be imagining this, she prayed. But when she looked up again, the parchment was still there in front of her. With a trembling hand, she took it.

'Shall I read it for you?' The concern was clear in Tempsanus' voice.

'No.' Cracking the seal, she unrolled it. Dimly, she heard Tempsanus demanding his note. After that, her attention was locked on the neat script that covered the page.

'From the hand of Caius Licinius Stolo, agent of Lucius Vibius Melito and Julius Tempsanus in Rhegium—'

It wasn't from Lucius. Aurelia's fear reached new heights.

'I send greetings to Aurelia, wife of Melito.'

Her eyes sped on, skimming the pleasantries. The words 'watching the loading of a ship', 'iron ingots' and 'a rope snapped' leaped out at her. Full of fear now, she read on. Stolo wrote that her husband had been gravely injured. The surgeon had diagnosed a shattered pelvis, multiple cracked ribs, two broken legs and a fractured arm, but it was Melito's head injury that was giving rise to the most concern. 'In the hours since the accident, he has rarely been conscious. When he does awake, it seems that he has no idea who he is, or where he is.' Aurelia felt sick; she struggled to finish reading the letter. It closed with an attempt at reassurance, telling her that no efforts were being spared with regard to Melito's care. She was to remain calm; to pray, especially to Aesculapius, and to wait for more news.

Aurelia took a moment to rally her strength before pinning the messenger with her eyes. 'Did my husband yet live when you left?'

'Yes, mistress.'

'How many days ago was that?'

'Four. The message would have been sent by ship, but the weather was too severe.'

It was then that Aurelia took in the lines of exhaustion on his face, the dirt that was ingrained in every patch of exposed skin. The man must have ridden like a demon, and changed horses many times. She would have to reward him well, she thought absently. Four days. For someone with such severe injuries, it was a lifetime ago. Aurelia's eyes moved to Tempsanus. She saw the same awareness there. 'He could already be dead,' she said, her tone flat.

'Let us not think like that, my lady,' he urged. 'Lucius is a young man; he's at the peak of his physical strength. It will take time, and the help of the gods, but he may yet recover.'

Aurelia nodded, trying to believe him. Inside, however, she was terrified that Lucius was as dead as her mother. She felt an overwhelming need to hold Publius, to feel his breath warm her cheek, to know that he at least was still with her. It was also obvious what else she had to do.

'I shall set out for Ostia in the morning, and there take ship for Rhegium,' she heard Tempsanus' voice saying. 'The Bark of Isis was launched last week, so the winds should be with us.'

'I want to travel with you,' said Aurelia.

Tempsanus gaped. Regaining his composure, a fatherly, knowing expression crept across his face. 'I cannot countenance that, my lady. You must celebrate the sacred feast for your mother in nine days. Besides, your husband would not approve of you leaving Rome.'

'I need to be by his side.'

'Your devotion is to be admired, my lady, but the sea journey is too perilous. Bad weather sinks many vessels. Syracusan and even Carthaginian vessels can be found in the waters off Rhegium. It's no voyage for a woman of your station to undertake.'

Aurelia began to object once more, but Tempsanus was having none of it. 'Your grief is clouding your judgement, my lady. It is time for you to return home, to your son. You need rest and sleep. I will call on you in the morning, before I leave.'

Aurelia didn't have the strength to argue. 'Very well,' she whispered.

'Mama, Mama!' cried Publius the instant that Aurelia emerged from the *lararium* and into the courtyard. He was playing by the central fountain, with Elira in watchful attendance nearby.

Aurelia had seen him briefly upon her return from the funeral, but had left him since in the care of Elira. She needed time to try and absorb her mother's death and the news about Lucius. On this occasion, however, there was to be no escape. Publius scampered over, his arms outstretched. She stooped to pick him up, grateful that his innocence would not see through her false smile. 'Hello, my darling.'

'Come and play,' he ordered.

She gave in. 'What are we to do?'

'Splashing in the water.' It was one of his favourite games.

The simple pleasure that Publius took in playing by the edge of the fountain, and the endless repetition of what he demanded she do – flicking water over his hands and arms, and occasionally a few drops on his face – took up all of Aurelia's attention. It was a relief not to think about her mother, about Lucius, about anything other than amusing her son.

The approach of the doorman a short while later was an unwelcome distraction. A strapping Thracian bought by Lucius upon their arrival in Rome, he lingered unhappily on the edge of her vision, not quite prepared to intervene on the domestic scene. Eventually, Aurelia could ignore him no longer. 'Publius, quiet for a moment. Who is at the door?' she demanded. 'Another itinerant soothsayer who wants to peddle his lies? Someone purporting to sell the finest perfumes in Rome?'

'No, mistress,' he mumbled.

'Who then?'

'He wouldn't say.'

'In that case, send him away!' she snapped.

'He's i-insistent.' He stumbled over the word. 'He asks to speak with you, mistress. Aurelia, daughter of Gaius Fabricius.'

Aurelia's head spun to regard him. In Rome, few people indeed knew her father's name. 'What else?'

A helpless shrug. 'Nothing, mistress.'

There was no point interrogating the Thracian further. 'Let the man in. Search him for weapons, and bring him to me.'

'Mistress.' The Thracian was already backing away.

'Time to play with Elira again, my sweet. Go and find her. I will be back soon.' She planted a kiss on Publius' head and walked into the *tablinum*. There she would find some privacy.

She paced to and fro, wondering who was this visitor with knowledge of her family. With a sudden dart of fear, she thought of Phanes, the moneylender her mother had talked about. Before Cannae, he had made their lives a misery. She dismissed the idea. He wouldn't have the balls to come here. Nevertheless, Aurelia was relieved to see that the man following the Thracian was not Phanes. He had the same dark complexion, but his black hair was tight and curly, not in oiled ringlets. Aurelia didn't recognise him. Composing herself, she took up a position by the lararium, asking the household gods to watch over her.

The Thracian stopped a few paces from her. 'He had a knife, mistress, but he gave it up easy enough. Nothing else on him, apart from a purse.'

Aurelia nodded her approval. 'Remain here.'

The Thracian stepped to one side, allowing the visitor to approach. He bowed courteously. 'Have I the honour of addressing Aurelia, daughter of Gaius Fabricius?'

'And wife of Lucius Vibius Melito. You do, yes. Who are you?'

He looked up, revealing deep blue, wary eyes. 'My name is Timoleon. I am an Athenian merchant.'

'I know no Athenian merchants. Perhaps you have come to see my husband? He is not here—'

'I am here to see you, my lady. I bring you a message.'

Aurelia felt a familiar flutter of fear in her belly. This could not be more bad news from Rhegium. Could it? 'From whom?'

'A friend.' He cast a sideways glance at the Thracian.

Aurelia understood. 'Return to the atrium,' she ordered. The Thracian looked unhappy. 'You've got his knife, haven't you?' she cried. 'If I need you, I will call out. Go!'

With a final glare at Timoleon, he shuffled off.

'Approach,' Aurelia directed.

Timoleon drew near. 'Thank you, my lady. My real name is Bomilcar.' He paused. 'It's Carthaginian.'

Aurelia's throat tightened. 'Hanno sent you?' she whispered.

'I am here on . . . other business, but Hanno asked me to seek you out if I could.'

'D-does he not think that I am still in Capua?' she stammered.

A slight upturn of his lips. 'With the city gone over to Hannibal? He knows that you and your family will always remain true to Rome.'

She felt her cheeks grow warm, and not just because Hanno had guessed where her loyalties lay. She thought of their embrace, the kisses that they had shared on the night of their chance encounter. 'How did you find me then? How could you know where I had gone?'

'I didn't. My mission was to come to Rome, and while I was here, I made some enquiries. As you might imagine in a city of this size, they came to nothing. I gave up eventually. Two nights ago, however, I fell into conversation with a group of stonemasons who were drinking at my inn. One of them happened to mention that he'd been commissioned to erect a tomb to a lady named Atia, the wife of a man called Gaius Fabricius. He didn't know much more, but I gambled that there wouldn't be too many individuals by that name in Rome. It was easy enough to persuade him to tell me where your mother lived. A bronze coin placed in the hand of a slave there gave me your name and address, and here I am.'

'You are a resourceful man.' As Bomilcar smiled in recognition, Aurelia gave thanks for his persistence. 'Is Hanno well?'

'He is. Hale and hearty. He commands a phalanx of Libyan spearmen. Hannibal favours him too.'

Even the mention of Rome's worst enemy and his soldiers, who had laid waste to half of the Republic, could not stop a creeping joy stealing over her. Hanno was alive and in good health! The gods had not abandoned her completely. 'What message did he give you?'

'He asked me to tell you that he thinks of you often. Often.' Bomilcar let those words sink in before adding, 'He said, "Tell her that with the gods' help, we will see each other again one day."'

Aurelia felt her knees grow weak. 'I hope so. One day,' she murmured.

Bomilcar smiled. 'May my gods and yours see that it happens. Now, with your permission, I must go.'

Aurelia had to stop herself from crying out: 'No!' She longed to ask Bomilcar more, to get him to tell her everything about Hanno, yet she held her peace. Bomilcar was an enemy spy, in the heart of enemy territory. 'You have risked much to come here. I offer you my heartfelt thanks, and the blessings of this household. Go in peace, and may your return journey be swift and safe.'

He gave her a grateful nod.

'Can you take Hanno a message from me?'

His face grew sorrowful. 'Alas, my lady, I cannot.'

'Why?'

'I am not at liberty to say.'

'I swear, upon my mother's grave, that I will not tell a soul,' she beseeched.

A wary look, a sigh. 'Hanno has gone to Syracuse.'

'On Sicily?' Her heart leaped. Rhegium was close to the island, where Quintus was. Now Hanno would be there too.

'That is already too much information. I cannot tell you any more.'

'Very well. Thank you,' she said, bowing her head.

'Farewell.'

When she looked up, Bomilcar was gone. An aching hole opened in Aurelia's heart, and she longed to run after him. The encounter had been too brief, yet to delay Hanno's friend would endanger his life. Receiving a message from Hanno out of the blue was enough good fortune, she told herself, and it gave her even more reason to go to Rhegium, to Lucius' side. Aurelia felt only a little guilt. There was no chance of seeing Hanno or Quintus – how could there be? – but it would be comforting to be so close to them, even if it was for but a short while. No one else would know her underlying purpose; to all intents and purposes, her journey would look like that made by a devoted wife.

The main obstacle in her way was Tempsanus, but Aurelia had a feeling that she knew how to get around him.

'You can say what you wish,' said Aurelia, the next morning. 'You are going to delay leaving until the feast in honour of my mother has been held in eight days' time. Then I'll be coming with you. So will my son, my body slave and my father's old overseer, who has just been manumitted.'

'The delay—' he began.

'Is acceptable.' It was what she'd told herself repeatedly. Aurelia was not prepared to leave her mother's funeral unfinished. 'The day and hour of our arrival will not influence Lucius' recovery. Only the gods can do that.'

Tempsanus sighed, looking apologetic. 'I am sorry, my lady, but I will not allow it.'

Aurelia was ready. 'Nothing in life is as important as those whom we care for,' she said passionately. 'I am not from Rome. What have I here?

Other than my son and a few slaves, nothing! If you will not take me, I shall find my own way to my husband's side.'

'What do you mean?'

'I will go to Ostia and find a ship that's sailing south.'

'No captain will take you!'

'For the right money, anything can be bought,' Aurelia retorted. 'Someone will be willing to afford us passage.'

'You can't do that,' said Tempsanus, with genuine alarm. 'For all you know, they might plan to steal your money, or sell you as slaves! Worse, perhaps.'

'The gods will protect us,' Aurelia declared breezily.

'No. You cannot do this, my lady. As much as anything, Lucius would never forgive me.'

'It's none of your concern, Tempsanus. You are to leave today, is that not so? Once you've left, I will follow on behind. You can't stop me.' She gave him her most determined stare.

There was a short pause before resignation began to set into Tempsanus' eyes and Aurelia knew that she had won.

'Very well,' he said with a sigh. 'May Fortuna watch over us.'

'And let Lucius still be alive when we reach Rhegium.' He would recover faster with her there to care for him, she thought, and while he did, she could dream of seeing her brother again.

And Hanno.

Chapter V

H aving taken leave of his brothers – parting from Bostar had been especially hard – Hanno had travelled to the western coast of Bruttium. In a tiny fishing village, he had found a crusty old sailor called Alcimos, in whose small boat he now found himself. Hannibal had ordered Hanno to make his journey as secret as possible, and his general didn't have many ships at his disposal anyway. It was therefore best to arrive in Syracuse unannounced. There would be spies everywhere in the city; it was even possible that they'd try to kill Hanno before he met with Hippocrates and Epicydes. Making his own entrance, without any warning, gave him the best chance of success.

As Alcimos steered the little craft out to sea, Hanno stared at the coastline of Italy, and thought of his men and, most especially, Mutt. Their farewell had been far more difficult than Hanno had anticipated. The two had never shared that many secrets – it was only recently that Hanno had mentioned Aurelia to Mutt – but their experiences in combat had forged a strong bond between the two men.

'You're going then,' Mutt had said.

'Yes.' Hanno had shifted from foot to foot, feeling awkward and stupid. 'It's time.'

'Aye, sir.'

'Look after the men.'

Mutt's brows had lowered. 'You know I'll do that.'

'Yes,' Hanno had replied, too fast. 'Take care.'

'I will, sir. You too.' Mutt's eyes had met his for a moment, before they flickered away.

'Gods damn it!' Hanno had stepped forward and enveloped Mutt in a bear hug. After a slight hesitation, Mutt's arms had come up to grip his back. 'I'll miss you,' Hanno had muttered. 'You're an excellent officer.'

'So are you, sir.' Mutt had released his grip; quickly, Hanno had done the same. Mutt had gazed at him, without smiling, as was his way. 'The gods protect you, sir. You'll need it, where you're going.'

'I'll be fine.'

'Fortune seems to favour you, that's for sure, sir.' Mutt's excuse for a smile had appeared. 'The gods grant it always be that way.'

'And the same for you.' Hanno had wanted to say more, but didn't have the words.

Mutt's eyes had been understanding. 'Go on, sir.'

'May we meet again.'

'I hope so, sir. One day.'

Swallowing the lump in his throat, Hanno had walked away. When he'd glanced back, Mutt's hand had been raised in farewell.

Tears stung Hanno's eyes at the memory, and he was glad that Alcimos was looking the other way.

He studied the horizon, searching it for sails, but saw nothing. Hanno had been a little surprised to see signs of the war on the sea. A Roman liburnian, one of the fastest ocean-going craft, had rowed north the day that they'd set out. He'd had no idea what it was doing until Alcimos muttered something about 'official messages' being sent to the Senate in Rome. Hanno had fantasised about taking the liburnian, and its communications, to Hannibal, but even if it had been possible, this was not his mission. They had been passed several times by Roman triremes, powering south to join the fleet being assembled near Syracuse. On the first occasion, Hanno had been very nervous. From a distance, he looked the same as any other fisherman – deeply tanned and clad in only a loincloth – but the vessel was so tiny that there was really nowhere to conceal his gear. Even the most cursory of searches would find his gear and sword under a pile of netting.

The trireme hadn't even slowed down. The lookout had seen them, and called down to the deck; Hanno had seen the captain at the helm raise a hand to his eyes and stare in their direction, but that had been it. Each of the other warships had treated them in the same manner. So too had the great transports, of which there had been many, lumbering empty down the coast to Rhegium where they would be used to ferry soldiers, equipment and supplies across the straits to Messana. Eventually, Hanno had grown more relaxed about the sight of a sail. Thanks to the number of Roman ships on the waves, pirates in these parts were now rare. The fact that he was soon to go ashore wrenched him back to stark reality. This part of Sicily was possibly in Roman hands – Hanno had no idea how the war here had been going of recent days – and from the moment his feet hit the beach, danger would beckon.

A sense of melancholy stole over him. If anything went wrong from hereon in, there would be no salvation. Mutt and his soldiers, his brothers and Hannibal were all a long way away. Until he gained the walls of Syracuse, everyone he met was likely to be an enemy. He threw up a prayer to Tanit, the goddess who protected Carthaginians and their homes, asking for her help, and clutched Hannibal's ring through the fabric of his undergarment.

'We're nearing the shallows. I don't want to linger,' said Alcimos. 'Ready?'

'Yes.' Hanno glanced over the side. The water was crystal clear, and the rocky bottom was no deeper than his height. The shore was only a hundred paces distant. He fumbled in the leather bag that contained his clothing, sword, dagger, money and food. He took a gold piece from his purse; it was worth far more than the cost of his passage, but he had been given plenty by Hannibal, and Alcimos was a good man. 'Here.' Sunlight glittered off the coin as he proffered it.

Alcimos' eyes narrowed. 'Are you sure?'

'Take it, and forget that you ever saw me.'

It disappeared into Alcimos' gnarly hand and for the first time since they'd met, a broad smile creased his weather-beaten face. 'I am blind to you, my Carthaginian friend.' With the ease of long practice, he furled the small sail. At once the boat slowed in the water; only the slight swell kept it moving towards the beach. 'It's chest deep. In you go. I'll pass you your bag.'

It would be so easy for Alcimos to sail away with his possessions, thought Hanno, but a man had to trust sometimes. There was no simple way to get in other than jump, so that's what he did. Knowing that the water would be cold made little difference as he went in. It took Hanno's breath away, and he was grateful that his feet soon touched the bottom. When he looked up, Alcimos was holding out his bag. Hanno felt ashamed that he had even considered him capable of treachery. 'My thanks,' he said, placing it on his head to keep it dry.

'May your gods keep you from harm. With luck, you'll make Syracuse before sunset.'

Hanno nodded gratefully. 'Let your return voyage to Bruttium be swift.'

'I'll take that, and full nets too, if I can.' Alcimos was raising the sail again.

By the time that Hanno had waded ashore, the fisherman and his boat were five score paces offshore and more. As if he were already fulfilling his promise to forget Hanno, Alcimos didn't look back. Hanno blocked the feeling of loneliness that rose in his chest. His mission had begun. Hannibal was relying on him. A glance up and down revealed that the beach was still empty; apart from Alcimos' craft, so too was the sea around. Hanno delved in his bag again. A few moments later, he had clad himself in a worn labourer's chiton. A neck cloth covered the scar on his neck, and a thin strip of leather served as his belt, and to hold his dagger at his waist. His intention, as he walked towards Syracuse, was to look like just another homeless peasant, carrying his worldly possessions on his back. If he was stopped by a Roman patrol, well . . .

Don't even think about it. It won't happen.

Willing his hope to be true, Hanno struck inland, off the beach.

Hanno's troubles began when he'd reached the Hexapyla gate, the main entrance on Syracuse's northern wall. He'd arrived outside the city the evening before, having seen no Roman patrols. The sun had been right on the horizon when the Hexapyla had come into sight, however, and he'd heard the guards calling to each other as they began to close the great wooden doors. Travellers seeking entrance to a city at such a time were far more likely to fall under suspicion, even more so when there was a war on. Despite the fact that he carried Hannibal's ring and letter of introduction, he *looked* like a ragged-arse peasant without an obol to his name. It wasn't impossible that he would be accused of stealing the items, and his sword, but until he had the ear of a sympathetic or alert officer, it paid to be cautious. Frustrated and hungry, he had found a discreet spot under a tree some distance from the road, and there he had curled up in his woollen cloak.

After a poor night's sleep, he had risen stiff and cold the following morning. Careful monitoring of the traffic on the road towards the city allowed him to approach the Hexapyla at the same time as a good number of others. The Romans might be near at hand, but people needed to enter and leave. Farmers and merchants had produce to sell, and labourers their time to offer. There were other travellers too, groups of soldiers returning from patrol, and conscripts from the surrounding countryside, answering Syracuse's summons. Hanno tagged along behind a group of the latter, hoping that the guards wouldn't pay him any heed.

His tactic didn't work. Most of the sentries were enjoying rude banter with the conscripts, but one eagle-eyed individual saw that Hanno was on his own. 'You there!' he barked in Greek.

Hanno considered running for it, into the city, but it seemed unwise. Ignorant of Syracuse's layout, he risked immediate capture as a 'spy'. The wise thing to do was to stay calm and see what happened. He should have nothing to fear. That knowledge didn't stop his pulse from beating a pounding staccato at the base of his throat. He looked up, casually, vacantly. 'Me, sir?' he said, answering in the same tongue.

'That's right, fool.' The guard's thick black eyebrows met in a frown. 'I'm not looking at anyone else, am I?'

'No, sir.'

'Come here. Quickly!' A man in middle age, he wore a dented bronze cuirass and a Boeotian helmet in similarly poor condition. He was armed with a sword and a long thrusting spear. Hanno had seen his type before. Given a little bit of power, and without an officer present, the guard liked to act as if he were Zeus Soter himself. Prick him hard enough, and he'd deflate like a goatskin bladder of wine. For all that that appealed, Hanno wasn't in a position to do so. Appease the cocksucker and get into Syracuse, he thought.

'Now, I said!'

As fast as he could, Hanno threaded his way past a farmer in a mule-drawn wagon who had just been waved inside. 'Sir?' he asked, avoiding eye contact.

'Name?'

Hanno's mouth opened to say 'Alcimos', but Thick Eyebrows jabbed him in the chest with a finger. 'Cat got your tongue, peasant?'

Furious, Hanno decided it *was* time to reveal who he was. 'Hanno,' he said, pitching his voice so that the people walking in behind him could not hear. Some could be Roman spies, and he had no wish for it to be known that a Carthaginian was entering Syracuse in disguise.

'What's that? Speak up!'

Hanno leaned forward. 'My name is Hanno; I am a Carthaginian officer. I've been sent by Hannibal Barca, with messages for your generals, Hippocrates and Epicydes.'

Thick Eyebrows looked incredulous for a moment, then he laughed. 'And I'm fucking Appius Claudius Pulcher, propraetor. What's that on your back?'

'My things. Clothing, food, a sword.'

'A sword?' Shoving Hanno backwards, Thick Eyebrows levelled his spear. 'Alarm! I've got one with a weapon!'

Shouts of panic rose as the travellers around Hanno broke and ran, both into and out of the city. Within a few heartbeats, he was alone within a ring of grim-faced guards, all of whom were threatening him with spears. Hanno dropped his bag, threw his dagger down and raised his hands in the air. 'I'm unarmed,' he said loudly. Thick Eyebrows was shouting that they should kill him there and then; a good number of his comrades appeared to agree. Thankfully, the rest seemed fearful but indecisive. Beyond them, people were crowding in to see what was happening. 'A spy! A spy!' he heard a man say.

The circle of spear points wavered. Thick Eyebrows cursed and took a step towards Hanno.

Hanno fought to stay calm. 'I need to speak to your commanding officer,' he said, even louder than the previous time.

'We'll decide what to do with you, vermin,' snarled a voice from behind him.

Hanno began to turn, but a heavy weight smashed into the back of his head, and he knew no more.

Hanno gasped as a bucket of water was emptied over his head. He came to, lying on his side, bound with ropes like a pig for the slaughter. A blinding headache beat an unpleasant rhythm inside his skull, and his mouth felt dry and sticky. Rolling on to his back, he found himself being regarded suspiciously by four men. One was Thick Eyebrows. Two others were also ordinary soldiers, but the last was an officer, clad in a polished breastplate and pteryges that protected his shoulders and groin. Hanno's relief died away as the officer pointed at his neck. 'You're a slave?'

Hanno's nerves jangled. He hadn't noticed that they'd removed the protective piece of cloth, in the process revealing the 'F' mark that Pera had given him. 'F' stood for *fugitivus*. 'No! I was captured by the Romans some time ago, and tortured. This was one of the results.'

'A likely story,' said the officer.

Yet it didn't take long for Hanno's story to appear more believable when he mentioned Hannibal's ring and letter. They hadn't been found when he had been searched. When they were produced – by stripping him naked – the officer scowled at his men. 'How did you miss these?' They hung their heads resentfully. Hanno ignored them, concentrating instead on speaking rapid, fluent Greek to the officer, telling him a little of his mission. The officer made to open the seal on the letter. 'Do that at your own peril,' warned Hanno. 'It's to be read by Hippocrates and Epicydes alone.'

The officer halted. As if to convince himself, he asked Hanno a couple of questions in hesitant Carthaginian. The speed of Hanno's answers seemed to provide the last proof he needed. The officer had the grace to flush a little as he ordered Hanno to be freed and his clothing and possessions to be restored to him – apart from his weapons. 'My apologies for the confusion. We have orders to be on the alert for Roman spies.'

'I would hardly have made myself known, and as a Carthaginian, if I'd been sent by Marcellus,' said Hanno sarcastically as he got dressed.

'I know. I'm sorry. My men will be disciplined.' Here, a scowl at Thick Eyebrows, who looked away. 'I'll take these to Hippocrates and Epicydes.'

Hanno eyed the ring and letter with some alarm. 'I had thought to present them in person.'

'I'm just doing my duty,' replied the officer awkwardly. 'It shouldn't take long. In the meantime, can I offer you food? Drink?'

'Yes, thank you. A drop of something for the pain too, if you have it. My head is splitting.' Hanno aimed a poisonous stare at Thick Eyebrows and his fellows.

'Of course.' The officer barked an order that sent the soldiers hurrying from the room. 'I'll return as soon as I can,' he said with a friendly nod, before locking the door behind him.

Hanno swallowed down his anger. Being confined to a prison cell after being assaulted by Syracusan guards was not how he'd expected his visit to the city to begin. The fact that the officer believed him clearly wasn't enough. He hoped that Hippocrates and Epicydes realised that his letter and the ring were genuine, or his stay in this bare, dank room might turn out to be permanent.

His spirits were lifted a little while later by the arrival of a slave bearing a platter of bread, olives and wine. A surgeon was next to enter. He tutted with disapproval when Hanno told him how he'd received the wound to the back of his head, but pronounced after an examination that it was not serious. Three drops of poppy juice in Hanno's wine would dull the pain but not make him drowsy, he said, unstoppering a tiny glass vial.

Some time passed – in the windowless cell, with just an oil lamp as light, Hanno had no idea how long – before the officer reappeared. He was smiling. 'I'm to convey you to the generals,' he said. 'Are you rested? Is your head any better?'

'I'm fine, thank you. They read my letter?'

'Yes. They want to meet you at once. I must apologise again for your treatment and this period of . . . *detention*. Twice, assassins have made attempts on Hippocrates' and Epicydes' lives.'

'I understand.' It made sense, thought Hanno, even if Thick Eyebrows was an imbecile. He smoothed down his chiton and smiled. 'I'm ready.'

The officer half bowed. 'If you could follow me, then.'

A pair of soldiers fell in behind them as they exited the cell. Hanno's sword and dagger had not been returned to him either. The brothers' trust only went so far.

The four walked down a long corridor lined with flagstones. The whimpering sounds from behind some of the doors on each side made Hanno's skin crawl. He remembered Victumulae, and he reached in reflex under the cloth, to his scar.

Emerging into daylight, Hanno squinted. As his eyes adjusted, he saw that they were in a large courtyard, which was bordered by stables, barracks and workshops. Soldiers were everywhere, talking, cleaning gear, being chivvied by their officers. The cells were in a building that had been erected as part of the defensive wall, and the great limestone blocks he'd seen on his approach were just as impressive from the inside.

'We're in the east of the city. This is part of the garrison's quarters,' explained the officer. 'Hippocrates and Epicydes live close by. It'll be quickest to go there via the ramparts. No one will see you this way, and you'll appreciate the view.'

Hanno's interest grew as they climbed a stone staircase that ran up the side of the cell block to the top of the defences. A sentry guarding the last step saluted as the officer reached him. Nothing could have prepared Hanno for the magnificence of the sight that greeted him. A little gasp escaped his lips, and the officer chuckled. 'Most react in the same manner.'

'It reminds me of Carthage,' said Hanno, feeling a little homesick. They were facing eastward, and the mid-afternoon sunlight had turned the sea into a blinding white mirror. That didn't stop him from making out the shapes of dozens of ships in the anchorages far below, and the finger of land that edged out to meet a little fortified island. 'That must be Ortygia.'

'You're well informed. It's named after a quail, because of its shape. Here we overlook part of Achradina. The harbour that lies on this side of Ortygia is the small one. On the other side, out of sight, lies the great. It's far more protected from the weather, and can hold hundreds of ships.' He beckoned.

'There must be a Roman blockade, surely?' As he walked, Hanno scanned the sea, but the intensity of the reflection from its surface meant that he couldn't see a thing.

'Oh yes, they're out there somewhere. Ten, twenty, sometimes more triremes. They never go away, but there aren't enough of them to seal off the city completely, thank the gods. Your people have been very generous to us. They have sent regular convoys bearing supplies.'

'I'm glad to hear that.' Hanno wondered about taking passage on a Carthaginian vessel, back to his home. Fleeting bitterness took him. There would be no family, and few friends of his there. His mother was dead, and most of his childhood companions would be in one or other of Carthage's armies.

Reaching a broader section of wall, his attention was drawn to a twin-armed catapult positioned a few steps to the rear of the walkway. It wasn't manned, but neat piles of large stones lay all around, and its mechanisms looked well oiled. The catapult was ready for use, that was plain. Another stood thirty paces on, and then a third and a fourth. More were visible beyond. He whistled. 'How many of these are there?'

The officer looked pleased. 'I'm not sure exactly. Hundreds, at the very least. They line the walls for their entire length, and that's more than two hundred stadia. These are only the small ones. The larger ones have to be set at ground level. You'll see one in a moment. If it hadn't been for Archimedes, we wouldn't have half the number that we do. He spent his time nagging Hiero about building more of them. I think Hiero had some built just to shut him up, but we'll be damn glad of them soon.'

'The Romans are coming?'

A short laugh. 'Oh yes. Every so often, deserters make their way here. The word has it that it won't be long before Marcellus moves his legions. It was inevitable, but at least the waiting will be over. We'll be ready. These walls won't fall in a decade of siege.'

'The defences are truly impressive,' agreed Hanno, thinking with pride of his own city, and its fortifications, which were even greater. It would never see a besieging army, though, as this one would. Hippocrates and Epicydes would hold Syracuse, and he'd play his part in helping to accomplish that. Armies would arrive from Carthage, and the tide of war on Sicily would flow in their favour.

A short distance further along the rampart, they were halted by a group of soldiers. These individuals were a different stamp to the guards such as Thick Eyebrows. Their equipment and weapons shone in the sunlight, and they carried themselves in the manner of men who knew their business. The lead one, a man of Hanno's age, wore an old-fashioned *pilos* helmet topped with a fantastic five-spined crest. He saluted as he blocked the officer's path and said politely, 'Password, sir.'

'Herakles.'

Pilos-wearer stood aside with a nod. 'You and your guest may continue, sir, but your men stay here.' His comrades parted in the middle, allowing Hanno and the officer to pass between them. More security, thought Hanno. The problems he'd had made more sense now, if even ordinary soldiers were not to be trusted.

Just beyond the sentry point, the walkway broadened out into a great square; it was the roof of a massive dwelling, even a palace. The whole surface had been decorated with swirling patterns of black and white mosaic tiles. Huge clay pots containing vines, lemon and fig trees had been arranged around the sides. Timbers had been set into the floor, their purpose to support a lattice framework that held some of the vines. The ingenious technique had created plenty of shady spots, and mimicked the appearance of a garden. There was even a fountain, the centrepiece of which was Poseidon astride a great dolphin. How the water reached this height, Hanno had no idea.

The officer saw his surprised look. 'More of Archimedes' work. A wheel with leather buckets set over a well carries the water aloft.'

'He must be a man of great talent.'

'You haven't seen the half of it.'

A number of figures could be seen near the fountain. Two were reclining on couches. As they drew closer, Hanno saw that two of the party were manacled, and on their knees. Soldiers with drawn swords stood behind them. He could hear questions being asked. When one of the prisoners didn't answer quickly enough, one of the soldiers kicked him in the back. He fell forward on to his face, moaning, and didn't try to get up. A question was hurled at his companion, who flinched.

'Our Carthaginian!' called one of the men on the couches. 'Bring him here, Kleitos.'

The officer ushered Hanno in front of him and together, they approached.

Hanno realised that the reclining men were Hippocrates and Epicydes. The brothers were as Hanno remembered seeing them at the time of Cannae, although he could not recall who was who. One had a beard, while the other did not, but that was the only discernible difference between them. Both had tousled black hair, and slender, almost feminine features. They were each clad in a richly embroidered himation, a mark of their status, and calf-high boots that reminded Hanno of those worn by Hannibal.

Ten paces from the couches, Kleitos touched him in the back. Hanno took the prompt and stopped. He bowed. 'Greetings, O rulers of Syracuse.'

'Rulers?' said the bearded one with a chuckle. 'We're merely two of the generals who form the ruling council.'

Hanno glanced at Kleitos, but his face was a mask. 'I don't understand.'

'Hippocrates is jesting with you,' said the clean-shaven man with a laugh. 'It's true that the other generals are our equals, but they tend to *defer* to our judgement.' The emphasis on the word 'defer' was light, but the unpleasant gleam in his brother's eyes suggested that the relationship wasn't altogether cordial.

Hanno wondered if any of the other leaders enjoyed the pleasures of this rooftop garden, but he kept that to himself. 'I am honoured to meet you, Generals. My name is Hanno of Carthage. I come from Hannibal Barca, as you will have read in my letter.'

'I have it here.' Epicydes flicked a hand at the low table before him, where Hannibal's ring lay upon the unrolled parchment. 'You are most welcome to our city. My apologies for the manner in which you were treated on your arrival. The guards on the gates can be a little jumpy.'

And stupid, thought Hanno. 'I understand, General. These things happen.'

'You bring no soldiers with you?' asked Hippocrates in a truculent tone.

'Regretfully, General, no. For the moment, Hannibal needs every man he has. With every passing season, the Romans raise new legions.'

Hippocrates made a *phhhh* of contempt, but Epicydes smiled. 'We have sufficient numbers to defend the city, and a little more. When the armies that Hannibal speaks of arrive from Carthage, we shall sweep Marcellus' forces into the sea!'

'May it turn red, as the waters did at Trasimene,' added Hippocrates.

'I look forward to that day,' said Hanno. 'I will do my utmost to help you both achieve that end.'

'Were you there, at the lake?' asked Hippocrates, his eyes eager.

'I was, General.' Hannibal had absolved him and the other phalanx commanders of blame after their units had been punched open, allowing thousands of legionaries to escape the carnage, but Hanno still felt a trace of guilt.

'As were we. I don't recall your face.' This in a slightly accusatory tone.

'I was present, nonetheless,' said Hanno, his temper rising a little. Hippocrates seemed argumentative, and impossible to please.

'No one can remember one face out of many thousands! His word is enough. Hannibal states that you're an experienced infantry officer,' said Epicydes, his eyes appraising.

'That's true, General. I fought at the Trebia, Trasimene and Cannae, and most of the battles in between and since.'

'It's a mark of Hannibal's esteem that he picked you for this mission, and that he gave you this.' Epicydes picked up the ring and admired it. 'Here.' He tossed it to Hanno, earning a scowl from Hippocrates.

'I was going to keep that.'

'It's not yours to keep, brother,' said Epicydes.

'My thanks, General,' said Hanno, clenching the ring in his fist, and hiding his growing dislike of Hippocrates. 'How can I be of service?'

Epicydes regarded Hippocrates. 'What think you, brother? Shall we give him the command of a unit of infantry?'

'I suppose,' replied Hippocrates with poor grace. 'But what damn difference one officer is going to make, I don't know.' He got up and walked to stand over the prisoner who was lying on the floor. 'What have you to say?'

The only answer he got was a whimper.

'Ignore him,' said Epicydes to Hanno, meaning Hippocrates. 'You can take charge of some of our less experienced foot soldiers. They'll benefit from the training you can provide. If you could help other officers to do the same, I'd be grateful. When the siege begins, I'll give you a section of wall to defend.'

'It would be an honour, General.' Hanno warmed towards Epicydes, who was courteous at least. He was unsure what useful intelligence would come his way when fulfilling that role, but there was little he could say.

'Your role will come into its own when the promised forces from Carthage arrive. We'll need an officer who speaks both Greek and Carthaginian, won't we, brother?'

That's more promising, thought Hanno.

'Yes, yes,' answered Hippocrates, sounding uninterested. He kicked the prisoner. 'If you won't give me any information, you're no damn use to me.' He glanced at the soldiers who were guarding the captives. 'Throw him over the edge.'

Epicydes made a vaguely apologetic gesture to Hanno as the sobbing man was hauled by his arms to the battlements and without hesitation, flung to his death. A despairing cry carried to the garden for perhaps two heartbeats after he disappeared, before abruptly stopping.

Gods, what a way to die, thought Hanno. Keeping his expression neutral, he asked, 'What had he done?'

'Ha! Not told me what I wanted to hear, that's what,' replied Hippocrates, looking irritated.

'He was a suspected traitor,' said Epicydes. 'So is his companion.'

'Suspected?' The question had left Hanno's lips before he could stop it.

'Correct.' Epicydes' voice had lost its friendly edge. Meanwhile, Hippocrates had ordered the second prisoner taken to the spot where his comrade had gone over, and was making all kinds of threats.

'The other one will be more likely to talk now, I'd wager.' Hanno laughed, as if he'd enjoy watching.

'No doubt,' said Epicydes, his good humour returning. 'Hippocrates can be very persuasive.' A moment later, the screams began, proving his point, but Epicydes made no acknowledgement of them. 'Kleitos will find you rooms, weapons and equipment. We will meet again soon.'

Hanno knew when he had been dismissed. 'Thank you, General. And my new unit?'

'I'll send a messenger with the details.'

Hanno bowed and muttered more platitudes. As he walked away with Kleitos, he couldn't help but glance at Hippocrates. He wished he hadn't. The prisoner had just had his ear sliced off. Hippocrates examined it for a moment before tossing that over the edge and remarking that if the man didn't want to follow it, he'd better start talking.

Hannibal had been right, Hanno decided. Hippocrates was dangerous. For all of his friendliness, so too was Epicydes. He had been sent to live in a nest of vipers.

Chapter VI

By the time that their vessel had been at sea for a day, Aurelia was beginning to wonder if her decision to travel to Rhegium had been a wise one. Her restricted existence as a wife and mother had long irritated her, but it was easy to rail against such things from the safety of Rome. Now she was at the mercy of the elements, which were controlled by the gods, a set of beings with whom she had a troubled relationship. Since Cannae, she had been careful not to voice such feelings, yet she worried that the deities could discern her mistrust. She had made plentiful offerings before their departure, partly penitence for her behaviour, partly to ask that her husband might live – indeed, might recover from his injuries – and lastly, that they had a trouble-free voyage.

Neptune and the wind gods appeared not to have heard her requests. Within an hour of leaving Ostia, the bright, sunny weather had vanished; squalls and rain showers had battered the open-decked merchantman until well into the afternoon. The boat's constant rocking motion had made Aurelia feel sick, but poor Publius had been worst affected, vomiting until nothing came up but bile. Tempsanus was little better, while Agesandros seemed completely unaffected. If anything, his mood lightened with each mile that they travelled south.

Things improved as the sun fell in the sky. The choppy winds died down, and a breeze from the north settled in at their backs, pushing them towards their destination. They made a good distance before the captain, a balding man with a little paunch, chose an anchorage for the night. Aurelia's misgivings vanished on the second day, as they all but flew south on a gentle sea, under a blue sky. A school of dolphins rode in the ship's bow wave for a time, delighting everyone, and veritable proof of Neptune's favour.

At dawn on the third day, the captain announced that if the wind held and they saw no hostile vessels, sunset would see the end of their journey. Mention of 'hostile' forces set Aurelia's nerves jangling, but hours passed without sight of anything other than an occasional fishing boat. Eventually, the lookout called that Sicily was in sight. They'd be docking at Rhegium within two hours, Tempsanus said with a smile. Aurelia's mood lifted briefly, but her mind turned to Lucius, and fresh worry racked her. Was he even still alive? She prayed that he had not been claimed by Hades, that he would pull through. Such dark thoughts were averted by Publius, who escaped Elira's grasp and scampered to her side. It was a welcome relief, and Aurelia began a game of Hide and Seek, using the mast to conceal herself from a delighted Publius.

'Sail!'

Engrossed in the game, Aurelia didn't pay much attention to the lookout's call.

'Where?' asked the captain.

'To the south, sir. It's in the straits.'

'Is it on its own?'

'Seems to be, sir.'

'What type of vessel is it – can you see?' demanded the captain.

His tone caught Aurelia's attention. She looked up the mast to where the lookout clung like a monkey, his hands gripping the wood and feet braced against a band of encircling rope.

'I can't see, sir. It's too low down on the horizon.'

'Neptune's hairy arse crack,' said the captain under his breath.

Pushing a laughing Publius towards Elira, Aurelia went to the captain's side. 'You're worried,' she said as Tempsanus joined them. Agesandros had somehow managed to put himself within earshot too.

'There's no point lying. I am.' The captain made a sign against evil.

'Marcellus' ships dominate these waters, so more than likely it's one of ours. But there's no guarantee. The Syracusans send out vessels from time to time. It could even be a gugga trireme, blown north. The point is, we won't know until we've got a lot closer, perhaps even entered the straits. If it does turn out to be unfriendly at that point, we'll be so near that it might be able to run us down.'

'What should we do?' asked Tempsanus, his normal jovial expression absent.

'Go a little closer, perhaps. See if the sail gives us an idea of its identity. Or we could just turn about, and row north. If it doesn't follow us, so much the better. We can anchor off one of the Lipari Islands overnight and set sail before it gets light. We'd be in Rhegium in no time.' The captain's tone left no doubt that the latter option would be his choice, but he was not the master. Tempsanus was, because he'd chartered the vessel. Aurelia's pulse beat a little faster as she glanced at her husband's partner. She wanted to reach their destination as fast as possible, but not at any cost.

'Avoiding trouble seems the best option,' said Tempsanus, casting a look at Aurelia. 'One more day won't matter.'

Aurelia smiled in acceptance. I'll be with you soon, husband, she thought. Hold on.

The captain was noticeably relieved by Tempsanus' words. He cupped a hand to his mouth. 'Reef the sails, and look lively about it!'

A dozen of the crew scrambled to the lines, but they had barely touched them when the lookout shouted 'Sail!' for the second time.

'Where?' yelled the captain.

'Behind us, sir. It's come out of nowhere. Must have been in the lee of one of the islands.'

All eyes turned to the ship's stern. Perhaps a mile to their rear, a square sail, larger than theirs, could be seen plain as day. The captain cursed, and Aurelia felt a little sick. She didn't need to be told that the newcomer had the wind behind him. If it was using its oars as well, they'd be overtaken before long.

'Leave those lines be!' roared the captain. He glanced at Tempsanus. 'That one's not friendly, sir, not the way he appeared. I don't want to hang around to check, which leaves us no choice.'

'To run south, and pray that the ship there is not an enemy?' said Tempsanus.

'If that's all right with you, sir.'

'Do as you see fit. A thousand extra drachms for you if we make Rhegium tonight.'

The captain's teeth flashed. 'I'll do my best, sir.' He stalked down the catwalk, ordering the fifty crewmen to their benches and for the oars to be run out. 'I want us at top speed,' Aurelia heard him tell the second-in-command. 'Our best chance of outrunning them is now. You know what the wind's like when we enter the strait—'

'Unreliable as a Phoenician moneylender in a bad mood, sir.'

'If it's blowing to the south, we'll be laughing. But if it's the other way around?' The captain grimaced.

Aurelia's fear grew a fraction more. Prayer was her only resource. She tried not to feel hopeless about that.

Before long, their fortunes had taken a further turn for the worse. The ship behind them had caught up sufficiently to block their route north, and the sail that they'd seen to the south turned out to belong to a trireme. Bigger, faster, with more than three times the number of oarsmen, it scythed through the waves towards them. The painted eyes above its ram were hideous, and its decks bristled with soldiers and archers. A standard near the prow revealed it to be Syracusan.

Fear blossomed on Aurelia's ship. The oarsmen slowed their stroke, yet no one said a thing. 'They must row!' said Tempsanus, a sheen of sweat decorating his brow.

'What's the point?' retorted the captain. 'We're done.'

Tempsanus seemed about to protest when a voice speaking bad Latin carried across the water: 'Heave to, or we'll ram you!'

Throwing an I-told-you-so expression at Tempsanus, the captain ordered the oars shipped.

'Can we not fight?' demanded Tempsanus.

'That lot? We're sailors, sir, not soldiers.'

The trireme closed to within a long bowshot. It was aiming to come in beside their vessel. Men were clustered at the side rails, ready to board the instant that the two craft closed with each other.

'I'll make it worth your while.'

'We'd be massacred, sir. Sorry to say, but your drachms are no longer worth a thing.'

Aurelia fought to stay calm. For a change, she was grateful for Agesandros' presence by her side. 'What will happen?' she asked the captain, pleased that her voice was steady.

'With a little luck, lady, they'll just seize the ship and force us to serve as its crew, with a captain and officers of their own.' He hesitated before adding regretfully, 'As for you passengers, well, I couldn't say.'

Aurelia's gaze moved to Tempsanus' face, which was twisted with fear.

'We'll be enslaved,' grated Agesandros. 'Killed if we're unlucky.'

Aurelia locked her knees to keep them from folding. I've been so stupid, she thought. I should have taken Tempsanus' advice, and stayed in Rome.

'I can kill you now,' muttered Agesandros. 'And your son. It would save you both a lot of suffering.'

Horrified, Aurelia checked his face. The offer was genuine, she saw. So too was the concern in his eyes.

'Terrible things could happen to you. You have no idea—'

'No.'

'What if Publius is sold to someone else? Have you thought about that?'

'That will not happen! I will appeal to the captain. He'll recognise that I'm a noblewoman.'

'That will make little difference,' said Agesandros.

'You're not killing us,' she hissed. 'What will you do?'

'Let myself be taken. Slavery's nothing new to me. I'll escape when my chance comes. If I can help you then, I will.'

Aurelia swallowed, and prayed harder than she had at any time since before Cannae. *Spare me and my child. Spare us all.*

Another order came over, in the same poor Latin. 'Lay your oars in!'

The captain hastily repeated the command, and the crew heaved in their sweeps, the port-side ones completing the task just as the trireme came gliding in alongside. Its oars had already been neatly shipped. *Thunk, thunk, thunk.* Timber ground off timber as the two hulls met. The Syracusans didn't wait for their ship to stop moving. Half a dozen, then a dozen soldiers leaped on to the merchantman's deck, their weapons drawn. 'Throw down your arms!' yelled one in mangled Latin. He repeated the command in Greek.

The few crew on the deck fell to their knees, begging for mercy. The men at the oars didn't even lift their eyes. The captain raised his hands in the air and said in passable Greek, 'We're unarmed. The ship is yours.'

Agesandros stepped in front of Aurelia, who had beckoned Elira and Publius to her side. To his credit, Tempsanus did the same. 'Stay calm, my lady,' he whispered. 'I will defend you.'

'No, Tempsanus,' she protested, but he had stepped forward. 'We are civilians,' he began.

The lead soldier's reply was instant, and brutal. He shoved his sword into Tempsanus' belly, right up to the hilt. There was a terrible '*Ooooffff*' of pain, which quickly became a scream. Using his shield, the soldier pushed Tempsanus off his blade, and down into the midst of the oarsmen. There he roared in agony. The soldier eyed Agesandros, who was next, with cold eyes.

Aurelia felt Agesandros tense. Despite their troubled history, there was no point in him throwing away his life like this. It would achieve nothing. 'Stop,' she whispered, before stepping around him. 'I am a Roman noble-woman,' she said loudly in Greek. 'Harm me at your peril.'

'I've never fucked a Roman matron. Didn't think to find one on this tub either,' declared the soldier with a chuckle. 'My luck's just changed, brothers!'

His comrades laughed, and Aurelia felt her bowels loosen. Agesandros stirred beside her, and this time, she didn't have the resolve to stop him.

'HOLD!' shouted the same voice that had ordered them to heave to. 'No one is to be killed, or fucked, until *I* have had a look at them.'

Frustrated, the soldier stayed put and Aurelia breathed again. Another pair of feet thumped on to the decking and, a moment later, she found herself face to face with a handsome Syracusan officer. He hadn't even bothered to draw his sword. 'You are?' he asked in an arrogant drawl.

'My name is Aurelia, wife of Lucius Vibius Melito,' she said, as calmly as her thumping heart would allow. 'I am of the equestrian class, and I demand to be treated as such.'

'You'll *demand* nothing.' His tone's silkiness made it even more threatening. 'If I but give the word, my men here will do every kind of vile thing to you, and to your female slave. Your child – by your expression I can see that he's yours – will see every bit of it. I suggest that you shut your mouth, and give us no trouble.'

Aurelia could not remember ever being so scared, but was damned if she'd let him see it. She nodded.

The officer pushed past, pausing to look at Publius and Elira. 'Bind them all, except the child,' he ordered. 'Transfer them to our ship.'

Aurelia found her voice again as the soldiers swarmed in. 'Where are you taking us?'

'Syracuse, of course.'

Aurelia shivered. She had been such a fool. She'd be lucky to escape this unharmed, and with Publius by her side. Who knew what would happen to any of them?

'Mama?' Publius' reedy voice echoed through the dungeon. 'Mama?'

'I'm here, love.' By now Aurelia's eyes were so used to the gloom that she had no trouble walking to the moth-eaten blanket that served as their bedding. Elira was also there, asleep. 'It's all right, I'm here,' Aurelia whispered.

She stooped to pick him up, savouring his small-child smell, his warmth. They reminded her of normality in this hellhole. Six other women shared the tiny space they had been thrown into after their arrival in Syracuse: skinny wretches in ragged clothing. Despite Aurelia's attempts, none had spoken other than to say they'd been seized on a ship the previous week, and that they got fed once a day. Aurelia had no idea where Agesandros, the captain and the crew were. Poor Tempsanus was lying on the seabed, food for the fishes. And Lucius? Only the gods knew if he was still alive. *Let Hanno find me, somehow,* she prayed. The notion was crazy, but it was all Aurelia had.

'I'm hung-y, Mama. I'm hung-y.'

'I know, love, I know.' Aurelia's own stomach was rumbling. The blackness made it impossible to judge the time, but it had to be meal-time soon. 'They'll bring us something any moment, you'll see.'

'I want sau-sages.'

'Maybe they'll bring sausages. I don't know, love. It might just be some bread, but that would be nice, wouldn't it?'

'Bread! Bread! I want bread.'

'Soon, my love, soon.' Stroking his hair, Aurelia walked the eight steps to the cell's back wall, turned and returned to the tiny grille that opened on to the corridor. No one was there. It had been the same since their arrival. Moans and cries from other cells haunted Aurelia as she paced to and fro. At last Publius fell asleep. Worried that his hunger would wake him, she didn't stop until the muscles in her arms were screaming for a rest. Thankfully, he didn't stir as she laid him on the blanket and covered him up. She stared down at him, almost able to hear her mother's voice, reprimanding her. 'Impetuous behaviour will get you nowhere, child.' Aurelia rallied what was left of her courage. It was done now. She had decided to travel by sea to Rhegium, and all of them would have to live with the consequences. Remembering the misery of the slave market in

Capua, which she had seen as a child, Aurelia prayed: At the very least, let me stay with Publius. Being separated would be worse than anything, even death.

Death. Is that what it would come to? she wondered numbly.

All the mental preparations in the world could not have equipped Aurelia for the following morning. Along with the cell's other occupants, they had been escorted by soldiers to a courtyard. Perhaps a dozen more women arrived soon after. The entire group was ordered to strip naked by the same officer who had taken their ship. Quiet sobbing filled the air as the reason behind this sank in – they were being readied for sale – but the women had little choice.

Trying to reduce Publius' distress, Aurelia pretended that it was nothing but a game. In reality, of course, it was unbelievably degrading. She had not been without clothes in public since she was a small child, and the soldiers' comments and groping hands only added to her distress. Buckets of water were hauled up from the well, and they were ordered to wash themselves. Worse was to follow. Their feet were dusted with white chalk, to signify their status, and they were bound with rope at the wrists and neck. Gods, give me strength, thought Aurelia, avoiding all eye contact. This is inhuman. It was what Elira, and Hanno, had both gone through, and Agesandros. So too had the slaves that her family and Lucius owned. Her previous attempts to empathise with slaves had been utterly romanticised. Nothing could have prepared her for this.

'Why Mama tied up?' asked Publius, his bottom lip jutting.

Aurelia was glad that the guards didn't speak Latin. 'It's part of the game, my love,' she said, forcing a smile. 'We have to go to a special place now, and find our clothes.'

'Where?' demanded Publius.

'I don't know, love. Follow me.' *Let it not be far, please.*

To her relief, she heard one of the others say that the slave market was only a quarter of a mile away. The officer and several of his soldiers led off, carving a path through the busy streets, and the rest took up the rear. Bizarrely, the experience wasn't as horrific as Aurelia had expected, because few people even noticed their passage. It was yet more bitter medicine to swallow: slaves weren't worth looking at. They were the lowest of the low.

Publius was happy to trot alongside at first, but as the crowd grew denser, it became difficult for him to match the adults' pace. At one stage, Aurelia had to stop to allow him to catch up. The rope that connected her to the next woman went taut, unbalancing her. Aurelia's tearful apology to the soldiers and a promise not to do it again were enough – just. All she got was a heavy cuff around the ear. From then on, she made Publius walk in front of her, which forced him, complaining, to maintain their speed.

Before long, they arrived at the marketplace. Aurelia was grateful for this tiny reprieve. Publius' limits wouldn't be tested further, in this at least. A gate in the outer wall, and the strong smell of the sea, revealed the site to be adjacent to one of the city's harbours. Seagulls screeched and cried overhead, concentrating on the food stalls that lined one side of the roughly rectangular space. Lines of slaves filled the central area, separated according to sex, age and also by owners. They were all the colours and races under the sun: fair-complexioned Romans, Gauls and Germans, brown-skinned Greeks and Egyptians. There were Nubians, black as pitch, and even a pair of yellow men with black hair and slanted eyes – Seres, Aurelia thought they were called. The slaves were old, middle-aged, in the prime of life, stripling youths, children, and babes that were still at the breast. Every single one was naked; most bore the same numbed, blank expressions. Some of the women and children were crying, but their vendors were quick to silence them with threats or blows, or both.

'Is this where we get our clothes back, Mama?'

'No, my darling. First, we have to go with someone to find them.'

'Who?'

'I don't know yet.'

Publius' attention had already moved on. Seeing a heavily built man chewing on a piece of grilled fish, he announced, 'I'm hung-y! I want fish.'

'Shhhh, my love,' Aurelia urged, but fortunately none of the soldiers heard. After a little negotiation, the women were made to stand in a line close to a podium that stood in the very centre of the market. She managed to distract Publius by getting him to draw in the dust at their feet.

Time passed in a haze of fractured images. The purchase by an officer, for a few coins each, of a handful of old, sick-looking men. Every soldier in the garrison was needed for the city's defence, the officer told the slaver. The wretches were to be set cleaning out a section of the sewers that had blocked. If they died on the job, it wouldn't matter. A mother and her small son being sold separately; the screams of distress from both as their buyers forced them off in different directions. A raddled-looking man, perhaps a brothel-owner, mauling every young woman he could find, including Aurelia and Elira. She breathed again when his attention settled on a blonde Goth and her companion, an auburn-haired, full-breasted woman. He bought both, along with one of the youngest girls in Aurelia's group.

The one constant, and oddly what kept Aurelia sane, was Publius' whingeing. He was hungry, he wanted to go home, he wanted to cuddle with Aurelia, then Elira. Where was his daddy? Aurelia managed to keep him from wailing or crying, and Elira, who was beside them, played her part too. Yet desperation began to steal over Aurelia as tell-tale red marks appeared on Publius' cheeks, and his voice grew a little shrill. He was tiring. Their ploys would not work for much longer. The guards were beginning to look irritated. She had seen at least one crying child ripped from its mother and sold to the first bidder, just to get rid of it.

'Agathocles! It's good to see you.'

Aurelia's head turned. The officer who'd captured them was talking to a thin, well-dressed man with neat black hair. From the smiles and easy conversation, the two knew each other. A pair of soldiers, Agathocles' bodyguards, stood nearby.

'What are you looking for this morning? More women?'

'Aye. Hippocrates has grown jaded with the last crop.' Agathocles gave an expressive shrug. 'You know what he's like. Never happy.'

'What have you become, brother?' The officer lowered his voice. 'Procuring fresh meat for Hippocrates? You should have joined the army, like me.'

'Don't start! You're here, selling slaves on the generals' behalf, aren't you? There's nothing to choose between us.' Agathocles clapped the officer on the shoulder. 'Let's see if you have anything worth taking to Hippocrates this morning.'

'There's a Roman matron down the line. She's reasonably attractive,' said the officer, and Aurelia's blood ran cold. 'So is the Illyrian who was her female slave.'

Aurelia's spirits lifted a fraction. She glanced at Elira, saw the same hope flare in her eyes. Fortuna, watch over us in this moment, Aurelia prayed. If we're together, it won't be as bad.

Agathocles selected one of the first women in the line, but he passed on the rest without a second look. 'You haven't many beauties here today, my friend.' He came to a halt before Aurelia and looked back at the officer. 'Perhaps I was being a little hasty.'

'I told you. Hippocrates will like that one. She's haughty.'

Agathocles caught Aurelia's chin with one hand and turned her head from side to side. She tried not to show her outrage, but he noted the tension in her neck. 'You don't like that, eh?' he said in Latin.

Aurelia didn't reply.

He let her go and in the same instant, backhanded her across the face. 'I asked you a question, you Roman bitch!'

Publius began to cry, and Elira tried to comfort him. 'I don't mind you touching me, no,' Aurelia whispered.

'Liar.' His smile was all teeth. 'My friend has the right of it. Hippocrates will enjoy breaking you, more especially because you're Roman.'

'She's a noblewoman,' called the officer.

'Even better. I'll take her.' One of his hands lingered on her breasts.

'And my child,' said Aurelia at once.

Agathocles laughed. 'Hippocrates is many things, but he's no pederast!'

Aurelia sensed that in this place of desolation and broken hearts, pleading would make no difference. *I cannot lose Publius!* She pitched her voice so that Publius couldn't hear. 'If you take my son as well, I will pleasure Hippocrates as he has never been before.' She prayed that the techniques taught to her by Elira when she'd first got married, and used successfully on Lucius, still worked.

Agathocles' eyebrows rose; then he scowled. 'You'll do that anyway, or I'll have the skin flogged from your back.'

'The horse that's rewarded for obeying makes a far better steed than the one that's whipped,' replied Aurelia. She licked her lips, scarcely believing what she was about to say. 'I could do the same for *you*. So could my slave.'

Agathocles' eyes shot to Elira, and Aurelia's heart lurched in her chest. Elira had every right not to play the part that she'd just been given. Another owner might treat her more kindly. Aurelia could have wept when Elira flashed a seductive smile at Agathocles and said, 'You won't regret it, sir. I swear it.'

Agathocles studied Aurelia again, and Elira. He gave a brusque nod. 'Go and stand by my men.' Even as she gave silent thanks, he grabbed her by the throat. 'Your brat best know how to keep quiet. If Hippocrates hears him, you'll wish that he'd never been born.'

'He's a good boy,' whispered Aurelia, genuinely terrified now. 'No one will know he's even there.'

He waved her away.

A monumental wave of shame and disgust washed over Aurelia as she, Publius and Elira made their way towards the soldiers. *I'm no better than a whore. And a whoremistress, to treat Elira so.* Yet part of her was glad. She had managed to keep Publius by her side. For the moment.

Despite the fact that Kleitos was Hippocrates' and Epicydes' man, Hanno still found him likeable. After finding Hanno a small but

well-furnished room in one of the barracks, with a window that over-
looked the courtyard, Kleitos had insisted that they visit an inn. 'Your
weapons can wait, but this cannot,' he'd declared, offering a brimming
cup of wine to Hanno. 'To friendship, and to Syracuse's alliance with
Hannibal and Carthage!' Hanno had responded with gusto, and they
had had several drinks, each time swearing friendship between their
two peoples, and victory over the Romans. Kleitos, thought Hanno,
was a friend in the making, and a more decent individual than
his masters.

Well lubricated, the two had then gone to the garrison's armoury. There
Kleitos had demanded the finest kit for 'one of Hannibal's best men'. Hanno
knew that word of his arrival would spread fast, but Kleitos' declaration
made sure that everyone in the city would know it by the next morning.
Part of him didn't care. The Syracusan soldiers were delighted by his
presence, and asked repeatedly how many men he'd brought with him. His
previously prepared answer, that forces from Carthage would soon arrive
on the island, seemed to satisfy.

Hanno chose a plain but serviceable bronze breastplate, and an Attic
helmet. Kleitos was amused by his request for a Roman scutum and *gladius*.
'What's wrong with our Greek equipment?'

'You may laugh, but we found out the hard way at Trasimene what
happens when phalanxes meet Roman infantry. Hannibal had us arm
ourselves afterwards with the weapons and armour taken from the enemy
dead. We retrained to fight in blocks, as the legionaries do. It worked
too.'

Kleitos' face grew thoughtful. 'No one can argue with what Hannibal
did at Cannae. Still, it's a different war here. We're defending a city, not
engaging the legions face-to-face.'

'That day will come,' said Hanno fiercely. Making improvements such
as this was part of what Hannibal had sent him here to do. 'And when it
does, the Syracusans will have more chance of victory fighting as the
Romans do, rather than the way they always have.'

'Something tells me that Hippocrates in particular would not want his entire army retrained.'

'I could just start with the soldiers of one phalanx.'

'Hmmm. Let's talk more about it, over some wine.'

'What about my duties?'

Kleitos laughed. 'They can wait. The Romans aren't here yet, and Hippocrates and Epicydes won't bother their arses asking what you've done. Seeing the best inn in Syracuse is far more important.'

'If you're sure . . .?'

'I am. I order you to come with me. All we need to do is dump your kit in your room.'

It had been a long time since Hanno had been in a friendly city, with no concerns other than getting pissed. He grinned. 'Well, if you put it like that . . .'

A short time later, they were wending their way down a street that led to Ortygia and the small harbour. Kleitos returned the greeting of a man in charge of a party of naked female slaves, but kept walking. Hanno gave them a casual glance as they strode by, but they were all staring at the ground. Poor wretches, Hanno thought. 'A friend?' he asked.

Kleitos shook his head in denial. 'Agathocles? No. He's an arse-licking busybody. Works for Hippocrates, finding him women. For, you know . . .'

Hanno gazed after the line of miserable women, his dislike of Hippocrates increasing. Don't think about it, he told himself. You're here to aid him and his brother in the fight against Rome. Everything else is irrelevant. Yet an unpleasant taste remained in his mouth. 'How far is it to this inn of yours?' he demanded. 'I'm parched.'

'Ha! That's what I like to hear. It's just around this corner.'

Hanno increased his pace. After a skinful of wine, he'd have forgotten his worries.

*

Mixed feelings continued to batter Aurelia in the two days that followed her arrival into Hippocrates' part of what had been Hiero's palace. There was overwhelming relief that she and Publius were together, and that Elira was with them. They had been supplied with fine clothing and plenty of food and drink. She had made use of the baths more than once. Publius enjoyed them too, although Aurelia was careful to take him early in the morning, before anyone else made use of the facility. Guards prevented them from leaving the set of interlinked rooms, but they did not offer any violence, sexual or otherwise. For the most part, the other occupants, four beautiful women, ignored them. There were occasional barbed comments, and plenty of hostile looks, but that was all. Physically at least, they wanted for nothing.

Mentally, it was a different matter. She belonged to Hippocrates now, and her only purpose was to serve as his concubine. It was not a matter of 'if' she would have to attend him, but 'when'. It was the same with Agathocles, who whispered frequent lewd suggestions to her. This made every moment, every hour of waiting, of not knowing when she would be summoned, pure torture. The longer it dragged on, the worse she felt.

It wasn't just that of course. Her promise in the market to send Hippocrates to Elysium and back would have been relayed to him already, of that Aurelia was certain, and she was terrified she would fail this test. Her experiences of lovemaking had been with Lucius, and bar one or two occasions, they had been short-lived encounters absent of passion. Lucius' wellbeing, which had so concerned her, now rarely crossed her mind.

Desperate, Aurelia sought Elira's advice one afternoon when Publius was napping. Their relationship had changed since their enslavement. Elira still deferred to her, but with less respect than before. Whether that had anything to do with her promise to Agathocles, Aurelia had no idea. She had apologised abjectly for it; Elira had brushed her off, saying that she would have done the same if she'd had a child.

Aurelia was much relieved when Elira readily gave her some new tips and techniques to try. 'Once you learn what men like, they're easy to please,' Elira liked to pronounce. Aurelia hoped that it was so with Hippocrates. After Elira's fruity description about to how keep a man from reaching climax, she even managed to find some humour in the situation. 'Like that? You're not serious.'

'I'm telling you, they love it. Just try it and see.'

Aurelia giggled, but it didn't take long for brutal reality to sink in again. How life could change, she thought miserably. If someone had told her a month ago that she'd be in Syracuse, a prisoner *and* concubine to one of its rulers, she'd have called them insane. Yet here she was.

As was so often the case, Publius saved the moment. He woke up and crawled across the bed to her, sleepily demanding a cuddle. Aurelia clutched him to her, wishing that she could transport them both away to safety.

The reprieve didn't last. Agathocles came later that day. Aurelia was to be ready by sunset. She was to dress in a seductive manner. Hippocrates would receive her on the roof of the palace. 'Disappoint him and you'll pay,' he advised in a steely voice. 'Or more likely your son will.'

Aurelia flashed him a confident smile. 'There's no need for threats.'

'We'll see about that later. Don't think I've forgotten what I owe me either.'

'I'm looking forward to it,' Aurelia lied, caressing his face and wondering how she was going to get through the impending degradations with not one hideous man, but two. When Elira later offered her a cup of wine laced with a little poppy juice – obtained from one of the other women – she didn't refuse. She had avoided it since the news from Cannae had shattered her world, but needs must. The pleasant, numbed feeling that it granted might help to block out the worst of what was to come.

Elira helped her to get ready, giving opinions on which dress to wear, the best way to style her hair, and which perfume to apply. Under normal circumstances, Aurelia would have enjoyed the experience – since having Publius, and with Lucius away, occasions to dress up had been rare – but the reason behind it threatened to drag her spirits into the abyss. She supped more wine and poppy juice, grateful to feel disembodied, able to look down on the surreal situation as if it weren't she who would have to go through with it.

A short while after the first watch had been sounded, Agathocles arrived. Telling Publius that she would kiss him good night when he was asleep, Aurelia left him in Elira's care. Elira gave her a reassuring look; Aurelia clutched on to the encouragement for dear life. Someone cared about her, thought of her as something other than a piece of meat. She was grateful that Agathocles did not try to engage her in conversation as they walked down a long passageway, past a number of sentries, finally reaching a set of stairs.

'Remember what I said,' warned Agathocles, his foot on the bottom step.

Aurelia didn't trust her voice, so she nodded.

The view at the top took her breath away. It wasn't the patterned mosaic underfoot, the fruit trees and cultivated vines, the murmuring fountain with Poseidon astride a dolphin at its centre; the staircase had brought them out on the edge of the palace's roof, where they were able to look out to the east, over a harbour full of ships, and the bright, sunlit sea beyond. Aurelia fancied that she could even see the coastline of Italy in the far distance. Her heart bled; she had to force her legs to keep moving, following Agathocles towards the figure that lay on a couch near the fountain.

'General.' Agathocles bowed from the waist.

'Yes?' Hippocrates sounded irritated.

'The woman you wanted. The Roman. I have brought her.'

'Leave us.'

'General.' Agathocles performed obeisance again. With a stony glance at Aurelia, he walked away.

'Approach.'

Her mouth was dry; she could feel sweat trickling down her back. Aurelia walked the few steps to Hippocrates' couch. He was a slim man, perhaps twenty-nine or thirty years old. A close-shaven black beard couldn't conceal his slender features. There the softness ended, however. His lips were thinned; his eyes glittered black and cold. She made sure to meet them for a moment before dropping her gaze. 'I am at your disposal.' The words tasted bitter in her mouth.

'Agathocles said you were a looker.'

She didn't know how to reply. Did he agree with the sentiment or not? 'Sir.'

'You are, I suppose, in an unusual way. I hope that your reputation is deserved. Get undressed.'

Aurelia couldn't stop her gaze from flashing to the guards, the nearest of whom was only fifteen or so paces away. What did it matter? she thought. Many more people than these had seen her naked at the slave market. Doing her best to appear graceful, she slid the top of her dress off her shoulders. Slowly, she let it fall to her waist. There she paused, aware of Hippocrates' keen eyes upon her. Swaying her hips, she walked to stand over him. He stared up at her, his lips open. He wasn't ugly, Aurelia decided. It was a tiny consolation. When his hands reached up to pull her dress down further, she didn't resist. Instead, she smiled.

Gods, help me through this, she asked. Gods, help me and Publius.

Chapter VII

Even at a distance of more than half a mile, Syracuse could impress. Its wall filled the whole southern horizon, the limestone blocks that formed it turned golden by the setting sun. Westward from the sea's edge it ran, across the coastal plain and up on to higher ground beyond, where it disappeared into the orange haze. According to the messengers who carried orders between the Roman camps, it extended for a good twenty miles around the city. Quintus and his comrades had only seen this section, opposite the vast camp that their legion had built on its arrival, but it was more than enough to impress. Assaulting it by land or sea would be no easy matter.

Quintus, Urceus and their tent mates were standing on the packed-earth rampart a short distance from their unit's tent lines. A sentry would move them on soon, but until then the view was worth it.

'Which is worse?' asked Quintus, belching. 'Having your skull smashed by a stone from a catapult, or drowning when your ship sinks?'

Urceus drank deep and smacked his lips in appreciation. 'That's not bad stuff,' he said, proffering the wine skin. 'Like some?'

His friend was dodging the question, but Quintus wasn't surprised. He and the rest of Corax's maniple were part of the force that would assault the defences of Achradina, which lowered over the smaller of Syracuse's two harbours. They would be attacking by sea, and Quintus had no doubt that there would be catapults and bolt-throwers aplenty where they'd land.

'Give it here.' He lifted the skin up by its end. Misjudging how much there was in it, he was unprepared for the tide of wine that rushed down his throat. He managed to swallow a couple of gulps while hurriedly lowering the leather bag, but couldn't stop himself from coughing a good amount of it on to the ground.

There were chortles from the rest.

'Don't waste it,' Urceus cried, grabbing the skin from Quintus.

'Sorry,' muttered Quintus, hating the burning feeling of the wine that had gone up into his nostrils. He'd drunk more than he had thought. It was all in an effort not to think about the hell that awaited them the day after tomorrow.

'I'd rather drown,' pronounced Felix, a skinny man with buck teeth. Forever dogged by misfortune – mainly at gambling – he was always being ribbed about his name. 'Unlucky,' everyone called him. 'I can't swim. I wouldn't know a thing about it after a few mouthfuls of water.'

'You'd know more than you would if your brains were splattered ten paces in every direction by a stone from a *ballista*!' challenged Quintus.

'What if I saw it coming, though?' retorted Felix with a shudder. 'No. Drowning would be better.'

A couple of the other men voiced their agreement, but Wolf gave a vehement shake of his head. He was a taciturn man who'd been a sheep farmer before enlisting, and who still wore the strip of wolf skin on his helmet that had marked him out as a veles. 'I hate every bastard wolf that lives and breathes,' he'd say to anyone who listened. 'This bit of skin reminds me of the day I get my discharge. The first thing I'll do is to go hunting.'

'What is it, Wolf?' asked Quintus.

Wolf ran a dirty fingernail down the links of his mail shirt. 'Imagine trying to get this damn thing off as you sink. I can't think of a worse way to die.'

Unlucky snickered. 'That'll teach you to go all fancy with your armour. For once, I don't mind only having a breast- and back plate.'

'You'd like a mail shirt too, Unlucky, admit it! If you weren't so shit at dice, you'd have had one long ago. Two of them, even,' Wolf flung back at him to a chorus of laughter.

Unlucky flushed and muttered something under his breath, but he didn't dare challenge Wolf, whose unpredictable temper had won him few friends.

Even though Wolf was right, Quintus felt a little sorry for Unlucky. Nearly all the hastati in the maniple had mail shirts now: bought with their saved pay, won on a bet or through gaming, or pilfered from the dead after battles. Unlucky had taken one once from the body of a bandit that he'd killed, but lost it the next day in a wager. If Corax hadn't been such a disciplinarian – missing pieces of equipment was *not* tolerated – Quintus reckoned that Unlucky would have long since gambled away his square chest and back plates too. His desire to wager was like a disease. He'd bet on anything: two slugs crawling on the ground, who'd fart the most times in one sentry watch, what the weather would be like the next day. As a consequence, he never had two obols to rub together. Wine was a luxury beyond him. 'Give Felix a sup,' Quintus said to Urceus.

Urceus popped the stopper in and flung the skin through the air.

Unlucky shot a grateful look at Quintus as he caught it. 'Which do you fear more?' he asked Quintus.

'Drowning, for sure.'

'Why?'

'I'm not good at swimming and, like Wolf says, our mail shirts are damn heavy.'

'Don't wear it, then,' advised Urceus with a leer.

'If I did that, I'd get a sodding arrow in the chest,' said Quintus.

'It won't make any difference what you do,' said Wolf. 'If Hades has picked your name, he's picked it. You can't do fuck all about it.'

Everyone laughed and Quintus finally let himself smile. There was no point in brooding over the coming offensive. It was going to happen, and he would be part of it. He had survived the fields of blood, had he not, and the years of war since? Plenty of men would die when

Marcellus sent them to take Syracuse, but he didn't have to be one of them.

'Enjoying the wine?' asked a familiar voice.

They all swung around, mumbling, 'Yes, sir.'

'At ease, at ease,' said Corax, clambering up on to the rampart. He jerked a thumb at the skin, which Unlucky was still holding. 'Anything left in that?'

'Yes, sir.' Unlucky passed it over.

Everyone watched as Corax drank several mouthfuls. 'It's not complete horse piss,' he pronounced at length. 'Who stole it?' He eyed Wolf first, who was known for his ability to purloin everything from spare pieces of kit to rounds of cheese.

'Not me, sir,' protested Wolf, grinning.

'You, Crespo?'

'No, sir!' replied Quintus.

'I actually bought it, sir,' said Urceus. 'Thought I'd spend a bit of money on some half-decent stuff before the attack. In case, you know—'

'That's as good a reason as any.' Corax lifted the skin. 'Can I have another drop?'

'Drink away, sir. Finish it if you like,' urged Urceus.

'I'm not about to do that. You might not say, but it'd piss you off,' replied Corax after he'd slugged a final mouthful. 'I need you on my side, to watch my back when we're fighting those Syracusan bastards.' He threw the skin back to Urceus.

'I'd do that anyway, sir, you know that! We all would.' A rumble of accord rose from the others. 'See, sir? We look after you, because *you* look out for us.'

'Damn right,' said Wolf.

'Aye!' added Unlucky and Quintus. There were other loud echoes of agreement.

Corax seemed pleased. 'Ah, you're good lads,' he growled. 'May Mars keep his shield over every last one of us the day after tomorrow.'

Quintus wasn't alone in repeating a quiet prayer in response.

'Are the ships seaworthy, sir?' asked Unlucky. 'You know, the ones with those *sambucae*, the bloody great ladders, on them?'

Everyone's eyes swivelled to the centurion. On Marcellus' orders, six pairs of quinqueremes had been lashed together. Long, hide-encased scaling ladders had been laid on the decks of three, attached at their base to the ships' bows. Pulleys and ropes secured the ladders to the vessels' masts. When they were raised into the air, the structures resembled lyres, the musical instruments that had given rise to their nickname: sambucae. The three remaining pairs of quinqueremes, similarly attached to one another, had had siege towers several storeys tall placed on their decks. Every soldier in the army had been down to the water to see the outlandish-looking vessels. They were the object of morbid fascination, if not downright dread, and innumerable wagers had been made about how many men would die on them.

'The sailors and carpenters have been readying those ships for weeks,' answered Corax. 'They've tested them out a few times. None have sunk yet.'

'They haven't had hundreds of soldiers on board, though, sir,' said Quintus, emboldened by the wine.

To his relief, Corax didn't bite his head off. 'I'm not overly keen on the idea of setting to sea on ships with contraptions like the sambucae on board either, Crespo, but orders are orders. At least we don't just have to sit below the battlements like the archers and slingers will, on their sixty ships. They'll be easy targets for the enemy artillery. And it's a huge honour for our unit to be selected as part of the initial attack. Imagine being the one to win a *corona muralis*! The Senate might not allow us the real things, but Marcellus has promised one of his own design, and a purse to match.'

Quintus didn't dare to utter what he was thinking: that scores of men, if not more, would die before anyone reached the enemy rampart, let alone became the first one to scale it.

Mention of the crown had struck a chord with his comrades, however. 'I wouldn't mind one of them, sir,' said Unlucky, grinning.

Corax winked. 'Even you wouldn't gamble an award like that away. The money, yes, but not the decoration.'

'Never, sir!' protested Unlucky to guffaws from the rest.

'Well, may the gods grant that you or one of the others gets the opportunity to win a corona,' declared the centurion. 'And whatever happens, I know you'll do me, and Rome, proud.'

Urceus raised the wine skin high. 'For Rome, and for Corax!'

'CORAX! CORAX! CORAX!' Quintus and the six others roared back.

'Enough,' said Corax, but his voice held none of his usual iron. He raised a hand in acknowledgement of the acclaim, letting it wash over him for a moment or two. When it died down, he nodded in a pleased way at Quintus, Urceus and the rest. 'I'd best move on, talk to some of the others. Enjoy your night.'

'Thank you, sir,' they all replied.

'What a fucking officer,' pronounced Urceus when Corax was out of earshot. 'I'd follow him down a bottomless well.'

'Aye,' said Quintus. 'Me too.' He dreaded the day when he was promoted out of the unit to the *principes*. A centurion like Corax made what was to come more bearable. Often soldiers died in battle because their officers made stupid decisions, or because they couldn't see how to react to the enemy. It wasn't like that with Corax. I'll be all right, Quintus thought. We all will.

Two days later, they were packed like sardines on a quinquereme, and bound for Syracuse's smaller harbour, which lay a short distance to the south. The city's imposing ramparts ran along to starboard, perching 'on top' of the sea as if by magic. Most men were studiously ignoring them. It was easier to concentrate on the glittering water on the port side, and the flotilla of vessels around them, or to talk among themselves of women or lovers left behind in Italy.

Because a set of oars had been removed from both ships, half of each quinquereme's rowers had been left behind. On Quintus' vessel, it was the port banks, and on the craft that it was lashed to, the starboard banks. The missing oarsmen's cramped positions on each ship were now filled by 140 soldiers. The remainder of Corax's maniple, twenty-odd hastati, who could not fit below, stood on the deck alongside the quinquereme's complement of forty marines, and another half-century of men from another maniple. Quintus and Urceus were among these fortunate ones. Packed together they might be, thought Quintus, but at least he could see the sky, could see where they were going. Having the menacing enemy fortifications in sight was better than being crammed together for the entire voyage like beasts in a market pen.

Urceus grimaced. The normal ruddy colour of his cheeks had changed to grey. 'I hope it doesn't take much longer,' he muttered.

'Still feeling sick?' For the hundredth time, Quintus cast an eye over the side, some three paces below. The sea was barely moving, yet Urceus wasn't alone in looking queasy. Wolf seemed unhappy; so did Unlucky and many of the faces around him. Men aplenty were vomiting below.

'Of course I fucking am! I'm not used to being on a ship.'

Quintus nodded in an understanding way, though on another day, he might have enjoyed the passage. It was a beautiful day, with scarcely a cloud in the sky. The temperature was pleasantly warm, but their destination ensured that there was no enjoyment to be had from it. As that Syracusan officer he'd interrogated with Corax — what was his name? Kleitos? — had admitted, the walls they would soon have to attack would be lined with catapults and bolt-throwers. As if to prove the Syracusan's words true, a catapult twanged on the ramparts, some five hundred paces to their right. A few heartbeats later, the stone it had loosed came down in the water, a decent bowshot away. Quintus' own stomach, which had been fine until that point, did a neat roll. We're out of range, he told himself. 'At least we're on deck. Not below, with the others.'

'Aye, I suppose,' replied Urceus, but his eyes were on the spot where the rock had landed.

No more missiles were launched, and Quintus tilted back his head, grateful for the sea breeze.

The deck crew, men with nut-brown, weather-beaten skin and calloused feet, slipped between the soldiers as they went about their duties, resigned looks on their faces. They didn't like the presence of the hastati on their ship any more than the hastati did, nor the purpose of their journey. The captain and helmsman stood together at the stern, talking to Corax. From time to time, the captain held a shouted conversation with his counterpart on the quinquereme to which they were attached. Beside him, a pair of flautists played the tune that had been agreed beforehand, a slow, easy-to-follow refrain that would not confuse the oarsmen on the two different vessels.

Quintus was determined to take Urceus' mind away from his seasickness. 'At least we're not on one of those,' he said, pointing. Three score quinqueremes were leading their ship and the others towards their destination. Their decks were packed with archers, slingers and javelin men. Every one of them had at least two light catapults as well. Their job was to rain down a covering barrage that would keep the city's ramparts clear of enemy troops as the vessels with sambucae on board made their way to the base of the defences.

'True,' said Urceus. 'Those poor bastards are going to have to sail right in under the walls and fucking stay there. At least we can move once we get into position.'

'Like Wolf said to me the other night then, shut up,' ordered Quintus with a crooked grin.

Urceus went to nudge him in the ribs, but wary of Quintus' mail, held back. 'Smartarse.'

'It's good advice. Whingeing just makes an unhappy man unhappier.'

'A shame there isn't room to play dice,' chipped in Unlucky from the rank behind them. 'That'd pass the time.'

Quintus twisted around. 'Got your dice with you?'

Grinning, Unlucky pulled up a little leather bag on a thong from inside his tunic. 'Always!'

'Madman,' said Quintus.

'They bring me luck in battle. Fortuna might cheat me out of all my money, but she's always true when it comes to saving my skin.' Unlucky kissed the bag reverently.

Quintus nodded. Even Wolf didn't pour scorn on Unlucky, for this, his little habit before combat. Wolf's was to rub the strip of skin on his helmet. Quintus' was to ask Mars for help. Urceus repeated the same short prayer over and over. Corax – even he – had a ritual: snapping his sword half in and out of its scabbard.

'There it is,' said Urceus. His tone made Quintus turn at once.

The walls to their right had begun to curve inwards, away from them. Quintus peered, eager to see what had previously been a sketch drawn by Corax in the dirt. Together with the island of Ortygia, which was connected to the rest of Syracuse by fortified bridges, the fortifications before them formed a three-sided harbour. Ortygia's defences made up the southern side, while the western and northern ones were composed of part of the city's main wall. The anchorage was exposed to the east, meaning it could not be used when inclement weather was coming from that direction. The lower or great harbour was much more protected from the weather, but the battlements there were a great deal higher, which was why Marcellus was directing his attack here, at the smaller harbour.

'See that, boys?' shouted Corax. 'Achradina! By tonight, gods willing, we'll be on the other side of those walls. For now, enjoy the view, and the sun on your face.'

His men laughed and cheered, but their reaction was a little subdued. Quintus felt the same way. The defences were the height of five men standing on each other's shoulders, and they were manned by thousands of the enemy, whose armaments included an unknown quantity of artillery. Quintus knew some of his comrades – at the very minimum – would die today.

Corax made no recognition of their muted response. He waited until they had quietened. 'You know the drill, but I'll tell you again anyway. Check the straps on all of your kit. Helmet, breastplates if you have one, baldrics and belts. The straps on your shields. Don't forget to look over your sandals: laces and soles. It'd be damn stupid if you slipped off the ladder because of a loose hob.'

There were a few nervous chuckles at this.

'Run your hand down the shafts of your pila to make sure that there are no splinters. Your swords need to be loose in their scabbards. Have a piss over the side. A shit, if you need one. I for one don't want someone's mess all down my face when I'm climbing.'

'No one would dare take a dump on you, sir. Not after the roasting you gave that lad who sneezed on you,' called a voice from behind Quintus – Unlucky?

More laughs, happier this time.

Corax's lips twitched; he let them enjoy the joke. 'You're probably right, soldier, but my advice remains the same. Odd things happen to a man's guts when he goes into battle. It's best to get bodily functions out of the way beforehand. There's no shame in it. We've all seen each other's cocks at this stage, and how small they are. Except for mine, of course, which rivals that of Priapus.'

The hastati below decks joined in the eruption of laughter that followed. Even the crew did.

Corax allowed himself a little smile. 'Get on with it,' he roared. 'Down the back, where you won't be pissing straight on top of the oarsmen.'

Soon a line of men had formed up on the port side of the deck, just behind the point at which the last sets of oars protruded from the hull. Jokes and insults flew, especially at those who needed to empty their bowels, but it was good-humoured. Morale had been preserved yet again, thought Quintus admiringly. 'How does he do it?'

'May the gods grant that he's always there to look after us,' said Urceus. 'Fuck knows what would happen to us if he was—'

'Don't say it,' interrupted Quintus.

Urceus cursed and reached for the phallus amulet that hung around his neck. He rubbed it furiously, as if that would retract his words.

Offering up a prayer of his own that their centurion would come through the assault safely, Quintus went to join the line. Urceus chased after him. Quintus had emptied his bladder before they had embarked, but he needed to go again. It was always the way. Still, he thought, watching a hapless soldier squatting at the deck's edge as hoots of derision rained down on him, there was always time to lighten the mood by making fun of someone. 'Get a move on,' he roared. 'Some of us want to fight rather than shit!'

His comment was met with widespread laughter. The crouching soldier finished as fast as he could and made his way past them, glowering with embarrassment.

A number of paces from where the friends were standing, the captain called across to his counterpart; they agreed a new course. The hastati muttered to each other as the helmsman spoke with the flautists, who changed their tune. The rowers on the starboard side smoothly lifted their oars from the water while those on the port continued to row. The quinquereme began to turn. Half a dozen heartbeats later, the flutes reverted to their previous refrain. The starboard oars slid back into the sea with soft splashes, and with barely a break in the rhythm, took up the same stroke as the port ones. Quintus peered towards the prow. They were heading straight for the centre of the little harbour. At least thirty of the quinqueremes with missile troops occupied the water ahead. Two of the ships with sambucae were a short distance in front, while the three vessels with siege towers were strung out behind with the remainder of the protective quinqueremes. They would follow as soon as there was space to do so.

A hush settled over the hastati as the walls, on either side now, drew closer. Even the sailors' conversations became subdued, leaving the flutes' music and the noise of the oars to fill the air. It would have been a beautiful accompaniment to any voyage, thought Quintus grimly, if it weren't for the reason that silence had fallen. Every man aboard knew that at any moment, they would come within range of the enemy artillery.

'Four hundred paces,' said Urceus in a low tone. 'That's how far a good artilleryman can aim a large catapult. We've got to be close to that already.'

'Aye.' Quintus wished that Urceus hadn't mentioned it.

Twang! All eyes shot towards the walls to their left. The stone came through the air in a blur, moving so fast that it was almost impossible to track. Quintus was relieved to see that it would come nowhere near their ship.

His relief lasted no more than a heartbeat.

Twang! Twang! Twang! Twang! Twang! The sound was coming from both sides, faster and faster. Suddenly, the sky was full of stones and arrows. Beneath the noise, Quintus could hear men shouting: the officers and men who judged the range of each shot. *Twang! Twang! Twang! Twang!* Quintus fought his fear, doing his best to ignore the deadly chorus. It was impossible of course. Beside him, Urceus was mouthing savage curses. Others were praying. Back where they'd been standing, Unlucky had the bag containing his dice clenched in his fist. Wolf was staring fixedly at the deck. Corax, on the other hand, was stalking from man to man, slapping their backs and telling them what fine soldiers they were. Quintus took heart, but he was relieved a moment later when it was his turn to piss over the side. There was far more urine than he'd imagined there would be. Job done, he hurried back to his position. Urceus wasn't far behind him.

Fortunately, their captain had taken the decision to direct the ship down the middle of the entrance to the harbour. This kept them at the outer edge of the enemy catapults' range. A good number of the quinqueremes in front and to the sides were not so lucky, however. The enemy artillerymen had ranged their weapons well. Quintus could not be sure of the size of the stones being hurled, but the damage they were causing was significant. He could see a number of vessels that had been holed, some near the waterline. One was sinking slowly, its crew and passengers jumping off in scores. Another ship had had its mast cracked; the tall piece of wood now leaned at a crazy angle. Shouts of dismay rose from the vessel's crew. To continue, they would have to chop the mast down, thought Quintus, and the flotilla was so close together that that ran the considerable risk of hitting another quinquereme.

Crash! A stone struck the deck of a quinquereme perhaps a hundred paces off their port side. As if by magic, a gap appeared in the densely packed soldiers on board. The stone shot into the sea between the ships with a loud splash. The roars of pain reached Quintus a heartbeat later.

'Shit, that's not a pleasant way to go,' said Urceus.

'How many men did it kill?' asked Quintus, fascinated and horrified. 'Five? Ten?'

'At least,' replied Urceus with a grimace.

Crash! Crash! The enemy artillerymen were focusing on the quinquereme that had just been hit. Two more rocks landed, clearing swathes more space on its decks.

Quintus' gorge rose, and he knelt and busied himself with the laces on one of his sandals. After that, he tried not to look at what was going on. His comrades were doing the same. It was an act of self-preservation. Nothing could block from their ears the screams of the injured and the piteous cries for help from the soldiers who were in the sea, however. Quintus gritted his teeth and wondered if it had been wise to wear his mail shirt. Even the strongest of men would struggle to swim wearing one. Mars, let us reach the bottom of the walls soon, he prayed. Do not let me die in the water.

Their ship ploughed on, with death and destruction showering down on either side. A stray stone ripped a great hole in the mainsail, but they took no other direct hits. There was a near miss with a quinquereme that had suffered heavy casualties among its oarsmen, and which could not move out of their way. Luckily, the soldiers at the front relayed the message, allowing the captains to order their rowers to back water. They came to a halt less than a javelin throw from the stricken ship. Many of the hastati shouted abuse at its crew, telling them to get the fuck out of the way or they would sink their damn vessel themselves.

Long moments passed, during which their craft had to sit motionless. It soon became a target for the enemy catapults. A number of stones smacked into the water just to the front of it, and two hit the decks of the quinquereme that their one was attached to, killing a dozen soldiers. Quintus and his comrades were helpless, able to do nothing but study the walls on both sides in utter dread, wondering when the next barrage would be launched. It was pure good fortune that their ship and, more importantly, the great ladder with which they would launch their attack, were not hit. After what seemed an eternity, the damaged quinquereme in front limped from their path, allowing them to continue.

'That was a close one, lads,' said Corax as he prowled past. 'Be a shit way to die, colliding with some of our own, eh? Or to be mown down while we sat there?'

'Yes, sir,' the pair muttered.

There was to be no respite. More and more stones and arrows rained in. The enemy artillerymen had ranged their weapons by stages, Quintus concluded. There was no other explanation for their concentrated volleys to have been so efficient. Finally, inevitably, their ship's luck ran out. Two men in the ranks ahead went down, both their skulls smashed by the same stone. Another was thrown to the deck, skewered through the chest by a bolt as thick as two of Quintus' fingers. Blood pooled rapidly beneath his twitching body as he choked and gasped his way to oblivion. It left a crimson stain on the deck timbers. On the neighbouring quinquereme, a trio of soldiers were hurled overboard, falling into the gap between the two vessels. The screams as they were crushed to death or pushed under the water by the ships' momentum were horrendous. Quintus prayed; around him, his comrades did the same. Corax seemed oblivious. He paced to and fro between the men, making no acknowledgement of the enemy artillery at all.

Corax was made of iron, Quintus decided. He himself managed not to soil his undergarment, and to appear calm, yet it was quite another to do as Corax did, and to defy death. Despite the centurion's example, Quintus was grateful that they were nearing their destination. Hades beckoned in numerous new ways, but at least he'd have his feet on dry land.

Twang! Twang! Quintus held his breath; he did not look up. It was better not to. Wolf had been right. If the gods had marked him out to be wiped from existence, there was nothing he could do about it. Blood pulsed behind his eardrums nonetheless; fear gnawed at his guts. *Crash!* The roars of agony that followed were some distance to his rear; Quintus felt guilty relief that the stone had not hit him or Urceus, and then immediate terror about where the second stone would land. *Crash!* The deck trembled beneath his feet; there was the unmistakeable sound of a body hitting the ground, right behind him.

'Wolf!' wailed Unlucky.

Blood sprayed over Quintus' lower legs as he turned; he winced at the sight. The stone had taken Wolf's head clean off; there was no sign of it, or his helmet with its signature strip of fur. His truncated corpse sprawled before them, unrecognisable as their comrade. The severed arteries in the stump of Wolf's neck pulsed with each slowing beat of his heart, showering the area with droplets of blood. A great gouge had been taken out of the deck planking beyond Wolf, but fortunately for the other hastati, the stone appeared to have bounced on into the sea.

'Wolf,' whispered Unlucky, his face as grey as week-old snow. '*Wolf.*'

'He's gone,' grated Quintus, seizing Unlucky's chin and forcing his gaze away from the mangled body. Quintus stared into Unlucky's eyes. 'He's gone. The gods will take care of him now. Get a grip of yourself.'

For a moment, it seemed that Unlucky would crack, but then he knuckled away his tears and nodded. 'I'm all right,' he muttered. 'I'm all right.'

'Good.' Quintus released him, noting that Unlucky's grip on his dice was so tight that his knuckles were glistening white through the skin of his fist. 'Thank the gods that the wretch will be behind us on the ladder,' he said to Urceus in an undertone. 'Otherwise we'd have him falling on top of us.'

'You're not wrong there. Gods grant that it is soon.' Urceus made an obscene gesture at the defences. 'Wait until we get up there, you whoresons!'

Quintus felt the same fury. If he lived long enough to reach the enemy, he would make them pay dearly for Wolf's life: yet another comrade to be avenged.

Chapter VIII

'We're nearly there, boys!' Corax's shout could not be ignored. The centurion was pointing at the imposing stone walls that were looming above them, some 150 paces away. 'Steady yourselves. Pray to your favourite deities. When the captain gives me the order, the crew will raise the ladder. The instant it hits that rampart, I want you scrambling up there as fast as you fucking can. Do you hear me?'

'YES, SIR!' they roared at him, their nerves, their desire for vengeance adding volume to their voices.

Whizzzz! Whizzzz! Whizzzz! The noises came from straight ahead. Quintus had stood before enough enemy volleys to recognise the sound of arrows. His gaze shot to the top of the wall, took in the slits positioned below the actual ramparts. His stomach clenched. 'They've got more artillery, sir,' he yelled. 'Short-range pieces!'

Corax had already seen. Bounding to the captain's side, he bellowed in his ear. 'Increase rowing speed. NOW!'

A flurry of missiles began to land all around them: in the water, skittering off the oars and slicing through the fabric of the mainsail. These ones were long iron arrows, and they were striking men aplenty too, ripping their flesh apart like a hot knife through cheese. A flautist had his jaw shorn off right in front of the captain. Keening like a grief-stricken madman, he ran to the edge of the deck and leaped into the sea. Shaken, the captain roared at the remaining flautist, and then at his counterpart on the other quinquereme.

He should have done it the other way around, thought Quintus in alarm.

It took a few heartbeats for the captain's demand to register and within that time, the oarsmen on Corax's vessel had begun to row at ramming speed. The rowers on the second ship tried to take up the same rhythm, but they were a pace or two off the beat. As a result, the paired quinque-remes' prows turned and aimed at a different part of the wall.

'It's higher in that section,' hissed Quintus in dismay. 'Will the damn ladder reach to the top?'

'I fucking well hope so!' snarled Urceus. 'If it doesn't—'

'RAISE THAT LADDER!' yelled Corax. 'I want it in the air, and I want it there now. We'll have fuck all time to get up it before the enemy start dropping rocks and the gods know what else on us. MOVE!'

The groups of sailors who'd been assigned to the task didn't wait for confirmation from the captain. They went to work with alacrity. Grabbing the thick ropes that lay ready at their feet, they began hauling them through the pulleys that had been fastened to the timbers. The slack section sped through their hands, and the cable grew taut. For a moment, nothing happened. Shit, thought Quintus, it's too heavy. Fear gave the crewmen extra strength, however. That, and Corax's vine cane, which was slapping down on their shoulders.

The top of the ladder lifted a hand span from the deck, and then another.

'Put some effort into it, you fucking maggots!' roared Corax. 'Our damn lives depend on it!'

The purple-faced sailors bent their backs and heaved. The ladder moved up again, until even a tall man couldn't touch the end of it. It didn't stop this time; the men lifting it had found their rhythm. Up it went now, silhouetted against the sky, directly overhead. Quintus had to squint as it flashed across the glaring orb that was the sun.

'HOLD!' bellowed Corax. 'HOLD IT, I SAY!'

The ladder jerked to a halt.

Quintus' eyes shot to the base of the wall, which was about fifty paces away.

The captain conferred with his counterpart, and they both ordered the flautists to slow their tune. The oarsmen obeyed at once, and the vessel slowed in the water.

Whizzz! Whizzz! A pair of bolts shot in at an acute angle from the slits in the wall in front of them. One thumped into the deck by Corax's feet, the other hit a sailor holding one of the ropes holding up the ladder. It passed straight through his body and drove into the belly of the man behind him. Both dropped to the deck, roaring in agony, and the ladder lurched to one side as its weight proved too much for their comrades.

'The filthy dogs are aiming at the sailors on the ropes,' Quintus spat.

'Hades take them!' cried Urceus.

'Two men! I need two men here!' Corax had leaped in and taken the place of one of the casualties. 'I want a dozen more holding their shields up to protect the sailors. MOVE!'

None of them wanted to unsling their *scuta* from their backs, where they had put them in order to be able to climb the ladder. Putting them on again would be tricky when packed as tightly on the deck as they were. But if they didn't obey Corax's command, there would be hell to pay – and likely no ladder to climb. Quintus and Urceus shoved their way forward; Unlucky followed. With some of their comrades, they formed a line alongside the sailors. Quintus was near the front of the file, Urceus was right behind him and Unlucky to his rear.

Quintus swiftly undid one of the two straps that suspended his shield, and with the ease of long practice, twisted the opposite shoulder so that the scutum slipped around to the front. *Whizzz! Whizzz! Whizzz! Whizzz!* Heart thumping, Quintus grabbed the shield rim, and then the grip on the inside. He lifted the curved scutum up and over himself and the sailor to his right.

Thump! Bang! Bang! Thump! The bolts landed. More screams, more choked sounds of pain, more bodies hitting the deck. Thankfully, none were close to Quintus. Because of the throng, he could not see the base of the walls. 'How far have we to go?' he yelled to no one in particular.

'Almost there,' Corax replied. 'Hold steady, lads!'

Whizzzz! Whizzzz! Whizzzz! Now Quintus could hear the cries of the defenders. He made out shouted orders in Greek, curses and demands for more ammunition. The air filled with agonised shrieking; there were splashes as men who'd been hit fell overboard. Quintus' guts roiled, and he closed his eyes, offering up yet another beseeching prayer. *Mars, keep your shield over us still.*

'Urceus?'

A wave of relief washed over him when his friend replied. 'I'm all right. You?'

'So far, yes,' said Quintus, grinning like a fool.

With a solid thump, the ram on their quinquereme struck the rocks that formed the breakwater at the base of the fortifications.

This is it, thought Quintus. This is fucking it. His eyes shot to those of the sailor whom he was shielding. In them, he saw utter fear, but determination too. 'Do your job,' the sailor muttered, 'And I'll do mine.'

Encouraged, Quintus nodded.

'LOWER THAT LADDER!' Corax cried.

The sailor beside Quintus began to let the rope slide between his fingers. Quintus watched it with a mixture of dread and fascination. When it went slack, the ladder would be resting against the enemy battlements. The artillery barrage would become even heavier, and he and Urceus would be stuck here, on the deck, which was not where he wanted to be.

Clunk. Amid the crescendo of sound, Quintus somehow heard the ladder come to a halt.

'UP! UP! UP!' yelled Corax. 'Fast as you can!'

If Quintus turned his head away from his shield, he could see beyond the sailor to a section of the ladder which extended from about his own height to ten paces above him. Already the wood was creaking and moving beneath the weight of men ascending it. A heartbeat later, he saw the first hastatus appear. It didn't surprise him that it was one of the oldest and steadiest men in the maniple, a veteran who wouldn't have flinched from Corax's order to take the lead. Gods, but I'm glad that it isn't me, thought

Quintus. 'Fortuna be with you,' he shouted, but the soldier didn't hear him. A scowl of determination twisted his face as he went up the rungs as fast as a man could with a scutum on his back and a long sword dangling from his right hip. A moment later, he vanished inside the hide framework that extended almost to the ladder's top. Its purpose was to shield the attackers from enemy missiles, and it would now be put to the test.

Another hastatus immediately came into view, and then another and another. The rain of enemy bolts and stones was still hammering down, but Quintus couldn't resist a look around the side of his shield, up at the wall. It towered above their position, an imposing rampart of stone blocks that was at least thirty paces in height. The defenders' faces were clearly distinguishable: so too were their arms as they leaned out and hurled spears or loosed sling bullets at their foes. Quintus recalled again the Syracusan officer he had interrogated. Where was Kleitos? Looking down at him right now? *Twang!* went a catapult that he could actually see. He jerked back in reflex as it shot a bolt at the ladder.

'Up you go, that's it! Come on, brothers!' roared Corax. 'To the top!'

Five or so men fitted on the ladder. More than a score were waiting their turn at the bottom. He and Urceus wouldn't have to move for a bit yet. Quintus' head twisted. To their left, another pair of quinqueremes had come to rest; its crew were in the process of elevating its *sambuca*. Bolts and stones were hissing down in response. He saw a number of sailors killed, but the officers on board soon did as Corax had, rushing soldiers forward to protect the crew on the ropes. Hastati began swarming up the rungs the instant that it reached the ramparts. Quintus' stomach lurched as he saw a group of defenders push a long, forked piece of wood out from an embrasure to one side of the point where the ladder met the defences. 'Look out!'

Of course he was too far away to be heard, too far away to do anything but watch in horror as the fork made contact and was swiftly pushed outwards, forcing the ladder into a vertical position. There it stayed for a sickening moment before the Syracusans heaved again and tipped the ladder backwards. The hastati at the bottom were able to jump clear, but the rest were hurled to their deaths on the deck of their own ship, or in the sea. The ladder came to rest against the mast with one soldier still hanging on for dear life near the top. 'Thank the gods,' whispered Quintus. 'Hold on.'

An enemy bolt lanced out from the walls and punched the hastatus clean off the ladder. He dropped into the water below without a sound.

Quintus swallowed and looked away. Forget him, he told himself. Concentrate on what's happening here. *THUMP!* The force of the impact threw him back on his heels. Regaining his balance, Quintus gaped at the barbed head that had slammed through his shield. It had missed his left fist, holding the central grip, by two fingers' width, and his head by less than that.

'Are you hit?' shouted Urceus from behind.

'No! A bollock hair nearer and I would have been dead, though,' Quintus gasped. He wouldn't be able to hold up his shield for long, that was clear. The weight of the iron bolt was already telling on his arm muscles. With a few wrenches, he managed to tug the thing through his scutum and drop it to the deck. A large hole remained in the shield, but at least he was able to raise it aloft again.

'Your comrades have a foothold up there, lads!' roared Corax. 'Keep climbing!'

Quintus peered around the edge of his shield again. To his delight, he saw that their centurion was correct. Somehow, a handful of hastati had reached over the battlements and secured the top of the ladder so that others could follow. His heart leaped. Perhaps they would make it after all?

His hopes continued to rise as two and then three more of his comrades clambered over the defences to join the fray. Corax continued to urge his men onwards, but they had seen what was going on. Now, they were eager to ascend.

A moment later, Quintus' heart stopped. 'What in fucking Hades' name is that?' he heard Urceus say. An outlandish-looking device was emerging over the edge of the ramparts. It was a long, broad piece of wood, about fifty paces in length. From its end dangled a chain and a great three-pronged hook. Even as he watched, the chain was lowered down, towards their ship. Quintus had never seen anything like this before, but he didn't need to be told what it might do. 'Fuck!'

'Is it going to pick us up?' growled Urceus.

'I'd say so.' Quintus looked at his mail shirt and cursed. The bloody armour would be the death of him. Urceus' decision to wear a chest and back plate like Unlucky's seemed more than wise now.

Corax had noticed the new weapon too. 'Climb that ladder!' he screamed. He blew his whistle to try and attract the attention of the soldiers on the battlements, but they were enmeshed in their own struggle for survival.

Plus, Quintus reckoned, those men were too far from the device to make a difference anyway. At least a hundred paces and scores of defenders separated them from its position. It couldn't be taken. Perhaps the hooks could be cut off the arm? he wondered desperately.

The air was filling with shouts of dismay. Everyone had seen the iron claw.

'Crespo, Urceus, Unlucky. Put down your shields. With me.' Corax went striding past, towards the prow. Towards where the hook looked as if it would hit.

Sweat sluiced down Quintus' back the way it might if he were in a caldarium. 'Here.' He handed his scutum to the sailor whom he'd been protecting and hurried after Corax. 'What's your plan, sir?'

Corax's expression was bleak. 'I don't have a fucking plan, Crespo. But if we don't stop that thing, we're all going to drown.'

They weaved their way to the front of the ship, through their fearful comrades. Quintus studied the hook as it loomed overhead. There appeared to be no cables or bindings that they could use their swords on. Panic bubbled up inside him. What could they do with their bare hands? A quick glance at Urceus and Unlucky told him that they were no less unhappy. They were here, as he was, because of their devotion to Corax. Quintus' lead foot caught on something and he stumbled forward, narrowly avoiding falling overboard. Cursing, he kicked at the coiled length of rope that had been responsible, and then an idea flashed into his mind. 'Sir!'

Corax turned with a scowl. 'What?'

Quintus lifted the rope. 'If we could throw this around one of the prongs, we might be able to pull it out of the way. Stop it grabbing hold of the ship.'

'That's bloody clever! Bring it here!'

The men nearest the prow didn't need to be told to make way. A space cleared around Corax, Quintus and the rest as they unrolled the rope and tied one end into a great loop with a sliding knot. 'Are any of you used to roping cattle?' asked Corax.

Feeling stupid, Quintus shook his head. 'No, sir,' muttered Urceus, 'but I'll give it a go.' Unlucky didn't say a word.

Corax's lips turned downwards. 'Fuck it. It's my job.'

'I can do it, sir,' said Unlucky out of the blue.

Their eyes turned in unison. 'Speak up. Quickly!' ordered Corax.

'It's been a few years, sir, but I used to help round up the cattle on our farm every summer. Time was that I could catch a cow from thirty paces away.'

'Now's your chance,' said Corax, handing over the rope.

Quintus shot an encouraging glance at Unlucky, who looked as if he wished he'd said nothing. Urceus slapped him on the back. Unlucky moved to stand in front of them, hefting the loop of rope in his right hand. The hook was now little more than twenty paces over their heads. Quintus was alarmed to see that it no longer appeared to be aiming for the deck. Instead, the men controlling it were going to try and snag the bronze ram that protruded from the front of the ship. Unlucky's task had just been made immeasurably harder. His first attempt failed. So too did his second, and Quintus' hope began to vanish. Then, against all odds, the loop landed on the hook and caught on one of its prongs. Unlucky yelled with delight and tugged on the line, sliding the knot closed. 'I've done it, sir!'

'Grab the rope, all of you!' roared Corax. 'Pull on it like you've never pulled your cocks!'

Quintus, Urceus and Corax made to seize the rope. Their fingers were just closing on it when an arrow took Unlucky in the chest, to the left of his pectoral plate. Whoever had aimed the shot – no coincidence, surely – was a master bowman. Unlucky's grip on the rope slackened; it pulled through his palm, leaving the others scrabbling to catch it. Unlucky's eyes bulged with pain; he looked down at the rope, knowing he had to keep hold of it. Instead of regaining control, however, he dribbled pink-red froth from his lips and let go entirely. Before their horrified gaze, the rope ran over the side, where it dangled from the hook into the sea. Unlucky dropped to the deck in a tangle of limbs. Corax bellowed his frustration. Quintus stooped and picked up another length of rope. 'Here!' he said to Urceus. 'You have a go. We might still manage to grab it.'

Cursing, Urceus tied a running knot as before. Holding the rope with both hands, he approached the point where the low rails that ran along the ship's sides came together at the prow. Quintus watched with jangling nerves. Already the hook was being lowered into position over the ram. Urceus threw and missed; he pulled in the rope and tried again. That attempt failed too.

'Help us, Fortuna,' Quintus cried. He wanted to add, but didn't dare, 'You old bitch, like you should have helped poor Unlucky.'

Urceus was readying himself for one last effort when an enemy bowman – the same one who'd slain Unlucky? – loosed an arrow that scythed down to take him through the left arm. With a scream of pain, he dropped the rope. Even as Corax and Quintus grabbed for it, the hook struck the ram with a resounding clang. It was raised at once, but it hadn't found a purchase and rose into the air again. The men operating it manoeuvred the hook a fraction and lowered it once more. Corax threw the rope, but it fell short, into the sea. With a despairing curse, he hurled it a second time. Quintus didn't see it miss, because his eyes were locked in horror on the hook, which dropped neatly into the water alongside the ram. The chain suspending it began to rise a heartbeat later and Quintus almost vomited when it jarred to a stop. It had snagged the ram.

'It's caught. Pull as you've never pulled!' The shout in Greek, from above, could not be missed.

Insults and roars of triumph carried down from the battlements.

'The arm's going to shoot up in the air, sir!' Quintus roared at Corax.

'Save yourselves,' yelled Corax at the gaggle of soldiers and crew who were watching them. 'Jump! Jump overboard!' He began shoving men towards the rail. 'There's no time. Jump, if you want to live!'

Quintus looked down at his mail shirt, which would pull him under, and then at Urceus, whose injured arm would be the death of him in the water. He wouldn't be able to help his friend with his armour on, but with it off, he had the slimmest of chances. Moving as fast as he could, he unbuckled his belt and baldric, grabbed the hem of the mail and heaved it up to the middle of his chest. He stooped. Normally, this was the point when a comrade grabbed it with both hands and pulled it over his shoulders. On one's own, it was damn tricky. Quintus shook his torso, but nothing happened. His bladder twinged painfully, and he tried not to panic. Drowning would be bad enough, but to die with a mail shirt over his head was a horror that plumbed the depths. He could have wept with relief as he felt a hand – Urceus' good one – take hold of the armour and wrench it up towards his head. Quintus used all the strength in his arms to force it up and off his body. It landed on the deck with an almighty crash.

'Mind my feet,' said Urceus with a crooked grin.

'You mad fuck!' retorted Quintus. Already the deck had started to tilt upwards. Men were shouting in alarm, leaping into the sea. Corax was shoving anyone who came within his reach after them. 'Hold on to me,' directed Quintus. He reached out to Urceus' right side and grabbed him around the midriff. 'To the edge of the deck.'

They had just reached the railing when the world turned upside down.

The decking beneath their feet came up to meet them; the sky tilted at a crazy angle; both of them lost their balance. In quick succession, Quintus saw the prow rise up until it was almost vertical, the ramparts lined with cheering defenders, a jumble of men and weapons and armour – the other soldiers on the ship – the sun, the sea and Urceus' mouth, which was screaming a curse that he could not hear.

And then he was falling, falling into the sea.

Quintus hit the water still somehow gripping Urceus. At the last moment, he held his breath, hoped his friend did the same. The force of the impact ripped them apart; Quintus had no time to react, to hold on to Urceus. He was lost at once in his own war for survival. Buffeted, spun this way and that, he lost all sense of direction. Swirling streams of air bubbles surrounded him; the bodies of men, alive and dead, flashed past too. What filled Quintus with more terror, however, was the knowledge that when the claw was released from the arm – for that was surely its purpose – anyone beneath it would be drowned. The instant that he'd stopped sinking, he began kicking his legs like a maniac. Up, he had to get up to the surface and away to the side. But which way? Underwater, he had no idea where the ship lay. He twisted his head frantically, and through the debris of weapons and corpses, was rewarded with the sight of a great black mass – the stern of their quinquereme, which was pointing down into the depths.

It moved a little, shifting towards a more upright position, and Quintus wasn't sure if he wet himself with fear. He began to swim away from the ship, arms and legs powering him with all of his strength. Neptune, I beg you, he prayed. Do not drag me down to your kingdom.

One, two heartbeats later Quintus felt rather than saw the quinquereme being dropped. A wall of water hit him from behind. He was picked up and bowled along like a twig dropped on to the surface of a fast-flowing river. His feet swept past his head as he was turned end over end. Everything went light, dark, light, dark as the depths and the sky above flashed by Quintus' straining, disorientated eyes. *Thunk*. Something solid – a man, an oar? – struck him in the midriff. Pain lanced through him and it took a mighty effort not to suck in a lungful of seawater.

Then another object hit him on one shin – *smack* – and Quintus' lips almost opened in reflex agony. He couldn't take much more. His lungs were bursting with the need to take in fresh air. He had to get to the surface, quickly. Another impact was a certainty, and when it happened, he would die. I'm not going to make it, he thought. Let go and all of the pain will go away . . .

Somewhere deep inside, he found a last glowing ember of hope. *One last effort. You can make one last effort.* Quintus twisted his head, saw the light, prayed that his mind was not playing him false and struck out for it. Kicked with his legs. Swept forward with his arms. Did it again, and again. Blackness tugged at the edge of his vision. He took another stroke, and another, but the strength was fast leaching from his muscles.

Just as he had lost all faith, his head burst out of the sea. Quintus gasped in air as he'd never done in his life, great juddering mouthfuls of it. He inhaled some water, but he was able to cough it up. His nose ran, his eyes stung from the salt, but he didn't care. He was alive.

His eyes swivelled, trying to make out what was going on. Around him, scores of heads bobbed on the water. Men roared at each other, cursed and pleaded with the gods, cried for their mothers. Quintus saw few faces that he recognised. Of Urceus and Corax there was no sign. Beyond the survivors, some fifty paces away, floated the battered shape of his quinquereme. Half its oars had been shorn away and the mast had been smashed. The ladder hung out over the side, like a tree blown down in a storm. The decks were empty. Everyone had been hurled overboard, thought Quintus numbly.

Whizz. Whizz. Whizz. Fresh fear clawed at him. A heartbeat later, the missiles struck the water nearby. A muffled cry signified another man who would now either drown or die from his injuries. Quintus' gaze shot upwards. Bastards, he mouthed. It wasn't just the artillery that was aiming at them: the ramparts were lined with archers and slingers who were determined not to miss out on this fresh sport. It would only be a matter of time before they singled him out. I'm fucked, he thought. The rocky shore at the foot of the walls offered some solid ground: he could see men hauling themselves up on it, but the defenders had seen them. Soon boulders had been heaved up on to the edge of the parapet and dropped on the unfortunates below, maiming some and killing others. There would be no respite there, or anywhere along the shoreline below the city's walls. Quintus remembered the distance that they had rowed in from the open sea, far beyond which lay their camp, and despair filled him. Even without his armour, he wasn't that strong a swimmer. What other option did he have, however? It was that, or tread water until an enemy missile sent him down to Neptune with the others.

Quintus struck out towards the east, offering up more prayers. It was ironic how he made requests of the gods in times of danger, he knew. At other times, he barely believed in their very existence – they never really offered proof of such – but now, here, he wanted every scrap of hope that might be on offer. Let Urceus be alive somewhere, he asked. Corax too. And as many of my maniple as you can spare. Do not take them all, please.

'Help me, brother!' croaked a soldier to his left. 'I can't swim.'

Quintus forced himself to look the man in the eye. 'I'm not a good swimmer. If I help you, we'll both drown. I'm sorry.'

The soldier reached out an arm. 'I don't want to die. I don't want to die.' His tone was frantic, and Quintus knew that if the man grabbed hold of him, they would both sink faster than a stone. Without a word, he swam away as fast as he could. Guilt tore at him, but he did not let up until the man's pleas had vanished into the crescendo of voices and the noise of missiles landing.

After a time, he stopped for a rest. There were fewer projectiles coming down here, because the enemy artillerymen were concentrating on the Romans directly below their positions. Some way off to his right, the sambuca on the craft that had come in at the same time as theirs had just been grabbed by another iron claw. Quintus' eyes were riveted to the horrifying sight. Soldiers on board were frantically trying to do what he and his comrades had done – land a rope on it – but they too failed. It didn't take long for the Syracusans to catch one of the quinqueremes' rams. Commands rang out at once from the rampart, and a few heartbeats later, the chain holding the claw snapped taut. The prow of the ship was jerked out of the water, pulling the vessel a substantial distance into the air as well. Shrieks filled the air. The tiny figures of men fell away from the decks like ants falling off a disturbed log. That was bad enough, but as the claw was released another arm appeared over the battlements. This one bore a massive stone, the size of three men's torsos. Fresh wails rose from the men who had survived the fall as they saw a new terror looming over them. Quintus could bear to watch no longer, but he was unable to block his ears to the noise of the block striking the ship and the wave that followed in its wake.

Clenching his jaw, he began swimming again. The pain from where he'd been struck in the midriff and leg slowed his progress, and he began having to rest more often. During these breaks, he scanned the area, hoping to see a ship that might be able to pick him up. His search was in vain. Every vessel within sight had either been wrecked beyond redemption by the enemy's missiles, or was in the process of sinking to the bottom of the harbour. Not since Cannae had Quintus seen such wholescale carnage.

He studied the faces of the closest men, praying that he would recognise no one. He didn't. There was no point examining the corpses – there were too many. So when Quintus bumped into yet another body, he gently pushed it away. The man, who was lying on his back, bobbed off to his left. Quintus was about to swim on, when something made him look again. The dead soldier's ears stuck out from his head. He blinked. It was Urceus.

He swam to his friend's side, grief tearing at him anew. Urceus' eyes were closed, his mouth slightly open. He looked dead, but Quintus placed two fingers on the side of Urceus' neck, just under the angle of his jaw. Heart thudding, Quintus waited. For a moment, he felt nothing, but then, to his utter joy, he sensed a weak pulse. 'You're as tough as an old fucking sandal, Urceus,' he muttered, uncaring that tears were running down his face. 'Thank you, Neptune, for leaving this man to float rather than sink.'

Quintus' joy was short-lived. There was no chance that he could support Urceus all the way to the mouth of the harbour and beyond. Despair began to creep over him once more. 'Stop it,' he whispered savagely. 'Urceus wouldn't give up if it was him helping me. Think of something!'

He glanced about, trying to ignore the horror, trying to see a way out. His gaze settled at last, unwillingly, on the vessel that he and his comrades had arrived on. It lay in the water like a dead thing, useless to everyone. The realisation hit Quintus from nowhere. The pair of quinqueremes didn't appear to be sinking. Yes, they could not move anywhere. Yes, they were right under the enemy's noses, but therein lay the beauty of it. In the Syracusans' eyes, there was no need to continue raining missiles on the pair of ships because they presented no further threat to the city. 'We'll be safe there,' Quintus murmured to Urceus as he hooked an arm around his friend's chest from behind. 'For a time at least.'

It seemed to take an age to reach the nearest quinquereme. Quintus could have reached the stricken ship sooner if he'd aimed for its middle, but there were still missiles landing there. At the stern, perhaps even in the gap between the two vessels, they would be hidden from the ramparts entirely. The enemy artillerymen's attention was concentrated on visible targets. As they drew near to the back of the ship, he spotted a cluster of heads in the water. Quintus' spirits rose a little. The more of them there were, the more hope they had of surviving. He redoubled his efforts. The arrow in Urceus' arm needed to be looked at. Extra pairs of hands would make that possible. 'We'll get you sorted out soon, you'll see,' he said to Urceus, longing for his friend to answer.

There was no response, and Quintus' worries surged back. He fumbled again for the pulse in Urceus' neck and was mightily relieved to find it. Then he heard a distinctive voice among the group. Corax! All was not lost, he decided. The gods had not completely abandoned them. It was as well, because he was weakening. Much further, and he would have begun to struggle with Urceus.

About twenty paces from the stern, he called out: 'I have an injured comrade here. Can anyone help?'

Faces turned, and three men struck out towards them.

The first one to arrive had black hair and blue eyes. Quintus recognised him as a hastatus in the other century of their maniple, but he didn't know the man's name. 'Where's he hurt?' the newcomer asked.

'He has an arrow through the left arm. But he's been unconscious since I found him, so there might be a head injury I haven't seen.' Do *not* let that be the case, Quintus prayed.

'Let me take him,' said the black-haired soldier. 'Head for the centurion. He's the—'

'I know,' Quintus butted in. 'Corax is my centurion, thank all the gods.'

'Seems like a good man.' With great care, the black-haired soldier took ahold of Urceus around his chest. 'I've got him.'

Happy that Urceus was in good hands, Quintus swam towards Corax. The hastatus and his companions followed.

When the centurion recognised Quintus, an expression of real pleasure crossed his face. 'Look who Neptune just spat out! By all the gods, Crespo, it's good to see you.'

'And you, sir,' replied Quintus fervently. 'I didn't think you'd made it.'

'Nor I you. I haven't seen a man of my century until you showed up. This lot are mostly from the unit that split itself between our ship and the other one. A few sailors too, and a handful of Vitruvius' lot. Who have you got there?' He gestured behind Quintus.

'Urceus, sir.'

'More good news,' said Corax, smiling. 'Is he badly hurt?'

'I'm not sure, sir. He's unconscious.'

Corax's face blackened with anger and concern. 'We'll have to do our damnedest to make sure he survives then, eh? Hades can fuck off if he thinks he's taking a soldier as good as Jug. I've lost too many good men today already.'

The faces to either side registered shock at Corax's blasphemy, but Quintus didn't share in their opinion. Corax was here, alive, and that was what mattered.

'Let's get him tied to this for a start,' ordered Corax, lifting a rope out of the water. Quintus saw that it ran in a big loop, giving everyone something to hold on to. It was secured to an iron ring that hung from the timbers of the stern, just above their heads. The black-haired soldier swam in with Urceus a moment later, and using a short length that Corax produced, they looped it around his comrade's chest.

'Which arm is it?' enquired Corax.

'His left, sir.' Quintus reached down and felt for Urceus' hand. Gently, he lifted it sideways, away from his friend's body, so that the arrow wouldn't catch his torso. As it emerged, he blinked. The front half of the arrow had snapped off, leaving only the feathered end sticking out of Urceus' flesh.

'That's a stroke of luck and no mistake,' muttered Corax. With a steady pull, he withdrew the shaft. A thin stream of blood followed it, and Urceus moaned. His eyelids fluttered open.

'Urceus, can you hear me?' asked Quintus.

Urceus' eyes came into focus. 'Fuck . . . my head is sore. I must have . . . hit it on something in the water.'

Quintus wanted to laugh and cry at the same time.

'Are you hurt anywhere else?' demanded Corax.

Urceus registered the centurion's presence, bobbed his chin respectfully. 'Er, no, sir. I don't think so.'

'Excellent. One of you rip a strip off your tunic,' Corax ordered. 'I want a bandage tied around Urceus' arm, to stop the bleeding.'

The black-haired soldier was first to proffer a piece of fabric, and Quintus warmed to him further. 'What's your name?' he asked as Corax set to tying it in place.

'Mattheus.' He saw Quintus' surprise. 'I'm as Roman as you are, but my maternal grandfather was Hebrew. I'm the last of four boys. My mother nagged my father until he gave in about the name.'

'Crespo, they call me.' He reached out a hand, and they shook. 'I'm one of Corax's men, as you can tell. You?'

'I'm in Festus' maniple.' A grimace. 'Or I was. He's probably as dead as the rest of my lot.'

'You were at Cannae?'

'I wouldn't be here in fucking Sicily if I hadn't been, would I?' Mattheus winked to show he meant no offence.

'There have been some new recruits, but not that many, I suppose,' replied Quintus, relieved that Mattheus was a veteran, like him. 'We're going to need more of them after today, and that's no lie.'

'Don't get cocky, Crespo. Don't think that those bastard Syracusans won't be on the lookout for survivors later, when we try to get away,' warned Corax. 'We'll have to be as sly as you like to succeed.'

'You painted us a picture like that at Trasimene, sir,' croaked Urceus. 'And Cannae.'

'And you got us out both times, sir,' added Quintus. 'You'll do it again.'

'Damn right,' said Urceus.

For once, Corax seemed at a loss for words. He muttered something like, 'Don't go getting your hopes up,' before swimming to peer around the stern, towards the city walls.

'You trust him then?' Mattheus' expression was appraising.

'He's saved my arse even more times than this reprobate here,' growled Urceus. He gave Quintus a grateful glance that needed no words.

'Mine too,' said Quintus. 'He's the best damn centurion in the whole army.'

'I'd heard him spoken of highly,' said Mattheus, nodding. 'It's good that he's in charge, eh?'

'Aye.' Quintus was thirsty, sunburnt, up to his neck in the sea, and grief-stricken because of the comrades he'd lost. Thousands of the enemy were only a few hundred paces away. That didn't stop his heart from singing.

They would see tomorrow. Somehow, he was certain of that.

Corax was here.

Chapter IX

'I come with an invitation.' Kleitos shoved the door open without knocking.

'Tanit's tits, you startled me!' Hanno had been dozing on his bed.

'My apologies.' Kleitos didn't sound remotely sorry. 'You won't want to miss this, my friend.'

Still half asleep, Hanno felt a little irritated. 'Miss what?'

'Hippocrates and Epicydes are throwing a party this evening in celebration of our famous victory,' Kleitos announced, beaming.

'We've been doing that since it happened!' Following the sinking of the Roman fleet outside the city walls, the festivities had been riotous. Hanno had drunk more wine in the previous few days than at any time since the debauched sessions he and Suni had used to indulge in in Carthage.

'Maybe so, but this will be an official do, in the rulers' palace. There will be unlimited food and wine. I'm told that flute girls will be laid on too.'

Hanno woke more fully. 'Who's invited?'

'Every nobleman in the place. Also the commander of every unit, whether infantry, artillery, navy or cavalry.'

'The cavalry shouldn't be allowed,' Hanno joked. 'They've done nothing so far!'

'We'll give them plenty of shit for that during the evening, don't worry. It's to begin with Hippocrates and Epicydes each making a speech. There'll be awards for some of the most courageous soldiers, and then . . .' Kleitos paused. '. . . we can all get smashed!'

'Count me in.' Hanno's mission was proving to be altogether more enjoyable than he'd imagined, but this time would not last. The Romans had not pulled out of Sicily, merely back to their camps. They would return. Oddly, if Quintus had survived Cannae, and the naval assault, he might be among their number. Kleitos had told him of the harsh punishment imposed on the survivors from the fields of blood. He's probably dead, Hanno told himself. Poor bastard. He put Quintus from his mind. There were more pleasant things to think about. If Hippocrates and Epicydes wanted to thank their soldiers for their valour, who was he to object? 'When does it start?'

Kleitos winked. Beneath Hanno's curious gaze, he walked out, returning with a large earthenware jug and two cups that he must have concealed in the corridor. 'Right now!'

Hanno mock groaned. 'It's going to be a long night.'

They set to with a will. The wine didn't last long, and Hanno suggested that they refrain from drinking any more until the party got under way. 'It might be all right for you, but I'm here to impress. How would it look if I arrived pissed? Hannibal would have my balls.'

'Hannibal would never know!'

'Unless one of the brothers told him. Even if they didn't, what would *they* think?'

Kleitos grumbled, but he relented.

The two went instead to the garrison's baths, where they relaxed in the hot pool before enjoying a massage by slaves. Conversation flowed readily. Neither talked about the war; instead, the topics drifted from the best nights' drinking they could remember, to their youth and what they had got up to with their friends. Inevitably, they argued about the beauty of Carthaginian girls compared to Syracusan ones. As a matter of pride, neither would acknowledge the other's point. The topic grew a little heated, and in an effort to avoid an argument, Hanno said, 'Roman women can be very attractive too.' He pictured Aurelia.

'Most of the ones I came across – before the war, naturally – looked like mules, and brayed like them too.'

'They know their own minds, that's for sure, but they're as pretty as any Carthaginian or Syracusan I've seen.'

Kleitos gave him a knowing smile. 'You're talking about a particular girl. Tell me who she is, you dog!'

Embarrassed now, Hanno flushed. 'Nothing much ever happened.'

'It doesn't have to, for Eros' arrow to sink deep.'

'It's foolish even to think of her. I'll never see her again. This damn war . . .' Hanno gestured in exasperation.

'Aye. It has affected me in that way too. About two years ago, I had managed to persuade my parents to agree to my marrying a girl from Enna whom I'd met and fallen for at a festival to Demeter and Persephone. She was from a poorer family than mine, but I didn't care. We were to be wed not long after Hieronymus came to power.' His face darkened.

'What happened?'

'Hieronymus became unpopular. There was a lot of unrest – you must have heard about that. When he was assassinated, things went crazy in the city for a time. Scores of nobles were murdered; no one knew who'd be next. Marriage was out of the question. When the brothers seized power, things calmed down. That's one of the reasons I support them. They might not be the nicest of men, but they've kept the peace.' He chuckled. 'Apart from with Rome, that is.'

'Where is she?'

'In Enna, with her family. We send letters to each other when we can.' Kleitos' expression grew a little sad. 'We'll wed when the war's over.' The slave who'd been cleaning his skin with a strigil finished, and he sat up.

'That will be a happy day.'

Kleitos threw him a grateful look. 'Perhaps you *will* see the Roman girl again. When Hannibal has beaten the Romans, you could seek her out.'

'She's married,' said Hanno more sharply than he'd meant.

'Well, who's to say that her husband won't have fallen in battle?'

'I've thought the same thing more than once. But even if we did meet, she wouldn't be interested in me – a dirty gugga, one of those who had humbled her people.' Aurelia had never called him that, but Hanno was trying to harden his heart against further pain.

'Don't be so sure. You'll never be as handsome as me, for example, but I dare say even the flute girls tonight could be persuaded to lie with you.'

Hanno grabbed one of the drying cloths from the pile and flicked it, catching Kleitos on the arse. 'Cheeky dog!'

Kleitos took the challenge with a whoop. Like two boys, they ran around the room, thrashing each other with their cloths. The slaves looked on, bemused.

Kleitos called a halt eventually. 'Let's not miss the start of it. I want to hear what the brothers have to say.'

The bath and massage had sobered the pair up, to Hanno's relief. Kleitos had awakened Hanno's devilish side, which wanted to go on an almighty bender. But a public affair like this required his best behaviour, at least for the early part of the night. He did his best to keep this uppermost in his mind as they set off.

Hanno had seen few rooms as grand as the immense banqueting hall in which the party was held. Its grandest feature was the mosaic floor surface – a set of magnificent scenes depicting the war between Greece and Troy: Paris eloping with Helen; Menelaus' thousand ships setting sail; Achilles defeating Hector; the Trojan Horse full of soldiers. To Kleitos' amusement, Hanno insisted on wandering around, studying the lot.

'Carthage is bigger and more beautiful than Syracuse,' Hanno said. 'But we have nothing like this!'

'You Carthaginians are famed for your city, your wandering natures, and your ability to make money where others can't.' Kleitos clinked his cup off Hanno's in salutation. 'My people's skill in war may not be what it was in the days of Xenophon, Leonidas and Alexander, but we are still masters of the arts and culture.'

Hanno studied the room, trying not to be awestruck. The ewers of wine and of water carried by the slaves were made of gold or silver. So too were the kraters being passed between the guests. From the hardwood couches

and serving tables to the richly painted walls and gilded lamp stands, everything in the room exuded quality and class. His family were wealthy, as
was Quintus', but not on this scale. And despite his stature, Hannibal did
not go in for shows of riches. This was the first time that Hanno had been
inside the palace of someone – Hiero – who effectively had been a king.

'Ho, Kleitos!' called a short man with almost no hair, who was reclining
with a group of nobles on a set of nearby couches. 'Brought a friend?'

'Come.' Kleitos beckoned to Hanno. 'I'll introduce you to some of my
comrades.'

By the time that the sixth krater had been passed around, Hanno was feeling
rather inebriated. The wine was watered down, but perhaps not as much
as he was used to. He would pass the next time it appeared in front of him,
or he'd soon be puking. What time it was, he had no idea, but it had to
be late. Not long after his and Kleitos' arrival, the brothers had appeared,
to rapturous applause. Epicydes' speech had been witty and acerbic, and
Hippocrates had waxed long and proud about the gathered men's bravery.
Both discourses had gone down like a house on fire. Toast after toast had
been made, and the floor was now awash thanks to the wine that had been
poured out as libations to the gods. There had been a spontaneous rendi-
tion of the paean, the Greek hymn of triumph, which had set the hairs on
the back of his neck atingle. Kleitos' friends, who seemed a decent lot, had
been welcoming and interested to talk with him. Annoyingly, he had heard
nothing that would interest Hannibal. Flute girls and dancers in diaphanous
robes had moved through the crowd, pausing here and there to perform,
and accompanied by musicians with lyres and pipes. Slaves kept the wine
flowing without pause. The food, served on silver platters, had been plentiful and delicious: fish and shellfish of all kinds, baked with herbs, stuffed
and grilled. There had been spit-roasted lamb and pork, and plenty of
fresh-baked flatbread to mop up the juices. If it hadn't been for the food,
Hanno would have been on the floor some time past.

It had been a mistake, he thought blearily, to start drinking when they had. He'd peaked early, and despite the break at the baths, it had all been downhill since then. His plan of retreating to one of the more secluded parts of the room with one of the many attractive flute girls still appealed, but he wasn't sure if his body was up to the task. His bladder went into spasm, reminding him that he hadn't yet been for a piss. It seemed perfect timing. If he took his time going and coming, and downed a cup of water taken from a passing slave on the way, he'd start to sober up. Carefully, he got to his feet.

'Has one of the girls taken your fancy?' asked Kleitos, leering.

'More than one. But I need to empty my bladder.'

'Do it in a corner. No one will notice.'

'Speak for yourself,' retorted Hanno. It was unlikely that Hippocrates or Epicydes would hear about it if he did such a thing, but he wasn't that desperate. 'Where's the latrine?'

'Somewhere over there.' Kleitos waved vaguely through the crowd at the opposite end of the room.

Hanno hadn't gone far when he was accosted by a man who introduced himself as Thick Eyebrows' commander. He made a hearty apology for his men's behaviour and insisted on sharing his krater of wine. After what he considered enough time to be polite, Hanno made his excuses and left. This time, he was careful to avoid eye contact with the other revellers. His bladder felt as if it were about to burst. Even the sight of a voluptuous flute girl performing a naked dance for a rapt audience of noblemen couldn't make him pause.

He wandered down a well-lit hallway, trying various doors. They were either locked, or opened into storage rooms. Finally, though, his luck was in. A grander arrangement than he'd seen in an age, the latrine had several wooden seats that emptied into a large-bore angled pipe. Hanno exchanged pleasantries with the other occupant, a fat man whose poisonous farts had Hanno pissing as fast as he could. A little disappointed that his trip hadn't taken longer – he did not feel any less drunk – he headed in the opposite direction to the banqueting hall. A pleasant breeze cooled his cheeks; Hanno hoped it was coming from a spot where he could sit for a while and let the wine's effects subside.

Fortune smiled on him. The small balcony that he came upon through a pair of open doors was unlit. By sitting to one side of it, he could avoid being seen from the corridor. With a sigh of relief, he sat on a stone bench and peered out at the city. Slivers of moonlight traced the outline of tiled roofs; shadow filled the spaces in between. Overhead, innumerable stars shone. Off to one side, he could make out the line of the rampart. Now and again, a dog barked. From a distance came the sound of waves lapping against the breakwater. It was the most natural thing in the world to close his eyes.

He woke, shivering with cold. Knuckling away his weariness, Hanno studied the moon. It had started to fall in the sky. Melqart's beard, he thought, I must have been asleep for hours. He was about to stir, but a movement from the corner of his eye stopped him. He wished that he'd ignored the order to come unarmed, but his concern eased as the shape on the neighbouring balcony, which he hadn't noticed until that point, was revealed to be a woman. She had a child in her arms, and was rocking it gently to and fro. 'There, there,' she whispered. 'It was a bad dream, my love. Mother's here. There, there.'

Hanno blinked and listened again. She was talking *Latin*, not Greek. A Roman woman here had to be a captive or, worse, one of Hippocrates' whores. Every instinct was telling him to back away silently, and return whence he came, but sympathy – and curiosity – made him stay put.

'Mother?' asked the child, a boy.

'Yes, my love?'

'When are we going home?'

'I-I don't know, my love. Soon, I hope.' The boy might have missed the catch in his mother's voice, but Hanno did not. A memory tickled the edge of his still befuddled mind, like a feather.

'Mistress?' A second woman spoke from the room which gave on to the balcony.

'Yes, Elira?'

Hanno felt as if someone had thrown him, head first, into a pool of icy water. He had not heard the name 'Elira' since he'd left Quintus' family home, more than four years before. She'd been an Illyrian, he remembered. How many women of that race, of *that* name, could serve a Roman mistress? It couldn't be. Could it?

'Aurelia?' he whispered. 'Aurelia?'

There was a sharp intake of breath, then a frightened voice said: 'Who's there? Who is it?'

Hanno cursed his stupidity. She couldn't see him, couldn't know who it was on his balcony. 'Do not fear. I'm just a weary guest from the party. Is your name Aurelia?'

'How could you know that?' she demanded, retreating further.

Now Hanno *knew* it was she. He spoke quickly, in case she grew even more alarmed. 'Because I am Hanno, he whom your brother Quintus picked out in the slave market in Capua. You were there too.'

'Hades below! H-Hanno?' Her voice cracked again.

He went to the edge of the balcony so she could see him better. 'I'm here.'

She moved towards him, still clutching her son. 'I'd heard that you might be in the city, but to meet you is beyond all hope!' She began to weep quietly.

It was Hanno's turn to struggle with disbelief. 'Bomilcar found you?'

'Yes, in Rome.'

'Who are you talking to, Mother?' The boy's voice was sleepy.

'Just a man, my love.' Aurelia glanced at Hanno. 'Give me a moment.' She disappeared from view.

While she was gone, the hideous image of Agathocles and the women he'd bought – for Hippocrates – filled Hanno's mind. This could be the only reason for Aurelia's presence here, in the palace. A rage such as he'd never felt before burst into flames in his belly. *Hippocrates, the filthy fucking bastard.* He *had* to get her away – how, Hanno had no idea, but doing nothing was not an option.

'How long have you been in the city?' She was back.

'A few weeks. And you . . .?' Hanno didn't know how to phrase it delicately. 'You were taken prisoner? Is that how you came to be here?'

'Yes. Our ship was taken by a Syracusan trireme. My husband's partner was killed. I have no idea what became of Agesandros, but Elira and I were chosen by one of Hippocrates' men as . . . *concubines*.' She said the last word with utter venom.

Hanno longed to enfold her in his arms, to tell her that everything would be fine. 'Let me into your room.'

'I can't, Hanno. I'm sorry. We're locked in.'

He mouthed a silent, savage oath. 'Then I'll kick the door down.'

'And if the guards come?'

Again Hanno cursed. What chance would he have, pissed and unarmed, against Hippocrates' soldiers? Even if they could be avoided, there were plenty more at the palace's main gate. There was *no* way that he, Aurelia, her son and Elira – Hanno had no doubt that Aurelia would insist she came too – would be allowed to leave. He wanted to scream with frustration. 'I can't leave you.'

'You must. For now.'

'But that monster, Hippocrates—'

'He can't hurt me any more. Not when I know you are here.' Her hand reached out, and he seized it, trying to send all he felt for her through his fingers and into her flesh.

'I'll devise a plan for us to escape.'

'I know you will.' Her voice had a serenity to it that he wouldn't have thought possible. It helped to calm him. 'How can I get word to you?' he asked.

'There's a baker's near the agora that sells sweetmeats and pastries. They're the best in Syracuse, or so everyone says. Elira is allowed to go there occasionally, if Hippocrates is pleased with us. That's the only thing I can think of, unless you can grow wings, and fly up here.'

'I'll find her.' Again he was staggered by her apparent equanimity. Fresh rage washed over him. When Hippocrates 'is pleased' with them? Hanno made a spontaneous, heartfelt vow. The filth would die for this. But first, he had to get them out of here.

'Hades, that hurts!' grumbled Urceus.

'Stop being such an old woman. I'm being as gentle as I can.' Two days had passed, and Quintus was unwinding the bandage that covered Urceus' wound. The last of the wrapping came away, and Urceus couldn't quite mask his concern.

'Well?' he demanded.

Quintus eyed the inner parts of the bandage, and then the hole on either side of Urceus' triceps. The fabric was stained with blood, but there was no trace of green. Both wounds were reddened, but their edges weren't angry-looking. There was a little discharge from each, but it was pink-red, not purulent. 'It looks good. There's no smell. The surgeon must have been right.'

Urceus grunted. 'Aye, maybe salt water is good for killing infection.'

'Well, that and the *acetum* he sluiced in there. You squawked when he did that,' jibed Quintus.

'As if you wouldn't have! You're the one who whines when he gets a stone in the heel of a sandal.'

'True enough.' Quintus' grin was rueful. Picking up the roll of linen that lay by his side, he began to cover Urceus' wound again. 'Another week or two and you'll be able to return to duties, I'd wager.'

'Good. I want to get back into training with you and the rest of our brothers.' Urceus made a face. 'What few of them remain.'

They both fell silent, remembering Wolf, Unlucky and the dozens of others who had died in the carnage of their assault on Syracuse. Their maniple had not been alone in suffering heavy casualties. Exact numbers were always hard to come by, but the word was that more than two thousand legionaries and a similar number of sailors had died in the water that day. The attack on the Hexapyla gate had fared no better, the artillery barrages there being every bit as accurate as in the harbour. Marcellus, it was said, had been incandescent with rage when the news reached him. Upwards of a legion had been lost in total; that didn't take into account the hundreds who had died of their injuries since. The wounded who yet lived still filled the beds of the makeshift hospitals. Men such as Urceus, whose arm no longer required the attention of a surgeon, had been sent to recover among their comrades. His friend's improvement had definitely speeded up since then, thought Quintus.

The assault's failure and the loss of life had badly affected the soldiers' morale. The name of Archimedes, previously unknown, had become a byword for evil. Men spoke his name with trepidation, or not at all. For a couple of weeks after the failed attack, if as much as a length of wood appeared over the edge of the battlements, widespread panic broke out. It had taken the legionaries a while to appreciate that the Syracusans were taunting them with nothing more than planks. Their courage restored by this realisation, men had started advancing towards the walls to hurl insults a day or two before – which was when the enemy artillery had sent over a heavy barrage that had killed a dozen soldiers and sent terror lancing into the hearts of the remainder of Marcellus' troops. The losses had seen the issuing of an order that no one was to cross the line of the Roman circumvallation unless commanded to do so by a centurion or other senior officer.

Quintus didn't have a problem with that. Nor did any soldier he knew. Even Corax was happy enough to stay out of harm's way for the time being. 'Attacking the walls again would be suicidal,' he had growled one night as he'd passed through the maniple's tents on his rounds. 'Marcellus is right to have us wall the bastards in. If an assault that big couldn't take the city, there's no reason to think that another would go any better.'

'Not to worry,' said Quintus, tying off the new bandage on Urceus' arm. 'We'll have plenty of time to get to know our new comrades in the months to come.' He winked at Mattheus, who had indeed turned out to be a decent sort, as well as a better cook than anyone else in the reconstituted *contubernium*. Mattheus' presence had come about thanks to Marcellus' practical response to his army's heavy casualties. The units in which the senior officers had been killed had been amalgamated with those whose commanders had survived. Mattheus and more than two score of his comrades now formed part of Corax's maniple. In turn, Quintus and Crespo had four new tent mates, among them Mattheus, and a soldier called Marius.

Urceus inclined his head. 'The food's better since you arrived, I grant.'

Mattheus performed a mock bow. 'You say that the defenders will starve, but the twenty-mile long wall that we're building doesn't stop the arse-humping Greeks from receiving supplies by sea.'

Quintus scowled in acknowledgement. Urceus spat on the ground. 'Let's hope that the promised naval blockade is in place soon.'

'I won't be holding my breath,' said Quintus. 'Corax told Vitruvius this morning that the headquarters gossip is that the Senate has authorised more ships, but not enough for Marcellus to seal off the approaches to both harbours night and day.'

'So the siege will drag on.' Urceus didn't seem unhappy. No one did, thought Quintus. He wasn't prepared to admit it out loud, but he too was relieved. For all that he wanted Rome to win the war, the brutality of the naval attack had drained him of the desire to fight. Once Quintus would have been overwhelmed by guilt for feeling this way. Now he felt but a twinge.

'It's not so bad here, is it?' asked Mattheus, smiling as heads nodded. 'We're miles from the swamps that the men to the south of the city have to live beside. We've got well-drained latrine pits, plentiful food, and the wine that Crespo manages to produce over and over.'

Everyone laughed at this, especially Quintus. Of recent days, he had developed a skill at bartering for supplies of wine. Sometimes he even stole it from the locals who sold such things in the camps outside theirs. On one occasion, he had even pilfered it from the back of the quartermaster's tents. If Corax suspected, he said nothing. As long as his men followed orders and didn't thieve from the units to either side of his maniple, he didn't care. The hastati loved him even more for this indifference.

'All we have to do is finish the wall and the ditch, and stay alert for enemy patrols,' Mattheus went on. 'I'm happy to do that for a few months, regardless of how the Syracusans are doing, and if you don't think that way too, you're bigger fools than I imagined.'

More laughter.

'We'll each of us be a long time dead,' agreed Quintus, thinking of poor Unlucky. 'So it's best to enjoy life while we can, eh?'

'That', declared Urceus with a meaningful stare at Quintus, 'is something that needs to be toasted properly.'

Everyone's eyes turned to Quintus. Mattheus rummaged among his utensils and produced a clay cup, which he held out expectantly. 'Fill her up!'

Quintus thought for a moment. They had already done their drill and weekly ten-mile run. The contubernium was on sentry duty that evening, but that was hours away. The chances of Corax requiring them before then were slim. 'Damn it, why not?' He ducked into the tent, emerging with an amphora that fitted under one arm.

'Is that the one you stole from the quartermaster's tent?' hissed Urceus, who knew perfectly well that it was.

A round of applause broke out, and Quintus grinned. Gods, but what had he been thinking? Full, it had weighed enough to slow him right down as he'd sloped off into the darkness. If he'd been caught, well . . . 'I couldn't say,' he replied with a smirk. 'Now, who wants some?'

His offer was met with a roar of approval.

Life wasn't so bad, Quintus decided. He was alive. So too were Urceus, Corax and the rest. They weren't going to be killed in the immediate future either, which felt very good indeed.

Making contact with Elira proved more tricky than Hanno had hoped. His duties – training his and other officers' men – meant that he had little free time. It was several days after the celebrations before he had an opportunity to search for the baker's shop. At first, things went well. The bakery proved easy to locate: a couple of questions to passers-by in the area sent him straight to its door. Real excitement gripped him as he waited outside for an hour, and then two, but as time passed he had to admit to himself that it would be pure luck if Elira came along while he was there. Hanno realised he needed someone to wait there every day. Gods, but he wished that Mutt and his men were with him. It would be the easiest thing in the world to order a couple to remain outside. His soldiers here seemed a decent lot, but there was no way he could trust any of them with such a duty. Abducting two of Hippocrates' concubines would carry the severest of punishments: his and Aurelia's relationship would count for nothing in mitigation. Never had he felt more alone. He wondered about bribing the baker, a jolly type with a paunch that revealed he enjoyed his own produce, but decided it was too risky. The city was alive with rumours of enemy agents, and of troops who wanted to defect to the Romans. No one could be relied upon, least of all someone he didn't know.

Hanno had another reason for caution. A way of communicating with Aurelia might be a means to an end, but he was no nearer knowing how to get her, her son and Elira out of the palace. Even if that seemingly impossible objective had been achieved, what would they do then? His duty to Hannibal meant that he had to stay within the city, and that would be dangerous in the extreme.

A week went by. The loss of so many men had ensured that the Romans were silent. Epicydes seemed pleased with Hanno's training of the troops, and he was kept busier than ever. His offer to become more involved with the city's defences – a ruse to discover information for Hannibal – was politely ignored, so Hanno bit his tongue and said nothing. He visited the baker's at every opportunity, but not once did he see Elira. In desperation, he visited a temple to Zeus, one of many in Syracuse. A few silver coins placed in the hand of one of the priests saw a plump lamb sacrificed, and his entreaty that a female friend 'find her way to his side' requested of the god.

The calm bestowed on Hanno by this offering lasted as long as it took him to leave the temple complex. The entrance was clogged by a crowd of the usual type of supplicants. As he threaded his way between them – the man with inflamed eyes, come in search of a cure, and the distraught mother, carrying her sick babe – he was overcome by bitterness. It was the same here as it had been at the shrines in Carthage, and, he suspected, at the temples of all gods in every land under the sun. The needy, the unwell, the dying, the jealous and the grieving came with a wide variety of offerings, from coinage to food, glassware and pottery, and what did they receive in return? Platitudes from a priest, and Hanno was tempted to think 'nothing else', but he didn't quite dare. The gods were the only ones who could help him. It was they who had engineered the meeting between him and Aurelia. They would not – could not – leave things to continue as they were. Hanno told himself this a hundred times a day, but he was still riven by doubt.

Several more days passed. Hanno thought he caught a glimpse of Aurelia on her balcony one evening, but he dared not wave in case anyone saw. Impotent and furious, he determined to speak with Kleitos, his one friend in Syracuse. To do so would place his life squarely in Kleitos' hands, but by this stage, he was resigned to that risk. If he didn't act, Aurelia would continue to suffer degradation at Hippocrates' hands indefinitely.

He pitched up at Kleitos' door later that day, bearing a small amphora of wine and a hunk of the best ham that money could buy. The gifts ensured that Kleitos' warm welcome became even more enthusiastic. Giving Hanno the only stool, he deftly cracked the wax seal on the amphora and filled two cups. Toasting each other, they drank deep.

'Hungry?' Kleitos jerked a thumb at the ham, which he'd placed on the table.

'Let's tackle it later, when we get back from the inn.'

Kleitos chuckled. 'Ah. We're going out, are we?'

'It might be good to, yes. My men talk about a little place on a back street in Achradina. It's worth the walk, by all accounts.'

'Poseidon's Trident, is that the one?'

Hanno felt a little disappointed. 'You've been there.'

'I've darkened the threshold of every tavern in Syracuse at one point or another.' Kleitos slurped some wine. 'I'd be happy to visit that one again, though. Especially if you're buying!'

'That was my intention,' replied Hanno with a wink. He hesitated, unsure, but the thought of Aurelia was enough to make him continue. 'I have a favour to ask.'

Kleitos set his cup down. 'I've been wondering if you had something on your mind of late. As long as it doesn't harm my city—'

'It's nothing like that,' said Hanno quickly.

'Then if I can help, I will,' said Kleitos with an expansive gesture.

'You might not say that when I've told you what it is.'

'Ha!' Kleitos raised a hand, stopping him. 'I need more wine.' When he'd filled their cups again and taken a large mouthful, he indicated that Hanno should continue.

'Do you remember the Roman girl, the woman, I told you about?'

'A while back? I think so. The one who was married.'

'That's right.' Hanno could feel his emotions rising, but he forced them down. This had to be done with a cool head. 'She's here. In Syracuse.'

'You're taking the piss!'

'I'm not. I saw her, about two weeks ago.'

'*That's* why you've been preoccupied! Been sneaking off to screw her, have you?' Kleitos roared with laughter, but he saw that Hanno wasn't joining in, and frowned. 'Of course. She's Roman, so she won't be roaming about freely. Let me guess – she's someone's captive or slave, is that it?'

Hanno nodded.

'That shouldn't be hard to sort out. Being a mid-ranking officer carries *some* perks. I'll come with you to see whichever prick it is who's bought her. Once his head's been smacked off the wall a few times, he'll see the wisdom in selling her to you. For a pittance, naturally.'

'My thanks. You're a good friend, Kleitos. But it's not that simple.'

'Why ever not?'

He had to roll the dice, and hope. 'Because her owner is Hippocrates.'

There was a sharp intake of breath. 'You're joking with me.'

'I wish I was.'

'You know that I've sworn to serve Hippocrates and Epicydes, both, with all of my strength, until my dying day.' Kleitos' voice was hard.

He had committed himself now. 'You've said before that Hippocrates can be . . .' Hanno struggled to find a suitable word. '. . . unpleasant. I'm concerned that he's doing the most disgusting things to Aurelia. I can't stand by and do nothing. I *have* to free her.' Kleitos said nothing, and Hanno's fear grew. 'This has nothing to do with the war against the Romans, or my loyalty to your rulers. If it comes to it, I'll die in the defence of your city. I swear that to you, on my mother's grave.'

His words vanished into the yawning silence between them. 'Damn it, Kleitos, she's the woman I love,' said Hanno. He could almost see Hippocrates' guards coming to arrest him.

He was stunned when Kleitos began to laugh. 'What's so funny?'

'Your passion, my friend. Your burning need to convince me that what you want will not harm the war effort.'

'So you'll help me?'

'How could I not? You'd aid me if I needed to free my lover, wouldn't you? If it didn't impact on your fight with Rome?'

'As Baal Hammon is my witness, I would,' said Hanno fervently.

'Right then. We need a plan,' Kleitos declared. 'But don't get your hopes up. Just because there are two of us now doesn't mean this will succeed. We're more likely to end up being flung over the walls while Hippocrates watches.'

The dire warning couldn't stop Hanno from grinning.

He was no longer alone.

Chapter X

'I could get used to this,' said Mattheus, turning his face to the sun, which was dipping down to the western horizon. 'Warm sun all afternoon. A nice breeze off the sea. Not an officer in sight.'

'No sign of the fucking Syracusans either,' added Urceus, spitting over the timber ramparts in the direction of the besieged city.

Quintus wasn't going to argue with his comrades' sentiments. It was true that over the previous weeks, life had become a little sedate, but after the horror of the failed naval attack on Syracuse, there was nothing wrong with that. Besides, it had been sheer luck that their commander Marcellus hadn't taken their unit with him when he'd recently marched off to teach a lesson to the cities who had declared themselves for Syracuse. Megara Hyblaea had been taken by assault and then burned as an example of the fate that awaited those who defied Rome. While that victory had seen more than one town change sides yet again, there had been a good number of Roman casualties. *Stop thinking like that!* At times Quintus wondered if he'd lost his nerve, which made him feel ashamed. He didn't admit this to a soul, not even Urceus. It flared up now, though. 'It'd do us no harm to face an enemy attack,' he said fiercely.

'Eh?' Mattheus looked at him as if he'd gone mad. 'Why the fuck would you wish such a thing?'

'Soldiers grow rusty if they don't see enough active service,' snapped Quintus.

'Madman,' said Mattheus, tapping his head. 'I'm happy enough leaving off fighting for another while.'

Irritated, and a little worried that anyone would see beneath his bravado, Quintus stalked off along the rampart. The section that they were guarding was near the main camp, and ran up to and over one of the regularly placed gates that faced towards Syracuse. The portal was only ever opened when a patrol was sent out to investigate possible enemy activity. Thankfully, that was rare. Even now, men still had a healthy respect for Archimedes' lethal artillery. Why risk soldiers' lives in no man's land when no assault was to be made on the city walls? thought Quintus. Marcellus was no fool. He was conserving his forces for a time when they would be needed.

Rumour had it that an enemy fleet was on its way to Sicily from Carthage. It would land in the southwest, men said. That made sense. The towns of Heraklea and Akragas were on that coastline, and they had been Carthaginian strongholds until near the end of the last war. If the stories were true, Marcellus would not take the challenge lying down, Quintus decided. No doubt that was why he'd been subjugating towns such as Megara Hyblaea. If too much of the island went over to Syracuse and Carthage, the Romans' position on the island would become untenable, especially if thousands of Carthaginians were soon to arrive.

'An obol for your thoughts,' said Urceus' voice, from right behind him.

Quintus spun, annoyed that he hadn't heard his friend and still unhappy with himself. 'Nothing much.'

'Liar.'

Stung, Quintus' mouth opened to issue a stinging retort.

Urceus spoke first. 'We're *all* shitting ourselves at the idea of yet another battle, brother.'

Quintus glanced up and down the walkway. To his relief, they were alone. 'Who said that that's what I'm thinking?' he demanded hotly.

'It's as obvious as the sun on your face, Crespo. Why? Because every last one of us feels the same way! Trasimene and Cannae were awful, and we'll never forget them, but the slaughter in the harbour was almost worse. All those men drowning . . .' Urceus grimaced. 'A man can't see things like that without paying a certain price. You never want to experience anything like that again. That's a normal response. We're all of the same mind.' He gripped Quintus' arm and squeezed, hard.

A host of emotions welled up inside Quintus. Terror. Relief and pride that he had a comrade like Urceus. Love for a man who saw his weakness and didn't judge him for it.

'You're still the same soldier you were. When the time comes to march and to fight again, your balls might shrivel up, but you'll stand with us, won't you?'

'Of course!' Quintus replied. Despite the possible consequence – death – not to do so would be unimaginable. His comrades meant everything to him.

Urceus' eyes met his. 'As we will, beside you. To whatever end.'

Quintus leaned his pilum and shield against the battlements and grabbed Urceus in a bear hug. 'You're a good friend.'

'As you are to me,' said Urceus, returning the embrace.

Quintus felt tears pricking at the corners of his eyes.

'I didn't know you two were a pair of *molles*!' called Mattheus.

Both Quintus and Urceus made an obscene gesture by way of reply. 'Watch out, or we'll ask you to join us!' advised Quintus with a leer.

At that moment, Marius, another of their new comrades, whistled the call that signified 'officer approaching'. Everyone in their section took an instant interest in the ground beyond the wall.

Hobs clattered on the nearest ladder, and Quintus risked a glance to his left. It wasn't Corax, or anyone he recognised. 'Look lively! It's not one of ours,' he shot from the side of his mouth.

Urceus took off along the walkway, as a sentry should. Quintus remained where he was, hoping that the officer, whoever he was, wouldn't stay long.

Annoyingly, the newcomer's footsteps came to a halt beside him. Quintus looked, turned and saluted. 'Sir!'

The officer, a centurion, gave him a critical stare. He was clean-shaven, square-chinned and nearing forty. 'As you were.'

'Can I help you, sir?' asked Quintus, standing at ease.

'So that is Syracuse,' said the officer, gazing at the distant walls. 'Its defences are impressive.'

'They are, sir.'

'After more than half a millennium, it's not surprising, I suppose. Did you take part in the initial attack?'

He had come with the reinforcements, thought Quintus in surprise. 'I did, sir.'

'Was it as bad as they say?'

'Yes, sir.' Quintus tried not to remember how Wolf and Unlucky had died, and failed.

A grunt.

'Have you just arrived, sir?' risked Quintus.

'Yes. The Senate ordered us from Cisalpine Gaul.'

Quintus felt a sudden kinship with the centurion. 'Were you also at the Trebia, sir?'

There was a flicker of annoyance. 'No. I was stationed at Victumulae, a town to the west of Placentia. I was forced to remain within its walls at the time of the battle at the Trebia.'

'I remember Victumulae, sir. It was one of the towns that Hannibal's army sacked after the Trebia. You were lucky to survive.'

Now the centurion's face blackened.

Why didn't he like that? wondered Quintus in surprise. He moved to remedy the situation. 'Fortuna must have been smiling on you that day, as she was on us in the harbour outside Syracuse.'

The centurion's expression softened a little. 'The goddess is a capricious sort at the best of times, but she must have been in a good mood with me when Victumulae fell.'

'You've been fighting Gauls since then, sir?'

'Aye, filthy savages that they are. It'll be a welcome break to battle Syracusans for a change. I hear we might even get to kill some guggas. That would please me.' The centurion's eyes had lit up.

'Me too, sir,' said Quintus stolidly. It wouldn't do to mention how welcome the time spent building the encircling wall had been.

'Pera!'

The centurion looked down. So did Quintus. Another centurion sat on a horse below, beside a tethered mount that had to belong to Pera.

'What is it?' asked Pera.

'I've been searching all over for you. A summons has been issued. We're to attend a meeting at the headquarters at sundown. Marcellus wants to meet us. Best get ready, eh?'

'Aye.' Without another word to Quintus, Pera made his way back to the ladder.

He seems like a tough one, thought Quintus. He wasn't sure why, but he didn't like Pera.

Urceus was by his side before Pera had reached his comrade. 'What did he want?'

'The usual: to look at Syracuse.'

'He's new then?'

'Yes. He and his unit have come in from Cisalpine Gaul. They missed the Trebia, which I think was a bit of a sore point.' At this, Pera glanced up, and Quintus' stomach twisted. *Shit, I hope he didn't hear that!* 'That's a fine mount you have there, sir,' he called by way of distraction, pointing at Pera's horse, a black with a white blaze on one fetlock.

Pera's lip curled. 'What would an ordinary hastatus know about horses?'

Stung, Quintus' own temper flared. He had ridden from a very young age, something that Pera might well not have – probably had not – done. It had been his choice to join the infantry, but at times like this, when he couldn't admit to too much for fear of being discovered, it really galled him. Without thinking, Quintus said, 'We had quite a few horses when I was a boy, sir.'

'You can ride?' Pera's voice was full of disbelief.

Quintus could feel Urceus' gaze on him, knew that his friend was silently shouting at him to end the conversation that very instant. A devil took him, however. *Fuck Pera. He's an arrogant prick.* 'I can, sir. Well, too.'

Pera glanced at his companion and chuckled. 'Hear this? We've chanced upon the only hastatus who should be in the cavalry!'

The second centurion laughed. 'A fine discovery! Maybe you and he should race against one another.'

'Now there's an idea!' Pera looked up at Quintus. 'How about it? You and I, tonight. Gaius here will let you have his horse, won't you?'

'Of course!' declared the second centurion.

'Thank you, sir, but I couldn't,' replied Quintus, sensing that the situation was slipping out of his control, fast.

Pera's face hardened. 'Why ever not?'

'An ordinary soldier can't race against a centurion, sir,' Quintus flailed.

'He can if he's bloody ordered to,' snarled Pera. 'Do you want me to go to your centurion about this?'

Quintus had half a notion that Corax would tell Pera to piss off, but if that happened, he would feel like a child whose father had stepped in to protect him from a bully. Again his pride surged out of control. 'No, sir,' he said. 'I'll ride against you.'

'Crespo! Are you fucking insane?' whispered Urceus.

'Later, then,' said Pera. 'Here, at the turn of the second watch. We can use the ground outside the wall.'

'Very well, sir.' Already realising he had been unwise, Quintus watched as the two centurions rode off, joking with one another.

'You're a damn fool!' snapped Urceus. '*What* were you thinking?'

'Who does *he* think *he* is?' answered Quintus in an angry undertone. 'My father put me on a horse's back before I could walk. I could ride him into the ground.'

'Maybe you could, but you won't! Not unless you're even more of an idiot than I take you for. The man's a centurion! The likes of you and me are nothing compared to him.'

'Jug is right,' said Mattheus, who had just arrived. 'If you beat him, he'll make your life a fucking misery.'

Marius rumbled his accord.

Quintus nodded his head in furious, reluctant agreement. 'I hear you.' His comrades were right. Standing up to Pera had been rash. He would have to let the centurion win. His sour mood deepened and, for a moment, Quintus regretted leaving his exalted position as an equestrian behind four years before. The idea vanished in a few heartbeats. I wouldn't have my comrades, or Corax as my commander, if I'd stayed in the cavalry, he thought. Are they not more than enough? Bitterness filled him, however, as he pictured the race to come. Not only would he have to lose, but he would have to endure being humiliated by Pera.

Quintus cursed himself for not keeping his mouth shut.

'Ready?' asked Gaius, the centurion who had accompanied Pera earlier.

Darkness had fallen some time before, and the Roman fortifications loomed bright in the moonlight. If one looked hard, it was possible to make out the sentries as they walked to and fro. The usual night-time noises carried from the camps on the other side: cavalry mounts nickering at one another, men's voices and occasional bursts of laughter.

Astride Gaius' horse, a steady chestnut with a luxuriant mane, Quintus' throat was tight with tension. He nodded firmly.

'More than ready,' said Pera, smirking. He sat on his mount, ten paces to Quintus' right.

'As agreed, you will ride to where the torch has been stuck in the ground, five hundred paces yonder, and back. The first man to reach my line' – Gaius pointed with his sword tip to the dirt at his feet – 'will be accounted the winner. Agreed?'

'Yes,' both men replied.

'On the count of three, then,' declared Gaius.

It was a beautiful night, thought Quintus. Cool, but not too cool. No wind. A clear sky above, with a waxing moon to provide light. The ground that they were to race upon was for the most part flat. He'd walked the course earlier, and there were few places where a horse could break a leg. The conditions were perfect for a clandestine race. Unsurprisingly, news of it had travelled fast. More than a hundred soldiers had gathered to watch. Despite the fact that such activities were prohibited – especially because they were outside the siege wall – there were plenty of infantry officers too: *optiones*, *tesserarii* and centurions. Quintus thought he had spied Corax among them, wearing a hooded cloak. He didn't know whether to feel relieved or worried that his centurion hadn't tried to end his participation in the race.

A number of men moved through the throng, offering odds, taking bets. Quintus half smiled. If Pera hadn't been his opponent, he would have given Urceus all of his money and told him to wager it on him, the naïve hastatus who was going up against a centurion. Of course he'd done nothing of the sort. Instead, he would ride as if to win, but near the end, he would lose. Beating Pera might provide him with a moment of glory, but having a centurion as an enemy would be downright dangerous. *Damn it all! I should have kept my peace.*

'One,' said Gaius.

Quintus leaned forward and stroked his horse's cheek. He'd had a chance to trot it up and down a little beforehand. It was a calm beast, but he wasn't sure that, even if he'd wanted it to, it had the legs to beat Pera's mount, which looked fast. 'Do your best, boy,' he whispered. 'Don't fall and hurt yourself, or I'll have your master to answer to.'

'Two.'

Quintus glanced at Pera, who mouthed a curse of some kind at him. Like Quintus, the centurion was dressed in nothing more than a light wool belted tunic. He also had a whip gripped in his right fist, a tool that Quintus had never liked using on a horse.

'Three!'

In spite of the requests by Quintus' comrades that they remain quiet, the spectators let out a low cheer. Hoping that the race would not be discovered by a senior officer who wasn't in the know, Quintus urged his horse towards the spot of light – a torch – that marked the turning point of the race. Alongside, Pera was already wielding his whip, striking it off his mount's sides with sibilant little cracking sounds. The black surged into the lead, and Pera shot a triumphant glance over his shoulder at Quintus.

'Come on! We can't let the whoreson get away with that,' Quintus muttered to the chestnut. He flicked the reins and, to his delight, the horse responded with gusto. Its hooves pounded off the ground faster and faster. By the time that they had ridden perhaps half the distance, Quintus judged that the gap between them and Pera had narrowed. The torch was more visible now, flickering in the light breeze. The devilment of earlier returned, and Quintus grinned. There could be no harm in scaring Pera a little, surely? The centurion was still going to win after all. 'Faster,' he urged the chestnut. 'You can catch the black. I know you can.'

Gamely, his horse increased his speed. This beast is faster than he looks, thought Quintus with delight as the night air rushed by his ears. He smiled again as Pera threw an alarmed look back at them. By the time that the torch was a hundred paces away, they had caught up with him. Side by side, no more than an arm's length apart, they galloped towards the halfway mark. Quintus took great pleasure from the anger on Pera's face. Does he realise yet that this is no mistake? That I could beat him? he wondered.

Crack! Quintus heard the sound in the same moment that his cheek erupted in agony. He reeled, almost losing his balance. Only his grip on the reins prevented him from falling off the chestnut, which slowed instinctively.

'You piece of filth!' cried Pera. 'That'll show you!'

As Quintus regained his seat, the centurion's mount surged ahead, towards the torch. He lifted a hand to his stinging cheek, winced as he felt the warm stickiness of blood under his fingers. Pera clearly wanted to win, but Quintus hadn't been expecting the bastard to use his whip as a weapon. White-hot rage surged through Quintus, and he thumped his mount's chest with his heels. It was if the chestnut sensed his desire to catch Pera; it rushed onward once more, its hooves hammering the hard ground in a mesmeric rhythm. Quintus wished that he had a spear to throw or, failing that, a chance to knock Pera from his horse and beat the centurion into a bloody pulp.

Despite the pulse beating at his temples, Quintus knew such a reaction would result in a death sentence. How he longed then to win the race instead, to teach Pera a lesson in horsemanship. The chestnut was doing him proud; at this rate, it might well catch the black soon after they had both turned for home.

Quintus took a deep breath; then he let it out slowly. The option of succeeding against Pera was also impossible. Best to ride on, keeping his mount under a tight rein. He could give a good account of himself, accept the jeers of Pera and his friends at the end, and consign the whole race to bitter experience. Draining an amphora of wine with his comrades afterwards would help to put the whole sorry episode from memory.

Quintus' good intentions were challenged a few heartbeats later when he saw Pera slowing his mount and wheeling it in a tight turn – a full two score paces from the torch. Even as the chestnut closed in on it, Pera and the black were galloping back towards them and the finish line to Quintus' rear.

'HEY!' roared Quintus in outrage. 'You can't do that!'

'Who's checking?' snarled Pera as he rode past him.

Quintus forgot everything other than the desire to win. 'Yah!' he shouted, lunging the chestnut forward. 'Come on!' His horse responded with gusto, pounding towards the torch with even more speed than it had managed before. It showed no fear as he hauled it in a turn so tight around the burning brand that the heat from the flame was uncomfortable. Five hundred paces away, the glimmer of light marked where the spectators and Gaius' line were. Quintus squinted, searching for Pera. A shape moved against the glow in the distance, and his heart banged off his ribs. 'He's a long way off, brave heart,' he said as the chestnut began to recover the speed lost in the turn. 'I don't know if even you can catch him. If you can, however, I will find you the sweetest grass on Sicily to eat. That, and a bag of apples. Can you do it?'

Its hooves immediately beat out an even more rapid tempo, and in that moment Quintus loved it. The chestnut wanted to race! Gripping its chest with his thighs, he leaned forward over its neck the way he'd done on his horse as a boy, competing against his father in the big flat fields near their house. He had never ached to win one of those races the way he did this one, though, which made the short time that followed last an eternity.

Quintus was profoundly aware of the warmth of the horse beneath him; of his breath, shallow and fast, contrasting against the rhythm of the chestnut's hooves; of the moon, and the stars glittering above; of the dark line that was the Roman rampart off to his left; of the flicker of light from the distant walls of Syracuse on his other side. And most of all, he was conscious of the moving outline that was Pera and the black. *Cocksucker!*

They were closing on the centurion, that was clear, but what was also apparent was that Pera's lead was too great. However game the chestnut, it was not Pegasus. Quintus didn't know how far they had come, but it had to be more than half of the return distance, and Pera was still at least sixty or seventy paces ahead. 'Fuck him to Hades!' There would be no point in accusing the centurion of cheating. The word of a mere hastatus against such a senior officer would count as nothing. Pera would beat him.

They sped on regardless, horse and man in a synergy that Quintus hadn't experienced since he'd been in the cavalry. Gods, but he had missed this feeling. However good it was to stand in the midst of his comrades as they went into battle, it wasn't the same as riding a horse at full gallop. If he closed his eyes, he could imagine Calatinus and all of his former companions, could feel the ground tremble beneath the weight of hundreds of hooves.

An odd sound made Quintus open his eyes. He blinked. Pera's outline, which had been readily visible thanks to the background light from the spectators' torches, had vanished. The realisation hit him as the chestnut ran on: the black had stumbled and fallen on one of the rough patches of ground. Within a score of paces, the truth of this was made apparent. Curses filled the air as Pera's standing shape loomed out of the darkness. Beside him, his mount was struggling to its feet. 'Up, you useless fucking mule!' Pera screamed, using his whip.

Pera hadn't walked the course beforehand as he had, Quintus realised. Slow down, his cautious side advised. Let Pera overtake you again. *He must win, not you.* The wind caressed Quintus' cut cheek, sending fresh darts of pain down the side of his face and into his neck. The sensation rammed home the lowliness of his position, brought into sharp focus his helplessness before Pera's rank – which was when temptation got the better of him. For victory to be his, all that was needed was a little inaction on his part, a failure to rein in his horse. With a last look over his shoulder at Pera, who was still trying to clamber aboard the black, Quintus let the chestnut do as he wished. Perhaps a score of heartbeats later, he had his revenge. To the sound of thunderous applause from the ordinary legionaries, they crossed the line that Gaius had drawn in the dirt. Revelling in the ovation, Quintus brought his chestnut to a gradual halt and slipped off his back.

'Well done, boy, well done.' He patted the horse's neck.

Quintus wanted to greet his friends, who were yelling 'CRE-SPO! CRE-SPO! CRE-SPO!' at the tops of their voices. Some of them had clearly wagered on him despite knowing he would try to lose. Gaius, the adjudicator, was waiting at the line, however. 'He's a fine beast, sir,' said Quintus, walking back to meet him and raising his voice to be heard. 'My thanks for letting me ride him.'

'I'm not sure that Pera will be happy with me, but those who wagered on you will be well pleased.' Despite his words, Gaius was amused. 'Credit where credit is due. You rode a fine race.'

'Thank you, sir.'

'Did Pera's horse trip?'

'Aye, sir, on a patch of uneven ground.' Quintus saw no point in mentioning how Pera had cheated. There seemed little point.

'If it hadn't been for that—'

'You fucking trickster!' cried Pera, emerging from the darkness. He rode his horse straight at Quintus, who had to dodge out of the way to avoid being knocked over. Gaius had to move smartly not to be struck as well. *Crack!* Pera didn't miss with his whip, landing a stinging blow across Quintus' shoulders; he shouted with pain and staggered away from the centurion. The chestnut reared up, whinnying, and Quintus had to grip its reins hard to stop it from running off in panic.

A shocked silence fell over the gathering.

Pera flung himself from his mount, and gestured at the nearest soldiers. 'Seize that piece of shit! I'll have him beaten within a hairsbreadth of his life.'

Four men strode towards Quintus, who thought about fighting, or fleeing, before deciding neither option was wise. Impotent rage – and fear – bubbled up in his throat. Nothing he said or did would help. The punishment that was coming could leave him crippled. Why hadn't he been able to keep his damn mouth shut?

Gaius frowned. 'A moment, Pera,' he said. 'The hastatus crossed the line first. He won.'

Pera's face went purple. 'He only fucking won because—'

'Wait!' The deep voice carried through the air.

Everyone's gaze turned to a cloaked man who came striding in from the direction of the torch. The figure came to a halt before Gaius and Crespo and threw back his hood. It was Corax. Quintus felt fresh sweat dampen his back, and dared to hope.

'Crespo won because your horse fell. You were neck and neck until that point,' declared Corax. 'At least that's how it seemed to me, from where I was standing.'

Pera's mouth worked furiously. 'Where were you?' he managed.

'Somewhere out there.' Corax waved vaguely into the blackness.

'It's a pity that your black stumbled. Before that, it was a well-matched contest.'

Quintus struggled to contain his surprise, and his anger. Corax had seen Pera cheat; Quintus was sure of it. Why else would he have come running back? It was good that Corax was defending him, but why wasn't he also revealing what Pera had done?

'That's what it looked like from here too,' said Gaius, appearing relieved. 'It wasn't the result any of us expected. You ought to have won, Pera.'

'Damn right!'

No, you shouldn't, you cheating cocksucker, thought Quintus. I had you beaten a long time before your mount fell.

'The gods do as they wish,' declared Gaius.

'It's not for us to divine their purpose,' Corax agreed.

Pera muttered an obscenity. He seemed about to hurl more accusations, but a glance at Corax and he fell silent.

Gaius barked an order at the throng of soldiers to disperse. Looking confused, they did as they were told. 'Time for a few cups of wine,' said Gaius. 'Come on, Pera. It'll be my treat.'

Quintus was aware of Pera's hate-filled eyes boring into him, but he was careful not to meet them. 'Why did you lend the dunghill rat your chestnut anyway?' he heard Pera demanding of Gaius as the two centurions moved off. 'You should have given him your other horse.'

The instant that Pera was out of earshot, Quintus spoke. 'Did you see what happened at the torch, sir?'

'I saw,' replied Corax.

'Pera cheated, sir! He turned a long way from the halfway point. If his mount hadn't gone down, he would have won – by cheating!'

'I know.'

'Why didn't you say anything, sir?' Quintus knew the bitter truth even as he asked.

Corax gave him a hefty shove in the chest. 'Watch your mouth! It's thanks to your stupidity that this whole damn enterprise came about. What came over you to decide to race against a centurion? Do you really want men like Pera to discover that you're of noble birth?'

Quintus had wondered for some time if Corax suspected, but to hear it said out loud was truly shocking. 'You knew, sir?'

There was a derisive snort. 'After this long with you under my command, it's as clear as the nose on your face. Your accent used to give you away; so too did your manners, however hard you tried to act like the rest. You speak Greek well, and have some understanding of battle tactics. You can ride a horse. What else could you be but an equestrian?' Corax's eyes were amused as he looked at Quintus. 'Close your mouth, soldier, or a fly will go in.'

'You haven't told anyone, have you, sir?'

'You must have your reasons for wanting to serve among the hastati, Crespo. As long as you didn't murder someone' – here Corax raised a hand in acknowledgement as Quintus began to protest – 'it's not for me, or for anyone else, to stop you doing so. Besides, you're a good soldier, one of the best in the maniple. I need you.'

'I don't know what to say, sir.'

'Then say nothing, Crespo.' Corax chuckled. 'That's not even your name, is it?'

'No, sir. It's—'

Corax put a finger to his lips. 'It's better that I don't know. If anyone ever comes looking, I'll be able to deny all knowledge of you.'

'That will never happen, sir,' said Quintus sadly. 'My father died at Cannae.'

'I'm sorry to hear that,' said Corax. 'But do not think that you might never be discovered. You tried hard tonight to have Pera realise that you were of noble birth.'

Quintus felt his cheeks redden. 'I'm sorry, sir.'

'What's done is done. Be content that you were saved a beating, or worse. And watch out for Pera from now on. He will not forgive you for this, even if it was a fair victory. Did you know that he is related to Marcellus?'

'No, sir,' replied Quintus, shocked.

'It's distantly, I am told, but that's not to say that he won't try to bend Marcellus' ear about this.'

Quintus felt sure that Corax was telling him obliquely that as Quintus' commander, he too might attract unwanted attention from above. 'If you knew, sir, why didn't you tell me to back out beforehand? I'd have had to, if you ordered it.'

There was a fiery glint in Corax's deep-set eyes. 'You're not the only one who doesn't like to refuse a challenge, Crespo.'

'No, sir,' Quintus muttered, feeling proud yet again that Corax was his centurion. 'Can I go, sir?'

'You can. Call by my tent in the morning.'

'Sir?'

To his surprise, Corax winked. 'There were huge odds against you winning, but I thought it only fair to back one of my men. I'm not sure of the exact amount, but I'll be collecting something over four hundred denarii later. You can have ten.'

'Thank you, sir!' Despite the tiny fraction of his winnings that Corax was offering, Quintus straightened up. The memory of Pera's incandescent rage at being beaten was a consolation too. So what that Pera was Marcellus' third cousin or something? He was the centurion of another unit, with no power over him or any of Corax's men.

'Go on, then. Piss off and find your mates. No doubt they'll be wanting to spend some of their earnings on you.'

Quintus saluted and headed for the gate.

Chapter XI

'Mistress.' Elira's voice echoed in the bedchamber.

Aurelia barely registered it. All of her focus was locked on the crumpled little shape that was Publius, in the bed before her. She leaned over him, stroked the damp hairs off his forehead, telling herself that the dark red flush to his skin was because he was too hot. The cool breeze that blew through the palace most evenings couldn't come quickly enough today. If only they were in Rome, if only she hadn't decided to travel south. None of this would have happened. *Stop it. You have to stay strong, for Publius' sake.* 'There, there, my darling. You'll soon be better.'

'Mistress.' This time, Elira shook Aurelia's shoulder.

She tore her eyes from her son. 'Is the surgeon here?'

'No, mistress. He said he couldn't come again until tomorrow, remember?'

'But the medicine he gave Publius hasn't worked.'

'That was the best treatment he had. Malaria is very hard to treat, mistress, especially in the young.' Elira's tone was very gentle.

For the thousandth time, Aurelia's eyes moved around the well-appointed room, looking for a way out. Along with an adjacent living area and a latrine, this was her entire world. Her prison. Apart from the times that Hippocrates summoned her, that was. It was fortunate that Elira was the current focus for his lust, she thought dully. With Publius so sick, there was no way that she would have been able to entertain him as she had before.

Publius coughed, and her attention reverted to the present. 'Bring me a damp cloth.'

'Of course, mistress.' Elira scurried off.

By the time that she had returned, Publius had wet himself. A large stain was spreading across the sheet, surrounding the lower half of his body. Without a word, they changed the bed linen and wiped him down. With the sheets removed, it was impossible to ignore how the malaria had ravaged him. He was nothing more than a bag of skin and bones, and the yellow tinge to his skin was mild in comparison to the jaundiced colour of the whites of his eyes. Somehow, Aurelia blanked it all out, ignored Elira's concerned glances. Refusing to acknowledge how ill Publius was made it easier to imagine his recovery.

'I know it's difficult, mistress, but I need to talk to you.'

The unusual sharpness to Elira's tone pierced Aurelia's mental haze. 'What is it?'

'I was given another message when I went out this morning.'

Hanno. 'At the baker's?'

'Yes. From a soldier, as before. I made sure to give him your reply to the first letter.'

Aurelia took the proffered tiny, rolled parchment with trembling hands. It had seemed an eternity since her chance meeting with Hanno until the first one had come. Although it had not offered a way out of the palace – Hanno had said that he was planning that with a friend – its arrival had helped her to go on. This was the second message, come two weeks after its predecessor. Maybe Hanno could get another surgeon to attend Publius? she wondered. She dismissed the idea at once. He could no more do that than spirit three people through the walls of the palace. The familiar, yawning pit of despair opened up before her. Do not give up hope, she told herself. This letter is proof that the gods have not forsaken us completely. We will escape, somehow. Cracking off the little blob of sealing wax and unrolling the parchment, she began to read.

'To Aurelia: Greetings. My apologies for the long delay in getting this second missive to you, but my friend has few soldiers whom he trusts enough with the duty of giving it to Elira. I pray that you are enduring as best you can.' Aurelia's eyes moved to Publius' form. She had to concentrate to see him breathing, and a stab of pain pierced her heart.

> I regret to say that we are still searching for the best way to rescue you, your son and Elira. Clearly, force cannot be used, and the number of guards within the palace means that subterfuge will not work either. We need a way to get you all into the city proper. My friend says that if this becomes possible, your escape is certain.

Her gaze roved down the remaining lines, to Hanno's signature. Each of the phrases 'stay strong', 'the gods will protect you' and 'we will meet again soon' felt like hammer blows to the last of her hope. Publius was gravely ill, and they would never leave this place. She would be at Hippocrates' mercy until he tired of her. After that, Agathocles – whom she had already had to couple with once, hurriedly – would want his share of her flesh. Despairing, she let the tears that often threatened begin to fall.

'What does it say, mistress? Is it bad news?'

Aurelia wiped her eyes. 'Not so much that, more that nothing has changed. Hanno can find no way to break us out of here. For now. But we are not to give up hope.'

'That's easy for him to say!' spat Elira. 'He's not the one who has to lie with Hippocrates every night.'

'He's doing what he can.'

Elira's temper vanished, leaving in its place sorrow. 'I know, mistress. It's so hard, though. Just waiting, waiting, all the time.'

Rather than improving as Aurelia had hoped, Publius' condition took a sharp turn for the worse. In the ensuing hours, his fever rose and rose until his entire body was burning hot to the touch. Seizures followed: horrifying wild jerks and spasms of his limbs that terrified both women. It was fortunate that the surgeon had warned them of this possible development, or

Aurelia might have thought him possessed by a demon. Instead, she knew that trying to lower his temperature might help. There was no ice to be had, so they had to make do by repeatedly bathing Publius in cool water. When the fits finally stopped, Aurelia hoped he might have turned a corner. Instead, he lapsed into complete unconsciousness. Then an area around one knee, which had banged against the floor during a seizure, developed into what looked like a bruise. Soon it was apparent that there was bleeding under the skin. At this point, Aurelia threw caution to the wind and went to the guard who stood outside their door. Prepared to do just about anything, she was relieved when he agreed to send for the surgeon because her child was seriously ill. She had no doubt that it was due in part to Publius' cheerful nature and admiration of the guards' every move. He had charmed a good number of them. More than one had smuggled in extra food and sometimes even a small wooden toy for her son.

The surgeon's poor humour at the hour of his summons fell away the instant that he saw Publius.

'Why did you not call for me sooner?' he asked, and then sighed. 'You don't need to answer that. Tell me what he's been doing.' Calling for more light, he knelt by the bed and listened to Aurelia's explanation. He immediately subjected Publius to a close examination, placing his ear on the boy's chest to monitor his breathing, checking his pulse and the colour of his gums, and lifting his eyelids to examine his conjunctivae. The process made Aurelia so nervous that she had to take hold of Elira's hand.

At last he was done. 'When did the child last pass urine?'

Aurelia regarded the surgeon blankly. 'Urine? I don't know. A long time ago. Six hours? Eight?'

With another sigh, he checked Publius' pulse again. When he looked up, his expression was sombre. 'I'm sorry. There's nothing more I can do.'

Aurelia felt as if someone had punched her in the solar plexus. She gasped, and sank to her knees. 'What do you mean?' she heard Elira ask.

'It's classical, severe malaria. A high fever, followed by seizures and other nervous signs. I suspect that he fell into a coma after that. This mark on his knee shows that his blood is not clotting. From what you say about his urination, I suspect his kidneys are also failing.'

Aurelia could not speak. She stared at Publius, at the surgeon, at Publius.

The next time she looked, the surgeon's face had softened further. 'He's dying, I'm afraid. There's nothing that can be done.'

'Dying?' she repeated.

'Yes. I've never seen an adult recover once this stage has been reached, let alone a small child. I'm sorry.'

'Will it be long?'

The surgeon shook his head, sending Aurelia into a daze of grief. She scarcely noticed his light touch on her shoulder as he walked out.

Sinking on to the bed, she enfolded Publius in her arms. Unbidden, a lullaby came to mind, one that she'd crooned to him as a tiny baby. Aurelia began to sing it, very softly. Over and over she sang it, until her voice gave out and she had to hum the melody. Grief overwhelmed her, and it wasn't long before the sheet had been saturated by tears. Apart from an occasional deep breath, Publius didn't move or stir. She was grateful that he no longer seemed distressed. It was easy for Aurelia to fall into a fantasy that he was sleeping off an upset stomach, and that she was comforting him. She was still enmeshed by this pleasant fiction when sleep took her.

When she awoke, it took no more than a heartbeat for her mother's intuition to tell her that Publius was gone. With infinite tenderness, she laid his head back on to the pillow. His eyes were half open, but his colour had changed from the angry pink of earlier to the grey of the freshly dead. Aurelia placed a finger on the large vein in his neck. By the time she'd counted twenty, there had been no pulse. It was a little late, but she put her mouth to his, to allow his soul to exit his body. 'Forgive me, my little darling,' she whispered. 'The gods grant you a safe passage to the other side. Let them reserve their punishment for me.'

'He has gone.'

Aurelia looked up at Elira, whose cheeks were running with tears. 'Yes,' she said dully.

'May all the gods bless him and look after him. He was a wonderful child,' murmured Elira, her voice breaking.

'We must see to the funeral arrangements. They won't deny me that, will they?' Aurelia felt her fragile façade begin to crack.

'I don't know, mistress. If they do allow it, this might be our chance to escape.'

It took a moment for Elira's implication to sink in. 'You mean, if we were to be allowed out of the palace?'

'Yes, mistress.' Elira's eyes glistened. 'Can you write a reply to Hanno? The soldier said that he would be at the baker's again today. I can persuade the guard who's on duty this morning to let me out. If Hanno knows about the funeral, he might be able to act.'

'But we don't know when they might let us hold it.'

'I know, mistress, but some information would be more useful to Hanno than none, surely?'

In that moment, Aurelia did not care about escape, or about Hanno. Her mind was full of Publius, and how desperately she would miss him. But she knew that this might be their first and last opportunity to get away. However she felt herself, it was not fair to condemn Elira to a lifetime of enforced prostitution. She took a deep breath and forced herself to think of the future. 'Very well. I'll do it.'

Chapter XII

After a discussion with Kleitos, Hanno had decided to take the soldier's place by the bakery that morning.

'It makes sense to change the person who does it,' he'd argued. 'People might remember your man from yesterday.' So now he was standing a few paces from the baker's, a warm loaf in his hand. Gods, but it was good to eat it fresh from the oven, he thought. There weren't many things that tasted better.

Yet his pleasure couldn't dispel his nerves. Despite the bravado he'd shown Kleitos, it was hard to act normal, and even harder not to be continually looking up and down the street for signs of trouble. Fortunately, nothing gave Hanno cause for concern. Housewives congregated by the door of the bakery, chattering. Slaves who'd been sent out by their masters saw their chance and slipped past them to jump the queue. A well-dressed youth emerged with a bag full of loaves, and two stray dogs sniffed up and down, hoping for a dropped crust from the customers who ate what they'd bought.

Some time went by, and the early-morning rush to buy bread died away. Hanno began to feel self-conscious again, and he was glad that there was an open-fronted inn on the little square opposite. None of the other customers gave him a second glance as he occupied an outside seat and ordered a cup of wine. An hour and a second cup, then another hour and a third cup, slipped past without any sign of Elira. Hanno's worries began to grow. Maybe something was wrong? Maybe Aurelia had been taken ill as well, forcing Elira to look after her? To distract himself, he went to empty his bladder in the tavern's facility – a section of its wall that lined one side of a tiny alleyway. As was commonplace, graffiti had been scratched into every visible part of the brickwork. Hanno grinned as he read. It was a combination of the usual: 'I had a good shit here'; 'Eumenes loves Agape'; 'The whores in this inn have the pox'.

Back at his seat, he resumed his study of the people who entered and left the bakery. It was with real shock that he saw Elira walking out, clutching a bulging bag. She was thinner than he remembered, and there were new lines of unhappiness that ran from the corners of her nose to her lips. Throwing back the last of his wine, he sauntered after her.

He waited until no more than three steps separated them before speaking. 'Elira.'

She spun, nearly dropping her bag as she recognised him. 'What a surprise,' she said in a low voice.

'Keep walking.' Hanno drew alongside. 'How is Aurelia?'

'Not good, sir. Her son Publius – he's dead.'

'What? How?'

'Malaria. He died during the night.'

'Gods, that's terrible.' At once Hanno felt torn. This was horrific news for Aurelia, yet now he had one less person to magic out of the palace. The realisation that that too might not be necessary sank home a heartbeat later. 'Will a funeral be permitted?'

'We don't know. With the gods' help' – here Elira put on her most seductive face – 'and mine, I hope so.'

Rage bubbled up inside Hanno, and he tried not to think of what Elira and Aurelia had been forced to do to survive since their capture. 'If you are, that is when we will strike. When will you know?' He heard how stupid that question was as it left his lips. 'You don't know that either.'

'No, sir.'

'No matter.' Kleitos had already mentioned a gang of street urchins who might be used to cause a diversion on the street. They could surely be paid to keep watch on the palace gates too. 'When you find out about the funeral, try to come to the baker's to let me, or one of the soldiers, know. If that proves impossible, you're to tell Aurelia that we'll be ready, regardless.'

Elira looked scared. 'How will you free us?'

'Leave that to us. Be ready from the moment you leave the palace gate. It will be done as fast and as bloodlessly as possible,' he declared, glad that Elira couldn't hear his thumping heart. 'Give Aurelia my deepest sympathies. Tell her—' He stopped. What could he say that would make any difference to her grief? 'Tell her that I'm sorry.'

'I will, sir. You'll be able to tell her yourself soon.' She gave him a tremulous smile. 'I'd best go now. I can't stay away too long, or the guard might become suspicious.'

'Stay strong.' It was harder than Hanno expected to watch Elira walk away, back to captivity. He consoled himself with the knowledge that within the next few days, she and Aurelia would have both escaped. Though quite how they would hide away from the search that Hippocrates' soldiers would embark upon afterwards, he had no idea.

'You're ready for this?' Kleitos' voice was muffled by the cloth that covered the lower half of his face. He was standing with Hanno and a group of children in an alleyway that lay near one of the city's main gates. It was a calculated gamble, the first of many, that Aurelia and Elira would come this way with Publius' body. Most of the tombs, and the largest area of graves, lay to either side of the road that led away from the city here.

'Course we are,' insisted the gang's leader, a crop-haired, broad-faced boy who went by the nickname of 'Bear'. His followers, nine children ranging from his age, which was about eleven or twelve, down to what Hanno reckoned was only around six or seven, muttered or shook their heads in fierce agreement. At first glance, they didn't look like much – apart from Bear, who was as stocky as many grown men. They were thin, clad in little more than rags, and with bones showing everywhere, but their appearance deceived. Kleitos had shown them in action to Hanno, descending like a pack of wolves on a hapless vendor of cheese who was dismantling his stall. It had taken them less than twenty heartbeats to floor the man, knock him half unconscious, and steal his purse and every last piece of his merchandise.

'Tell me what you have to do again,' ordered Kleitos.

Bear gave him a truculent stare that would have earned one of Kleitos' men a beating. 'When they're close enough, we grab hold of the wagonload of hay that's parked in the yard opposite and push it out into the street.'

'They need to be within thirty paces of the alley,' warned Hanno.

'I know, I know. We hone in on the soldiers who'll be guarding two women. Distract them, knock 'em down. It doesn't matter too much as long as we don't kill them.'

These children's lives must be brutal, thought Hanno. At least half of them had knives, and not one looked shocked by the idea of murder.

'What matters is that the women get away,' Kleitos said. 'You just have to delay the soldiers as long as you can, and not get caught. If *that* happens, you're on your own.'

'You don't need to tell us,' replied Bear, curling his lip. 'It's one of our rules. There's fuck all we can do if the soldiers take one of us, so we forget about whoever it was. Don't we, lads?'

'Aye.' 'That's right.' 'Better dead than captured.'

'Good,' said Kleitos, casting a look at Hanno. It was their fervent hope too that none of the urchins was taken. Both had worn masks and nondescript chitons every time that they'd met Bear and his gang, but there was still a risk that some of the boys could be overpowered. Under torture, they might remember a detail that would send armed men to Hanno's or Kleitos' doors.

'What's so special about these women?' demanded Bear.

'You're being paid enough not to care.' Kleitos held up a bulging leather purse. Because his native accent wouldn't sound out of place, it was he who'd done the recruiting, and most of the talking. The *chink, chink* sound from his bag drew every urchin's stare like a cat to an injured mouse. 'As we agreed, there's a gold piece for each of you if this is successful.'

Bear puffed up his chest. 'I want half now.' His followers moved a little closer to him, and Hanno saw some even lay hands to their daggers. *Little bastards.* He tensed, ready to fight.

'Don't piss about with me, *boy*. I gave you three gold pieces already as a goodwill gesture. That's more than you see in a fucking year of thieving. You'll get the money when we're done, as I said. If you don't like that, to Hades with the lot of you.'

Bear's eyes flickered to his companions.

'Lay hands on your weapons,' said Kleitos menacingly, 'and we'll gut half of you before you've taken a breath, and the rest two heartbeats after that.'

Bear glowered at Kleitos, and then Hanno. Both men returned the stare with equal intensity. After a moment, Bear laughed. 'I'm joking with you. Our deal is good. You pay me outside the temple to Demeter in Achradina, at the beginning of the third watch tonight.'

'You're wiser than you look,' grated Kleitos. 'Now, if you want to earn your gold, you'd best get some eyes on the streets around here, so that we get plenty of warning when they're coming. We'll stay here. Keep us informed.'

With a sullen look, Bear chivvied his gang out of the alley.

'The little shit would sell his own soul if it made him a profit,' said Hanno.

'So would any of the adult lowlifes in the city,' Kleitos said, and Hanno knew he was right.

'Will Hippocrates not punish the guards?' he asked, voicing the worry that they had argued over twice before. Those accompanying Aurelia and Elira were likely to be innocent of any wrongdoing against the two women.

'They'll be flogged afterwards, that's for sure, but I don't think it will come to more than that. Trained soldiers are priceless commodities at the moment. Besides, the coinage you gave me will more than compensate them. I will see that they receive it secretly, from an anonymous donor.'

They settled down to wait, as far from each end of the alleyway as possible. Hanno watched one direction, and Kleitos the other. They'd chosen the site with great care. The narrow passage was full of human waste, and therefore frequented only by those with chamber pots to empty, but that didn't mean they were safe from discovery. Two men wearing masks were bound to attract attention, yet they couldn't take them off for fear of the urchins seeing their faces. Added to this concern was Hanno's worry that Aurelia would be accompanied by too many soldiers, or that she would go to a different gate, or not come at all. It was a nerve-racking time. Conversation had to be kept to a minimum, so he could do nothing but brood.

Hanno's humour wasn't helped by the rank stench of shit and piss, and the squelchy feeling of both between his toes every time he moved. He focused his mind on the room that Kleitos had rented above a tavern in the far west of the city. News of the women's escape would take time to reach the area. With luck, the inn's owner, a man known to Kleitos, and whose hand had been well greased, would pay no heed. Kleitos' ploy was to say that Aurelia and Elira were flute girls, secreted away for illicit meetings with him and his friend (Hanno). After a little while, Hanno thrust that idea from his mind too. That part of their plan was also full of risk. Everything *had* to go according to plan, or it would end in disaster. Gods, but fighting a battle was easier than this, he thought sourly.

'They're coming!' One of Bear's smallest followers, a waif with protuberant eyes and a mass of curly black hair, stood before him.

'You're sure?' asked Hanno.

A confident shrug. 'I saw two women, one carrying a small body wrapped in linen. A couple of soldiers were with them. That's who you want, isn't it?'

Heart racing with excitement, and sorrow for Aurelia, Hanno shot a look at Kleitos. 'It's them. It has to be.'

'Only two soldiers! That's good. How far away are they?' demanded Kleitos, stepping to Hanno's side.

'A few blocks. They won't be long.'

'Bear and the rest are in place?' asked Hanno.

'Aye. We want our gold.'

'And you'll have it, if you do your job.'

'Never fear.' He grinned, revealing filthy, misshapen teeth. 'I'm to let Bear know when they're about thirty paces from the entrance to the yard.' He placed a thumb and forefinger between his lips and blew a low wolf whistle. 'I'll do that, but much louder. The instant that the wagon's rolled out, me and the lads will fall on the two soldiers.'

'Good. I'll see Bear tonight, in Achradina, as we arranged. He'll receive the money then.'

'I'll tell him,' said the urchin over his shoulder as he trotted off.

Kleitos nudged Hanno. 'Nervous?'

'Shit, yes! Aren't you?'

'My guts are churning like I just ate a dodgy plate of mussels.' Kleitos leered at him. 'By Zeus' beard, though, I feel alive!'

'Me too,' said Hanno with a tight smile. It felt good to be doing something for love, instead of for vengeance, or loyalty, or any of the other myriad reasons that men fought. If things went well, he and Aurelia would be reunited. He took a deep breath to calm himself down. Clear heads survived in combat, where overexcited ones did not.

'I'll grab the slave girl – Elira, is it? You take Aurelia, and her son.'

'And if Bear and his lot fail to bring down the soldiers?'

Kleitos stooped, ferreted around in the muck and came up with first one, and then a second, lump of brick. 'We use these. For gods' sakes, try not to kill them.' Kleitos set off towards the mouth of the alley. He stopped about ten paces in – enough distance to remain unseen to the casual glance of a passer-by, but close enough to be able to run out the moment they had to.

Since the war had begun, Hanno had waited in ambush on countless occasions. It was normal for time to become stretched, for his vision to reduce to a small tunnel in front of him, for his mouth to be dry, his palms sweaty and his guts in turmoil. Yet he'd never felt so nervous. It was due to Aurelia's involvement, of course, but knowing that didn't stop his heart from racing ever faster. He began to worry. If he was too nervous, he might screw it all up. *That* thought was enough. Biting deep into the inside of his cheek, he let the resulting, exquisite pain drive all else before it. His focus soon returned.

A different urchin sauntered into the alley's mouth. He stopped, and casually scratched at a dirty ankle. 'They're fifty paces away,' he hissed, and disappeared.

Hanno's nervousness must yet have been palpable, because Kleitos reached out to grip his arm. 'It will be all right.'

Hanno swallowed. 'Aye.'

'We've no idea how fast they're walking. I'll count down from thirty, so we're ready.'

Hanno nodded.

'Thirty. Twenty-nine. Twenty-eight.'

Kleitos' count went on. Hanno's gaze was locked on the tall, narrow portion of street that he could see. An old man tottered by, leaning on a stick. In the house opposite, a woman leaned out to beat a small carpet off the iron railings of her balcony. 'Fresh, hot sausages! Just cooked! Who wants some?' called a stallholder.

'Nineteen. Eighteen. Seventeen. Sixteen.'

In the sky above, a seagull screeched contemptuously, and was answered by several others. The waif wandered past without looking into the alleyway. A man pushed a little cart full of ironware past, muttering under his breath about its weight. Two girls stopped to admire something in a shop that abutted on to the alleyway, chattering about who fancied which guard on duty at the gate.

'Six. Five. Four. Three. Two. One,' said Kleitos.

Neither spoke. They stared at the street, took a couple of steps towards it. The background noises dimmed in Hanno's ears; he could feel a pulse there, as well as in the base of his throat.

Fweeeeee-feeeeeerrrr. The wolf whistle was far louder than Hanno would have thought possible from someone as small as the waif.

It had begun.

Baal Hammon, watch over us. Baal Saphon, grant us your protection, and your strength, Hanno prayed as they moved to the end of the alley.

Rumble, rumble, rumble. The noise of iron-bound wheels off cobbles came from off to their left. Bear was playing his part so far, but Hanno's eyes weren't searching for the wagon. They were desperately scanning the street to his right. He could sense Kleitos behind him, doing the same, but the damn priest and his party were blocking their view. Ten steps away, three urchins stood together, making a bad pretence of inspecting the wares displayed in the entrance to a carpenter's workshop. Two more loitered on the other side, playing dice in the dirt. The others were probably with Bear.

'Look out!' shouted a man's voice. The rumbling sound grew louder; shouts of alarm went up, and Hanno heard the wagon thump into the wall of a house on his side of the street. Bear laughed. 'We did it!'

Hanno was far from happy. *If Aurelia's guards have seen, they might turn and run.*

To his immense relief, a soldier pushed his way past the priest. He was followed by a stone-faced Aurelia, carrying a small, cloth-wrapped bundle. Elira was next, and then an officer whom Hanno recognised, but couldn't place.

There was a savage curse from behind him. 'Agathocles! If he spots me, I'm fucked.'

Shit! thought Hanno. The officer was Kleitos' acquaintance, the one they'd met with the group of female slaves. Yet another risk factor had been added to their enterprise.

Right on cue, Bear and the rest of his urchins appeared from behind them. They swept towards the first soldier, who let out a scornful laugh. 'Don't make me kick your arses!' He hadn't seen the rest of the children, who were swarming in from both sides.

'Remember what I told you!' Bear shouted at his companions. Darting in before the surprised guard could react, he grabbed the man around the back of one knee and jerked it forward, upending him on to his backside. Four urchins leaped on top of the guard, pummelling and kicking.

Hanno and Kleitos sprinted out on to the street. Elira had begun screaming, but Aurelia scarcely seemed to notice the mayhem. Agathocles elbowed his way past them, his hand already pulling at his kopis. 'What in Hades' name is going on?' he roared. 'You little bastards!'

It went against all of Hanno's training not to look at the enemies he faced, but he kept his gaze fixed on Aurelia, who still seemed unaware of what was going on. It wasn't until he reached her side that she even saw him. With a sad smile, she lifted the bundle in her arms. 'This is Publius. You'd have liked him.'

'Aurelia. Come!' He took her arm.

'I have to hand him to someone at the gate. I'm not to be allowed to leave the city. To see him cremated.'

Hanno hadn't considered that her grief might have rendered her dazed. 'We can make the arrangements later,' he said gently, pulling her away. 'But we must go. *Now.*'

She didn't move, and Hanno began to panic. The first soldier was behind him. From the grunts of pain and the shouts of glee from the urchins, he was receiving a good kicking, but Agathocles, who had also been floored, had somehow struggled to his feet again. He'd seen what was going on. It was the heroic efforts of Bear, who had slit his baldric with a knife and hurled his sword down the street, that had prevented him from wading into the fray with a weapon. Armed or no, he was heading in Hanno's direction. Bear and three other urchins were darting in and out around him, but Agathocles swatted them away like annoying wasps. In desperation, Hanno grabbed Publius' body from Aurelia. She gasped in shock, and he hissed, 'Follow me!' before turning and running for the alley. He kept his eyes locked on Kleitos and Elira, who were a dozen paces in front of him.

Hanno had all but reached the safety of the passage when he realised that she wasn't behind him. Spinning, he was stunned to see Aurelia seize a dagger from one of the urchins and plunge it into Agathocles' groin, below the protection of his pteryges. Agathocles roared in pain, and she stabbed him twice more. 'You whoreson!' she screamed.

'What the fuck is she doing?' cried Kleitos.

'I don't know,' Hanno replied as Aurelia left Agathocles to collapse to his knees, blood running in thick streams from his wounds. With great calm, she walked to the first soldier, who was still lying on the ground. Her blade rose and fell, rose and fell, and the man's shouts came to a gurgling end. There was a clang of metal off stone as she let the knife drop. At last her gaze travelled towards Hanno, who had stepped outside the alley again.

'This way!' he urged.

Aurelia's face was serene as she walked, not ran, towards him. Around her, confusion reigned. The urchins had vanished from sight, but shop-keepers stood in their doorways, craning their necks to see what was going on. One man had gone to Agathocles' aid, but the other passers-by stood in shock, mesmerised by the sudden, random violence. 'Hurry!' urged Hanno, pulling up the cloth hiding his face.

When she reached him, Kleitos gave her a sharp look and then headed into the alley, Elira by his side. 'Get a move on!'

'Ignore what's underfoot,' said Hanno to Aurelia. 'It isn't far to the other side.'

'I knew you would come,' she breathed.

'How could I not, knowing you were captive here in the city? I'm sorry that it took so long.' His eyes fell to his burden, Publius. 'If only I could have done it sooner.'

Kleitos beat a criss-cross path away from the ambush, for the most part taking alleys that led from one thoroughfare to another. With their masks removed, few people paid them any attention, but Hanno didn't want to leave things to chance, so he wrapped Publius in the old cloak that Elira had been wearing. Kleitos' circuitous route meant that he lost all sense of direction, and it wasn't until they emerged on to a main artery that led to Epipolae, the western part of the city, that he regained his bearings. Kleitos rounded on Aurelia almost at once. 'Why did you kill those men?' he demanded in Latin. 'They were guarding you, not taking you to your execution.'

'What do you care?' she shot back with more spirit than Hanno had expected.

'They're Syracusan, like me. I also knew the officer. There was no need for them to die. The urchins had them distracted.'

'Agathocles didn't just select me to be Hippocrates' property. He forced me to lie with him. He wasn't gentle either. Elira suffered the same from him, and from the soldier. What have you to say to that?' Aurelia's eyes blazed, and her face was distorted with fury.

'I see,' Kleitos said heavily. 'I am sorry.'

But Hanno was glad that Agathocles was dead. 'They can't talk to anyone, which reduces the chances of us being found out.'

'I suppose I never liked Agathocles much,' admitted Kleitos with a shrug. 'There's not much we can do about it in any case. Let's hope that Hippocrates has more things to worry about than seeking vengeance for this.'

Conversation ceased until they had reached the room that Kleitos had rented. He went on ahead, waving to them when the coast was clear so they could go up the rickety stairs without the inn's landlord seeing them.

'The less he knows, the better,' said Kleitos to Hanno as he ushered them into the small, dingy space, which contained little more than two beds, a table and one chair. A chamber pot sat beside the tiny window that opened on to the street below. 'It's not much, but it will do.'

'Thank you,' Elira ventured in poor Greek.

'Forgive me. I spoke sharply earlier,' said Aurelia. 'I'm very grateful for what you've done. This room might not be large, but it's ours, and it's not a prison. That counts for more than you could know.'

Kleitos inclined his head. To Hanno, he said, 'I'll leave you to it.'

Hanno gripped his shoulder. 'My thanks, brother.' In a whisper, he added, 'We'll need to bury or, better, cremate the child. D'you think that's possible?'

'Inside the walls? You never have easy problems to solve, do you?' Kleitos sighed. 'Leave it with me. We'll talk later, or tomorrow.'

When Kleitos had gone, Hanno laid Publius on one of the beds. 'We'll arrange his funeral as soon as possible.'

Aurelia had grown calm again. 'What then?'

'I'm not sure. A lot depends on Hippocrates' reaction.' The best thing would be to stay here, he decided. Besides, where could they go? He had no friends in Sicily apart from Kleitos.

'Can we not leave?' she asked. 'It's well known that the Roman blockade is incomplete.'

He coughed. 'It may well come to that, but we'd best stay where we are. For the moment.'

'Because they'll be looking for us?'

'Partly that. And partly because Hannibal sent me to serve Epicydes,' he said uncomfortably, before adding with even more reluctance, '. . . and Hippocrates.' She didn't reply, which added to his discomfort. Maybe she didn't want to be with him, he thought. Maybe she desired nothing more than to be reunited with her husband, and to grieve over their dead child. He had to respect that. 'Things will have calmed down in a couple of days. I'll see about finding you a boat that can carry you to the Roman positions. They'll make sure that you reach your husband,' he said heavily.

'Lucius is probably dead. Even if he isn't, I have no reason to go back to him.' She stepped right up to Hanno, and drew his arms one by one around her. '*This* is where I've wanted to be ever since you appeared outside our house near Capua.'

Hanno's heart beat a staccato rhythm off the inside of his ribs. He was dimly aware of Elira retreating to the window to give them some privacy. He embraced Aurelia, breathing deep of her scent. 'Oh gods above. It's what I've wanted too. I'm just sorry that it had to be like this. With all that's happened.' One of her fingers came up and touched his lips, silencing him.

'Hold me,' she whispered. 'When I'm here with you, I feel safe.'

Chapter XIII

News of the two guards' deaths, and Aurelia's and Elira's escape, reached Hippocrates soon after Hanno's arrival at the barracks. Hippocrates was said to be incensed, but to Hanno's relief, his anger hadn't translated into much action. Patrols within the city were doubled for a short while, and a number of street urchins were captured and tortured, but that seemed to be it. As time passed, Hanno concluded that Bear and his cronies remained at large, or if they *had* been caught, that they hadn't had enough information to incriminate either him or Kleitos. Aurelia and Elira remained safe in their room throughout.

By the third day, Kleitos judged it safe enough for Hanno to take Aurelia out of the city to cremate Publius. Kleitos had checked the duty rosters beforehand to ensure that the soldiers who had seized Hanno upon his arrival weren't on duty. If stopped, the couple's pretence was to be that they were man and wife, the boy their deceased son, and Elira a servant.

Aurelia had retained her poise since her rescue, but the moment that she, Hanno and Elira began their sad journey, it cracked. 'If only Quintus could be here too,' she whispered. Hanno stared blankly at her. 'He's here on Sicily,' she said, dissolving into floods of tears, clutching the linen-wrapped shape that was Publius. Elira also began to weep. Hanno instinctively went to put an arm around Aurelia, but, worried that she would think it inappropriate, he stopped. It wasn't long, though, before he did it anyway. She didn't tell him to stop, so he walked alongside her, his arm around her waist. Feeling an unexpected depth of sadness, for he had never met the child alive, he supported her all the way. It felt odd that Quintus was stationed here on the island, but at least they would never meet. Hanno didn't want to face that possibility, especially considering his feelings for Aurelia.

He needn't have been worried about the guards, who took one look and waved them on. What he didn't like was hearing the announcement, repeated several times as they walked through, that at the slightest risk of danger, the gate could be closed without notice.

Standing outside the walls, therefore, felt most disquieting. Hanno half expected to see an enemy patrol appear. Yet despite the siege, life here – and death – had achieved a kind of status quo since the failed Roman assault. From the vantage points on their fortifications, enemy sentries could see anyone who came along the road that led to the north, but their fear of the Syracusan artillery meant that they did nothing. It meant, too, that funerals were held as they always had been, among the innumerable tombs that lined the thoroughfare.

There were roadside stalls where religious trinkets, wood for pyres, animals for sacrifice and even hot food could be bought. Priests, orators and professional grievers offered their services. Musicians played dirges on flutes and lyres. A soothsayer in a greasy leather cap promised a good chance of favourable readings in the entrails of any animals he examined. Whores and other lowlifes congregated around the less well-kept tombs. It was similar in many ways to Carthage, although there were none of the ornamented masks that went into the afterlife with the dead. Hanno's apprehension about where they were gradually eased. He, Aurelia and Elira were just three mourners in a crowd. No one paid them any attention, and the Romans weren't going to either.

A few extra coins saw the pyre built, and tended by the son of the man who'd sold him the wood and charcoal. Before long, the heat from its flames forced them to retreat. Hanno and Elira stood a little distance back from Aurelia, who was so locked in her own world that she didn't notice. They remained there for some time, the background noise of music, other mourners and the roving vendors filling the air.

'Life can be so cruel,' said Aurelia at last.

Hanno moved closer. 'It can,' he replied sombrely. 'I have no children, but I can imagine that losing one must be terrible beyond belief.'

Fresh tears rolled down her cheeks. After a moment, she said, 'I wasn't just talking about my little Publius. My mother died about two months ago. Right after that, Lucius was badly injured in Rhegium. The last I heard, he'd been unconscious for days. To lose one's loved one is bad enough, but two – as well as one's husband? And Quintus is probably no more than a few miles away.'

Hanno felt too awkward to talk about Quintus. He put an arm around her again. 'I had no idea that your mother was dead. I'm sorry.'

'It was a growth in her belly, on her liver, that took her. She wasted away in a matter of weeks.'

'Atia was a good woman. Your father must be grieving still.'

A bitter laugh. 'Of course! How could you have known? Father is gone too. He died at Cannae.'

'Damn it, Aurelia, I'm sorry. My father was also killed that day.'

She squeezed his hand. 'And your brothers?'

'They survived, thank the gods. I left them in good health when I departed for Sicily.'

'It is good that you have living flesh and blood.' Her voice changed, becoming wistful. 'Do you ever think of Quintus? He's stationed on the island, you know. He might be close by.'

'I have wondered whether he could be here,' said Hanno, realising that his relationship with Aurelia meant that he could never now regard Quintus as an enemy. Had he truly ever done so? he wondered. 'May the gods keep him safe.'

It took a number of hours to burn Publius' body, and several more until the embers had sufficiently cooled. By this point, Hanno was keen to regain the safety of the walls. After so long at war, it felt foolish to remain in such an exposed position. Just because the Romans had never staged an attack along this route didn't mean that they mightn't try. Yet the sun had almost set by the time that they set out for Syracuse, Aurelia clutching an urn full of her child's ashes. The area had already emptied, and they were among the last people to enter the city before the gate was closed for the night.

Life settled into an odd kind of routine as the heightened security over the soldiers murdered by Aurelia died down. She and Elira began venturing outside. They never went far, but, as they told Hanno, anything was better than being cooped up day and night. He visited once a day, often twice. Kleitos sometimes came with him. The urn and the makeshift shrine in the corner were reminders of what had gone before, but Aurelia's mood remained if not happy then stable, and a touch less sad than it had been. Thinking that a distraction from their confined existence might help, Hanno bought a kitten one day, a mewling bundle of tabby fur. To his relief, both women fell in love with it at once. Aurelia named it Hannibal, after its habit of ambushing the back of their legs from around the corner of the beds. Hanno found this hilarious, and even Kleitos' disapproval of the creature was half-hearted. Soon all of them were spending hours playing with Hannibal, getting him to chase a trailed length of wool, or to pat a ball of it around the floor. Hanno would admit it to few people, but caring for the tiny creature was a welcome break from his military routine.

He should have known it would never last. Since he'd joined Hannibal's army, Hanno had learned never to take things for granted. Life was uncertain, but war was a different beast altogether: uncaring, unpredictable, and far more savage. But being in Syracuse and freeing Aurelia had lulled him into a sense of false security. It was a city under siege, but it was easy to forget that. Apart from the presence of soldiers on the streets, and the shortage of certain foodstuffs, life went on as normal. When news came three weeks later that Himilco, a Carthaginian general, had landed on the island's south coast with thirty thousand soldiers, Hanno had to acknowledge reality. A day after that, a summons to the palace arrived. Despite what the order meant, his spirits rose. If there was ever going to be a chance for him to discover something of use to Hannibal, it would be now.

Hippocrates' and Epicydes' planned response to the Carthaginian landings changed everything. Hanno couldn't deny that there was sense in sending some of their strength to join with Himilco. Breaking the siege would be made easier if a massive, friendly force were to attack the Romans' rear while the garrison sallied forth to assail them from the front. Yet Hippocrates' order to accompany him meant that Hanno would have to leave Aurelia behind. That mightn't have been so bad – in terms of the task set him by Hannibal, it was good news – but Kleitos had also been chosen to go.

Troubled, he went to talk with Kleitos upon his return from the palace. 'What should I do?'

Kleitos regarded him with lowered brows. 'Leave her here.'

'After all that she's been through?'

'She's a resilient woman, and so is Elira. They've got each other. There'll be no threat from Hippocrates, because he's leading the expedition. If Epicydes even knows of her existence, I doubt he cares. What other dangers could there be, other than the normal ones of living in a city? We'll pay the innkeeper to have someone keep an eye on them. That should be more than enough, my friend. She'll scarcely even know you're gone before you're back again, having helped to drive Marcellus' legions into the sea.'

'What about taking her with us?'

Kleitos gave him a scornful look. 'The only women who follow armies are cooks or whores. Usually, they're both. There's no place for them among the soldiers.'

'I know, but—'

'This will be no gentle stroll in search of an enemy,' warned Kleitos. 'The damn Romans could have troops anywhere in the hinterland. We'll be marching at speed, and anyone who can't keep up will be left behind. Imagine if that happened to Aurelia.'

Hanno was all too aware of the carnage that resulted if soldiers came upon 'enemy' camp followers. Aurelia's status as a Roman noblewoman would mean nothing to battle-crazed legionaries. 'Aye, you're right,' he said with a sigh.

'She'll be safe inside the city, never fear. Safer than she would be with us.'

Hanno nodded reluctantly.

What he hadn't counted on was Aurelia's vehement reaction when he told her.

'I'm not staying behind. Nor is Elira.' She listened as Hanno re-explained the dangers of accompanying an army on campaign. 'I don't care,' she declared. 'It's worth the risks.'

'You have no idea of the risks,' retorted Hanno, frustrated.

'I'm not going to hide in this room while you march off, to return gods know when, if at all.'

His temper flared. 'I forbid you!'

She recoiled.

'I'm sorry, Aurelia. I could wish for nothing more than for you to come, but it's too dangerous. If there was no other option, then maybe we'd have to consider it, but there is another way. You can stay here with Elira, in relative safety. I'll be back within a few months.'

Her chin wobbled, but she didn't argue further. 'Very well. You must swear to return. If you didn't, I don't know what I would do.'

'I give you my oath,' said Hanno, hoping that the gods were listening, and in good mood.

Aurelia seemed satisfied. She hooked her fingers around the back of his head and drew him close. 'If you're to be gone for some time, we should become better acquainted.'

Summer had arrived as they had left Syracuse, and with it had come blue skies, burning sun and baking heat. This was the fifth day of their march through the hilly region to the west and south of Syracuse, a fertile, beautiful area of vineyards and farms. Hanno had had little time to admire the scenery, however. His unit had been placed midway down the column of eight thousand men, and the great clouds of dust sent up by those in front hid much from view. He wiped at the sweat that had trickled from under the felt liner beneath his helmet, and his fingers came away brown with moist dust. Was this what hell was like? he wondered. His throat was dry with thirst, his lips were cracked, and it felt as if he was cooking in his bronze breastplate. How good it would feel to be in Aurelia's bed instead of here. But she was back in Syracuse, and he was here.

Thus far, there had been no news of Himilco's force, which meant that their journey had to continue. It didn't bear thinking about that once they had united with Himilco, the whole distance would have to be marched again, in reverse. At least there'd be some Carthaginian officers whom Hanno might know. Seeing some of his own kind would be a welcome change. He hoped that Hannibal would be pleased with the message that he'd sent via a Carthaginian trireme that was bound for southern Italy, telling him of the patrol, and their mission to join up with Himilco. Hanno hoped too that Himilco and Hippocrates got on with one another, or his job would prove a difficult one. Few things guaranteed defeat faster than commanders who argued.

It was fortunate that their cavalry had seen no enemy forces since their night-time departure from Euryalus, the westernmost fort in Syracuse's defences. They never spent that long in the field, which concerned Hanno. How far did they ride from the column? he wondered. Nonetheless, his nervousness that they would be the victims of a Roman ambush had eased.

Every day had been the same. There was an inviting cool period in the early morning that lasted as long as it took them to rise and break camp. If near a stream or river, the soldiers drank as much as they could before setting out. The first couple of hours' march were bearable, but after that came the hottest part of the day, a torment that had to be endured. The ball of fire that was the sun sapped men's energy even as it burned their skin and drenched them in sweat.

At midday, there was a short but welcome halt, to force down some food and to drink a couple of mouthfuls of blood-warm water. This lifted their energy levels somewhat, and then there was the slog until they had reached the spot where their camp would have to be built. Built? thought Hanno with contempt. Their disorganised encampments weren't built, they were more half assembled, like a wooden toy house abandoned by a child before it was finished. He had yet to see a defensive ditch completed, or for any order in the tent lines to exist. The slapdash arrangements were worrying, but his biggest concern every evening was that Hippocrates posted too few sentries. Hanno had mentioned it not once, but twice; Kleitos had backed him. The second time, Hippocrates had told them to shut their damn mouths, or he'd have them shut for good. That had been that. His prayers would have to suffice, Hanno decided. Keep the Romans a safe distance away, Baal Saphon. Let us have word of them only after we've united with Himilco.

'Where do all the damn flies come from?' grumbled Amphios, the ugliest of Hanno's soldiers, swatting a hand at the cloud of little black dots around his head. 'They fucking love me!'

'They can sense that you're full of shit,' jibed Deon, Amphios' best friend and the unit's joker.

All the soldiers within earshot laughed. 'They should congregate around you instead, Deon, because you're an arsehole,' Amphios shot back. 'A big, fat, hairy one.'

More hoots of amusement.

'I love you too, Amphios,' Deon retorted, grinning.

Hanno didn't interrupt. His men were marching forty stadia per hour, and coarse banter like this was normal. In some ways, he had grown to love it; the repartee also helped to maintain morale through the long periods of dusty discomfort.

No one spoke for a while, however, and the heat began to irritate Hanno again. His lightest wool tunic still felt as thick and uncomfortable as the one he used in the depths of winter. He was grateful for the distraction when Amphios asked, 'Remember that farmer's daughter you screwed the other day, Deon?'

'How could I forget?'

A barrage of catcalls followed. Deon encouraged it by raising his spear in the air for everyone to see. 'Think this is stiff?' he shouted. 'It's nothing on me when I'm excited!'

Amid the jeers and whistles Hanno pretended that he couldn't hear a thing. Deon had earned every soldier's admiration for managing, while out with a foraging party, to persuade a local girl to lie with him in her father's hay shed. At least, that was what he swore had happened. The junior officer in charge had been none the wiser, Deon had said, and he had even come away with two fat hens for the pot.

'What was her name?' Amphios cried.

'Aphrodite!' said a voice. 'A veritable goddess, she was.'

Their comrades loved that; more insults and foul comments followed.

Deon waited until the clamour had died down a little. 'Do you want to hear what she was called or not, brothers? And the details of what I did to her?'

'We do! Tell us!' came the chorus.

Like everyone, Hanno had heard it before. Most, if not all, of it was probably lies – according to one soldier who'd been near the hay barn, Deon had come out at speed, pursued by a fat, gap-toothed peasant girl armed with an axe. That wasn't the point, however. It was a great tale, and it helped to distract them from the march. Unfortunately Deon's story was turning Hanno's mind towards Aurelia once more, and what he'd like to do with her. Smiling inwardly, he sought out his second-in-command, a solid career soldier called Bacchios, and told him to take charge of the men. Then he set off to find Kleitos. He would know how much further it was until they could set up camp.

Chapter XIV

anno was woken when the sun's rays, shining through a small gap between two tent panels, lit upon his face. Deep in an erotic dream about Aurelia, he turned over and tried to go back to sleep, but it proved difficult. All around, the morning noises had begun. Men were farting, coughing, muttering to one another. Someone nearby announced that if he didn't have a piss that moment, his bladder would burst. His companions told him in no uncertain terms what would happen if he urinated in the tent.

As the dream receded, Hanno scowled and decided to get up. His bad mood didn't last longer than it took him to get dressed. Filling in the missing details of the dream would relieve the drudgery of the march to come. He wouldn't need to listen – yet again – to Deon's outlandish claims about what he'd done with the peasant girl.

Two vultures were circling over the western edge of the valley. It was early to see them. They must have found a carcase, he concluded. Ordering Amphios to prepare his breakfast and to take down his tent, in that order, he hurried down to the stream for a quick dip. The pleasure of a swim in fresh water was simply too good to miss out on. When Hanno got back a short while later, he was pleased to see that his soldiers were busy taking down their tents. The mules stood in a line, head ropes on, ready to be loaded. Some of what he'd been banging into their skulls had gone in, he thought, accepting the stale bread and cup of warmed gruel that Deon handed him. The same couldn't be said of the units around them. Most of the men he could see were still standing around fires, eating. They hadn't even put on their armour, let alone dismantled their tents. There was little point feeling frustrated, but Hanno couldn't stop himself.

'It's the same every damn morning, eh?' As he'd approached, Kleitos had seen where Hanno's gaze had wandered.

'You read my mind. I'd wager that your lot are ready, though.'

Kleitos performed a mock bow. 'Some of us Syracusans have standards.'

'I didn't mean to offend,' Hanno said quickly.

'I have taken none. I share your exasperation with the troops' discipline, my friend.'

'It's what might happen when we meet the Romans in open battle that concerns me. Defending a city is one thing, but going head-to-head with legionaries is another. From what I've heard, many of Marcellus' soldiers are veterans of Cannae. They won't be shy when it comes to butchery.'

'I know,' said Kleitos, frowning. 'Which is why it's good that we're going to meet with Himilco. Do you know much of him?'

'If it's the man I'm thinking of, he's a popular type, but he doesn't have a great deal of combat experience. Sadly, most of the men who do are with Hannibal, in Italy.'

'Still, he's got thirty thousand men, and some elephants. That's better than nothing.'

'It is. With any luck, he'll listen to what I've got to say.' Until that point, Hanno hadn't considered his own battle experience, but it was considerably more than Himilco's. 'Hannibal's letter and ring should help convince him of my worth.'

Kleitos snorted. 'Unless he's an arrogant piece of shit like Hippocrates.'

Hanno chuckled. 'Careful. Someone might hear.'

'I'm beginning not to care. I could lead this army better with a blindfold on.'

'I know you could, but it pays to be cautious.'

'Sage words,' admitted Kleitos. 'I'll stitch my lip – for now. I'll tell you something, though. Hearing what Aurelia went through opened my eyes to what a whoreson Hippocrates really is. Epicydes is all right, but it's as if they were born of different mothers. In my mind, the sooner Hippocrates falls in battle, the better.'

'As long as it doesn't mean that we're defeated, I agree with you.'

'I'll drink to that with you later. Right. Best get back to my men. See you on the march, no doubt.'

'Aye.' Hanno's eyes drifted upwards, to the brilliant blue sky. The pair of vultures had been joined by two more. He felt a tickle of unease. 'How far is it to the western edge of the valley?'

'I don't know. Five stadia, maybe a little more. Why?'

'Look.'

Kleitos' eyes followed his arm. 'Four vultures. So what?'

'There were only two there a little while ago.'

'They always gather where there's meat on offer. It'll be a dead deer or the like.'

'How far out were the sentries told to go?'

'To the mouth of the valley, I think. No alarm has been sounded.' Kleitos scowled. 'Do you think——?'

'It won't cost anything to send some soldiers to look, will it?'

'No. My men or yours?'

'Mine are right here. Deon! Amphios! Gather up half a dozen of your fellows.'

A few moments later, his soldiers had hurried off to the west, over the waist-high rampart and into the shallow ditch that lay beyond it. Hanno eyed the unfinished defences, and then the crowds of half-dressed men and the ramshackle tents that stretched through the camp. A queasy sensation roiled in his belly. 'Be ready,' he said to Kleitos.

'You think they'll find something?'

'I'm not sure, but I'm worried.'

Kleitos gave him a firm nod. 'Fine. If it proves to be a false alarm, we'll still have shown the rest how real soldiers should behave.' He strode off.

Hanno began bawling orders. 'I want those tents taken down! Before that, though, I want you all armed and ready, as if for a fight.'

He saw soldiers in other units looking. *Good. Their officers might take some notice.*

'Do you know something we don't, sir?' called a voice from behind one of the tents.

'No. I just want you to show the rest of this sorry shower that you're better soldiers than they'll ever be.' That got him a cheer, and his men moved to where their equipment was stacked. Hanno went and fetched his helmet.

From beyond the ditch, a cracked voice – Deon's? – shouted something in Greek. Hanno didn't catch the words, but the alarmed tone drew his attention like a bather's eye to a turd in a public baths. A heartbeat's delay, and several more voices joined in. Hanno saw the men around him take notice. He began running towards the edge of their position, where he would be able to see what was going on. 'Arm yourselves! Form up in front of the tents! MOVE!'

His soldiers responded fast, but those in other units merely looked on. The shouting from the far side of the tents had grown louder. Some men were already tearing in Hanno's direction. They all looked terrified. 'The enemy is coming!' one cried. 'Romans! Thousands of them!' yelled another. A cold pool of acid formed in Hanno's stomach. Had they really seen something, or had they just been panicked?

'FORM UP!' he roared over his shoulder. Despite pushing without regard for those around him, he emerged from the press far slower than he would have liked. His gaze travelled over the ditch, and up the gentle slope that led westward. Deon, Amphios and the rest were sprinting towards him, their faces twisted with fear. What made Hanno's mouth go dry, however, was the sight behind them. Some five hundred paces distant, the valley's entire width was filled with infantry, moving his way at speed. They were too far away to recognise uniforms, but that didn't matter. These were no friendly forces.

Hanno came to a number of stark realisations at the same time. Hippocrates' cavalry had not done their scouting as they should. The vultures had been circling over their dead sentries, of which there had clearly been not enough. Their half-built camp could not be defended. His men might be ready to fight, but the majority of the Syracusans were not. With thousands of Romans closing in, that meant the battle was almost definitely lost. Hanno agonised, aware that with every passing moment, things were deteriorating further. Men were starting to push and shove at one another, as they tried to move *away* from the enemy. Shields and even swords lay on the ground, further evidence. In situations like this, panic spread as fast as a bushfire at the height of summer.

Deon, Amphios and the rest hurled themselves into the ditch and over the rampart. To Hanno's relief, they didn't look as scared as he'd expected. 'What shall we do, sir?' asked Deon, his chest heaving.

That made his mind up. These men trusted him with their lives. There *was* time to lead them, to see if a rout could be prevented. Kleitos and others would be doing the same, of that Hanno had no doubt. If they could hold the Romans back for even a little while, the majority of the force would have time to get across the ford. Hanno shoved away his uncertainty that this was the biggest gamble of his life. 'Back to the rest of the men.' At the milling soldiers around them, he shouted, 'Everyone who wants to fight, follow me.' It was disheartening that only a handful of men obeyed, but that was better than nothing.

In a small but disciplined block, they waded through the mob, and soon reached their tents. Hanno's heart sank a little. Less than half his unit stood waiting. He didn't need to ask where the rest had gone. Fucking cowards, he thought. The men who had stayed looked none too happy either; more than one's gaze was on the retreating crowd. He had to grab them, or they too would run. 'Listen to me, O brave men of Syracuse!'

Their eyes wandered back to him.

'A lot of you want to run right now, I know that. But if you do, the likelihood is that you'll die.' They didn't like that, but he pressed on. 'Have any of you seen what the Roman legionary is capable of doing to a fleeing enemy? I have. Those bastards are disciplined. They don't do what you and I do when the battle's been won, which is to stop and look for wine or coin, or women.' There were a few laughs, and he took heart. 'Romans stay focused, like a damn hawk on a pigeon, and they don't stop until they've killed every poor fucker who comes within reach.'

'So you reckon we should stay and die *here* instead, do you, sir?' cried Amphios.

A chorus of unhappy murmurs rose up.

'What I'm saying is that we should stand and fight for a while at least. That way, most of our comrades will get away. Once they get over the river, they can head up into the broken ground, as can we. The Romans will have difficulty finding us up there.' *I hope.*

There was silence for a moment, and Hanno thought he'd lost them.

Amphios stood forward. 'Tell us what to do, sir.'

Deon moved to stand alongside him. 'I'm in, sir.'

Hanno could have kissed the pair. Shamed by their comrades, the rest nodded or muttered their willingness to fight. 'We must be quick,' he said. 'To the ditch. There we can form a line, and at least we'll have some kind of obstacle to slow the Romans down. Have you all got shields?'

'Yes, sir,' they yelled.

'With me!' Ignoring his churning guts, Hanno ran towards the enemy.

Twenty strides from the ditch, the first Roman whistle blew. It was followed by another, and then more of them than he could count. *Peeeeeep! Peeeeeep! Peeeeeep! Peeeeeep!* Shouted orders in Latin followed, and a swelling roar went up from the legionaries. Hanno's bowels churned. He was used to standing in the middle of a battle line to face a Roman charge, but to do so when his companions were a ragged group of men whose mettle was uncertain *and* they were outnumbered by hundreds to one was utterly insane.

At the ditch, he bawled orders. His men spread out, one rank deep. Hanno glanced to either side, felt the impotent rage pulse behind his eyeballs. Other officers had rallied their men to the ditch as well, but they were few, too few. There were gaping holes everywhere in their line. 'Move to the right,' he roared. 'Move! Join up with the next unit!'

Fortunately, his soldiers realised his intent and scrambled to obey. By the time that the Romans had closed to two hundred paces, perhaps ten score Syracusans had banded together. Hanno couldn't see Kleitos, but the camp was large enough for his friend to be standing elsewhere with his men. He'd had the briefest of chats with the other officers present: they had agreed to hold on for as long as possible, before retreating in the best order they could. Whether this would happen, no one knew, but it was better to have a plan than not. Hanno took his place in the centre of his soldiers. It was the best vantage point, and kept him closer to all of them than any other position. He scanned the Roman line, which was closing steadily. It was far wider than the Syracusan front, which meant that they risked instant envelopment. *What the fuck are we doing?* 'Ready your shields, lads,' Hanno shouted. 'It'll be javelins first – two volleys – and then they'll charge. Stay close to each other. Punch with your shields and thrust with your swords, the same as they do.'

'We're dead,' said a voice. 'Every one of us.' Fear rippled through the soldiers; Hanno could taste it in his own mouth.

'HOLD!' he roared. 'Remember your comrades. HOLD!'

To their credit, Hanno's men held as the legionaries slowed to a walk and from fifty paces, launched their first javelins. They held as the missiles hummed down upon them, damaging shields and injuring some. They held as a second shower of barbed metal rained in, wrecking more shields and inflicting new casualties. They even held as, at thirty paces, the Roman officers ordered their men to draw their swords and charge. They began to waver when the legionaries' war cries rent the air. They could take no more when the wall of enemy scuta, topped by hundreds of feather-crested helmets, closed in, when the ground shook from the weight of thousands of hobnailed sandals. Wailing in terror, they broke. From what Hanno could see, so too did the other Syracusans.

It was hard to blame them. Hanno had been close to death on many occasions, but rarely had he seen its jagged teeth, or smelt its fetid breath, so close. It was time for all of them to run. There would be no holding the Romans, no period of grace for those who'd already fled. No chance of holding his men together. The only ones who would survive were those who possessed enough strength and determination, and on whom the gods smiled. Desperation clawed at Hanno as he wondered if he was one of those few. 'RETREAT!' he shouted. Then: 'Deon, Amphios, the rest of you. Stay close if you can.'

Turning, he drove back the way they'd come. Fortunately, one of the paths that led back into the camp was right behind him, for the press was savage. It was as if Hanno had jumped into a river in full winter flood, when torn-down trees, bushes and other detritus are bowled along, head over heel, top over bottom, from left to right. He had no control, could do nothing other than be swept along by the current. Within a short distance, his shield was ripped from his grasp. It was as much as he could do to retain his sword. Hanno's feet scrabbled to remain in contact with the ground beneath and he fought the bubbling panic in his chest: if he lost his balance, it was all over. When Deon appeared by his side, it was as if the gods had sent him. The pair locked arms, allowing them to stay together as the mob swept towards the far edge of the camp. Of the rest of his men, there was no sign.

Hanno wasn't sure what distance they had travelled when the first screams rang out behind them. It was impossible to see how near the Romans were, but it was close, far too close. From this point, he thought grimly, the Syracusans would be like hens in a coop when the fox gets in. An animal sound of fear rose from the fleeing troops, almost as if they realised this too. Everyone began to shove even harder. To his right, Hanno saw a soldier stumble and fall to his knees. He had no opportunity to offer help – the tide of fleeing Syracusans behind was inexorable. No one behind the fallen man even slowed. There was a despairing cry as they trampled over the top of him, and he was gone. A moment later, Hanno barked his shins badly on a discarded shield. But for Deon's support, he might have tumbled to the ground.

'We're never going to make it, sir,' Deon shouted in his ear.

Hanno's instinct was screaming the same thing. A glance to either side. The tents to the left were far closer. 'We get off the path, and into the tents. Go through them.'

'Aye, sir.'

'On my count. One. Two. Three.' Hanno slipped his arm from Deon's, turned and drove to the left as if his life depended on it. Which it did. The first soldier in his path snarled a curse as Hanno tried to get past.

'What d'you think you're doing?'

Asking the gods to forgive him, Hanno smashed the hilt of his sword into the man's cheek. Eyes glazed, he dropped from sight. Hanno shoved into the space he'd left, felt Deon right on his heels. The next soldier saw his raised blade and thought better of challenging him. Hanno slipped past and elbowed another man in the face, and then he was free of the madness. Deon joined him a heartbeat later. 'Have you seen Amphios?' asked Hanno.

'Not for a bit, sir.'

'Any of the others?'

'No, sir.'

'Shit.' Hanno surveyed the chaos before them. After a moment, he recognised a number of his men in the throng, but they all looked mad with fear. There was no way of knowing if Amphios would pass by. If he was even alive. 'We can't look for him.'

'I know, sir.'

That was the only confirmation Hanno needed. Lifting his sword, he slashed a great hole in back of the nearest tent and stepped inside it, into the reek of men's sweat and old farts. Deon hurried right behind him, over the confusion of bedding that lay within. Hanno took care at the doorway not to barge out without looking. The coast was clear, however, and he raced across the gap, over a stack of plates and a pot of still warm stew, and through the open flaps of the tent opposite. At its end, he sliced a tear large enough to climb through, and so it went on. At times they met another soldier, who invariably ignored them. Once, Deon had to threaten a burly man with crazed eyes, but the rest of the time, it was a simple case of moving from tent to tent. Hanno's fear subsided a little, giving him time to marvel at the sheep-like behaviour of the troops who were milling and shoving and screaming on the paths to either side. All they had to do was think – what he and Deon were doing was so obvious – yet almost none had come to the same realisation.

Hanno stifled his pity. He wished the Syracusans no ill, but their bad fortune was his good, and he would need every last drop of that if he was to see the day's end alive. Memories of the bloody routs he'd participated in before filled his mind. If their enemies were disciplined – and the Romans were – few men survived when they broke and ran. It was sheer stubbornness that kept Hanno going. That, and the rolls of the dice that had seen Deon stay by his side and permit their mad, exhilarating run through the abandoned tents. On he went.

It came as a shock to emerge from a tent, panting, and find another half-constructed ditch before him. They had reached the far edge of the Syracusan camp. Beyond the earthwork, the ground ran gently down to the river in which he had swum, a lifetime ago. Hanno's eyes shot to the ford, where the mass of fleeing soldiers was concentrating. The Romans hadn't yet reached it, but that wasn't preventing tragedy from unfolding. It was a natural pinch point. Men were already dying there. All sense of discipline had vanished. Hundreds of Syracusans pushed and shoved to get into the shallows, where they could cross, and escape the enemy. The injured or weak were being thrust aside or knocked over into the deeper water, where they drowned. Some soldiers were so frantic to get away that they had come to blows with one another. Blades rose and fell; fresh blood spilled on to the dusty ground. Bodies lay face down in the current, colouring the river scarlet. Those who had been injured roared their distress. Hanno's heart clenched. In a mêlée such as this, such men stood little chance of surviving.

Movement on the far bank caught his eye. Scores of riders were streaming away to the east. Beyond them, Hanno saw hundreds more – it was the cavalry, which had managed to escape. 'Look,' he said in disgust. 'Hippocrates didn't even try to fight. The coward ran and left the rest of us.'

Deon scowled. 'The filthy bastard.'

'That's what he is, and no mistake.' It was another reason to hate him. *Gods, bring him within reach of my blade, just once.* 'We'll head for a place downstream of the ford. Our best chance is to swim across. Can you do that?'

Deon's lips twisted. 'I'll do my best, sir.'

'Never mind. I'll help you across.'

Deon nodded his thanks.

Staying close to one another, they threaded their way down the slope. Discarded weapons and shields littered the ground. Injured men who could go no further lifted their hands in supplication, beseeching those who passed for help, or for an end to their suffering. With clenched jaw, Hanno ignored them all. They were still some distance from the bank when loud wails of dismay dragged his eyes back up towards the camp. 'Fuck,' he heard Deon say as his own throat closed with fear. This entire bank was about to become a slaughterhouse.

Scores of legionaries had burst into sight from various points in the camp. They'd done the same as Hanno and Deon had, cutting their way through the tents. The officer who had ordered that was a smart bastard, thought Hanno. It was the type of thing that Quintus might do. Could he be here? Hanno wondered fleetingly. Just then, it didn't matter. The Roman move had been made to get ahead of as many of the fleeing Syracusans as possible, and it had worked. Utter panic broke out among the soldiers who were closest to the legionaries and, in a seething, disorganised mass, they fled towards the ford. Behind Hanno, the struggle to cross became even more vicious.

'Get your armour off,' he ordered Deon. 'You'll float better.'

'Look, sir.'

Hanno's gaze followed Deon's outstretched arm. 'What is it?'

'There, sir, close to the soldier wearing the Boeotian helmet. Poor bitch.'

Hanno stared, and finally saw the man Deon had described, perhaps three hundred paces away, and halfway between their position and that of the Romans. His heart nearly stopped. A woman was stooped over another, tugging, trying to pull her upright. She had black hair. Her shape was familiar. Claws of terror raked his guts. Aurelia was in Syracuse. It couldn't be her. Could it? The woman glanced at the Romans, who were being marshalled into a line by their officers, and she threw a despairing look at the river. Hanno cursed savagely. It *was* Aurelia. 'Go,' he ordered. 'Save yourself.'

'You're not going up there, sir?' Deon's voice was incredulous. 'It's suicide.'

'That's my woman. I have to.' *I cannot just leave her to die.* 'Go! May the gods protect you.'

Deon's eyes were full of respect as he saluted Hanno. He turned and was gone.

Sword in hand, Hanno began running towards where he'd seen Aurelia. Oddly, there was a benefit to advancing into the maw of death. The tide of Syracusans thinned as he headed uphill, allowing him to move faster than before. Many of the retreating soldiers didn't even notice what he was doing. There were disbelieving stares from some; a couple of men told him he was insane. Hanno didn't bother to reply, keeping his focus on the woman's shape.

From above came the Latin command, 'Close order!' Other voices repeated the cry. His belly roiled with fresh fear as shields clattered off each other: the Romans were about to advance. Hanno began to sprint. A mad cackle escaped his lips as he spotted the woman, who had somehow managed to lift her companion off the ground. If it wasn't Aurelia, he would die for nothing. Of all the cruel jokes that the gods had played on him in his life, that would be the worst.

As he closed in, however, he felt a heartbeat's relief. It *was* Aurelia, and she was helping another woman, whose face was ashen in colour. This woman saw him first; she muttered something, and Aurelia's head turned. Her mouth fell open in shock. 'Hanno! How did you find us?'

'Pure luck, and a soldier called Deon.' What in all damnation are you doing here? he wanted to ask. Instead he demanded roughly, 'Is Elira here as well?'

'No. She wouldn't come.'

'She has more sense than you then.' He glanced at Aurelia's companion. 'How badly are you hurt?'

'FORWARD!' bawled a voice in Latin. Hanno winced, but he did not look at the Romans.

The woman had collapsed again. Her face was resigned. 'I think my left leg is broken. I tripped, fell, at the top of the slope.'

Hanno stared. Subcutaneous bleeding surrounded a nasty bulge on the inside of her left calf. *Shit.* 'It's definitely fractured.'

'I've been telling Aurelia to leave me,' said the woman in an odd, calm voice.

Twin points of red marked Aurelia's cheeks. 'I can't. It's not right. She's been helping me since we left Syracuse.'

Hanno peered up the slope. The legionaries had begun to descend. The only thing in his and the women's favour was that they were doing it at the walk. There were clear-headed officers in charge, he thought absently. No need to run down, risking life and limb. The Syracusans were going nowhere. Nor, at this moment, were they. He searched for moisture in his mouth, found none. 'We *have* to go now, or we're all dead,' he croaked. 'I'll carry you.'

'You can't,' said the woman.

Hanno could see the fear – and hope – in her face. He reached out. 'I can. I'll sling you over my shoulder.'

Her face hardened as she found new resolve. 'If you take me, we have no chance. Without me, you might make it.'

Aurelia looked horrified. 'We can't abandon you!'

'You have to. Even on the other side of the river, you'll have to move fast. I'll slow you down.'

Hanno glanced at Aurelia, hissed, 'She's right.'

Aurelia hesitated, before gripping the woman's arm in farewell. 'The gods be with you.'

'And with you.' From the folds of her dress, she produced a dagger. 'Maybe I can take one of them with me.'

Hanno dragged Aurelia away. Half walking, half running, he guided her down the slope, over the mass of equipment, weapons and bodies. When Hanno looked back, the woman's huddled shape had nearly been swallowed up by the wall of advancing Romans. It was a faint hope that she would die fast, but Hanno prayed for it anyway. It was the least she deserved.

They reached the water's edge a short distance from the ford, which had become impassable due to the number of men trying to cross. Hanno quickly took off his cuirass. Flanked by scores of others with the same idea, they managed to swim across. Once on the other side, like any prey that is being hunted, they looked behind them. The Roman line had almost reached the bottom of the slope. A moment later, there was a sickening crash as the legionaries struck the mass of Syracusans clustered by the ford. Hanno did his best to ignore the screaming that followed. He hoped that Kleitos in particular made it through what was to come. Urging Aurelia onward, he headed for the safety of the trees that fringed the valley's eastern end. Dozens of soldiers ran alongside them. The same haunted look was on all their faces. No one spoke, because there was nothing to say.

Hanno didn't come to a halt until the muscles in his legs were trembling with exhaustion. Aurelia had made no complaint, but she too looked ready to drop. They were deep in the forest, and a good height above the valley, level with the cloud of vultures that waited in the air overhead. In the distance, sounds of combat – men's cries, the clash of weapons – could still be heard, but they hadn't seen another soul for some time. 'Let's rest a little,' he said.

Aurelia sank to the ground with a groan.

Thank you for your protection, Baal Saphon, thought Hanno fervently. Stay with us.

After a while, Aurelia lifted her head. 'What should we do?'

'Not so fast,' said Hanno, finding his anger. 'What in all the gods' names were you doing in the followers' camp?'

She had the grace to blush. 'The thought of not seeing you for only the gods know how long was too much to bear. What if you hadn't come back at all?'

'When were you going to seek me out?'

'Once we made contact with Himilco. I didn't want to interfere with your duties before that.'

He wanted to shake her. 'Your foolishness nearly got you killed! If Deon hadn't seen you—'

'I know. I'm sorry.' She began to weep.

His anger melted away. He had rescued her; they had got away. Placing a hand on her shoulder, he said, 'You're here now. We're together.'

In a crazy way, life had just taken a turn for the better, he decided. If they could avoid the Romans, safety in the town of Akragas – a natural target for Himilco to take – beckoned.

Chapter XV

One bright morning, Corax and Vitruvius summoned their men at dawn. This in itself wasn't unusual, but the grim set to the centurions' faces as they went from tent to tent told its own story.

'I knew that things were too good to last,' grumbled Urceus under his breath as he clambered from his blankets.

'To be fair, we have had it easy enough since Hippocrates had his arse kicked,' said Mattheus, yawning. 'But it looked bad when Himilco and his bloody army arrived, eh?'

There were rumbles of agreement from the rest, including Quintus.

'But Marcellus knew what he was doing.' As ever, Mattheus was ready to talk from the moment his eyes opened. 'Why leave the safety of our walls when we could stay where we were and shout obscenities at the guggas. Off they went, soon enough, to try and ambush the new legion that had arrived from Italy.'

There were a few guilty chuckles at this. No one would have wished the reinforcements ill, thought Quintus. Indeed, they were very welcome, but his and his comrades' skins mattered more than those of soldiers whom they didn't even know. 'It was good, though, that Himilco missed catching them,' he said. 'Their commander's decision to take the coastal road was smart, because our fleet was able to follow the legion as protection.'

'Aye, they were a sight for sore eyes when they came marching in,' declared Urceus. 'Especially when the guggas arrived the following morning. Those were a tense few days, after, but Marcellus held his nerve, making us stay put behind our fortifications. When we refused to fight, Himilco couldn't do much else but piss off.' His face darkened again. 'Things have been nice and quiet since. Why do I suspect that that's about to change?'

Quintus nodded grimly. Corax had a plan. He prayed that it wasn't too risky. They would ultimately have to fight Himilco's soldiers, but for the moment, manning the walls around Syracuse was preferable to just about any other duty.

'You seem suitably pleased to see me on this bright morning,' shouted Corax when they had assembled before him. Wrong-footed, his men glanced at one another, and the centurion chuckled a little at his own joke. 'Marching up and down on sentry duty appeals, I know. But it won't win the damn war on Sicily, will it?'

'No, sir,' a few men replied.

Corax's eyes glinted. 'I'd like a little more enthusiasm than that.'

'NO, SIR!' they roared.

Corax seemed a fraction happier. 'We've all been wondering what that whoreson Himilco's next move would be. Word has come what it will be.'

In a heartbeat, Corax had everyone's attention. The defenders of Syracuse weren't going anywhere, but the newly arrived Carthaginian force was free to move where it wanted. Part of their duty was to ensure that Himilco didn't find this easy.

Corax paused, and looked around. 'Like to know where the dog is?' he said at last.

'YES, SIR!'

'He's taken his army to Murgantia, one of the towns we use as a grain store. It seems that when he arrived, the inhabitants rose against the garrison and delivered the place, and all of its supplies, to the Carthaginian cause.'

Corax did not need to drum up a response to that. Angry shouts filled the air. He nodded in approval. 'So when you don't have enough flour to bake your bread this winter, you know whom to blame!'

His men bellowed even louder.

'Are we to march on Murgantia, sir?' yelled Urceus.

'Sadly, no,' replied Corax. 'Marcellus has seen fit to give this maniple another duty. Other towns are under threat as well. Have you heard of Enna?'

'It's in the middle of the island, and is loyal to us,' said Quintus.

'Correct, but it's only loyal because of its Roman garrison. Its commander is a man called Lucius Pinarius, an able soldier who has done much to ensure that the town stays in Roman hands. For all of his hard work, however, intelligence has it that the inhabitants wish to switch their allegiance from Rome.'

There was a rumble of fury from the hastati.

'Pinarius has sent word to Marcellus, asking for reinforcements.' Corax paused, and let his words sink in. 'This maniple is to be part of the force sent to answer Pinarius' request. Our duty will be to reinforce the garrison of Enna and to follow Pinarius' orders in all things.'

'Until when, sir?' called a voice.

'Until Pinarius judges that we are no longer needed.'

The soldiers glanced at one another, uncertain what to feel. The duty could either be soft beyond compare – being quartered in a town offered far more luxuries than in a siege camp, women being foremost among them – or dangerous in the extreme. If Himilco arrived to take Enna, they could be trapped, killed even.

'How many other soldiers, sir?' shouted Urceus.

'One other maniple will march with us, that of Centurion Pera.' Corax's voice gave away nothing, but his eyes were flat and angry.

'The same cocksucker whom Crespo beat in the horse race, sir?' called a voice from the very back of the maniple. Titters of laughter met the comment, and Quintus thought he saw the corner of Vitruvius' lips twitch.

'Just this once, I'll pretend that I didn't hear that,' snapped Corax, but with less iron than might have been expected. 'Pera is known to you, clearly. He's an experienced centurion, and I will not tolerate any disrespect towards him. Is that fucking clear?'

'YES, SIR!' they shouted.

Quintus could not believe his bad luck. Of all the centurions in the damn army, why did Pera have to be picked to accompany them on their mission? He shot a look at Urceus and mouthed the word 'Bastard', but there was nothing else he could do.

Corax nodded in satisfaction. 'We leave within the hour. Enna is just over eighty miles from here, and I want us there in four days. Travel light. Take only enough food for the march. Dismissed!'

The hastati scrambled to obey.

Quintus' comrades were already dreaming out loud of the inns and whorehouses that they would frequent in Enna, but his mind was filled with the image of Pera's grinning face. He would have to be on constant lookout for trouble.

'Not quite what we imagined, is it?' asked Quintus, catching the eye of a local Enna man. His friendly nod was ignored; Quintus was sure that the man made an obscene gesture as he turned abruptly down an alleyway rather than walking past him and Urceus.

'No, it's fucking not,' growled Urceus, kicking out at a scrawny mongrel, which had bared its teeth at him. It yelped and ran before his sandal could connect with its flesh. 'Even the dogs dislike us.'

Quintus grinned sourly. Barely a week had passed, yet from the innkeepers to the shop owners, the whores to the wine merchants, no one in Enna seemed well disposed towards the Romans. They did not refuse them business – that would have been downright foolish given the legionaries' own angry mood – but it was done with a surly, discontented air. 'They didn't want Pinarius' men here, so it's no surprise really that they don't like us either.'

Hearing a noise above, Urceus looked up. A respectable-looking matron was staring at them with clear disapproval from the second floor of a large house. 'Want to suck my cock?' he shouted in awful Greek. Shocked, the matron withdrew and slammed the shutters. 'They can all go to Hades,' said Urceus, spitting. 'They pledged their allegiance to Rome, and that's that, whether they like it or not.'

Quintus found himself in agreement as he was forced to walk around a particularly large pool of human urine and faeces. Every street was the same. Usually only the poorest townsfolk disposed of their waste in this fashion, and even they tended to use the dungheaps situated in the tiny lanes between buildings. Not so in Enna. The inhabitants didn't dare to show their dislike openly to the Roman garrison, so they did it like this.

There were other ways too. Quintus wasn't alone in having smelt the whiff of urine from a jug of wine in the dingy inns that lined the back streets. These occurrences had resulted in a number of innkeepers having their premises ransacked by irate legionaries. This in turn had seen vociferous complaints to Pinarius from the town's leaders, and *that* had resulted in an order not to frequent such establishments on pain of a whipping, or worse. Of course this had not stopped the soldiers from doing so – Quintus and his comrades thought that Pinarius had merely issued the order for appearances' sake – but it had seen the number of violent incidents decrease. The innkeepers knew that if they served wine that had not been tampered with, their establishments wouldn't be smashed up beyond repair.

Reaching a fork in the street, he came to a halt. 'Which way to the agora?'

Urceus peered left and right, scowling. 'I don't think it matters. Both of them will get us there, won't they?'

'True.' Enna's strong position on a hilltop, contained within walls, meant that the city was quite small. The buildings sprawled beyond the fortifications, along the sides of the road that wound its way up from the fertile valley below, but the beating heart of it – the central agora, the temples, the rulers' palatial houses and offices and the best shops – lay within the protective circle of its imposing ramparts. 'It's not hard to find one's way around, even when you're pissed.' He headed left.

Urceus chuckled. 'We'll have to find that inn we were in last night. What was it called again?'

'It's down this way, I think. The Harvest Moon.'

'That's the one. The owner was far less sour than the other arseholes here, wasn't he? And that barmaid with the big tits definitely liked me.'

'Ever the optimist, Urceus. She smiled at you once!'

'That's enough to give a man hope. Better that than the reception we've had in most places.'

'True, but I still wouldn't trust a single one of them. I'm glad that Pinarius ordered us to remain armed at all times.'

'Aye. I wouldn't want to walk around here alone.'

Fifty paces further on, a small wooden sign had been nailed to the wall of a house on the corner of an alley. It depicted a crudely daubed sheaf of wheat beneath a full moon; below it were the Greek words 'INN' and 'GOOD WINE. PRICES REASONABLE'.

'There it is!' cried Urceus. 'Fancy a quick cup?'

'We're on duty.'

'So what? I can't see an officer, can you?'

Quintus walked past the sign.

Urceus grumbled a little, but he did the same.

Quintus had gone perhaps a dozen steps when a short cry – of pain – reached his ears. It was followed by a burst of laughter. He glanced at Urceus.

'That came from the direction of the Harvest Moon,' said Urceus.

The sound was repeated, and again the laughter rang out.

'It might be some of our lads in trouble,' Urceus began.

'Come on,' said Quintus. 'If it's just locals, we can always leave them to it.'

Even though it was the middle of the day, little light penetrated into the narrow alleyway, which lay between a pair of three-storey buildings. Broken pottery, animal bones and other refuse crunched beneath their sandals. 'Gods, I don't remember it being this filthy,' said Quintus. He sniffed. 'Or smelly.'

Urceus winked. 'It's amazing how a man's thirst before he has a drink and the glow of happiness around him afterwards make him unaware of everything else around him.'

'Please! Leave her alone!'

The anguished plea sent them pounding towards the entrance of the Harvest Moon. A group of locals, tradesmen from the look of their calloused hands and stained tunics, stood outside. They didn't seem happy. 'More fucking Romans,' Quintus thought he heard one say.

'What's going on here?' he demanded in Greek.

The locals were surprised to be addressed in their own language. 'Some of your lot are getting fresh with the barmaid. We protested, so they told us to leave or they'd gut us,' replied the man who'd muttered the insult. 'No doubt you've come to join in.'

'Watch your damn mouth!' Quintus snapped. 'How many of them are there?'

'Five,' came the answer.

Quickly, Quintus translated for Urceus. 'Can they be our men, do you think?'

'There's only one way to find out,' said Urceus, as a scream reached them.

They barged in through the doorway, shields at the ready, Quintus in the lead. It was much as he'd remembered it. The room was rectangular, and poorly lit by small oil lamps set in alcoves. A mixture of sand and reeds covered the dirt floor. Simple tables and benches served as its furniture. A bar made of planks stood at the back; on the wall behind, the prices of various wines had been scrawled. There was no sign of the proprietor; Quintus decided he was probably hiding in the back.

Five legionaries were gathered around a table off to one side; their backs were to Quintus and Urceus. Laughs and lewd jokes passed to and fro between them; under the banter, a woman's moaning could be heard. Quintus peered. Between the soldiers, he could make out the barmaid spreadeagled on the table. Her dress had been shredded from her body, and her arms and legs were tied with lengths of rope. One of the legionaries put a hand to her crotch and set her to fresh wailing. 'Shut up, bitch!' snapped another of her tormentors, cuffing her across the head.

'They're not from our maniple,' Quintus whispered to Urceus. 'Are they Pinarius' or Pera's men?'

'They've got to be Pera's. Pinarius' soldiers wouldn't ignore his orders so blatantly, would they?'

'I don't fucking know. Do we leave, or get involved?' Quintus wanted to help the girl, but he didn't want Pinarius on his back, nor to give Pera another reason to hate him.

The decision was taken from him by Urceus. 'What's going on?' he shouted in a good imitation of Corax.

A stunned silence fell. The legionaries turned. Their shock didn't last more than two heartbeats, however. 'What does it look like, idiot?' demanded one, a fat-lipped man with a deep tan. 'We're each going to take a turn with this whore.'

'She's no whore,' snarled Urceus. 'As you'd know if you had even asked her.'

Fat Lips glanced at his comrades. 'Do you hear this prick? We should have *asked* this slut if she'd let us fuck her!'

They all laughed, but their eyes weren't a bit friendly.

'This is against orders. Your commanding officer will hear of this,' said Quintus in a loud voice. He had already noticed that the legionaries' shields and javelins were stacked together by the door – behind him and Urceus. That was a small blessing.

'Centurion Pera told us to do as we wished, as long as no one complains,' drawled another of the legionaries, a slight man with a cast in one eye. 'We was planning to cut her throat afterwards. She won't say a word then, will she?'

His companions chortled. The barmaid must have spoken some Latin, because she began to cry.

'You can either join us, or piss off and leave us to it,' said Fat Lips. 'The choice is yours.'

'I see,' said Quintus nonchalantly, although his heart was thumping so hard he wondered if the legionaries could hear it. 'What shall we do, brother?' he asked Urceus.

'I'm not leaving her to be raped and murdered,' muttered Urceus. 'Are you?'

Trouble beckoned whatever they did, thought Quintus. But he couldn't stand by and let an unfortunate woman be killed like this – especially as these were Pera's men. 'No.'

'Javelins first?'

'Aye. I'll aim at Fat Lips. You take Squint Eye. We can deal with the others once they're down.'

The ceiling was just high enough for the pair to raise their pila overarm as they would in battle. 'Back away from the girl,' ordered Quintus.

'You want her all for yourselves? Greedy bastards!' said Fat Lips, but his fingers were straying to his sword hilt.

'I reckon we can take these whoresons,' said Squint Eye, leering. Fat Lips sniggered; their companions began to sidle away from the table.

The tension in the room rose several notches, and Quintus readied himself to fight. 'Take another step and my pilum will end up in your chest,' he shouted at Fat Lips. 'My comrade will take your cross-eyed friend, and we can sort out the rest with swords. It shouldn't be too hard, given that none of you fools have shields.'

No one moved for a heartbeat. Two. Three. In the background, the barmaid sobbed. From outside came the murmur of angry voices – the customers who'd been evicted by the legionaries.

Fat Lips glowered, but moved his hand away from his gladius. His companions looked similarly pissed off, but none reached for their weapons, which relieved Quintus. It was one thing to threaten one's own men and entirely another to injure or kill them.

'You're being sensible. Good. I want you to walk past us, one by one, nice and slow. Anyone who does something stupid will get a javelin point in the eye. When you're in the alley, you can piss off.'

Fat Lips' gaze flickered to Squint Eye. 'What about our shields and pila?'

'Do you think we're stupid, you arse-humping *mollis*?' retorted Urceus. 'Come back and get them later.'

With filthy looks, the five legionaries shuffled past the friends. Quintus didn't relax when they'd left the inn. Leaving Urceus to tend to the barmaid, he moved to the door and watched them walk up the alley, talking angrily between themselves and throwing frequent glances over their shoulders. The group of locals watched with evident surprise. Quintus hoped that they spread the news of what he and Urceus had done, that some good came of this.

'Are they gone?' called Urceus.

'I think so. We'd best go too, in case they come back with some of their friends.'

Together they moved the legionaries' shields and javelins. As he left with the last ones, Quintus saw the proprietor, a sallow-faced, middle-aged man, emerge from the shadows behind the bar. 'Lock your door until tomorrow morning at the earliest,' he said. 'If those soldiers come back, I couldn't vouch for your safety.'

The innkeeper nodded. 'Thank you, sir. She's my daughter.'

'It'd be best if she didn't show her face in here for a while. Male servers are less likely to be molested.'

'I understand.'

Quintus turned to go.

'Sir?'

He turned.

'I can never repay you for what you just did, but should you and your comrade ever visit this inn again, the wine will flow all night.'

Urceus smacked his lips, and Quintus grinned. 'One day, we hope to take you up on that.' He beckoned to Urceus, and they ducked out of the door.

'Gods, but her tits are fantastic,' said Urceus the instant that they were outside. 'And as for her—'

'Hades below, do you think of nothing else?' asked Quintus, laughing. 'We could have ended up dead.'

'What better thing to think of then than a body like hers? A man could die happy having seen that.'

'Come on, Priapus! We'd best get back, or Corax will start wondering where we are.' They kept their shields raised as they emerged on to the larger street, but there was no sign of the legionaries. 'Do you think they'll go to Pera?'

'I doubt it. Rats like that go to ground when they're exposed.'

'All the same, it'd be wise to tell Corax,' said Quintus, thinking of the dressing down he'd received after the horse race. 'We want him on our side in case those pieces of shit *do* bend Pera's ear.'

Urceus grimaced. 'Aye, I suppose.'

For all that they had done as Pinarius had ordered, Quintus felt the same reluctance to confess their actions to Corax. Their centurion valued them as good soldiers, but that didn't mean that he would refrain from punishing them if he deemed it appropriate. It was a shame that they hadn't had a quick drink before leaving the inn, he thought. An extra bit of courage would have done no harm.

In the event, Corax did not really punish them. He called them fools: busybodies who couldn't ignore business that wasn't theirs. He also banned the entire maniple from visiting drinking establishments of any kind for the foreseeable future, but he left it at that.

To the friends' relief, Pera did not make an appearance in the two days that followed. Tensions in Enna remained high. Rotten fruit and vegetables were hurled at patrols by assailants hidden on the rooftops. The sewers serving the houses requisitioned for the garrison mysteriously blocked. Much of the grain that had been set aside for the legionaries had to be replaced after unidentified individuals broke into the warehouse where it was stored and spoiled it with a mixture of cheap wine and rancid olive oil. Each morning, building after building had fresh graffiti cursing the

Romans, or depicting them being defeated by the Carthaginians. Deputations of the town's rulers went daily to Pinarius' quarters to make complaints about his men's heavy-handed behaviour and his continued refusal to hand over the keys to the city gates, which they had requested.

Corax told his men that Pinarius had had enough of trying to please Enna's rulers. 'We're not to do anything stupid, like smashing up taverns or killing without reason, but neither are we to take any shit from the inhabitants. Anyone who is caught engaging in criminal acts against the garrison is to be dragged before Pinarius. Suitable punishments will include flogging, amputations and, if necessary, crucifixion.'

Despite this tough stance, the legionaries' morale was affected by the hostile atmosphere. It was hard to live in a place where the normal rules of war did not fully apply, and where everyone wanted them gone. Gossip ran riot between the maniples that Himilco and his army were about to arrive at the gates, that the priests of the Palikoi, twin local gods, had been preaching against them, that the strong winds and heavy rain one night was a sign from Jupiter that they were to be punished.

By the time that he and Urceus came off duty the day after the storm, Quintus was feeling thirsty. The stock of wine he'd had was gone – donated to his comrades to placate them for Corax's ban on visiting taverns. He paced up and down the small room that had been allocated to his contubernium, part of an apartment in a *cenacula*-like building close to Pinarius' headquarters and the agora.

'Sit down, will you?' growled Marius. 'The noise of your damn hobs is giving me a headache.'

Quintus ignored him, and kept walking back and forth. The evening meal was over; they'd washed it down with water from the public fountain. The locals used that themselves, so no one had fouled it, but it wasn't wine. The day had been long and hot, and the inhabitants even more surly than usual. Gods, but what he'd give for a drink!

'What's got into you?' asked Urceus from his bed. Carpenters had been given the task of building bunks and now every contubernium had a set in their room. After months of living in tents, it felt properly luxurious.

'My tongue is hanging out for some wine.'

'Not for some pussy?' asked Mattheus. 'That's what I'd like!'

'I'd like both!' said Marius, and everyone laughed.

'Have some of mine.' Mattheus tapped the small amphora that protruded from beneath his bunk. 'There's still a drop left.'

'Thanks, but I can't,' said Quintus. 'That stuff's like liquid gold, what with the ban.'

'Stop whingeing, then,' advised Marius with a shrug. In some ways, he had taken Wolf's place as the one who wasn't afraid to say what he thought. He was friendlier than Wolf had been, but more dangerous, Quintus had decided. His skill with sword and shield was impressive; Quintus was glad that they were on the same side.

'I'm not whingeing.' Quintus aimed a half-kick at Marius, who had to roll to the far side of his bunk to avoid being hit. 'I'm planning something.'

Marius rolled right back to the near edge, his eyes agleam. 'What kind of something?'

Quintus glanced around and saw that he had the attention of every man in the room. 'It involves wine, as you might have guessed. And an inn — one where we will be welcomed.'

'The only place you'll find a place like that is back in Italy,' declared Mattheus scornfully.

'That's where you're wrong,' said Quintus, deciding that he *was* going to defy Corax's order. He could almost hear the wine at the Harvest Moon calling him.

'Bullshit!' said Mattheus. 'Who in this armpit of a town is going to give us free wine?'

Disbelief radiated from everyone else apart from Urceus, who was grinning. 'The other day . . .' and Quintus launched into a quick explanation of what had happened. There was a uniform rumble of approval when he was done.

'The innkeeper must love you,' said Marius, chuckling. 'We're in for a right session!'

Quintus had known that Corax wasn't around. He, Vitruvius and the optiones were in Pinarius' quarters, attending the daily debriefing on the day's events. The hastati who were guarding the door of the house that Quintus' contubernium was stationed in – two soldiers of their own century – weren't taken in by their story of going for a walk. 'Fresh air, is it?' one had asked, grinning. 'Eight of you, battle ready at this time of night?' Smiling, Quintus had told them to shut their damn mouths and get out of the way. Advising them that the wine, whores or both had better be worth whatever punishment Corax devised for them all, the pair of sentries had stood aside.

It was just after sunset, and the streets were empty apart from an occasional leper or stray dog. Even in small towns, people didn't like to be abroad once the light went from the sky. The seven men that Quintus had taken with him – his entire contubernium – didn't carry torches. It wasn't far to the Harvest Moon, and they didn't want to attract any more attention than they already would with their hobnailed sandals. Quintus heard the rattle of shutters above as they tramped down the main thoroughfare; he felt the unfriendly stares of those who watched from their houses. Sick of the inhabitants' antipathy towards him and his comrades, he ignored the sounds. Let them come if they dislike us that much, he thought fiercely. We're fully armoured, and they'll get a sharp iron welcome from my gladius.

They reached the entrance of the Harvest Moon without incident, however. The door was shut and barred from within. Not a chink of light came from behind its shuttered windows. Undeterred, Quintus hammered on the timbers.

There was no response.

'You've brought us on a fool's errand, Crespo,' said Marius. 'It's shut. There's no one at home, or if there is, he ain't opening for business tonight.'

Quintus banged on the door again.

Nothing.

His comrades stamped unhappily from foot to foot.

'Let us in!' cried Quintus. This time, he used the iron butt spike of his javelin on the door. *THUMP. THUMP. THUMP.* 'Open up, I say!'

'Or we'll burn your tavern to the ground,' said Urceus with a snigger.

The others chuckled, and Quintus was glad that they were his comrades, and were still sober. In different circumstances, especially if their blood was up, they might well be capable of such a thing. He used his javelin butt a second time. *THUMP. THUMP. THUMP.*

At last he heard movement within. Feet shuffled up to the door, stopped just the other side. There was silence for a moment. He's probably terrified, thought Quintus. We might be Pera's men, returned for our revenge. 'You have nothing to fear,' he said in Greek. 'It's the two soldiers who saved your daughter.'

A heartbeat's pause, and then a short laugh. 'You must be thirsty!' Iron grated off iron as the bolt was thrown back, and the door opened a fraction, revealing the innkeeper's face. He gasped at the sight of so many legionaries, and Quintus quickly said, 'It's all right, they're my tent mates. I'm not alone in being thirsty, you see.'

The innkeeper didn't look too happy, but he pulled open the door nonetheless.

Quintus, Urceus and the rest barrelled in, and the door slammed shut behind them. The room – empty of customers – was even more dimly lit than before, but the hastati didn't care. Setting aside their shields and pila, they sat themselves down at a couple of benches near the bar.

'What have you got for us to drink?' cried Marius, slapping his hand on the wooden top.

'Your finest vintage!' added Mattheus, leering.

'After what your friends did, I'm more than happy to give you an amphora of my best wine,' replied the innkeeper.

'Excuse my friends,' said Quintus. 'We'll drink whatever you give us.'

'Only the best for the men who saved my daughter's virtue.' He hurried off behind the bar, and Quintus shot a reproving look at Urceus, who was already waxing lyrical about the girl's attractions.

The wine produced by the innkeeper, whose name was Thersites, was delicious. The hastati raised their cups in appreciation, and he half bowed, clearly pleased. They set to with a vengeance, and before long the small amphora had been drained. Another was brought forth from the back, and it too was of fine quality.

Quintus felt a tinge of guilt. 'We'll beggar him if this keeps up,' he said behind his hand to Urceus.

'No chance! He's been in the trade for years; anyone can see that. The next amphora that comes out, or maybe the one after that, will be the cheap stuff. We won't be able to tell by then, and he knows that.'

Urceus' simple explanation made Quintus feel a little foolish. Even after years spent with ordinary soldiers, his privileged upbringing still showed him up on occasion. He began to watch Thersites like a hawk each time he appeared with fresh wine. Sure enough, the fourth amphora was newer looking than the previous ones. He nudged Urceus. 'It's clean, so it's from the most consumed stock – in other words, the cheapest.'

Urceus gave him a solemn wink. 'It'll do us fine, though, eh?'

'Aye.' Despite his best efforts, Quintus found it impossible to taste the difference between the fresh wine and that which they had drunk up to that point. 'It tastes good to me,' he said ruefully.

Urceus clapped him on the shoulder. 'That's because you're half pissed.'

'True.' He gazed around at their comrades and took in their flushed faces and loud voices. 'We'd best not have too much more, or Corax will string us up by the balls.'

'One more, for the road, and to ask the gods that we leave the shithole they call Enna soon!' declared Urceus, clinking his cup off that of Quintus.

Quintus drank deep, relishing the warm feeling as the wine slid down his throat.

At that point, Thersites emerged with a platter of bread, cheese and olives. The hastati descended on it with eager cries, Quintus among them. Another amphora of wine immediately followed, and he forgot about getting back to their quarters. Neither Urceus nor his comrades spoke up. The occasion was fast becoming one of those all-night affairs, when tomorrow is another day and the only thing that matters is the banter and the next drink.

Late on in the night, Quintus' fuddled gaze chanced upon Thersites. Something made him look again. The innkeeper appeared troubled. Assuming that he and his friends were the cause, he lumbered over to the bar.

'More wine?' Thersites was already reaching for the amphora on the rack behind him.

'I've had enough for the moment. You seem unhappy. Do you wish us to leave?'

'No, no. You can stay as long as you wish.'

The wine had washed away Quintus' inhibitions. 'What is it then?'

Thersites stared at him, as if in assessment, before saying, 'You're a decent man. So is your friend.'

'We try to do the right thing,' he admitted.

'And these men are your friends, so they must be the same.'

'I suppose,' said Quintus.

'The town's leaders tell us that all Romans are bloodthirsty killers, who are incapable of any kindness.'

'Well, that's not true,' replied Quintus, bristling.

'I've never really believed it. Having met you and these others, I now know it to be a lie. You are men, the same as us.' Thersites lowered his voice. 'Nor are the Carthaginians all good, as they would have us believe.'

Quintus suddenly felt very sober. 'They talk of the Carthaginians in that way?'

Thersites' eyes were dark pools of concern. 'Yes. Our leaders want the town to switch allegiances, as so many others have done of recent weeks. Remember the old days, they say, before Rome took Sicily for itself. Things were so much better then. Carthage is a more gentle master.' He gave a bitter laugh. 'As far as I remember, those times were no different to the years before this war began. Powers such as Rome and Carthage care nothing for places such as Enna, as long as the taxes are paid and the grain supplies flow.'

'What do you want, Thersites?'

A long sigh. 'I want peace. Peace, so I don't have to lie awake at night worrying about my two daughters being raped, or my inn being burned down around our ears.' He made a placating gesture. 'I refer not just to Romans. Carthaginian soldiers are more than capable of such things, I know.'

Quintus thought of his family estate, which had had to be abandoned because of Hannibal's incursions into Campania. Thersites was probably unable to leave Enna, as his mother and Aurelia were powerless to return home. The whole of Sicily was in conflict; thousands of innocent people were affected in the same way. 'War is a tidal wave that sweeps everything in its path away,' he said heavily. 'And there is nothing we can do about it other than try not to drown.'

'We can do other things,' ventured Thersites. He hesitated, and Quintus saw the fear in his eyes.

'Speak,' he urged.

'Keeping Enna in Roman hands would avoid a battle within its walls, which is what will happen if the town's leaders get their way. They want the keys to the gate so that they can admit Himilco's troops in the middle of the night. Pinarius is far too clever to hand the keys over, however, and our leaders are talking now of a siege by the Carthaginians, during which we could help them over the ramparts or some such madness. I've heard the stories from other towns where that happened. It wouldn't matter that we were coming over to Carthage. The place would be sacked, and the population murdered.'

'You want to prevent that? Even if it means that Enna remains in Roman hands?'

'I don't care who rules us if things can remain peaceful. If it means that a massacre can be prevented. One day, if you have children, you will understand.'

In his mind's eye, Quintus saw the battlefield at Cannae as they had fled. Most Roman families had lost a son there that terrible day. Feeling old, he nodded. 'I think I already do.'

There was silence for a moment.

'Why are you telling me this, and not Pinarius or another officer?'

Thersites' smile was knowing. 'Every wall here has eyes and ears. I couldn't go within a hundred paces of Pinarius' quarters without being taken for a traitor. Do you trust your commanding officer?'

'With my life.'

'And Pinarius?'

'He's a bit stiff, but he's supposed to be a straight type.'

'I thought that too.' Thersites licked lips that had gone dry. 'If I gave you the names of the main conspirators, could you pass them on to your commander?'

Quintus shot a look at his companions and was relieved that they seemed oblivious to his conversation with Thersites. 'I could, yes.'

'Would he be able to guarantee safety for me and my daughters? I think that the remaining leaders will want to side with Rome, and they can sway the townsmen. Some men may wish me ill if they suspect what I've done, however.'

Quintus swallowed. He couldn't lie. 'I don't know. I'm only an ordinary soldier, but I swear to you that I will do my best to ensure that that happens.'

Another sigh. 'I can ask for no more.'

The loud banter and laughs from behind him died away. Quintus was aware of a pulse beating behind his eyeballs, of the rough wooden counter under his fingertips, of the fear writ large on Thersites' face.

'Simmias and Zenodoros are the two most active voices in Carthage's cause. Along with Ochos.'

'Simmias? The merchant who supplies us with grain?' asked Quintus in disbelief. He had always seemed pleased to deal with the legionaries.

'One and the same.' Thersites began reeling off more names, and Quintus raised a hand to stop him. 'I'm too drunk,' he said. 'You must write them down.' Thersites looked horrified.

'You need not sign the parchment. I'll hand it to my centurion myself,' Quintus promised.

'Ho, innkeeper! More wine!' bellowed Marius.

'Of course!' replied Thersites. In an undertone, he said to Quintus, 'I'll give it to you the next time you go to empty your bladder.'

Already wishing that he hadn't drunk as much – reporting something this momentous to Corax, or more particularly, Pinarius, would not look good when hungover – Quintus made his way back to the table. No one even noticed him return, which suited him. For the moment, it was best that few people knew what he'd just been told.

He set about downing beakers of water in an effort to wash out the wine he'd drunk, and, when his head was a little clearer, and the piece of parchment from Thersites was safely stowed in his leather purse, Quintus began the lengthy process of persuading his comrades to leave the inn. He needed some rest, but he wasn't prepared to leave them behind – apart from Thersites' revelation, he wanted to make sure none tried to have a look at the innkeeper's daughter.

By the time that they eventually returned to their quarters, Quintus was drained, but sleep proved evasive. Shafts of light were coming through the gaps in the shutters when he managed to succumb. It seemed that he'd only been asleep for a moment before the optio was banging on their door and ordering them to get up, if they didn't want their arses kicked back to Syracuse.

Quickly, Quintus told Urceus what Thersites had told him. 'I wasn't dreaming,' he hissed, opening his hand to show his friend the parchment.

'Vulcan's fucking balls,' said Urceus, who looked as bad as Quintus felt. 'You've got to tell Corax.'

'That's what I'm about to do.'

'Fuck it,' growled Urceus. 'That'll be more punishment duty. Rather you than me, though.'

'Thanks,' replied Quintus sourly. He had the presence of mind to stick his head in a bucket of water and don his clean tunic before seeking out Corax. He still felt like shit, but hopefully he didn't look too bad. Hopefully.

The door to the centurion's quarters, an entire apartment on the first floor, was ajar. Through the doorway, Quintus could see Corax sitting at a table, wolfing bread and honey. His servant, a monosyllabic slave, waited upon him. As Quintus was about to knock, Corax's head turned. 'Crespo – is that you?' he barked.

'Yes, sir.' Quintus knocked, feeling foolish.

'Stop loitering outside. Come in.' Corax appraised him as he approached, and Quintus cringed inwardly, wishing again that he had been more temperate the previous night.

He came to a halt a few steps from Corax and saluted. 'Sir.'

There was a short silence, during which Quintus could feel beads of sweat trickling down his forehead. Of course, he had to ignore them, while Corax's eyes traced their complete path.

'You wished to see me?'

'Yes, sir.'

'Strange. You look as if you were on the piss last night.'

'Sir, I, er . . .' Quintus floundered. What was the point lying? he decided. Corax wasn't blind or lacking a sense of smell. 'Yes, sir.'

Corax's lips pressed together for a moment. 'This, despite my orders?'

'Yes, sir. Sorry, sir.'

'You didn't come here to confess what you'd done, though.'

'No, sir.' Quintus proffered the piece of parchment, which he'd been clutching unseen in his right hand.

'What is that?'

'It's a list of names, sir, of those who are plotting to turn the town over to the Carthaginians.'

At this, Corax looked decidedly more interested. 'Where did you get it?'

'From an innkeeper, sir.'

Corax's eyebrow rose – Quintus hoped it wasn't in disbelief – and he said, 'Not the proprietor of whichever hole you were drinking in?'

'Yes, sir.'

'This better be good, Crespo,' warned Corax, his voice hard. 'Explain everything – fast.'

At this stage, Quintus decided that wiping the sweat from his brow made no difference. That done, he related again how he and Urceus had saved Thersites' daughter; how the innkeeper's offer of free wine had been too much to ignore. Recounting how the sentries had let them out with barely a question, he thought that Corax's lips twitched. This was the centurion's only reaction until he had finished the entire tale, however. When he was done, Corax stretched out his hand. 'Give it here.'

Quintus hurriedly obeyed. His stomach churned as Corax read it. If the centurion didn't believe him, his entire contubernium was in for severe punishment. Even if he did, there would be a price to pay.

'Do you believe this *Thersites* character?'

'I do, sir.'

Corax ran a finger along his lips, thinking.

Quintus sweated some more.

After what seemed an eternity, Corax fixed him with his deep-set eyes. 'One thing I've learned over the years, Crespo, is that an honest soldier isn't necessarily the same as one who is good in battle. The reverse also applies. A good fighter isn't guaranteed to be a decent, honest type. For a soldier to be both is a rare thing indeed. Now we both know that you joined the hastati under false pretences, which means that you're a liar.' He paused, waiting to see if Quintus would try to deny the accusation.

Quintus bit his lip, and Corax continued, 'So why should I believe this crazy, wine-fuelled story of yours? Can you imagine Pinarius' reaction if I dragged you before him and this turned out to be a big, steaming pile of bullshit?'

'He wouldn't be happy, sir.'

'Ha! Pinarius does not suffer fools gladly.'

Another silence, during which Quintus felt it important to keep his eyes locked with Corax's.

'What punishment do you think is merited for what you and your idiot tent mates have done?'

'A whipping to start with, sir—'

Corax interrupted before he could continue. 'How many lashes?'

'Twenty at least, sir.'

'Or thirty,' added Corax coldly. 'What else?'

Quintus tried not to think about the degree of pain from that many lashes. 'Latrine duties, probably, sir. Extra sentry duties too. Rations of barley rather than wheat.'

Corax nodded in satisfaction. 'That would be about right.'

Quintus locked his knees, trying to ignore the nausea that was washing up from his protesting stomach. His attempt had failed. He, Urceus and the rest would suffer Corax's punishment, and it was down to the gods how many legionaries would die when the Carthaginians came stealing into the town some dark night in the near future.

'You may be a liar, but you're also no fool. And only a fool would come to me with such a madcap story when the consequences of revealing that he had disobeyed orders were so severe.'

'Sir?'

'I believe you, Crespo.'

'Yes, sir,' said Quintus, feeling even more stupid.

'You're not going to escape punishment, but if the pieces of shit on Thersites' list confirm what he told you, I will look at your case with a more lenient eye. Before we go to Pinarius, though, you're taking me to

Thersites. I want to assess him for myself.' Corax pushed the table away and stood. 'Breastplate,' he said to the slave.

Quintus dived in before his instincts prevented him from doing so. 'Your pardon, sir, but I don't think that's a good idea.'

Corax didn't look pleased, but he waved his slave back. 'Explain.'

'Thersites said that everyone is watching everyone else. If a senior Roman officer goes to Thersites' tavern for no apparent reason, suspicion might fall on him. By the time Pinarius acted, he could be dead.'

'I wouldn't shed too many tears at that,' retorted Corax. 'He's not Roman.'

Quintus rallied his courage. 'No, sir, but I promised to do what I could for him and his family. And his friends.'

'So, you take it upon yourself to disobey orders, and you also bestow Roman citizenship on half of Enna,' said Corax, his nostrils flaring.

Quintus didn't dare to respond. I tried, he thought.

'Put that back on its stand, damn it!' Corax gestured at his slave, who retreated, breastplate still in hand. 'Fetch my old cloak. The one with the hole in the back.' To Quintus, he said archly, 'Satisfied?'

Quintus studied the worn, hooded cloak that the slave had produced from a chest. 'It looks perfect, sir.'

'Good. I suggest that you take me to Thersites with all haste. There's to be a public meeting later this morning. Pinarius has called the bluff of the town's leaders and demanded that every adult male gather in the agora. A vote will be taken as to whether the keys to the town should be handed back to its people. It could be quite a volatile situation, clearly, so the entire garrison is to be present. Pinarius feels certain that those in favour of staying loyal to Rome will win, if only because the majority will be afraid to voice their opinion before our very eyes. Up to this point, I agreed with Pinarius, but what you've told me changes every-thing. They might riot. Even if the whoresons don't, it matters little if they vote for Rome today while planning to open the gates to our enemies the next night.'

Quintus nodded, wishing even more fervently that he had not drunk so much. Despite his efforts, bloodshed of some kind was not just possible that day, but likely.

Chapter XVI

Quintus was still feeling like shit. He was in Pinarius' quarters, with Corax. The good news was that Corax had believed the story that Thersites had told him; the bad that his centurion had dragged him along in case Pinarius wanted to question him. They had arrived in time for a meeting of all six centurions in the garrison. Leaving Quintus in the atrium of the large house that Pinarius had requisitioned, Corax had hurried into the courtyard where the other officers were already talking.

Quintus tried to distract himself from what Pinarius might do to him by wondering who owned the house. It had to have been built by a Roman, or someone who admired Roman building designs. It stood in contrast to most of the larger dwellings in Enna, which were styled in the Greek fashion — with a courtyard just inside the front porch, rather than the central position favoured by Romans. His efforts didn't work for long. The headache that had been threatening all day erupted into a full-blown skull-splitter. And no matter where Quintus stood, the death masks of the owner's ancestors seemed to glower at him from the walls to either side of the lararium. Unsettled by this and shaking from his severe hangover, he offered up a swift prayer to placate them.

'Crespo.'

His wait was over at least. Quintus spun to see Corax framed in the doorway to the tablinum. 'Yes, sir.'

'Pinarius wants to see you.'

'Sir.' Quintus moved to Corax's side. 'Did he believe you, sir?'

'He did, I think, but he wants to hear it from you as well.' He looked at Quintus and sighed. 'Why did you have to get so pissed? You look fucking dreadful.'

'I'm sorry, sir,' said Quintus, flushing.

'Don't be sorry. Be convincing.'

At this stage, Quintus felt wary of asking Corax anything at all, but he had promised Thersites that he would do his best. 'The innkeeper, sir? Will some soldiers be sent to guard him?'

'I might have to send a few of you lot, but yes,' came the gruff reply. 'It will only be until the suspects have been arrested, mind.'

'Thank you, sir.' Let that be enough, prayed Quintus. He couldn't be Thersites' permanent protector.

In the courtyard, they found Pinarius and the others by a pattering fountain. Pinarius was a short, thin man with a perpetually severe expression. Quintus had never seen him this close, but he had a reputation for being a martinet. He knew Vitruvius, and Pera, but not Pera's junior centurion or the centurion who was second-in-command of Pinarius' maniple. They all watched him as he and Corax approached. Vitruvius' was the one face showing any friendliness, and Quintus' stomach tied itself in new knots. His troubles weren't over yet.

They came to a halt before Pinarius. Quintus saluted.

'This is Crespo, the soldier who brought me the news.'

'The dog looks as if he's still pissed,' drawled Pera.

There were a couple of chuckles, but Pinarius didn't join in. 'You certainly look the worse for wear, hastatus.'

'Sir.'

'I am told that you came to your centurion with this news in the full knowledge that you would be severely punished for disobeying his orders. Which were to stay in your quarters, and not to visit any establishments that sold wine.'

'That's right, sir,' said Quintus, meeting Pinarius' gaze.

'Corax also says that a day or two before, you and a comrade prevented some other legionaries from raping the innkeeper's daughter?'

'Yes, sir.'

There was a short pause as Pinarius stared at him. 'Very well. You're either a good liar, or telling the truth. Corax is an officer of the finest quality, and if he vouches for you, that's good enough. Dismissed.'

'Sir.' Quintus saluted again and turned to go.

'Wait outside,' ordered Corax.

'Yes, sir.'

'Are you sure about this, Pinarius?' cried Pera as Quintus walked out. He moved as slowly as he dared in order to catch what was being said.

Pinarius' reaction was instant. 'I am. Are you calling into question Corax's word?'

'Of course not,' said Pera, sounding flustered.

'Then I suggest you keep quiet.'

Hiding his delight at Pera's embarrassment, Quintus made his way to the atrium. If things went to plan from this point, the men on Thersites' list could be seized before the meeting went ahead. Not only would the Carthaginians be prevented from taking the town at night, but a vote by the townsmen in favour of remaining loyal to Rome was far more likely.

His mood dampened a little. Despite this success, he and his tent mates were still to be punished.

And his head felt like a well-beaten piece of iron on the smith's anvil.

In the event, things did not go exactly as Pinarius would have wished. The Carthaginian sympathisers, Simmias and Zenodoros, were nowhere to be found. Ochos was not in his house; neither were most of the rest of the fifteen men on Thersites' list. Urged on by their centurions, small parties of legionaries searched Enna from top to bottom, but their attempts were hampered by their lack of numbers – an attempt not to raise the suspicions of the populace. By the time that the meeting in the agora was due to start, only two suspects had been detained. Both were taken straight to Pinarius' house. This news shot around the town as fast as legionaries could carry it.

Not long after, Corax's maniple started deploying in the agora, which was already more than half full. Most of the glances thrown in their direction were unfriendly, but no one hurled any insults or, worse still, missiles. A continuous stream of men emerged from the little streets that opened on to the space, meaning that no one lingered beside the legionaries. The new arrivals were a cross section of the population. There were labourers and farmers in short, dusty chitons, potters with clay-encrusted hands, butchers in stained aprons, black-faced smiths and well-dressed merchants with supercilious expressions. Old men with sticks limped along, complaining about the pace of their peers. Small boys darted in and out of the crowd, playing catch and annoying their fathers, while their older brothers made derogatory comments.

The press was greatest around the steps up to the temple of Demeter, one of the most important goddesses on Sicily. This shrine, a grand affair with an six-columned frontage, took up the northern face of the agora. Corax's hastati took up position along the southern side of the large, rectangular space, and Vitruvius' soldiers covered more than half of the eastern. Pera's maniple spread out along the western side. It wasn't long before a messenger from Pinarius appeared to the rear of Corax's maniple. He passed on a message quietly, and moved off in search of Pera.

Quintus and his comrades were close enough to hear Corax talking to Vitruvius after the messenger had gone. 'There was only time for a short interrogation, because of this damn gathering. They pleaded ignorance at first, but once one of them had his toes in the kitchen stove, he sang his heart out. The innkeeper was speaking the truth.'

'They were going to let the stinking guggas in at night?'

'So it seems,' replied Corax grimly. A rumble of anger erupted from the hastati, and he did nothing to quell it.

'Where are the rest of the treacherous arse-lovers on the list?'

'Here.' Corax waved a hand at the agora. 'We've got no hope of finding the fuckers.'

The sacred fountain at its centre was now all but obscured by the throng. Boys were clambering up on to statues to get a better view of what was going on. The colonnaded rows of shops and businesses that bordered its two longer sides were no longer visible. Even the steps to the minor temples which lay on the shorter faces, one of which was behind them, were lined with loudly talking men. Yet no one was standing close to the hastati. It was understandable, thought Quintus. Pinarius' deployment was meant to intimidate.

'They'll show their ugly faces when Pinarius starts to speak, surely? We can snatch them that very moment,' Vitruvius declared.

'We'd start a riot. No, we have to play it softly, as Pinarius said. Otherwise, things could get out of hand,' Corax muttered. 'One suspect mentioned that some of their supporters have armed themselves. We'd sort them out if it came to it, but it could be nasty. There are an awful lot more of them than there are of us.'

'What are we to do?' asked Vitruvius.

'Stay calm,' replied Corax. 'Keep our position. Any moment, Pinarius will get here. His soldiers will split up to cover the sections of the east and west sides closest to the temple of Demeter. He will address the townsmen on the issue of who should retain control of the keys to the gate, and then invite its leaders to speak. If they speak for Rome—'

'That won't happen,' hissed Vitruvius.

'True. If they speak against us, we're to do nothing as long as their words are peaceable. We'll let the assembly finish, and seal off all but two streets that lead away from the agora. Pinarius has the suspects with him. One will be placed at each exit point so that they can identify the bastards on the list. We can grab them one by one.'

'And if they say that we *are* the enemy? If the crowd turns on us?'

Every hastatus within earshot craned forward to hear Corax's response.

'If that happens – or if any other treacherous move is made – Pinarius will clench his fist by his waist. In that case, we are to fall on every man present with drawn blade.'

'Very well,' said Vitruvius grimly. 'If it comes to it, we shall do our duty.'

'Hades, I hope it doesn't come to that,' muttered Quintus to Urceus.

'So do I. But if it does, it does. They're not Romans, are they?'

It was shocking but true. The hastati would follow orders – no matter what. So would he. Corax was his superior, and he had sworn to obey him, even if the order was to slay unarmed men. Gods above, let this go off without violence, Quintus prayed, wondering if it had been wise to take Thersites' list to Corax. Yes, it had, he decided, harsh though that judgement was. If he hadn't, countless legionaries, his friends among them, would have had their throats slit in their sleep.

The tramp of studded sandals on paving stones drew everyone's attention. It was Pinarius, arriving at the head of his maniple. Sunlight flashed off his polished helmet and breastplate, and his crimson horsehair crest had been freshly dyed. He looked truly impressive. So did his men. In the midst of the soldiers, Quintus caught a glimpse of a pair of bruised, bloodied faces – the suspects, surely – before their heads were covered with old sacks and they were whisked off to the designated exits. Pinarius spoke a few words to Corax and then, in a clear exercise of intimidation, he marched his legionaries straight across the middle of the agora. The silent crowd parted like a block of wood split by an axe. Pinarius stalked up the steps of Demeter's temple with about twenty men. The rest of his maniple spread out until they met up with Vitruvius' and Pera's troops. All four sides of the agora were now manned by legionaries. The multitude of locals shifted about unhappily.

'We're prisoners in our own town,' one man near Quintus shouted. 'You can't frighten us,' cried another. 'Go back to Rome!'

Quintus wasn't the only one to tense. Corax paced up and down, glaring at the nearest locals. Thirty paces away, Pera snapped an order at his soldiers, who raised their scuta. When Corax saw, a vein bulged in his neck and he hurried over to Pera. There were angry gestures, and heated words, but Pera told his men to ground their shields. Corax returned, looking furious. 'No one makes a move unless I say so. Clear?' he barked.

'Yes, sir,' the hastati replied.

It took a moment before the calmer heads in the crowd quietened the unhappy ones. A troubled silence fell.

Corax and his men were positioned directly opposite where Pinarius was standing. They could see him, but it wasn't yet clear if they'd be able to hear his words.

The blare of a single trumpet pierced the air. It drew all eyes to where Pinarius stood, at the top of the temple steps. 'People of Enna!' he shouted. 'I thank you for answering your leaders' call and coming to this assembly.'

There were plenty of angry mutters. The crowd moved to and fro a little. Men spat on the ground, but that was all. For the moment, thought Quintus uneasily.

'The meeting today was called by the town's leaders,' said Pinarius in reasonable Greek. He raised a hand against the sun. 'If we are to talk, they must be present, but I see none here. Where are they?'

'We are here, Pinarius,' called a voice from the midst of the throng, some way off to Quintus' right. 'And here!' said another. 'I, Ochos, am here.' 'Simmias is present.' 'So too is Zenodoros!'

Half a dozen other names were shouted at Pinarius, who smiled. 'Come and speak with me here, where everyone can see us,' he said, gesturing at the temple steps.

'We'll remain where we are, Pinarius. You're here with your full strength, and with two of our number in custody. Only a fool sticks his head into the lion's mouth.'

Mutters of anger rose from the gathering. Corax moved up and down the ranks, muttering, 'Steady, brothers. Nothing has happened. Steady.' Quintus hoped that Vitruvius and the other centurions were following Corax's example, not Pera's.

'Those men are helping us with our enquiries about the grain that was tampered with,' said Pinarius smoothly.

'Do you expect me to believe that?' retorted Ochos.

'I do. If it hadn't been for this meeting, they would have been already freed. I merely have to finish questioning them,' Pinarius said. 'But we are not here to talk about grain. It's these that brought us here, isn't it?' He held up a bunch of long iron keys.

There was a loud *Aaaaahhhh* from the crowd.

Pinarius was playing a risky game, thought Quintus. The townsmen should be persuaded by his show of force, but it had become apparent that violence wasn't far away.

'I, Simmias of Enna, wish to speak!' cried a man near the sacred fountain.

The crowd subsided.

'Pinarius!'

'I am here.'

'I say to you that we, the people of Enna, entered into alliance with Rome as free men. We were not slaves handed to you for safekeeping. If we request that the town's keys be handed over to us, it is only right that you do so. Loyalty is the strongest bond of an honest ally and the Roman people and Senate will be grateful to us that we remain their friends willingly, and not by compulsion.'

Cheers broke out. Shouts filled the air. 'Simmias is right!' 'He speaks the truth!' 'Give us back the keys!'

Pinarius let the townsmen speak for a few moments before raising his hands. A reluctant calm fell. 'Worthy people of Enna! I was given this command and these keys by the consul Marcellus, the officer who governs Sicily for Rome. It is my duty to defend the town on behalf of the Republic. It is not for me, or for you, to decide what shall be done with the keys. The only person who can make a decision of that gravity is Marcellus. If needs be, a deputation of your leaders should petition him. His camp is not far, and I can promise you that he will receive you with all courtesy.'

'Ha!' cried Simmias. 'I know what kind of welcome we would get.'

'You'd get your arse kicked because of the extortionate prices of your grain!' bellowed a skinny man in a ragged tunic. 'Send an embassy to Marcellus, I say!'

There was a burst of laughter.

'Aye!' cried another ill-fed-looking man. 'Perhaps the consul can set the price of grain at a level that normal people can afford!'

Relief swept through Quintus as he saw many heads nodding. Some men seemed unhappy, but they were in the minority. More and more voices joined in the cry. 'Send an embassy! Send an embassy!'

'Give us the keys!' shouted Simmias, undeterred. His supporters repeated the demand, and the noise in the agora swelled as the opposing sides vied with each other to be heard.

Pinarius had his trumpeter sound a few notes, which forced a silence.

'Let us take a vote,' yelled Pinarius at the top of his voice. 'Those in favour of sending an embassy to Marcellus, raise your right hand!'

Go on, urged Quintus silently. A hand went up near him and he blinked in surprise. It was none other than Thersites. Quintus warmed towards the innkeeper. Despite his concerns for his personal safety, Thersites wanted to cast his vote, to help keep the peace. He was busily talking to those around him, and a moment later, a number of men in his vicinity raised their hands. They were joined by a group to Quintus' right, who were standing in front of Pera and his soldiers. In the following moments, it was as if a wind swept across the agora. Scores more hands went up, and then it was hundreds. Good numbers didn't lift their arms, but they were in the minority.

Quintus let out a gusty sigh. The crisis had been averted. The embassy would go to Marcellus. It would likely never reach him, for Pinarius would detain every man in it whose name had been on Thersites' list, but at least the arrests could be done out of the public eye. In the meantime, those leaders in the town who were well disposed to Rome could be set to work. Some blood might have to be spilled, but it wouldn't be much, and it wouldn't be here. Quintus felt glad. Thersites and his daughters would be safe.

'You're all cowards!' screamed a voice from Quintus' right. A young man, barely out of childhood, pushed his way free of the throng to stand in the space between the townsmen and Pera's position. 'Give us the keys!' he roared at Pera and his hastati. 'Give us the keys!'

'Fucking idiot!' hissed Quintus to Urceus.

The young man fumbled in the leather bag that he was carrying and produced an overripe fig. He cocked his arm and was about to throw it when an older, portly man with a beard stepped forward and grabbed him by the wrist. 'What do you think you're doing?' he demanded in Greek.

'Showing these Roman bastards that we're not all yellow-livered, Father!' He wrenched his arm free and threw the fig, hard. It shot through the air and burst in the face of a hastatus not ten paces from Pera.

Several things happened at once.

Pinarius smiled at the clear majority of men who were voting to send the embassy to Marcellus. The portly man cried out and threw his arms around his son's waist.

'You Greek filth!' shouted Pera, his face purple with rage. Somehow the young man had another fig in his right hand. His father tried to grab his arm again but the second piece of fruit flew straight and true, bursting on Pera's breastplate.

'Give us the keys!' yelled the young man.

Another voice joined in. 'Give us the keys!' Faces in the crowd turned away from Pinarius and towards what was happening behind them.

Pera's face twisted with fury. Stepping out of rank, he drew his sword and pointed it at the father and son. 'Get back! Get back, I say!'

'Move,' urged the father. 'Walk away.'

His son would not listen. 'Give us the keys, you Roman cocksuckers!' he said in poor Latin.

Pera didn't answer. Instead Quintus watched aghast as he strode forward and shoved his gladius deep into the young man's belly. A shocked, gurgling cry rent the air. The father screamed, 'No!' Pera twisted the blade for good measure and, using his left hand, pushed the young man away from him. His victim staggered back a step, moaning and clutching his bloody chiton. He fell to his knees, and then on to his face.

'Curse you! You murdered him!' cried his father, pointing a finger at Pera. 'For throwing a damn fig?'

'Get back!' ordered Pera, advancing.

The portly man retreated a step, but continued to shout accusations, tears streaming down his face.

Another youth darted out of the assembled men and launched a stone at Pera. It clanged off his helmet. With a muffled curse, Pera jumped forward. The portly man got in his way, and with another oath, Pera stabbed him in the chest. Blood gouted everywhere as he tugged free his sword. Without a word, the portly man toppled on top of his son.

A low, baying sound of fury rippled the air. It seemed as if every man in the crowd near Pera turned as one. Those in front of Corax's century did the same.

Pera retreated to the security of his men. 'Close order!' he bawled.

'You heard Centurion Pera!' shouted Corax. 'CLOSE ORDER!'

Shields rattled off one another as the hastati obeyed.

'HOLD!' Corax bellowed, his call clearly aimed at Pera as well.

'Give us the keys! Give us the keys! Give us the keys!' The chanting swelled in volume, until, in the confined space of the agora, it seemed loud as thunder.

Fear clawed at Quintus, and his headache receded before his desire to draw his sword. He could see the same longing in his comrades' faces, but Corax hadn't given the order. Remarkably, nor had Pera. Over the heads of the angry crowd, he could see Pinarius shouting in vain at the locals who were near him.

'Give us the keys!' A youth – a friend of the fig-thrower? – moved to stand by the bodies of father and son. 'The keys, you murdering bastards!' Without warning, he flung a stone at Pera.

Pera ducked behind his shield, and the piece of rock shot over his head and out of sight. Up came Pera like a striking snake. He grabbed a javelin from one of his soldiers and threw. At such close range, he could not miss. The youth went down, skewered through the chest, and the crowd screamed their fury.

'You stupid fool!' said Quintus under his breath.

Three, seven, a dozen stones were thrown, and then it was as if a dam had burst. The air went dark with the number of missiles. The legionaries scarcely needed to hear the order 'RAISE SHIELDS!' Every Roman in sight was being targeted. Vegetables, stones, bits of broken pottery, cracked roof tiles banged and thumped off scuta. Mattheus went down, struck by what had to be a slingshot bullet. Quintus and the rest roared their anger, and Urceus, who was nearest to their friend, began roaring, 'Mattheus! Mattheus!'

There was no answer. Quintus still hoped that Mattheus had only been injured, but when Urceus straightened, he just shook his head bitterly. 'It caved in his forehead. You fuckers!' he roared.

Over the rim of his shield, Quintus also stared across the agora. It's Pera's fault, he wanted to scream. Mattheus is dead, and it's all that bastard's fault! There was no way that Pinarius could have heard him, however. Even if he could, thought Quintus, the outcome would have been the same. Bloodshed was inevitable, and while many innocents would die, part of Quintus was glad. Mattheus was gone, and for that, men had to pay.

Their garrison commander had climbed to the top of the temple steps. His trumpeter stood alongside, his instrument at his lips. A word from Pinarius, and a clarion set of notes issued forth. It was the signal to attack. In the same moment, Pinarius clenched his right fist by his waist and screamed something that was lost in the general uproar.

Corax was ready. 'READY JAVELINS!' His order was being echoed to left and right of their position. 'AIM SHORT. LOOSE!'

The enraged legionaries drew back and threw their pila in a flat trajectory. Quintus did the same. This close, the javelins were deadly. They flew towards the densely packed mass of people, taking little more than a heart-beat to travel fifteen or twenty paces. They made soft thumping sounds as they landed. The townsmen had no armour or shields to protect them; they were cut down in droves. Scarlet flowered on dusty chiton and clean white robes alike as labourers and rich men bled and died together. Wails of pain and anguish rose from the injured and those whose friends or family had been hit.

Some stones and pila were thrown in retaliation, but they were few in number. The townsmen were reeling.

'SECOND JAVELINS, READY. AIM SHORT. LOOSE!' cried Corax.

Another cascade of pila went up; another wave of destruction followed. Old and young men, cripples and whole-bodied, it didn't matter. Whether screaming their defiance at the legionaries or begging for mercy, they were scythed down by the devastating close-range volleys.

Next came the order to draw swords, to stay close, to advance at the walk. Quintus followed the orders as if in a dream. As he had so many times before, he could sense the man to either side of him, could feel the top of his shield touching his chin and the reassuring solidity of his wooden sword hilt in his fist. The knowledge that they were not facing enemy soldiers but civilians was there, floating around his mind, but it was being swamped by fear, the desire to avenge Mattheus, and the will to survive.

'Murderers!'

Quintus hadn't seen the grain merchant Simmias until that point, but he recognised his distinctive voice. Thickset, with muscled, hairy arms, he still looked like the farmer he had been before turning to the more profitable buying and selling of grain. Gone was the friendly mien that Simmias had displayed on every previous occasion that Quintus had seen him. Simmias' face was dark with rage; his tunic was spattered with blood. A cloak had been wound around his left forearm in place of a shield, and in his right hand he clutched a sword. Close behind him came ten or more men, similarly armed. The crowd cheered their arrival, and Simmias levelled his blade at the line of legionaries. 'They're murdering scum, the lot of them!'

An incoherent, rumbling growl of anger left the throats of the nearest townsmen.

'Arm yourselves, men of Enna. Pluck the javelins from the flesh of your brothers,' ordered Simmias. 'KILL THE ROMANS!'

'Forward!' Corax yelled. 'Put the arse-lovers in the mud. All of them! Otherwise they'll do the same to us.'

A disorganised, writhing mass, the mob swept towards Corax's hastati.

Quintus was glad that Simmias had rallied his fellows and led them to the attack. They might be in the confines of a town, but this felt like war. *That* was easier to deal with.

A man in a smith's apron came running straight at Quintus, a pilum clutched in both fists like a harpoon. Quintus braced and met him head-on. The javelin punched through his scutum and skidded off his mail. The smith's momentum carried him forward until he collided with Quintus' shield: so close Quintus could smell the garlic on his breath – and see shock flare in the smith's eyes as he stabbed him in the guts. The blow would have felled most men, but the smith was built like a prize ox. With a roar, he tugged on the javelin so hard that it came free of Quintus' scutum. Time stopped as they stared at each other over its iron rim. Both were panting: the smith with pain, and Quintus with battle fever.

There wasn't time to withdraw his blade, so Quintus twisted it. Viciously, with all his strength. The smith groaned in agony, and his right arm dropped away. Quintus wrenched back his sword and stabbed the smith twice, less deeply this time, one-two. Down he went, screaming like a baby taken off the tit too soon.

Quintus was aware that his comrades to either side were also fighting. Shouts, curses, cries of pain and the sound of iron striking iron rang in his ears. A man wielding an axe replaced the smith, swinging his weapon from on high down at Quintus' head. It would have split Quintus' helmet in two, and with it his skull, but he met the blow with his shield. Pain lanced up his left arm from the massive impact; there was a sound of splintering wood; Quintus ignored both. He looked around the side of his shield and thrust his sword deep into the man's armpit. The axeman was dead – the large blood vessels in his chest sliced to ribbons – before Quintus pulled it free. Mouth agape, pink froth bubbling from his lips, he collapsed on top of the smith. He left the axe buried in Quintus' scutum.

By some small twist of fate, the hastati had pushed forward a few steps. There was no one immediately facing Quintus. Bellowing at his comrades to close up the line, he fell back a little and, having no earth to stick his sword into, used a body. Upright and by his side, he could grab it if needs be, whereas sheathing it could prove fatal. A moment or two of sweating, and he had freed the axe from his scutum. The shield was ruined, but it would suffice until the battle was over.

The slaughter, he corrected himself.

Urceus had just slain Simmias. Most of Simmias' followers had vanished from sight, either slain or injured. The remainder of the townsmen were not warriors. Dismayed, they turned and tried to flee. Except there was nowhere to go, other than the centre of the agora. They were trapped like a shoal of tuna in a fisherman's net. The hastati pursued them with fierce, eager cries. Quintus moved to join them before his heart stopped pounding and reason came back into the equation. There was no avoiding what had to be done now.

Thersites! his conscience shouted. He is here! A modicum of sense returned, yet there was nothing he could do. No way to stop the madness, no way to find Thersites and bring him to safety.

Afterwards, Quintus would recognise the time that followed as his most horrendous experience since joining the army. Among his comrades and the other legionaries, all sanity had been lost. What mattered was to kill, something that they were expert at. In an enclosed space against unarmed victims, their skill was terrible to behold. When it was done, the only living beings would be Romans. Shorn of everyone who could fight, the townsmen shoved and scrabbled to get away from the legionaries' hungry blades. They punched and kicked at one another, trampled the weakest underfoot and called on their gods for help. None of it made any difference. Quintus, his comrades and the rest of the garrison closed in, a lethal cordon of curved wood and sharp metal.

Punched from behind by shields, the townsmen sprawled forward, easy targets to stab in the back. Any that hadn't been mortally injured could be stamped on or run through again as the legionaries pressed on. Those few who turned to face the hastati fared no better. They died pleading, shouting that they were loyal subjects of Rome, that they had wives and children. Pierced through the chest, the belly, the neck; losing arms, legs and sometimes heads. Blood showered the air, misted over the living and slain alike. Soon the legionaries' right arms were red to the elbow, their faces daubed in crimson, their shield designs obscured by a glistening, scarlet coating. At one point, Quintus tried to wriggle the numbed fingers of his sword hand and found he couldn't, thanks to the gluey layer of blood that coated his entire fist. He shrugged and continued killing. His comrades were also beyond noticing their appearance, beyond caring if they had seen. Any person who came within reach of their blades was fair game.

When the slaying in the agora was done, the hastati ran down the nearest streets, yipping like wild dogs. The officers did not stop them; indeed some gave encouraging waves. Quintus was about to follow, his intention to participate as well. Then, at close range, he saw two hastati run a boy of no more than ten through, over and over. The boy shrieked and wailed, twisted and spun in his efforts to get away. All the while, he bled and bled, like a stuck pig. Quintus stopped in his tracks, aghast with horror. Thersites was dead – he had to be by now – but what about his daughters? Quintus' mind began to spin. It was bad enough that the innkeeper had perished. He could not leave Thersites' innocent daughters to their fate as well. Dropping his cracked shield, he ran alone in the direction of the Harvest Moon.

The carnage was spreading fast through Enna. Every street, every alley rang with the sound of doors being kicked in and the inhabitants' screams and pleas for mercy, which were all too often suddenly cut short. Mutilated bodies lay everywhere in the dirt: a slave with a spilled basket of bread and vegetables; an old cripple with a makeshift crutch; a small girl who still clutched a doll in one hand – ordinary people who had been going about their business when death arrived. Quintus saw a matron of his mother's age being pursued from her house by four legionaries. They caught her and ripped off her dress. Then, laughing, they urged her to run naked. When she would not, they slapped her with the flat of their sword blades until she did. Quintus averted his gaze and ran on, praying that the matron had a swift end, though he knew that was not what the legionaries intended for her. A few steps on, new horror confronted him. A woman of about Aurelia's age threw herself from the top of a three-storey building rather than be caught by a group of jeering hastati. After she'd broken her neck on the street below, they leaned out of the window and called down to Quintus: 'You can screw her first!' Nauseous, he didn't answer; instead, he put his head down and began to sprint.

As he reached the Harvest Moon, however, his heart sank. The door was ajar, and from within came the sound of smashing pottery and screaming. Quintus wished that Urceus were with him, but he was alone. Time for a deep breath, a moment of calm. He needed to take great care if he wasn't to end up oozing his lifeblood on to the inn's floor, as so many innocents were bleeding throughout the town. Pillaging soldiers did not much care whom they killed. Watch over me, great Mars, he prayed. With a tight grip on his gladius, he entered.

Only a couple of lamps were burning within. The room appeared empty, but Quintus did not let down his guard. Within a few steps, he came upon one of Thersites' daughters, on her back in front of the bar. Just beyond the slack fingers of one hand lay a rusty hammer. The floor around her was slick with blood. On tiptoe, Quintus approached. The girl was younger than Aurelia. He peered, gagged. Her throat had been cut. At least she had died before her assailants had had time to violate her, he thought.

The same didn't apply to Thersites' other daughter, assuming that it was she who was screaming. The thin, distressing sound was coming from behind the bar. He stepped over the eldest girl's body, feeling sick at what he was about to discover. She wasn't in the first chamber – the storeroom – which was filled with laughing hastati. Some were moving along the racks, smashing the necks off amphorae and sticking their open mouths beneath the tide of wine that flowed as a result. There was far too much for them to swallow; they were soon drenched in it, which seemed to amuse them even more. No one even noticed Quintus. He moved silently on to the second room. From the hanging pots and pans, oven and workbench, it appeared to be the inn's kitchen. At the far end, several more hastati stood over the bare arse of one of their fellows. Underneath him, Quintus could see a girl's legs.

Steeling himself to spill Roman blood, he stole forward, placing his feet down softly so that his hobs didn't give him away.

'You stupid bitch! This for your trouble!' snarled the soldier on the floor. There was a soft, choking sound, such as someone makes when their throat fills with blood, and Quintus knew with a horrible certainty that he had come too late.

'Hey!' cried one of the spectators. 'I hadn't had my turn.'

'You can fuck her now. She's still warm!' With a dirty chuckle, the soldier wiped his dagger on the girl's dress and sheathed it. He got to his feet, oblivious to Quintus' presence behind him.

'It wouldn't be for the first time,' added another hastatus.

Everyone except the thwarted man laughed.

Quintus fought back the bile that had rushed up his gullet. Part of him wondered about falling on the hastati with his blade, but he discounted the notion. Not only would he die here – there were at least ten soldiers in the inn – but it would not bring back Thersites or his unfortunate daughters. Lowering his sword arm, he called out, 'Ho, brothers! What have we here?'

The group turned as one, and their hard faces relaxed a little when they saw one of their own. 'You're not one of Pera's lads, are you?' demanded the hastatus with the dagger.

'No. I'm with Corax.'

'If you've come for pussy, you're too late, comrade.' A snicker. 'But there's plenty of wine in the storeroom yonder. I'd wager that we can spare you a drop, even if you aren't one of ours. What do you say, brothers?'

The other hastati whooped their agreement. 'Wine! Wine!' they shouted. Quintus caught a glimpse of a pathetic, bloody bundle of limbs before he was led away, and his heart wrenched. He could not let his emotions show, however. He stayed for a short time to avoid suspicion, swilling down wine with his new comrades and hoping the memories of what he'd seen that day would be wiped away. More than once, he let some wine spill on to the floor. It looked like an accident, but each time Quintus was pouring a libation to the gods revered by Greek-speakers such as Thersites and his family. Accept their souls into the afterlife, he asked silently, for they were innocent of any crime.

With toasts of eternal friendship that were feigned on his part at least, he left the hastati to their celebration.

New scenes of horror greeted him on the streets, and he was stricken with remorse for what he had done in the agora. Not initially, when the hastati had been attacked, but after that, when the fighting had turned to slaughtering. The situation could have been – should have been – averted. A new purpose gripped Quintus. Corax had to know that it was Pera's action that had pushed the crowd into violence. If it hadn't been for him, he thought with a mixture of fury and sadness, Mattheus, Thersites and his family would not have died. Nor would many hundreds of the town's inhabitants.

He went hunting for his centurion. Corax would have some chance of convincing Pinarius that one of their own was responsible for the rivers of blood that had been shed in Enna that day. What would happen after that, Quintus didn't know, but he wasn't prepared to stand by and do nothing.

His search ended before it had started, in the corpse-filled agora. Corax was on the steps of Demeter's temple, deep in conversation with Pinarius and all of the other centurions. Approaching him in front of both Pera and Pinarius was out of the question, so Quintus first set himself the miserable task of trying to find Thersites. He had only a vague memory of where he'd seen the innkeeper. Other soldiers were pilfering the dead, so he didn't look out of place.

His job was stomach-wrenchingly awful. Some of the men Quintus rolled over were still alive. Drenched in blood, maimed or with loops of shiny gut hanging out, they moaned and wept and begged him for help, or for an end to their suffering. This was something that soldiers did for fallen comrades when necessary, but Quintus could not bring himself to do it here. The savagery of what he and his comrades had done weighed too heavily on his conscience. To send yet more innocents to the afterlife was beyond him. He averted his gaze and moved on.

When he found Thersites, Quintus was relieved that he was already dead. The innkeeper had taken a thrust to the chest, which would have killed him instantly. It was a small blessing, Quintus decided sadly, in that he had not known what had happened to his daughters. He wanted to apologise to Thersites, but the words died in his mouth. It was futile. Thersites was gone.

Preoccupied, he did not see the figure behind him rise from the piles of dead.

'Murdering Roman filth!'

Quintus felt someone grab him by the right shoulder. At the same time, he felt a punching sensation in his lower back. There was a squeal of metal as the rings of his mail were put to the test, and then a blinding pain shot through his entire body. Crying out, Quintus lurched away a step and grabbed the hilt of his sword, tried to turn and face his attacker. A punch to his chin sent him sprawling on to his back, however. Quintus lay helpless as a slightly built man with a flesh wound to his face loomed over him, knife in hand. 'I'll take one of you to Hades with me at least!' He stooped and came up with a gladius. 'Slain by one of your own weapons. That seems fitting.'

Quintus kicked out with his sandals, but the bodies underfoot gave him no purchase. He closed his eyes, resigned himself to death. This was it.

But the killing blow did not fall.

Quintus opened his eyes and was amazed to see his assailant toppling from sight with a pilum buried deep in his chest. He scrambled to his feet and was shocked to find Pera watching him from about twenty paces away.

'I'd imagined that a veteran of your standing would watch his back better,' mocked Pera.

He was right, and Quintus flushed scarlet.

'Are you hurt?'

Quintus put a hand to his lower back and felt beneath his armour. Ignoring the darts of pain, he probed the area with his fingertips. His hand came away a little bloody, but the wound couldn't be that bad. The hole in his mail was too small, so only the tip of the knife had gone through. 'No, sir, I don't think so.' His brush with death had wiped out his deference to Pera's rank, for a moment anyway. 'I thought you would have been pleased to see me dead, sir.'

'For all that you're a piece of shit, you're still a Roman. That's more than can be said for the sewer rat who tried to kill you.' With a look that said things might have been different if it had been he who'd wielded the blade, Pera walked away.

Bewildered by what had happened, Quintus hobbled over to the colon-naded market. There he was pleased to find Urceus, swigging from a skin of wine. His friend helped him to take off his mail shirt. 'Pah!' Urceus exclaimed. 'It's only a scratch. A wash with some acetum and a light dressing will see you right. The blade must have been blunt, or the man wielding it a weakling.'

'He was skinny, that's for sure,' said Quintus, relieved.

'Fortuna smiled on you twice just now,' Urceus pronounced. 'If the knife had gone in there, you'd have bled to death inside or I'm no judge. Then for that cocksucker Pera to save your life too! Well—'

'Here, give me some of that.' Quintus reached out, suddenly very thirsty indeed.

They drank in companionable silence, oblivious to the scene of carnage that lay so close by. The pair were still there some time later when Corax came striding along, with Vitruvius in tow. He slowed up; a tiny grin creased his lips. 'I should have known you two would find some wine without having to stray far! Is it any good?'

'Not too bad, sir,' replied Urceus. Both of them struggled to their feet and tried to salute at the same time. 'Would you like some, sir?' asked Urceus. He glanced at Vitruvius. 'And you, sir?'

Corax held out a hand. 'I'll have a drop. I'm parched.' He and Vitruvius shared what was left in the skin. 'You're right, Jug, it was tasty. Best find yourself some more, eh?'

'There'll still be plenty to be had,' said Vitruvius with a wink.

Quintus knew that a better time for him to say something wouldn't present itself. 'Sir?'

'Yes?'

'About what happened here today.'

Corax's brow furrowed. 'It's clear what went on, isn't it?'

'I'm not so sure, sir. Pinarius wanted a decision on whether to send the embassy or not. Most of the men were voting in favour of that, sir. They were being compliant, not aggressive. A fool threw a fig at Centurion Pera, it's true, but the situation was far from lost at that stage.'

Corax's lips tightened. 'Go on.'

'It was Pera's killing of the fig-thrower that made the mob turn on us, sir. If he hadn't done that, I think the vote would have been carried.' Quintus hesitated before adding, 'The bloodshed could have been avoided, sir.'

Silence fell. Urceus' expression had gone studiously blank. Corax's face was worryingly dark, and Vitruvius appeared equally unhappy. The moments dragged on, and Quintus began to feel uncomfortable.

'If this had come from anyone other than one of my veterans, I would beat the man responsible until he was unconscious. Either that, or throw him off a cliff.' Corax paused and then added, 'Pera just told me how you were jumped by someone who'd been playing dead. You'd have been killed if it hadn't been for him, he said.' A glare. 'Is that right?'

Shit! He hadn't thought that Pera might tell Corax. 'Yes, sir,' he muttered.

'Yet you have informed on him.' Corax's matter-of-fact tone was menacing.

Quintus struggled to meet his gimlet stare. 'Yes, sir.'

'Because it's you, Crespo, I will answer you. I'm not interested in a blow-by-blow account of what went on earlier. Nor is Pinarius, and nor, I suspect, is Consul Marcellus – especially from the likes of *you*. Today, Centurion Pera helped to kill a crowd of rebellious townspeople who would have sold us out to the guggas. That's all.'

Quintus felt foolish, and more than a little scared.

'I *never* want to hear of this again, Crespo.'

'Yes, sir.'

'Piss off out of my sight. You too, Jug.'

Quintus beat a hasty retreat.

'Sometimes I worry for your sanity,' hissed Urceus the moment that they were out of earshot of Corax. 'I hate Pera. Corax probably does too, but to criticise the man in front of him? He was only ever going to defend his own.'

'I know,' said Quintus with a sigh.

'Consider yourself lucky that he was in a good mood. It's time to put your head down and forget about Pera, and what happened here today.'

PART TWO

Chapter XVII

I t was sunset, and on the southern ramparts of Akragas, Hanno and
Aurelia walked hand in hand. The whole city was bathed in the
glorious, golden light of autumn as they wandered eastward along
the wall from the fifth gate, Hanno's officer's uniform keeping the regularly
placed sentries away. The smell of incense from the nearby massive sanctuary to Demeter and Persephone was thick in the air, and the chants of
the devotees within mixed with the cries of the vendors outside, selling
wine, trinkets and autumn fruits.

Ten stadia to the south, fishing boats were putting to sea from the
city's busy port. Nearer to the walls, hundreds of tents belonging to
Himilco's soldiers sprawled to either side of the shrine of Asklepios.
From the edge of the camp, an elephant bugled. A short distance from
Hanno and Aurelia loomed a magnificent temple, a number of which
had been built in a line along the ridge that formed Akragas' southern
limit. But it was the second, the one built in honour of Olympian Zeus,
that drew Hanno's admiring gaze. The city's residents loved to boast
that it was the biggest Doric shrine in existence, but it was a shame, he
reflected, that his people's annexation of Akragas had prevented it from
being finished.

'An obol for your thoughts,' said Aurelia.

He smiled. It had become one of their little phrases. 'Carthage is my
home, and I will always love it. But this place' – he gestured to his left,
from the grid of streets covering the two confluent hills that formed the
city's backbone, then down the slope, over the agora and the grand

bouleuterion, to the temples – 'it's just magnificent. It has stolen my heart.' He smiled down at her. 'As you have.'

Her fingers entwined further with his. 'Don't you think that it's also because we're here?'

'You could be right,' he admitted, grinning.

It had only been a month since Himilco's and Hippocrates' decision to end the year's scrappy, inconclusive campaign and march west to Akragas, once again a major Carthaginian stronghold on the island. It had become a halcyon time for them, so it felt far longer. That didn't mean Hanno had forgotten the Roman ambush on Hippocrates' force, or the days that had followed it. Gathering up more than a dozen survivors, he and Aurelia had headed west, towards the area where Himilco was supposed to be. They'd had to take constant care to avoid enemy patrols. Soon after that, they'd had their first encounter with Carthaginian scouts – what a joyful occasion for Hanno that had been. By that stage, his band of stragglers had swelled to more than fifty. Among them, to his pleasure, had been both Kleitos and Deon, and a few more of his men.

His reunion with Hippocrates had been far less amicable. Hanno had struggled to contain his contempt at Hippocrates' flight from the valley, while Hippocrates' disdain for his very presence had seemed to have grown. Once Hippocrates had established that Himilco spoke passable Greek, he had left Hanno out of their meetings. Hanno had tried speaking directly to Himilco, but it seemed that Hippocrates had earned the Carthaginian general's trust. Hanno's annoyance at being excluded from the two men's meetings had been eased by the knowledge that Aurelia was safe. With the war effectively suspended, Hippocrates had thrown himself into the city's brothels, where, by all accounts, he indulged his taste for the most attractive whores available. He was far too busy to bother with Hanno, or the Roman woman he'd once forced into his bed.

There were other reasons to be cheerful. By way of reward for escaping the ambush, Hippocrates had set him and Kleitos the task of regrouping the survivors into a few full-strength units outside Akragas. Pleasingly, Hanno had also been able to send word to Hannibal on a Phoenician merchant ship. The setback of the ambush on Hippocrates had not prevented him from joining forces with Himilco's vast army, Hanno had written. In the spring, they would smash Marcellus' legions apart.

'You've got to concede that the city is stunning. Rome doesn't even come close,' Hanno said. 'Nowhere in Italy does.'

'And Carthage?' she retorted.

'It's grander, but not as beautiful.'

Her eyes danced with mischief. 'Somewhere that's better than Carthage? How can that be possible?'

'Hmmm.' Hanno tried not to feel annoyed as she laughed, and failed. Aurelia was so much better at accepting perceived criticism of all things Roman than he was of anything to do with Carthage. Not wanting to spoil the mood, he diverted himself by admiring another of his favourite temples, the one dedicated to the goddess Hera. It lay on its own inside the southeast corner of the walls, and was a good spot to sit as it grew dark. Remembering the excellent inn near the third gate, which lay close to Hera's shrine, his good mood returned. They could eat there before returning to their rooms in the quarter that lay a short distance to the north.

Discipline in Akragas was far laxer than it had been in Syracuse, allowing Hanno to spend almost every night with Aurelia. These precious hours were filled with love and laughter. No wonder it felt as if he were on extended leave, he thought with only a trace of guilt. The slow pace of life seemed to be doing Aurelia good too. Her sorrow was still there, but Hanno was finding it harder to spot. He was glad for her. What she had been through – losing three family members in quick succession – was truly horrendous. While her decision to follow him had been rash, he was no longer angry about it: he simply wanted her to experience some happiness. Hanno did his best to add to that, wooing her as he might have done if they had met in more normal circumstances.

'It is a wonderful place,' she said happily. 'I could live here forever.'

'Your Greek is coming along. It won't be long before the locals think you're one of them.'

'Now you're teasing me,' she said, nudging him.

He grinned. 'Doing my best to, anyway.'

They walked on in companionable silence, enjoying the sun's heat on their backs. Hanno's eyes drifted to the lines of smoke rising from the vast camp that filled the flat ground below the walls. Thousands of soldiers there would be preparing their evening meal. Somewhere on the island, he hoped that Quintus would be doing the same. He felt a pang for Mutt and his Libyans, back in Italy, and hoped that they were alive and well. It seemed likely that they were. The summer had seen little action, so the stalemate on the Italian peninsula continued. Hannibal still needed a port large enough to allow reinforcements to flow from his homeland, while the Romans' every effort focused on chipping away at his allies: the cities and towns of southern Italy.

I'm not missing much, Hanno told himself. I'm doing my duty here. If Hippocrates and Himilco don't see fit to use me, what can I do? The excuse – for that's what it felt like – salved his conscience, but Hanno knew that by the time spring came around, he'd be raring for some action. Hannibal was also relying on him. He would try once more to gain Himilco's ear. Aurelia glanced at him and smiled, and his heart twisted. What would happen to her then?

As they sat by the temple to Hera, his worries slipped away. Aurelia had gone inside, promising to return soon. In all likelihood, she was praying about women's matters, but he wondered with a certain joy if it could be about marriage. The notion wasn't so shocking, thought Hanno. Life was short and, in these times, even more uncertain than normal. Either or both of them could be dead before the next year's campaign ended. A devilment took him. He'd ask her when she emerged. Kleitos was the only friend they had in the city, but that didn't matter. Marriage wasn't about having a large wedding feast, but about him and Aurelia, and their love.

Hanno's excitement vanished when Aurelia came out looking sad. How could he have forgotten about her husband Lucius? That she was so near to her brother, yet so far? Again Hanno cursed the war for interfering in his life. In peacetime, it would have been possible to find a merchant ship travelling to Rhegium and to pay its captain to enquire there after the health of a certain Lucius Vibius Melito. It was not so now. Rhegium was in enemy territory. There was absolutely no way of finding out if Lucius had died of his injuries, and Hanno doubted that Aurelia would even consider marriage unless she were certain.

He had asked so many times if she was grieving that it felt intrusive to do so again, so Hanno put an arm around her instead. Without saying where they were going, he guided them to the inn, which was called the Grape and Grain. By the time they reached it, Aurelia had not spoken, but her mood had lifted a little. She seemed happy to go in for a drink. Hanno was thirsty for some of the locally produced wine, which was better than any he'd had in an age. Kleitos had laughed when Hanno had begun praising the stuff to him one night. 'You wouldn't have had reason to know, but the vineyards in the hills around Akragas are renowned,' he'd said. 'They make the best wines in Sicily.'

Now, ordering a large jug of the best vintage in the place, he poured them both a measure.

Looking Aurelia in the eye, he raised his cup. 'To us.'

At last, the smile that made his belly flutter returned. 'To us,' she said.

By the time winter arrived, Hanno and Aurelia's life had settled into a smooth routine. To all intents and purposes, they lived as man and wife. His duties as an army officer kept him busy during the day, allowing her to run their small household. With Elira left behind in Syracuse, Hanno had mentioned buying a slave to do the menial tasks, but Aurelia had rejected the offer out of hand. 'Do you think I'm too grand to peel a vegetable or empty a chamber pot?' she'd asked. Hanno had coloured.

'Perhaps.'

She'd cuffed him then, gently. 'Well, I'm not. I changed Publius' underclothes myself from the first day. You wouldn't believe what comes out of a baby's bottom.' A wistful look had entered her eye, and she'd added, 'I have little enough to do when you're not here. Keeping the place in order gives me a purpose.'

In retrospect, this had seemed obvious to Hanno, and so he began to take more pleasure in the aromatic herbs that Aurelia hung from the walls, the coloured blankets that covered the bed, and from her amusing descriptions of the markets and shops in the city. He was less impressed with some of her attempts at cooking, but had the good sense to smile and tell her that the food was delicious.

When Kleitos came calling late one blustery afternoon, with an offer to take them out to dine, Hanno accepted with alacrity. Too late, he remembered that Aurelia had already begun preparing the evening meal. 'That is, if you would like to as well,' he said to her.

Her lips pursed; she lifted her reddened hands from a bowl of muddied vegetables. 'I'm nearly finished cleaning these.'

'They can wait until tomorrow, surely?' Kleitos darted to her side and kissed her palms. 'Get yourself clean, and let someone else do the hard work. Consider it a little repayment from me to you both, for being such good company.'

Hanno threw Aurelia a meaningful glance. He'd told her often about how hard Kleitos was finding life in Akragas. At first, it had been because there were few Syracusans of the same rank left among Hippocrates' men, and the local commanders and Himilco's officers were quite clannish. Then the news of the massacre at Enna had reached the city. By most accounts, fewer than a hundred of its inhabitants had survived. Among them, no doubt, had been Kleitos' lover. Kleitos had since been plunged into a spiral of impotent anger and overwhelming grief. His main way of dealing with it had been, and still was, to consume vast amounts of wine. He'd poured his heart out to Hanno during an all-nighter, but that had not alleviated his sorrow. This evening might be another chance for the poor bastard to unburden himself a little, thought Hanno.

Aurelia understood. She pretended to frown, before smiling. 'You've won me over, Kleitos.'

He peered at her handiwork. 'And saved you from the joys of preparing a somewhat mouldy cabbage and some extra-muddy carrots for the pot.'

Everyone laughed.

'Where are you taking us?' asked Hanno as he helped Aurelia don her heavy woollen cloak.

'A place near the sanctuary to Demeter and Persephone, called the Ox and Plough. It's an inn that I've not tried before, but its spit-roast lamb is reputed to be the best in Akragas.'

'And the wine?' Old habit made Hanno strap a dagger on to his belt. Kleitos was also wearing one and he'd placed a small cudgel by the door upon entering. Akragas was a friendly city, but after dark it was much the same as anywhere else. 'Is it any good?'

'Never fear, my friend. Its cellar is also respected.'

Hanno threw on his own cloak, a green hooded affair that he'd bought as the poor weather drew in. 'Lead on, then!'

Aurelia wasn't so eager. 'Is there nowhere closer?'

'Are you worried about *kleptai*?' Kleitos enquired. He saw her blank look. 'Thieves.'

'Well, yes. The longer we have to walk, the more risk that we meet some, especially on the way back.'

Hanno rummaged beneath their bed and came up holding the stout staff he'd found when they had moved in. 'I'll take this as well. Happy?'

She nodded reluctantly.

Kleitos' teeth flashed as he picked up his cudgel. 'I'd like to see the kleptai who'd take me *and* Hanno on!' Aurelia looked less than impressed, and he added, 'The Lenaia festival is also being held at the moment, so you have little to fear. The kleptai are the same as the rest of us, too busy getting pissed to think about much else.'

'I haven't heard of the Lenaia,' Aurelia said.

'It's held at the temple of Dionysos, and is celebrated by all married women. The whores—' Kleitos looked embarrassed. 'My apologies. I should have said *hetairai*. Courtesans. They are involved too.'

'What do the women get up to?' There was a mischievous glint to Aurelia's expression and Hanno hid his amusement. She *did* know something about the Lenaia.

Kleitos coughed. 'The proceedings start with a procession led by various priests, which is followed by the sacrifice of a goat. Some say that the women tear it to pieces, although I've never believed that myself. Maybe in the past, but not now.'

'And after that?'

'I couldn't really say.'

Hanno grinned. He'd never seen Kleitos so discomfited.

Aurelia giggled. 'Are you embarrassed, Kleitos?'

'A little.' He threw a glance at Hanno. 'Damn, but you picked a spirited one, didn't you?'

'I wouldn't have her any other way,' replied Hanno, smiling. Nonetheless, he was relieved when Aurelia gave up on her interrogation. According to his soldiers, who were congregating in inns near the temple complex, there was far more to the Lenaia. After the women had finished drinking and celebrating, men would be allowed into the sanctuary, whereupon priests and priestesses supervised an all-night orgy. It was one thing to consider that he, Hanno, might partake (if Aurelia hadn't been part of his life), but the notion that she might also set a jealous fire in his blood.

The rain and wind that they encountered on their journey put paid to any further conversation about the Lenaia, or anything else. If it continued, Hanno reflected, it would be further protection from any ill fortune befalling them on the way home. His lanolin-soaked cloak kept out the worst of the water, but he was still glad to reach the inn. 'This lamb had better be worth it,' he grumbled.

'I'm paying, so what do you care?' retorted Kleitos.

A quartet of muscled, gormless-looking men flanked the entrance. The lead one did his impression of a smile, which would have terrified most children, but told the three that they were being allowed in.

Kleitos held open the door, releasing a cacophony of noise and a blast of warm, fuggy air. 'Get your arse inside and stop complaining. Find us a table.'

As Hanno entered, he slipped his free hand under his cloak to the hilt of his dagger. Old habits die hard, he thought, scanning the packed room. There were casual glances from the nearest customers, but no one else seemed interested, which was reassuring. The patrons were a mixture of well-to-do types, from local merchants to officers from the garrison, Hippocrates' forces and Himilco's army. There were some women present, although they looked to be whores. When Hanno spotted two men leaving a small table by the left wall, not too near the bar, he made a beeline for it. Kleitos and Aurelia arrived a moment later. 'Sit here,' he said to her, indicating the single stool. 'Kleitos and I will take the bench against the wall.'

'I won't be able to see what's going on,' she complained.

'Maybe so, but we will. And fewer people will notice you.' Hanno had no need to explain further. Despite the peaceful atmosphere, the mix of customers was a recipe for potential violence.

'Relax,' said Kleitos, slapping his knee. 'Every man here is likely to have his mind set on one thing only. The Lenaia.'

Hanno could see that Aurelia was on the point of quizzing Kleitos again. 'Let's get some wine in,' he said loudly. Alert to danger, he scrutinised the room again.

Most customers appeared to be listening to a group of musicians with lyres and flutes, who had arrived accompanied by a singer with a reasonable voice. Others were eyeing a pair of heavily made-up whores who were working the crowd, batting away men's roaming hands and murmuring promises in their ears. Relaxing a little, Hanno caught the eye of a barmaid.

The wine that she brought soon after was excellent. Hanno began to enjoy himself. The company was convivial, the nearby fire's heat relaxing. Even Aurelia consumed more than normal. Kleitos drank as if he were dying of thirst, downing cup after cup of wine. Two more jugs of wine were ordered, and an hour or more had passed before they got around to ordering some of the famed roast lamb. A massive plate of it finally arrived, swimming in juices, and bordered by hunks of fresh, flat bread. They devoured it in complete silence, like small children who've unexpectedly been given a whole pastry.

'Gods, but that was tasty. This place's reputation is well deserved,' said Hanno. 'Well done, Kleitos.'

'It was good, eh?' Wiping his lips, Kleitos burped. His eyes shot to Aurelia's. 'My pardon.'

'Stop worrying about me,' she ordered. 'I grew up listening to my brother fart and belch at every opportunity.'

Kleitos grinned. 'If you hadn't spoken for Aurelia, my friend—'

'I'm a lucky man,' said Hanno, moving to kneel beside Aurelia.

'You're not the only one who's lucky,' she replied, leaning her head on his shoulder.

Kleitos' eyes grew sad.

'You will find another woman,' said Aurelia gently. 'It's obvious from a mile away that you're a decent, good man.'

'Maybe, one day.' Kleitos poured himself more wine. He raised the overflowing cup. 'But for now, my lover is this.'

An awkward silence followed; Hanno and Aurelia waited to see if Kleitos wanted to talk further, but he didn't.

'If the truth be told, I'm ready for bed.' Hanno stifled a yawn and glanced at Aurelia, who nodded. 'I'm no longer in your league when it comes to drinking, Kleitos.'

'Who said you ever were?' retorted Kleitos, but with an affectionate grin.

'That sounds like a challenge, yet it's one I'll have to answer another time.'

'If you're sure?'

'I am.'

'I'll walk back with you.'

'Don't you want to stay on for a while?'

'Aye. I'll return when I've seen you to your door.'

'The Lenaia is calling him!' said Aurelia with a wink.

'Maybe it is,' Kleitos admitted, the wine having banished his earlier embarrassment. 'These type of events don't come around too often, especially during a war. A single man must make the most of his opportunities, eh?'

Aurelia got to her feet. 'Come on. We mustn't delay Kleitos.'

Chuckling, Hanno led the way towards the door. The others followed, but Hanno didn't notice that after a few steps, Kleitos had stopped to talk with an officer he knew. Aurelia's shocked gasp also took him by surprise. 'Don't touch me!' she cried in Greek.

'I'll do as I damn well please,' said a man's voice. 'You're good-looking for a whore, I have to say. Why don't you and I go somewhere more private?'

Hanno spun, taking in Aurelia's outraged face and, over her shoulder, a pox-scarred local soldier in a wine-spattered tunic whose hand still rested somewhere on her. In two steps, he had moved around Aurelia to stand chest to chest with her assailant, who looked none too happy.

'What's your problem?' the soldier snarled.

'She's no whore, *and* she's with me,' growled Hanno. 'Piss off.'

Pox Face's lip curled. 'I think she'd prefer my company.'

'Come away, Hanno. Leave it.'

He caught the warning tone in Aurelia's voice; his eyes flickered to a nearby table. Pox Face had three friends, all of whom were watching proceedings with an intense, predatory interest. *Where the fuck is Kleitos?* Finally, he saw him, deep in conversation about fifteen paces away. Hanno cursed inside. If it came to a fight, that distance was as far as the moon. He decided that diplomacy was a better route to take. 'She's my wife, friend.'

'You're full of shit. No one takes their wife into a place like this during the Lenaia.' He leered. 'Unless you're planning to take her to the orgy afterwards!'

'Why don't we get started now?' asked one of his friends, standing up. Pox Face and the others laughed.

Hanno's fingers tightened on his cudgel, which was down by his side. If he brought it up quickly, he could down Pox Face with one blow. He'd probably take the first of his friends too, but only the gods knew what would happen when the last two reached him. Plenty of the customers were armed; they could well be too.

'Let's keep things friendly, eh?' Kleitos' voice had never been more welcome to Hanno's ears. His friend loomed behind the soldier who'd stood up; he pressed the tip of his knife into side of the man's neck. 'You can do what you like with the ladies at the sanctuary, but as you've been told, this one is spoken for.'

Pox Face's head turned; he saw Kleitos. His gaze wandered to his other friends.

Hanno seized his chance. Drawing his dagger, he nudged it against Pox Face's belly. The prick brought Pox Face's attention – fearful now – back to him at once. 'There's no need for trouble,' he said softly. 'We were just leaving. Sit back down and have a drink with your comrades, and we can forget that this ever happened.'

Pox Face wasn't without balls. 'And if I don't?'

'I'll bury this to the hilt in your guts. My friend will cut your mate's throat. After that, we'll sort out the others. Do as you wish. It's your choice.'

Pox Face studied him, as if memorising his features. Then, breathing heavily through his nose, he took a step backwards. 'I need a drink,' he announced.

A wave of relief washed over Hanno. Kleitos was a hard man; he was no slouch either, but fights in places like this were always risky. It would have taken little for a mass brawl to start, and with drink on board, men grew vicious. Sliding a knife between someone's ribs and slipping off into the confusion was easily done in such a crowded space.

Kleitos released his man, and joined Hanno. Casting warning looks at the soldiers, they headed for the door with Aurelia between them.

'Your woman's no Sicilian, is she?'

The question made Hanno turn. 'What's it to you?' he demanded.

'She's not dark-skinned enough to be a Carthaginian either, like you,' said Pox Face knowingly. 'Where's she from? I want to be able to ask for one like her in the whorehouse.'

'Go fuck yourself!'

The festival of Lenaia departed as quickly as it had arrived, although that didn't stop Kleitos from telling Hanno about it for days afterwards. It seemed that he'd had the time of his life, with two women simultaneously, one a priestess and the other a local noblewoman. Hanno wasn't sure he believed Kleitos, but it made a good story. Moreover, it seemed to have lifted Kleitos' mood.

In the weeks and months that followed, life inside the city returned to its peaceful ways. Lengthening days, buds on tree branches and warmer weather announced the arrival of spring. Hanno was glad to see the back of winter; after months of relative inactivity, he was chafing to get out of the city. Yet the knowledge that a new campaigning season would soon begin was not altogether welcome. Much of the time, it sat like a lead weight in his belly. If he and Aurelia weren't to be parted for months on end, taking her with him was the only option, but to do so would expose her to all kinds of danger. It had been pure luck that she'd escaped harm among the camp followers accompanying Hippocrates' patrol. In a vain hope that the issue would go away, he avoided mentioning it. Aurelia did not bring it up either, but it was clear from her ill humour that the prospect was also affecting her adversely. Ten days passed in this unhappy fashion, with neither caring to address the burning issue.

Matters came to a head one afternoon, but not as either of them might have expected. Hanno had been out since before dawn, drilling his soldiers, but he'd returned earlier than his new norm. Aurelia wasn't in their rooms; he assumed she was out shopping for the evening's meal. She still hadn't returned when he'd come back from a quick trip to the public baths. Unconcerned, for she had been befriended by a couple of women neighbours, he lay down on the bed for a short rest. Soon, he'd drifted off.

He was dragged from the depths of an unpleasant dream by the sound of sobbing. Aurelia was standing inside the door that led to the landing, which in turn gave on to the stairs to the street. He was at her side in an instant. She fell into his arms, weeping. 'Everything will be all right, my love,' he murmured, sure that her upset was to do with the upcoming campaign. 'I've been thinking. I'll buy a male slave, a strapping type who can fight. He'll travel with you, be your protector when I can't be with you.'

Her sobbing eased. She looked up, her tear-stained face full of confusion. 'That's not why I'm upset.'

'Oh,' said Hanno, feeling worried and a little foolish. 'What is it then?'

'It was someone on the street, just now. Do you remember that soldier who accosted me that time in the Ox and Plough? The one—'

'Yes, yes, I remember the cocksucker.' *Pox Face. He called you a whore.* 'You've seen him again?'

'By chance, yes. I nearly walked into him as I came out of the baker's down the street. He recognised me at once.'

Hanno felt a white-hot rage pulse behind his eyes. 'Did he touch you?'

'He tried mauling me, but he seemed a little drunk. I managed to slap him off.'

'The goat-fucking whoreson. I'll teach him a lesson he'll never forget.' Hanno scooped up his cudgel. As an extra precaution, he strapped on a belt and dagger.

'Hanno.'

Her sombre tone refocused his attention. 'Yes?'

'I shouted at him, and he realised from my accent that I was a Roman.

Then h-he . . .' She hesitated for an instant. '. . . mentioned something about his commander recently having drinks with Hippocrates, who was bemoaning the loss of a female slave back in Syracuse. A Roman woman. "I thought of you when I heard it," he said, smirking. "The whole thing's probably a coincidence, but it's worth carting you before Hippocrates to see if you're his missing piece of meat."'

'Did he see you enter the house?'

'Yes. I couldn't stop him from following me. I'm sorry, I was frightened.' She began to cry again.

'It's all right.' Despite his reassuring words, Hanno had broken out in a cold sweat. This changed everything. A beating was no longer sufficient. 'Was he on his own?'

'I think so.'

That was some consolation at least. 'Stay here. Bolt the door after me, and don't open it to anyone but me or Kleitos.'

'What are you going to do?' she asked, her voice trembling.

'Sort it out,' Hanno replied grimly. He went down the stairs two at a time, pushing past an errand boy, who dropped his basket of vegetables. Caution overtook Hanno at the entrance, and he peered out from the safety of a doorjamb. There was no one standing opposite, and his worry soared. *Let him still be close by, please.* The only people he could see to the left, however, were a couple of housewives chatting outside the baker's. To the right, a builder and his apprentice were unloading a small cart full of bricks. Pox Face had vanished. The first trace of panic rippled in Hanno's chest. If the soldier managed to speak with Hippocrates—

He quelled the thought, taking a moment to deliberate. Would Pox Face continue drinking, perhaps in the company of his fellows, or would he want to find out immediately if his discovery would reap any reward? Or would he do something altogether different, such as find a brothel? His heart battered the inside of his ribcage as he vacillated. Baal Saphon, help me, please, he prayed. Guide me.

When the answer came out of nowhere, it was so simple that he laughed out loud. He'd head for Hippocrates' residence, which lay about five stadia away. If Pox Face was going in that direction, Hanno would soon catch him up. If he had sought out his comrades and more wine, however, there'd be a lag period that would grant Hanno the time to return from Hippocrates' house and glance inside every hostelry for half a dozen streets around.

That was the plan, anyway.

He set off at a brisk pace, fighting his urge to run. It would be stupid to squander the only opportunity to silence Pox Face because his sandals' iron hobs had given him away. There was no question of intimidating his quarry. To be sure Hippocrates heard nothing, he had to murder him. At any other time, Hanno would have avoided slaying someone who was in effect one of his own. With his and Aurelia's survival at stake, he didn't give it a second thought.

At each alley or side street, Hanno slowed long enough to look for anyone with Pox Face's slight build. On one occasion, he followed a man thirty paces into a narrow lane to find that he had wasted his time. Hoping that the delay wouldn't cost him dearly, he ran for a bit to regain the ground he'd lost. Eventually, Hippocrates' house, a grand affair lent to him by one of the city's leaders, drew near. Hanno had passed scores of people, male, female, young, old, rich and poor, without as much as a sign of Pox Face. His initial optimism began to fade, but he rallied his courage. Maybe Pox Face *had* gone into a tavern to boast about whom he'd seen?

It was worth going right to Hippocrates' gate, Hanno decided. If Pox Face had reached the entrance, he could still be there. A lowly soldier would not be admitted without some kind of delay. There might be a chance to distract him, to force him into an alleyway.

The junction with the street upon which Hippocrates' residence was situated was no more than a hundred paces away when Hanno spotted a slight figure in a military tunic ahead of him. His mouth went dry, and he began to walk faster, stealing through the other passers-by to within a dozen steps of the man. Frustration filled him. Even at this short distance, he couldn't be sure from behind that it was Pox Face. Hanno ventured closer, his nerves taut as wire, wondering if he should act. But what if he killed the wrong man?

The gods smiled on him then. A woman laughed from a first-floor balcony, and his quarry's head turned, looking for the sound's source. In the process, he revealed his cheek, covered in characteristic pockmarks. Hanno exulted, but he had to act quickly – the junction was less than fifty paces away. His eyes darted left and right, spotted an alley that ran between a derelict building and a block of apartments. He had no idea if it would be empty, but he'd run out of time. It would have to do.

Drawing his dagger and holding it unobtrusively by his side, he ran forward. Too late, Pox Face heard Hanno's footsteps. His face registered first alarm, then recognition of Hanno, and last of all pure fear. He didn't make a sound, though, because Hanno had an iron grip on his left shoulder and a blade jammed up against his liver. 'Call for help, and you're dead,' Hanno muttered. 'Disobey me, and you're dead. Understand?'

Pox Face nodded.

'Left. Into the alley.' They'd drawn level with its mouth.

Pox Face hesitated, and Hanno jabbed the dagger's tip into his flesh. 'Move. I just want to talk to you.'

In the depths of terror, men clutch at the shortest of straws. Pox Face ducked inside the darkened space, which was no more than four paces wide. Broken pottery crunched underfoot. The air was fetid, laced with the smell of human piss and shit, and the rotten food that had been flung from above. Hanno glanced up and was glad to see none of the apartments' residents framed in the windows. He stopped Pox Face fifteen paces in. 'That's far enough.'

'Don't kill me, please.' Pox Face turned his head a little to try and catch Hanno's eye. 'Please.'

Hanno had been about to use his dagger, but at such close range, he'd cover himself in blood. That wouldn't do. He had to be able to emerge from the alley and walk away without raising suspicion. 'Shut up.' *Keep him thinking that he might live.* 'Where were you going?'

'Nowhere. I—'

Pox Face didn't get a chance to continue his lie. Releasing his grip on the other's shoulder, Hanno threw his left arm around Pox Face's neck and squeezed as hard as he could. Pox Face made a horrible, choking sound and fought back like a man possessed. He tried kicking backwards, smacking Hanno painfully on the knee a couple of times. His hands reached back, pulling at Hanno's hair, his ears, his arm. Tightening his grip, Hanno buried his face in Pox Face's smelly tunic to avoid getting a finger in the eye. All the while, he kept the knife ready as a last resort.

For a small man, Pox Face possessed considerable strength. Hanno had lost a few clumps of hair and had a bleeding ear before his opponent's struggling weakened. At last, though, his arms fell to his sides. He went limp in Hanno's grasp. Suddenly worried that there might be witnesses, Hanno glanced at the alley's mouth. There was no one there. Dropping his dagger, he threw Pox Face to the ground and rolled him over. His victim's eyes flickered and opened. Hanno met his gaze as he placed his hands around Pox Face's neck and began to choke him again. Pox Face's hands came up and pawed ineffectually at him.

'Thought that you'd sell out my woman, did you?' Hanno hissed, digging his thumbs right into Pox Face's Adam's apple. 'You piece of filth!'

He had killed many men, but never by strangling. It wasn't pleasant, but Pox Face *had* to die silently. Hanno watched, unmoved, as the other's face suffused with blood, as his engorged tongue poked out from between his lips. Pox Face's reddened eyeballs bulged from their sockets. They stared at Hanno with a mad, pleading intensity. 'Rot in hell,' he grated, digging in with his thumbs. There was a low *crunch* as the cartilage in Pox Face's throat gave way. His tongue retracted a little into his mouth, and the light went from his eyes. Hanno didn't let up. He didn't take his hands away until there had been no movement from his victim for another twenty heartbeats. Carefully, he felt for a pulse in Pox Face's purpled neck, and again over his heart. Nothing. Hanno let out a long, slow breath. He had done it.

The danger wasn't over, however. Noises from the street reminded him that there were people very close by. Replacing his dagger in its sheath, he brushed back his hair, dabbed at his bloody ear, palmed the sweat from his face. Hanno waited until he was stepping into the street before adjusting his tunic in the manner of a man who has been emptying his bladder. A carpenter crouched over a half-sawn plank looked up, and then returned to his work. No one else appeared to notice. With a little luck, thought Hanno, Pox Face's body wouldn't be found for a few days. By then, the rats would have been at him; it would be a miracle if he could even be identified. Hippocrates would remain unaware of Aurelia's presence in the city.

Hanno's step was light as he strode down the street, but scarcely thirty paces later, a familiar voice cried, 'Ho! Is that my Carthaginian officer I see?'

Hanno felt sick. *Of all the bad luck.* He turned and saluted. 'It is I, sir.'

Hippocrates drew near, with several of his cavalry officers close behind. Their breastplates glistened; their helmets and scabbards had been polished. They were going somewhere important. 'What are you doing here?' Hippocrates gave him a disapproving glance. 'And in such a state? You're filthy – and your ear's bleeding.'

Hanno ignored the curling lips of the officers at Hippocrates' back. 'I was just taking a stroll, sir. I wasn't watching where I was going. Tripped up, and landed on my head in the dirt.' He gave silent thanks as Hippocrates all but ignored his reply. Evidently, the general hadn't seen him until that very moment, had no idea of what he'd been up to.

'Walk with me,' Hippocrates ordered. 'I was going to summon you later.'

'Very good, sir.' Hanno looked around for the carpenter, the only person to witness him leaving the alley. To his immense relief, the man had vanished. Where, it didn't matter.

'The year's campaign is about to start.'

'Yes, sir. I'm looking forward to it.'

'As I'd expect,' came the sharp retort. 'Recent intelligence suggests that the Roman legions encamped around Syracuse won't be moving any time soon. Himilco and I intend to give them a nasty surprise.'

'That sounds good, sir!' Part of Hanno was delighted, part dismayed. He tried again not to worry about Aurelia.

Hippocrates' expression grew spiteful. 'Sadly, you won't be part of the attack.'

'I don't understand, sir,' said Hanno, fighting a sudden feeling of dread.

'My brother Epicydes must know of our plan, so that he can launch a simultaneous assault on the enemy. You will carry word to him inside the city.'

Now, Hanno struggled to conceal his pleasure. Getting through the Roman lines would not be without danger, but if he could take Aurelia with him, this would be a way to remove her from the twin dangers of being a camp follower, and having her identity revealed for a second time. It was also a chance to get away from Hippocrates, and if he could send word, Hannibal would be pleased to learn of this development.

'Have you nothing to say?'

'As ever, I will follow your orders to the last detail, sir,' replied Hanno stolidly, praying that in his message Hippocrates wouldn't try to poison Epicydes' mind towards him.

Hippocrates looked disappointed. 'Entering Syracuse will prove risky,' he warned. 'The blockade is much tighter than when we broke out. Epicydes *must* receive my letter, so I will send a number of messengers. One of you will make it,' he added with a touch more vitriol.

'At least one of us, sir,' said Hanno, giving thanks to the gods.

And if I have anything to do with it, he thought, two will.

Chapter XVIII

Quintus was pacing. The section of fortification that he and his tent mates had to man measured approximately eight hundred paces. The hastati marched in four pairs, and each set had a quarter of the distance to cover. Two hundred paces, six stops. At each, a pause to scrutinise the ground that separated Roman-held terrain from the walls of Syracuse. Quintus and his comrades had been patrolling the same part of the rampart since returning from Enna the previous summer. They'd tramped up and down for the whole winter. Now, in early spring, all of them knew it like the back of their hands.

Syracuse lay half a mile away, which meant safety from even the most powerful of Archimedes' catapults. Before the siege, the no man's land had been farmed, but the inhabitants had long since fled or been killed. Their grain had been reaped the previous autumn by the legionaries. No one had tilled the soil after that, or planted new crops, not on such dangerous territory. The harsh winter weather had rotted the stubble into the ground whence it came, leaving only mud.

It was a pity that there would be no wheat to harvest in the summer, Quintus mused, but the lack of vegetation made the sentry's job easy. Movement of any kind could be spotted at once. Not that the Syracusans ever ventured beyond the confines of their city. There hadn't been an enemy patrol sighted in this area since the previous autumn. With their defences secure, the Syracusans had no need to assault the Roman fortifications. It was far wiser to stay behind the safety of their massive walls, Quintus thought sourly, warmed no doubt by the fires in the regular towers that decorated the parapets. There had been no Roman attacks either, since that horrendous first day, almost a year previously. Instead Marcellus had tightened the blockade around Syracuse as much as possible. Frustratingly, that didn't stop the Carthaginians from running in regular supply convoys. In its current form, the siege would not end soon.

The wind whistled in from the north and Quintus hunched his shoulders. Yet again, he cursed the feathers on his helmet that prevented him from lifting up the hood of his cloak. Having a warm head wasn't worth the risk of taking the helmet off. If an officer saw him, severe punishment would follow. Wearing two woollen neck cloths, one overlapping the other, was the best he could do.

'Cold?' asked Urceus.

'Of course. You must be too!'

'Not at all.'

Quintus aimed a kick at Urceus, which he avoided by walking away. They played out the same types of routine every day. It helped to alleviate their boredom.

'How long left, d'you think?' asked Urceus.

Quintus aimed a look at the sun, which was nearing the horizon. 'Not long.'

'That's what I thought, thank the gods. Back to the tent. Warm blankets. A fire. Best of all, it's not my bloody night to cook!'

'Ha! You've forgotten whose turn it is, though.'

Urceus scowled. 'Not Marius?'

'How could you not remember that?' asked Quintus, laughing.

'Fuck. Burned bread. Raw meat, and boiled vegetables still covered in mud. I'll be lucky to escape a dose of the shits.'

'You could always offer to cook for him.'

'No bloody way!' retorted Urceus. 'I'll take my chances. Maybe tonight will be better than his last effort.'

They walked on, reaching the end of their section. There they met

Marius, and Mattheus' replacement Placidus, a sleepy type who suited his name. Urceus took the opportunity to rain abuse on Marius about his cooking. 'You'd better produce something edible tonight,' he threatened. 'Me and the boys won't eat any more of your slop.'

Marius laughed. 'Careful I don't piss in your stew, Jug.'

Urceus purpled. 'Do that and I'll shit in your blankets!'

Quintus and Placidus stood by and chuckled. This too was part of the routine. No one would do such a thing to the rest of his tent mates, but the same did not apply to the men in different maniples. Practical jokes such as dropping a dead mouse or a rotten cabbage into the cooking pot weren't unknown, although of late it had become increasingly difficult to get away with this. Soldiers in other units became suspicious if any of their neighbours came calling around meal times.

A trumpet blared from their camp, and they all grinned.

'Time to go!' said Urceus. 'I'm so bloody hungry that I'm even looking forward to the shit you produce, Marius.'

'You'll love tonight's offering,' declared Marius. 'Stewed neck of mutton, with vegetables. Delicious! It's an old recipe that my mother used to prepare.'

Urceus gave him a jaundiced look. 'No disrespect to your mother, but I'll be the judge of whether it's tasty or not.'

Some time later, the eight hastati were arranged comfortably around the ring of stones that formed the fireplace outside their tent. An iron tripod was still in place over the flames, but the bronze vessel that had contained Marius' offering for the night lay by Urceus' feet. Everyone had agreed that the mutton stew was good, yet it had been Urceus, Marius' greatest critic, who had insisted on scraping the pot clean. 'I'll expect that standard from now on,' he'd said. Typically, Marius had promised nothing of the sort.

'The weather's getting warmer,' said Quintus with a smile. 'It wasn't that long ago that we couldn't have sat outside like this.'

Urceus belched. 'Aye. Soon we won't need our blankets wrapped around us, or a fire, apart from to cook on.'

'There'll be a few weeks of lovely weather and then it'll be too hot again. Months of humping water from the river, sunburn all day and mosquitos all night,' said Placidus dolefully.

'Shut it!' growled Marius. 'Don't remind us.'

'Have some wine,' said Quintus, passing over the skin that they were sharing. 'And cheer up, for Jupiter's sake.'

Glowering at the laugh that this produced, Placidus took the skin and drank deep.

'Tell us a story,' said Quintus, feeling a little bad. As the newest member of the contubernium, Placidus bore the brunt of everyone's ribbing. His major redeeming feature, however, was his ability to weave a yarn.

'Aye.'

'I want the one about Hercules' Twelve Labours.' 'No, the tale of Romulus and Remus!' The tent mates' voices competed with one another.

Placidus seemed appeased. 'I'll choose,' he said importantly.

'Make it a cheerful one,' urged Urceus. 'I don't want to go to bed feeling miserable.'

Placidus thought for a moment. 'How about the one with Horatius, Herminius and Lartius on the bridge?'

'A good choice,' said Quintus. 'Don't start for a moment, though. I need a piss.'

'Me too,' added Urceus.

'Make it quick,' Marius ordered.

The two friends walked together to the nearest latrine trenches, which were situated under the ramparts in the camp's southeast corner. The sounds of ships being unloaded in the port of Trogilus, which lay close by, carried over the timber walls. The site from which their initial disastrous assault had been launched was now a supply base for the whole army. On the way back, they had to pass Corax's tent for a second time. Because of the angle of their approach, the pair were concealed by their centurion's tent until they were quite close. Quintus pricked his ears. It seemed that Corax had been joined by Vitruvius; the pair were deep in conversation, but in hushed tones.

Curiosity and a little devilment took Quintus. Nudging Urceus, he put a finger to his lips and indicated that they should go closer. Urceus looked a little unhappy, but he didn't walk away. Together they crept to within a few paces of Corax's position.

'Has there been any further development with Marcellus' pet Syracusan nobles?' asked Vitruvius.

'Not really. They've been trying to contact their friends inside the city, but Epicydes has spies everywhere. Anyone who's suspected of treachery is being denounced and killed.'

'Have none gone into Syracuse themselves?'

A derisive snort from Corax. 'They value their precious skins too much. So far, they've only bribed fishermen to carry their messages.'

'We need to get someone inside the city.'

'Aye, that's clear. But who?'

'What about a slave belonging to one of the pet Syracusan nobles? They must have plenty.'

'That's been suggested, but Marcellus doesn't trust a single one. Greasy Greeks, all of them. He thinks that they'll give themselves up to Epicydes' men and reveal their mission in the hope of manumission.'

'Bloody slaves. They never think about anything else. Why can't they know their station?'

'Human nature, Vitruvius. Unless he's a simpleton, what man wants to be the property of another? Why do you think that so many slaves volunteered to train as legionaries after Cannae?'

'Aye, well, maybe you're right. But the less said about slaves being manumitted to serve as legionaries, the better.'

There was silence for a moment.

'Putting pressure on the Syracusan nobles won't work either. They'd just enter the city and change sides. Tell Epicydes our troop numbers, the locations of our ships and so on.'

'Exactly,' said Corax. 'Whoever goes in has to be a Greek speaker, and as trustworthy as possible.'

'We need a reliable Syracusan deserter!' declared Vitruvius with a chuckle. 'Or better still, a Roman.'

'None of our men could do it,' said Corax.

'Why not? You mentioned some time ago that a couple of your lot spoke Greek.'

Quintus tensed. Vitruvius had to be referring to him – and who else?

'Crespo?' Corax responded.

'That's the one.'

'He's brave enough, certainly, but his educated accent would give him away. Epicydes would be torturing him within an hour of his arrival. I'd forgotten about Marius, though. He would suit.'

Marius speaks Greek? Quintus had had no idea.

'Marcellus would prefer two men,' said Vitruvius.

'True. Marius' accent is rough enough to pass notice, but not Crespo's.' There was a short pause – Quintus wondered later if it had been Corax's conscience? 'Still, he might do. I'll mention it to Marcellus.'

Fear began bubbling up inside Quintus. Being sent into Syracuse was tantamount to a death sentence. Even to his own ear, his Greek accent had been noticeably different to that of the Syracusan officer Kleitos. He tried to feel angry towards Corax, but failed. This didn't smack of vindictiveness on the centurion's part, more of doing what was right for Marcellus and the army. In the greater scheme of things, it didn't matter if he and Marius were lost on a spy mission. *Fuck it.* Jerking his head at Urceus, he tiptoed away from Corax's tent a few steps and then loudly walked back towards it, so that he could be heard. They rounded the corner and saluted. Quintus was relieved that neither centurion appeared suspicious.

'Shit, I'm glad I don't speak Greek,' muttered Urceus when they'd walked on.

'Aye, well,' said Quintus as stoically as he could, 'If I'm ordered to become a damn spy, I'll do my duty.'

'Make an offering to Fortuna. Maybe it won't happen,' said Urceus, clapping him on the shoulder.

Quintus grimaced. In his experience, such gifts did not affect the future, but he would not say so aloud.

The pair had to endure a barrage of insults for delaying Placidus' story-telling, but silence soon fell once he began his tale. It washed over Quintus, however, as dark thoughts of Syracuse filled his head. When it ended, he was still brooding.

Marius nudged him. 'A fine telling, eh?'

'Yes,' replied Quintus absently.

Marius gave him a shrewd look. 'You didn't hear a damn word! What's up with you?'

'It's nothing,' Quintus demurred, but Marius wouldn't let up. After a moment, he gave in. Marius was to be part of it, after all, and their comrades wouldn't think worse of them for not wanting to be sent on a suicide mission. To his amazement, though, Marius' face lit up at the prospect.

'How come you speak Greek?' asked Quintus.

'I grew up in Bruttium. Even today, Greek is the main language of many towns along the coast.'

Urceus let out a slow whistle. 'I know you have a Hades-may-care attitude, Marius, but to *want* to do this?'

'My time's not up yet.' Marius' grin was confident. 'And they say that the Syracusan women are stunning – as well as easy with their favours!'

'He's thinking with his cock again. A man's a lost cause when that happens. A *didrachm* that you come back without having buried it in a Syracusan's cunny.' Urceus stuck out his hand.

'Done!' Marius shook with him.

'Your word is your bond,' warned Quintus, smiling despite himself. 'No lying!'

'Agreed. May Vulcan hammer my cock into nothing if I lie.'

'That is something I would hate to watch. Your cock's so small that Vulcan would have trouble finding it,' said Urceus, smirking.

Marius' expression grew serious for a moment. 'It's not just the pussy. Imagine the thrill of it! And if we succeeded? There'd be promotions in it, for sure. We'd be able to get drunk on the story for months.'

Quintus tapped his head. 'You're mad.'

Marius laughed, and Quintus realised that for all his fear, he wouldn't be happy for Marius to be sent in alone. The man was his comrade, for better or for worse.

'Anyway, it won't happen,' said Marius. 'Marcellus will find better candidates than us, surely?'

Nothing happened for a couple of days, and Quintus' worries began to recede. Marcellus had found the men for his secret operation. When one morning Corax disappeared, leaving Vitruvius in charge of exercising the maniple, he did not feel alarmed. Centurions' meetings were common enough, and Vitruvius' ebullient mood didn't leave any time for thought. He soon had men running sets of sprints in full kit, while others had been ordered to fight one another with the heavy wooden weapons normally used by new recruits. Some were even wrestling in their armour – a chance, Vitruvius said, to freshen up their hand-to-hand combat skills. The hastati weren't happy – few centurions made their men train in this manner – but they went at their tasks with gusto, because Vitruvius was every bit the disciplinarian that Corax was. If he singled a man out for not trying hard enough, far worse would be on offer.

Quintus was finishing a set of sprints with Urceus and the rest when he heard Marius' name – and his – being called out. There were still four more lengths to run, but it was Vitruvius who was summoning them. They trotted over to the junior centurion, who had been standing with the optiones. A sense of foreboding began to sink in as Quintus spotted the soldier by Vitruvius' side. He wore the triple-disc breastplate of a Samnite, which made him one of the *socii*. The realisation hit home an instant later.

Corax was with Marcellus, and this was an *extraordinarius*, one of the finest allied soldiers who served as bodyguards to the consul.

Distinctly uneasy now, Quintus said, 'You called us, sir?'

'You're both to go with this soldier. Marcellus wants to see you.'

'Like this, sir?' He had no desire to meet the commander of all Roman forces on Sicily – whom he'd only ever seen from a distance – while red-faced and drenched in sweat. Even Marius looked a little less eager than he had a moment earlier.

'Yes,' Vitruvius snapped. 'Now.'

'Aye, sir.' Quintus saluted and eyed the bearded Samnite, who was only a little older than he.

'Follow me.'

Throwing a minute shrug at Marius, Quintus followed the Samnite. 'What's your name?' he asked when they were some distance from Vitruvius.

'Sattio.'

'Do you have any idea why we've been sent for?'

'The consul wants a word.'

Quintus gritted his teeth, but Marius seemed not to mind. Why can't I be as carefree? Quintus wondered. 'I know that,' he said lightly to Sattio. 'But why?'

'It's not my job to question the consul,' answered Sattio, his beard bristling.

Prick, thought Quintus.

'It's got to be because we speak Greek,' muttered Marius.

'Aye.' Quintus could think of no other reason that they would be singled out. We will return safely, he told himself. As they drew near Marcellus' *praetorium*, however, such confidence felt increasingly hollow.

Marcellus' headquarters was in the army's main camp, a vast affair that housed two legions. Reaching it, Quintus' apprehension soared. He had been inside such grand quarters once, it was true, but that had been an age before, when he was still in the cavalry. The man he'd met, Publius

Cornelius Scipio, who had helped to lead Rome's legions at the outset of Hannibal's invasion, had also been well disposed towards his father. Their meeting had been formal but pleasant; today's encounter would be radically different. Quintus' stomach knotted as they passed through the perimeter fence that ran around the praetorium.

At the entrance to Marcellus' tent, Sattio spoke with the officer in charge, a centurion of the *extraordinarii* who bore a passing resemblance to Corax. Multiple silver and gold *phalerae* adorned a harness over his mail shirt; a scar that ran from his right knee to his ankle was further testimony of his stature. The centurion eyed Quintus with distaste. 'You are Crespo and Marius, hastati in the maniple of Marcus Junius Corax?'

'Yes, sir,' they answered.

'And this is how you would meet your consul?'

'We were at training when the messenger arrived, sir. Our centurion ordered us to come at once. There was no time to change, sir.'

A *phhhh* of contempt. 'Come with me.'

The pair shared a resentful glance, and obeyed.

As Scipio's had been, the tent was opulently decorated. Thick carpets lined the floors, heavy candelabras hung from the ceilings, grand pieces of furniture were set out in style. Finely carved, painted statues – of gods, goddesses, satyrs and nymphs – eyed them from numerous vantage points. At the entrance to Marcellus' meeting chamber, the centurion called out their names. An order to enter was given. Quintus held his breath as they walked inside.

A large table occupied the centre of the rectangular space; on it, Quintus spied a detailed map of Sicily, and another of Syracuse. Both were dotted with black and white stones – marking the position of Roman, Syracusan and Carthaginian forces, he judged. That wasn't surprising. Nor was the presence of Marcellus and Corax. But Pera? What in Hades' name was he doing here? Fresh sweat ran down Quintus' back as they halted a respectful distance from Marcellus and saluted.

'These are the men you wanted to see, sir.'

'Thank you, centurion. That will be all.'

'Sir.' With a frosty look at Quintus and Marius, the centurion retreated.

Marcellus was a tall, thin man with neat brown hair. He wasn't dressed in uniform, but he looked every part the consul. His plain tunic, gilded belt and ornate dagger exuded quality. A magnificent ring decorated with a ruby flashed on his right hand; a bronze ram's head bracelet decorated the opposite wrist. He studied the pair for a moment. Both men squirmed beneath the scrutiny. From the corner of his eye, Quintus could see Pera smirking. He risked a glance at Corax, who gave him the smallest of nods. Quintus felt a degree of calm return. Perhaps they weren't here to be turned into spies?

Marcellus spoke at last. 'Your names?'

'Quintus Crespo, sir. Hastatus in Centurion Corax's maniple.'

'Gaius Marius, sir. The same.'

Marcellus eyed Corax, who said, 'They're both good soldiers, sir. Crespo has been with me since before Trasimene.'

Again the consul stared; again Quintus writhed mentally.

'Your centurion's opinion carries weight with me, hastatus,' said Marcellus.

'Thank you, sir.' If anything, Quintus' unease had increased. He hadn't been dragged here to be congratulated. Nor had Marius.

'Do you know why you and your tent mate have been summoned?'

Quintus glanced at Marius, and decided that feigned ignorance was the best option. 'No, sir.'

'It's because you speak Greek.'

New fear clutched at Quintus. Had Corax revealed his status? Beside Marcellus, Pera's expression verged on the hawkish. Quintus felt sick. 'Er, I do, sir. Yes.' There. He had admitted it. After more than four years, his status as an equestrian was about to be revealed.

'Corax tells me that your father died when you were but young,' said Marcellus in Greek. 'You had an old neighbour who was originally from Athens; the man taught you your letters, and also to speak his tongue.'

Quintus felt a rush of gratitude towards Corax, who *hadn't* given his game away. He'd been summoned here to become a spy, but not to be betrayed. 'That's correct, sir,' he replied, also in Greek. 'I haven't had reason to speak it much of recent years, of course.'

'Yet here we are, outside a Greek-speaking city.'

'That's true, sir.' Again Quintus contrived ignorance, but his heart had started hammering again. They *were* to be sent into Syracuse, then. Great Mars, protect us, he prayed.

'Direct attacks have got us nowhere. And while the guggas continue to sail in with supplies, our siege will not starve the defenders into submission,' said Marcellus. 'Treachery from within is what we need. It has always been the best method to take a besieged city.'

'I see, sir,' said Quintus, continuing to pretend not to understand.

'We need therefore to recruit men inside Syracuse. Men who will open the gates for us.'

'That sounds like a good plan, sir.'

'The Syracusan nobles who call themselves friends of Rome are too scared to enter,' declared Marcellus angrily. 'For weeks, I have been unable to find anyone who is trustworthy enough to take on this most important of tasks. That was, until I spoke to my cousin.' He glanced at Pera with a smile. Pera positively preened himself, and Quintus reeled. Marius, on the other hand, looked happy.

'Centurion Pera speaks fluent Greek. He has volunteered to go into Syracuse and locate those who might be persuaded to come over to Rome,' said Marcellus. 'You will both go with him.'

'Yes, sir,' the pair replied.

Their tone made Marcellus' nostrils flare. 'You *are* happy to do this, I take it?'

'Aye, sir.' Quintus hesitated for a heartbeat. Corax's eyes bore a degree of sympathy, but he hadn't protested. Pera's expression was gloating; that of Marius, excited. Quintus felt world-weary. His accent might give him away. Who knew what Pera was capable of? Kleitos might even see him.

This was a direct order from his consul, however, and Rome's need came before his life. 'I'd be honoured, sir.'

'Me too, sir,' Marius quickly added.

Marcellus looked more satisfied. 'Excellent,' he said. 'The Republic will be grateful.'

Quintus lay back and tried not to breathe. The stench from the fishing nets that covered him from head to toe was overpowering. Two nights had passed since Marcellus' edict, and now there was no turning back. They were on board a fishing vessel, heading from the western shore of the great harbour of Syracuse to the enemy-held eastern side. After a time, his lungs were bursting. He had to exhale. And inhale again. He gagged.

'Get used to the smell, hastatus. Find some way to breathe silently,' hissed Pera, who was lying beside him and similarly covered.

You filthy cocksucker, thought Quintus, wishing that it was Pera who was on the second boat, alone, and not Marius. 'Yes, sir,' he whispered.

'Quiet!' It was the old fisherman whose vessel they were on. Quintus felt the man's gnarly foot kick at the pile of netting. 'Quiet, or we're fucked.'

Quintus' pulse pounded an urgent rhythm at the base of his throat. Hard as it was to do, he lay back on the rough deck and forced himself to relax. His nostrils filled once more with the smell of fish and salt. The net's rough threads rubbed his cheeks. Under him, the planking moved gently as the little craft moved through the water. Timber creaked, water slapped off the hull and the fabric of the sail flapped in the breeze. The crew of three talked to each other in low voices. All was as it should be, but the knowledge gave Quintus no comfort. The danger wouldn't start until they crossed the harbour and drew near to the small jetty where the local fishermen — needed by the city's inhabitants, and 'ignored' by the Romans because of their usefulness in running messages into and out of Syracuse — docked their craft.

It was at that point that he, Marius and Pera would have to rise up and become Syracusans. Their first hurdle would be the guards at the gate through which the night's catch was taken. By most accounts, they paid scant attention to the fishermen – other than to collect their unofficial toll of a box of fish – but that didn't mean that there was no risk involved. Presuming it went well, however, the trio would stay for what remained of the night in the house belonging to the old soak who owned the boat.

After that, their work would really begin. Quintus felt a tide of bile rush up his throat. He could think of nowhere he'd like to be less than where he was right now. To walk, or rather sail into the middle of an enemy-held city, speaking their language with noticeable accent, reeked of stupidity. Yet the alternative – refusing a direct order from Marcellus – would have meant the *fustuarium* – him being beaten to death by his tent mates. He couldn't have let Marius go alone either. Damned if I do, damned if I don't, thought Quintus bitterly. May the girls be as beautiful as Marius says they are, he prayed, and may I get to lie with at least one before we're caught.

Despite his worries, things went smoothly in the hours that followed. The guards didn't even look up as they shuffled into the city, and they made their way to the old fisherman's house without hindrance. When they rose the following morning and went out on to the streets, no one gave them a second glance. The names and addresses they'd been supplied with proved to be accurate. Pera decided that he alone would enter the houses to talk to the nobles, which made Quintus wonder why they'd been made to accompany him. It proved truly nerve-racking to wait outside, wondering if every passer-by would denounce them. Nothing of the sort happened, though, and Pera never emerged with anything less than a pleased air. Moreover, Quintus and Marius rarely had to open their mouths, thereby risking discovery.

Quintus found it fascinating to be within the besieged city. It was clear that Marcellus' plan to take the place through subterfuge was a wise one. Morale seemed high both among the residents and the soldiers. The defences were in good repair, and the batteries of catapults even more numerous than Quintus had guessed. Syracuse had plenty of public wells, so water would never be in short supply. The market stalls weren't overflowing with fresh produce, but nor were they empty. Grain, oil and wine, the most important commodities, were available, and in a wise move, Epicydes had capped their prices. Fresh fish arrived daily, caught by the same fishermen who'd ferried the trio in. While the women were not as stunning as Marius had boasted, there were plenty of beauties to make their heads turn. Pera's short leash meant that there were no opportunities to pursue relations of any kind, however. The friends had to content themselves with just looking. When Pera couldn't hear, Quintus ribbed Marius mercilessly about his bet with Urceus. Marius' response was always the same: 'At least I'd have been in there. Women fall for my looks, but they run a mile from ugly bastards like you!' That was the cue to start trading insults. The banter helped them to while away the hours, to ignore the constant, gnawing fear.

Over the following five days and nights, in excess of a dozen high-ranking Syracusans were smuggled out and back in the fishing boats – ostensibly as crew – to talk with the nobles already with Marcellus. Once won over, Pera told Quintus and Marius, their mission was to convince more of their fellows to join the Roman cause. When there were enough to ensure that a gate could be taken by force at night, the time would be ripe.

'How many will they need, sir?' Marius asked. Quintus wanted to know too. With a core group recruited, it felt as if it were time to leave. The longer they remained in the city, the more peril they were in.

'I don't know, hastatus,' replied Pera, ambition glinting in his eyes. 'Sixty? Eighty?'

'Can the Syracusans we've spoken with not do the rest, sir?' ventured Quintus, his gaze wandering uneasily around the dingy tavern in which they were drinking.

'Maybe they could, but the task will be completed faster if we're also playing our part.' With a malevolent curve to his lips, Pera waited to see if Quintus would rise to the bait.

Chapter XIX

'There are close on eighty men involved now. That's as many as Demosthenes feels will turn readily,' Pera revealed to Quintus and Marius two days later. He'd just met with the chief conspirator in the agora. 'The gods are smiling on us, because the moon is on the wane. Acting tonight or tomorrow night would be best. Demosthenes will make the decision when it's dark.'

After so many days of living on his nerves, Quintus felt overwhelming relief. Oddly, a mad part of him exulted. It might be suicidal to stay, but it *would* feel incredible to be one of those who let their men into the city. The manic gleam in Marius' eyes told its own story about how he felt. Before Pera, however, Quintus put on a surprised face. 'We're to take part, sir?'

'Aye, we are.' Pera revealed his teeth. 'I think that we should have some wine to celebrate.'

Marius looked delighted, but Quintus held back. There was yet one more name on their list. Even a single man might be the difference between success and failure when they came to seize the gate, he thought. 'There was one last noble you were to talk to, wasn't there, sir? Attalus – was that his name?' Pera's scowl proved that he had forgotten all about him.

'We have sufficient numbers, damn it,' Pera snapped.

Quintus caught the warning shake of Marius' head and decided not to antagonise Pera further. 'As you say, sir.' Great Mars, let nothing go wrong from this point, he prayed.

After a quick drink, Pera had them retire to the fisherman's house, which had continued to be their refuge. The dwelling was located in a tiny lane populated entirely by the old soak's crewmembers and their extended families. From the first day, no one had paid them any attention, which had helped to relieve the strain that Quintus and Marius felt each time they'd ventured beyond the rundown quarter and into the city proper. Pera ordered Quintus to stay alert while he retired to his room.

Marius slipped Quintus a wink and whispered, 'If a nap's good enough for the centurion, it is for me too,' and disappeared.

Some of Quintus' concern slipped from his shoulders as he sat in the tiny, sunlit yard behind the house, watching their host repair his nets. Neither he nor the old man spoke, but Quintus enjoyed watching him. There was a hypnotic quality to the repetitive movement of needle and thread to and fro, the tying of knots, and the way that the fisherman used his last few teeth to bite through the ends each time he was done.

After a while, Quintus felt his eyelids droop. Normally, he would have fought the drowsiness, but in the calm of the yard, there seemed little harm in letting them close. They had finished scouring Syracuse for conspirators. Nothing would happen before nightfall, and the languorous feeling induced by the wine he'd drunk was proving too hard to fight. Quintus slipped into a most enjoyable dream; it involved Elira and her wondrously talented mouth.

A hand shook him.

Quintus dreamed that Elira had gripped his shoulder as they were locked together in passion.

He was shaken again, felt a hot breath on his ear. 'Wake up! Wake up!'

Quintus opened his eyes and recoiled. There was no perfume in the air, only body odour, no alabaster smooth skin, just the warty chin and the straggly beard of the old fisherman. 'What? What is it?' Quintus demanded.

'Soldiers. Soldiers are coming!'

Quintus' stomach did a neat somersault. 'How long have we got?'

'The warning signal came from my nephew's house, at the mouth of the alleyway. You have a few moments. Get on the roof' – he gestured at the red tiles above – 'and drop down into the lane beyond. Go right, and follow it until you come to the temple to Athena. From there, you'll know where you are. Make your way to my boat and hide yourselves. If they find no one here, their suspicions will be allayed. I'll take you across the harbour when it's dark.'

'My thanks.' Quintus was already on his feet, scrambling through the doorway to the room he shared with Marius. He considered not waking Pera – to seal the centurion's fate, he would have to do nothing more than that. Two things stopped Quintus: the fate of the old fisherman if Pera was found, and the fact that the centurion had saved his life in Enna. He owed Pera for that.

By the time that Quintus had roused the others, and the three had started climbing on to the house's roof, men's voices were audible outside. Pera, who had gone up first, reached down for Marius. You miserable fucker! thought Quintus. I save your hide and *this* is how you repay me?

A fist banged on the door, and a voice demanded: 'Open up, in the name of Epicydes!' The old fisherman, who was watching, indicated with his hands that he would take his time responding to the summons.

Marius crouched on the tiles and shoved out a hand. Quintus took the grip and scrabbled up the wall with his feet. One of the tiles half lifted from its position as he clambered up, and he cursed under his breath as it dislodged, fell to the floor of the yard and smashed into fragments.

Quintus and Marius looked at each other. Would the old man have time to clear up the broken tile? If not, things boded ill for all of them.

Pera beckoned from the outer edge of the roof. Then, without a word, he jumped.

The friends followed as fast as they could. The alley beyond was tiny and filthy but fortunately the drop was less than the height of two men. *Thud. Thud.* The mud softened the sound of their fall.

'Which way?' demanded Pera, his voice agitated.

'Right, sir, until we reach the temple to Athena.'

Pera turned and was gone.

'The prick is shitting himself,' pronounced Marius with a grin.

'I don't think he's realised the danger we were in until now,' said Quintus, also amused. His own fear was far more manageable knowing that Pera was terrified.

They took a moment to listen. Metal hobs clashed off the concrete floor, telling them that the soldiers had entered the house. Marius tugged at Quintus' arm, but he resisted. Knowing whether the fallen tile had caused suspicion or not was vital.

'What's this?' The angry cry needed no explanation.

'We can't stay in the boat,' Quintus muttered to Marius as they loped off. 'They'll come for us, sure as the sun rises in the east.'

'I've got a knife, but you don't even have that. What the fuck do we do?'

Instinct made both men slow as they came to the end of the alley. Running would draw attention. Quintus scanned the square beyond, which was dominated by the shrine that the old man had mentioned. It was as busy as he'd expect for the time of day. Stallholders proclaimed the quality of their wares; gossiping housewives walked together in twos and threes, inspecting what was on offer. Slaves carrying baskets of shopping walked behind the richer ones. Hawkers of everything from statuettes of the goddess to good-luck charms worked the crowd, smiling and bowing. A pair of cripples – soldiers who'd been injured in the defence of the city? – held up beseeching hands from their positions near the temple steps. Fresh blood glistened on the altar in the centre of the square. A small crowd watched as two acolytes manhandled a dead goat off it. A grey-bearded priest spoke with the merchant who'd paid for the sacrifice that had just taken place.

There was no sign of Pera.

'The fucker's gone and left us,' said Quintus.

'Maybe he thought we'd look suspicious walking together.'

'I suppose.' In Quintus' mind, however, this was proof of Pera's cowardice. 'I can't see any soldiers.'

'Nor I.' They set out across the square.

'How in Hades' name did the bastards know where we were?' asked Marius.

'Someone must have talked.'

They chewed on the rancid fat of that for a moment. The danger they had been in until that point was as nothing to what it would be in the hours that followed. Epicydes would ransack the city to find them, and all of the conspirators. 'The boat is our best bet,' said Quintus. 'Our only bet,' he added grimly.

'But what then?' hissed Marius as they headed in the direction of the fishermen's jetty. 'I can't sail, or swim. Can you?'

'I can swim, but I've never sailed.'

Marius mouthed a curse.

'Come on. It's our best chance,' urged Quintus. 'If necessary, I can help you.'

'If Pera can't swim, he'll order you to help him instead.'

'I'll leave the cocksucker to sink.' Waking him up had repaid the debt, Quintus decided.

Marius gripped his arm in gratitude.

They began to see parties of soldiers everywhere as they threaded their way through the streets – far more than usual. Quintus tried to tell himself that it was nothing more than coincidence but that idea was crushed when he saw one of the men whom they'd recruited being dragged from his house.

'I'm innocent, innocent, I tell you!' shouted the captive.

'Not according to what Attalus says,' retorted the officer in charge.

Quintus' head turned at the name. Had Attalus found out that he hadn't been included in the conspiracy and betrayed it out of pique? Panic flared in Quintus' guts as his captors headed in their direction. If the prisoner saw them, and said as much as a single word—

He shoved Marius into a street-side restaurant.

'This is no time to eat,' snarled Marius, but his outburst was quelled by Quintus' warning look. They took a seat at a nearby table and ordered soup from a serving girl. Quintus told Marius in an undertone what he'd seen.

'You mean this is Pera's fault?' Marius said indignantly. 'We should have left the stupid bastard behind.'

'Let's concentrate on getting out of here,' warned Quintus, but he still felt a stab of pleasure at Marius' solidarity. They kept an eye on the street as they waited. To their relief, the soldiers and their prisoner moved on without halting.

The soup appeared and they shovelled it down. Quintus slapped a coin on the counter and they set off again, studying the crowds with apparently casual eyes. Although they saw more soldiers, the friends spotted no other conspirators, which allowed them to pass unrecognised. They didn't see Pera. Quintus hoped that the centurion had been taken captive, that he would never see him again. Sweat drenched him as they neared the little gate in the wall that gave on to the jetty. He could sense the same tension in Marius. If the guards here had been alerted – by Pera, or by their own side – they were dead men. In silent consensus, they stopped by Arethusa's spring, a source of fresh water since antiquity. The place was a hubbub of householders coming and going with buckets. It was easy to pretend to be two passers-by, slaking their thirst.

'What do you think?' whispered Marius.

Quintus stared as he raised his cup, provided by an old crone in return for a copper. There were four soldiers by the gate, the usual number. That was good. So too was the fact that their spears were leaning against the wall. They didn't look any more alert than normal, but that didn't mean it wasn't a trap. Then one of the guards wandered out through the gate, saying that he was bursting for a piss. The most senior of the soldiers, a man whom Quintus knew by sight, didn't stop him. 'They don't know anything yet,' he said, explaining. 'I'd bet my life on it.'

'That's what you *are* betting, and mine with it,' retorted Marius sourly, but he didn't argue further. 'What's our story for going to the boat at this hour?'

'The old man found a leak last night. He wants us to take a look and sort it out if we can.'

'That tale isn't out of the realms of possibility, I suppose. And some of the guards know us by sight at this stage, which is something.'

'Let's hope that Pera hasn't already ballsed it up for us by spinning a different yarn.'

Marius frowned. 'What if they don't believe us?'

'We will have to kill them all,' Quintus grated, 'quietly enough that the men on the walls above don't hear us. Then we stroll to the boat. If Pera's there, he's there. If not, there's no point waiting for him. We can force a fisherman to sail us across the harbour.'

'Jupiter's hairy arse,' muttered Marius. 'I'm not even going to think about the catapults.'

'Good,' said Quintus, trying also not to imagine what it would be like helping Marius swim to safety. 'Come on.'

'If I don't make it but you do—' Marius began.

'Shut up!'

'Let me finish. Tell Urceus that I *did* screw a Syracusan girl.'

Quintus felt a smile push its way on to his lips. 'Very well. But you can tell him yourself.'

'With the gods' help. I'll have to admit that I was lying afterwards, though, or else Vulcan will hammer my cock to a pulp.'

Any trace of humour fell away as they approached the entrance, a narrow affair that was actually a tunnel protected by a gate at each end. Soon Quintus' pulse was hammering so fast that he worried it was audible. The fourth guard hadn't returned, which left three. The most senior was squatting on his haunches, playing dice with one of the others. The last man was the one monitoring who came and went. He eyed Quintus sourly, which wasn't any different to his normal manner. 'What are you doing here?'

'The chief found a leak in the boat last night,' mumbled Quintus, mimicking the Syracusan accent as best he could. 'He wants us to sort it out.'

'Ha! He sends you to do the dirty work while he sleeps, is that it?'

'Pretty much.' Quintus hawked and spat.

'It's always the same old story.' He rolled his eyes at the senior guard. 'On you go.'

Quintus felt overwhelming relief. He nodded his thanks and together, he and Marius stepped towards the tunnel that led through the wall to the jetty.

'Just a moment,' said a voice, and Quintus' fear resurged. He half turned, saw the senior guard getting to his feet. Quintus warned Marius with his eyes. 'Yes, sir?' he asked humbly.

'Bar their path, you damn idiot!' barked the senior guard at the man who'd let Quintus by. 'When their friend went through a little while back, he was going on about renewing the sail. Someone's telling lies!'

'I'll take the leader,' said Quintus in Latin to Marius. He leaped for the spears leaning against the wall. Grabbing one, he used it to skewer the senior guard through his padded cuirass. While he was doing that, Marius was stabbing the second man to death. Together they dispatched the last soldier before Quintus finished off his first opponent with a thrust to the neck.

The fight took barely fifty heartbeats. The instant that it was over, Quintus became aware of being watched. Every single person by Arethusa's spring was staring at them in complete shock. 'Shit! They'll alert the men on the walls. Let's go.'

'Look,' growled Marius.

Quintus' heart sank. A group of soldiers had appeared on the other side of the fountain. There were far too many to fight. 'Go!'

They barged into the tunnel, spears in hand. The narrow space echoed to their pounding feet and heavy breathing. It was perhaps thirty paces to the far side. Before they reached it, however, a shape loomed in the entrance. The last guard, thought Quintus.

'Pericles?' called the man. 'Is that you?'

'Yes,' Quintus replied from behind a hand. He readied his spear. Great

Jupiter, do not let the new soldiers shout out, he asked silently.

'You're in a damn hurry. Have you got the shits?' asked the guard with a snigger.

Quintus ran him through and pushed past. Marius stabbed him again for good measure. He fell, gurgling on his own blood. Quintus glanced back down the tunnel. No one was visible – but he could hear raised voices. 'It's a shame that we can't seal the outer door.'

'That's the least of our worries,' replied Marius, shoving him onward.

They emerged on to the rocks that sprawled below the base of the walls. The jetty poked out at sea level, a rickety arrangement of planking with ten or more fishing vessels tied up to it. A couple of fishermen were pottering about on their boats, and on the old man's craft, Quintus spotted Pera. With him was another figure, who appeared to be untying the mooring rope.

'Fucking Pera,' Quintus said.

'The piece of shit isn't waiting for us!'

'We can still make it!'

They scrambled down the rocks and thumped on to the planks, which swayed beneath them. 'Sir!' Quintus called out in a low voice. 'Wait!'

When Pera saw them, he muttered to the fisherman – a man Quintus didn't recognise – who pulled the last of the rope into the boat.

Quintus had no breath to curse, but rage filled him that Pera would desert them so deliberately. They began to sprint, with Quintus in the lead. He had covered half the distance when there was an almighty crack from behind him. Glancing over his shoulder, he was horrified to see Marius half disappear through a hole in the rotten timbers. He skidded to a halt, noticing soldiers emerging from the tunnel. *Fuck!*

Quintus glanced at the boat. It had only moved a length away from the jetty; the fisherman hadn't yet run up its sail. They might still catch it by swimming. He lay down and reached down towards Marius, swearing because of the splinters in the broken planks. 'Grab my hand!'

'I'm hurt,' groaned Marius as Quintus hauled him up.

'Up, up on your feet. We can look at you on board,' said Quintus. His gaze slid down below Marius' waist. So much blood and bone poking through the skin was really bad news, especially now that they needed to swim. His eyes lifted; he saw the soldiers already at the end of the jetty. He tried to grab Marius, but his friend pushed him away. 'Leave me.'

'No!' Quintus made another effort to pick him up, but there was nothing wrong with Marius' arms. He resisted fiercely.

'I'm done, Crespo! If you don't go, we'll both die. Where's the point in that?'

Quintus wanted to weep, but Marius was right. The first soldier was no more than twenty paces away.

'Get me up on my feet. I'll hold them back so that you can jump.'

Quintus' throat was closed with emotion. All he could do was nod. With an arm around Marius' shoulders, he managed to lift his friend upright. Marius roared with pain as he tried to stand on his injured leg. He took a deep breath, fixed Quintus with his eyes. 'Give me your spear.'

'Here.'

'Save yourself. Pera will pull you on board if you get to the boat. Go!'

'I will.' Quintus gripped Marius' arm hard. Then he turned and fled.

'Come on, you stinking Greek arse-humpers!' he heard Marius shout in Greek. 'One Roman is worth ten of you any day!' The Syracusan soldiers roared abuse in reply.

Quintus felt the timbers move as they advanced on to the jetty, but he didn't look back. He couldn't. There was an open space at the end of the planking and he hared towards it. The boat's sail was up now. Despite the shelter provided by the walls, there was some breeze to fill it. He would have one chance before the craft was beyond his reach.

Quintus slowed up enough to plunge into the sea head first, with his arms outstretched. He was no expert, but he'd often seen the men who dived for shellfish off the coast of Campania. The water was shockingly cold. Kicking out with his arms and legs, Quintus shot above the surface in a great spray of droplets. The boat was perhaps fifteen paces from him, and picking up speed fast. Pera was watching him, his face inscrutable. Quintus swam for the vessel with all of his strength. From the jetty came the sound of men fighting. Marius was still alive, then. Despite his growing distance from the vessel, new determination filled Quintus. His comrade's sacrifice must not be in vain.

Quintus' sense of time and space vanished. He felt the sting of salt in his eyes, the burn of it at the back of his mouth, and his limbs powering him along. Ahead, he saw only the boat. Finally, incredibly, he was almost within reach of it. With a huge effort, he swam close enough to touch its hull. The fisherman saw him, and Quintus prayed that it was he who reached out a hand. But it was Pera whose face appeared over the side, whose hand bore an oar like a weapon. Shocked, Quintus swallowed a mouthful of water and flailed backwards, trying to get away. *He's going to brain me.*

'Two people rowing would give us more speed,' said a voice – the fisherman.

Disappointment flickered in Pera's eyes; he changed his grip on the oar and extended it to Quintus. 'Grab a hold!'

Still wary, Quintus obeyed. To his relief, Pera pulled him in and held out his other hand. They shared a look – of mutual dislike, even hatred – before Quintus lifted his arm from the water towards Pera's.

'Quickly, quickly,' urged the fisherman as Quintus landed sprawling on the deck. 'The artillerymen won't sit about!'

Quintus' gaze shot not to the ramparts but to where Marius had stood. He saw only a bloody corpse. You died well, brother, he thought sadly. Several enemy soldiers had run to the end of the jetty, from where they hurled their spears. None had the range to reach the boat, nor, it seemed, did they know how to sail. Not a man among them climbed into any of the other fishing craft. Heartened by this, Quintus made obscene gestures at them. 'Fuck you, you whoresons!'

'Don't waste your breath.' An oar was shoved at him. 'Take this and row,' ordered Pera.

'Sir.' Quintus took the oar, little more than a length of wood with one end that was slightly thicker than the other, and lowered it into the crude rowlock, and thence into the water.

'On my count. One. Two. Three. Pull!' said Pera. 'One. Two. Three. Pull!'

With the wind filling the sail, their efforts helped the boat to travel over the waves at a respectable clip. It was two thousand paces to the far side, but at four hundred, they'd be out of range of the enemy artillery. Quintus judged that the boat had already travelled a quarter of that distance. He eyed the ramparts nervously. Still no activity there.

'I can't remember the last time there was an east wind in this harbour,' said the fisherman. 'It never happens.'

'Fortuna must have sat on Eurus' cock today,' Pera pronounced. 'He's in a good mood.'

Quintus had to smile, for all that he hated Pera. Eurus, the Greek god of the east wind, was regarded as the bringer of ill fortune, yet it was thanks to him that the boat was moving so fast.

Whizzzz!

The all-too-familiar sound made Quintus' gorge rise. There was a blur of movement some distance off to his right, and a splash as a large arrow scythed into the sea.

'Row! Row!' yelled the fisherman.

Quintus and Pera bent their backs. Their oars rose and fell in near unison, over and over.

It was as if the first missile had been a sign to the other artillerymen. *Whizzzz! Whizzzz! Whizzzz! Whizzzz!* The air filled with the deadly noise, and the water around the boat was struck again and again as the arrows landed. One hit the deck by the base of the mast, and another punched a hole in the sail, but that was the only damage. A second volley came close on the heels of the first, but again the little boat and its occupants escaped serious damage.

Just as suddenly as it had begun, the volleys ended. Quintus felt nervous rather than pleased. They were at the limit of the bolt-throwers' range, which meant that the stone-throwers would be next. They began shooting an instant later, yet this barrage too was desultory. About half a dozen rocks were loosed before the boat was left alone to complete its voyage.

Perhaps their ammunition was too valuable to waste on a couple of spies, thought Quintus. He didn't wait for Pera's command. Lifting his oar from the water, he slumped down beside it on the deck. The centurion glared, but then he too did the same. They sat in silence. Quintus couldn't put Marius' death from his mind, nor the image of Pera ordering the fisherman to move off from the jetty without them. His grief morphed into white-hot anger. 'You were going to leave us behind, sir.'

'Bullshit. I thought you had been caught.'

'Even when we were on the jetty, sir?'

'It was imperative to get the boat out into the harbour. I assumed you could both swim,' snapped Pera.

'Marius couldn't, sir.' He wanted to add, 'If you'd also been there, we might have saved him,' but didn't dare.

'Well, we've all heard the tale of how you saved a comrade from drowning. You would have been able to get out to the boat!'

Quintus didn't answer. What point was there? Pera would deny every accusation, and even more so when they got back to their own kind. There, Quintus' lowly status would render his testimony worthless. I should have left the prick to be discovered by the soldiers, he brooded. If I had, the guards at the gate wouldn't have been suspicious of us, and Marius would still be alive. Right then and there, Quintus considered killing Pera. As before, it was the presence of another that stopped him. To ensure that he didn't talk afterwards, Quintus would have to murder the fisherman in cold blood – and that he was not prepared to do.

'I wonder who it was that told Epicydes of our plan?' mused Pera.

That detail came crashing back, and again Quintus had to bite his lip. The officer in charge of the soldiers with the captive had mentioned Attalus. It couldn't be coincidence, Quintus decided. This was no longer just about Marius' death, and how Pera would have left them both to die. The whole damn conspiracy – Marcellus' great plan to end the siege – had gone up in flames because Pera had not been prepared to win over one more man. Gods, but what would Marcellus do if he found *that* out?

Quintus eyed Pera sidelong. The centurion hadn't heard what he had, or he wouldn't be wondering how their efforts had come to nothing. Yet Quintus couldn't say a word about that either, or Pera would try to murder him for the second time. A mixture of fury and frustration stung him. It would be best to keep his mouth shut entirely.

It was a bitter medicine to swallow. Even Urceus would have to be kept in the dark, in case his temper got the better of him. Quintus didn't want another death on his conscience. Impotent rage swelled within him now. Pera would emerge from this as the courageous officer who had risked his life for Rome, only to see his efforts come to nothing through events beyond his control. Quintus would be nothing more than the hastatus who had followed orders, and Marius the soldier who had died in the line of duty.

When an old adage that Quintus' father had been fond of came to mind, he was grateful. 'If the time to strike an enemy isn't right, stay your arm. Retreat if needs be. Keep your blade sharp. Keep it ready. One day, your opportunity will come.'

'Ho, Hanno!'

Hanno turned his eyes from the magnificent view of Ortygia and the Great Harbour. He was standing on the battlements of the Euryalus fort, and had been looking south. Kleitos was hailing him, so he walked to meet his friend, who was climbing the staircase from the courtyard below. 'What's brought you all the way over here?'

'The wine, of course!' Kleitos clapped him on the shoulder; Hanno did the same back.

Kleitos' unanticipated appearance in Syracuse a couple of weeks after his and Aurelia's return – a consequence of Hippocrates wanting further news relayed to his brother – had been a joy to them both. Their duties kept them apart most days, but they had made up for that in the evenings, meeting up for regular drinking sessions. Kleitos rarely mentioned what had happened in Enna, but it was obvious that he appreciated Hanno's company. With Kleitos still his only friend in Syracuse apart from Aurelia, Hanno felt the same.

'You were taking the air and enjoying the vista, I assume?' Kleitos gestured grandly over the rampart.

'Yes. It's not as spectacular as Akragas, but it's worth a look.'

'Aye. It was nicer there because there were no Romans in sight.' Kleitos spat in the direction of the enemy fortifications, clearly visible beyond the marshy land that led from the walls to the River Anapos, which discharged into the Great Harbour.

'That was part of it,' admitted Hanno. His command when he'd first arrived in Syracuse had been on the seaward-facing defences. After the initial naval assault, it had been unusual to see the Romans at all, apart from an occasional trireme in the distance. It was a different matter here and at his new unit's position, not far from the Hexapyla gate. Marcellus' enclosing walls were a constant reminder that the siege continued. 'But you didn't come looking for me to go on the piss. It's not late enough.'

'You know me too well.' Kleitos' face grew more serious. 'Is Aurelia about?'

'She's in the house. You know how it is,' Hanno replied, registering the first traces of alarm. Since her encounter with Pox Face in Akragas, she had stayed indoors as much as possible during daylight hours. It was hard on her, but they both agreed it was better than another guard recognising her from her time in the palace. Remaining incognito was another reason that they were living here, far from the centre of Syracuse. Hanno hadn't mentioned it to a soul, but he had also picked out Euryalus because of the network of tunnels that ran beneath it. Their main purpose was to allow defenders to appear from unexpected points and fall upon any attackers who made it within the strongly defended gates. But there was one – kept secret from all except senior officers – that ran under the walls for three stadia, emerging in a little defile. If the city ever fell, Hanno wanted a way out. Escape might be possible by sea, yet it was always best to have more than one plan. 'I hope you haven't come about her?'

'No, no. There's no reason to be concerned for Aurelia.' He saw Hanno's frown. 'Nor about yourself.'

'That's good. *You* know that I'm as loyal as anyone, but with all the denunciations, well . . . How many men have been executed now?'

'There was a real plot to turn the city over to the Romans, my friend. The spies killed a number of soldiers during their escape, and they were seen sailing off from the fishermen's jetty close to Ortygia.'

'I know.' Hanno had heard the tale of the three Romans who had tricked and fought their way past the sentries and stolen a boat. Two of them had managed to get completely away, somehow avoiding the artillery barrage. Brave men, he thought. 'So many of them confessed when they were arrested that Attalus must have been telling the truth. I've heard rumours, however, that some of the men who were seized were guilty of nothing more than being an enemy of his. I've had few dealings with him, but those that I've had have been unpleasant. He's a little rat of a man. We're fortunate that the conspirators didn't include him in their plot. If they had, Attalus would have had no cause to feel left out, and I'd wager that he would have happily joined them. By now, the city would be in Roman hands.'

'I won't argue with you about that,' said Kleitos. 'But Attalus wouldn't be stupid enough to accuse you. Hannibal sent you, for a start!'

For the first time in an age, Hanno thought of Hostus, one of his father's enemies in Carthage. 'Believe it or not, some of my people *would* sell us out to the Romans.'

'Maybe so, but you're not one of them. In fact, your loyalty is why I'm here.' He winked as Hanno's interest grew clear. 'A little bird told me that you're to be ordered to the palace in the morning. Epicydes is sending an envoy to Philip of Macedon, and he wants to talk to you about it before the messenger leaves.'

Surprise filled Hanno. Hannibal will want to hear about this, he thought. 'Really?'

'Maybe it's because that prick Hippocrates isn't here. He's the more dominant brother, but Epicydes has a cooler head on his shoulders.'

'He does,' replied Hanno. Epicydes hadn't mistreated him since his return, but nor had he asked anything of him but the most ordinary duties. 'It's excellent news that he's asking Philip for help. Once Hannibal secures a port, the Macedonians could land in Italy – as well as my people, obviously.'

'I hope to see that day. And if I have anything to do with it, Syracuse will also send Hannibal aid when the Romans have been beaten here.'

'This calls for a drink,' declared Hanno, delighted. 'You'll come back to the house?'

'Only if you insist,' replied Kleitos with a smile.

'Aurelia will be glad to see you. She finds the confinement hard.'

'Well, it won't last forever. When Himilco arrives with his army, the balance will tip in our favour again.'

'That's what I tell her, but she worries about what may happen when Hippocrates returns,' said Hanno, scowling. *May the gods grant me the chance to kill him then.*

'We'll keep her hidden until the Romans have been smashed, my friend, never fear. When your mission is complete, you can travel to Italy with her.'

Hanno nodded and made as if he were pleased, which he was – mostly. It wasn't ideal that Aurelia should become a camp follower once more, and follow him all over Italy, but it seemed the only way that they could avoid being parted.

Spotting the enemy camps in the distance, he put his concerns aside. It was pointless to cross bridges before they were reached. Until the Romans outside the city were beaten, everything else was irrelevant. In the meantime, he and Aurelia were still together.

Besides doing his duty, and sending messages to Hannibal, that was what mattered.

Aurelia was tired of secreting herself away, tired of the lack of company. She had been quick to seek out Elira when she and Hanno had returned, but had been upset to find that the Illyrian no longer wished to see her often. Elira's reason – which hadn't altogether surprised Aurelia – was that she had met a soldier in the months that Aurelia had been away. It was understandable that she wanted to spend her time with him, but it meant that the rare, joyful occasions such as Kleitos' visit the night before were all the more poignant. From the moment that Hanno left each morning, every passing hour felt like ten. I live in a prison, Aurelia thought bitterly, gazing around the main living area. She had to admit that it was large, and well furnished – Hanno had seen to that – and there were two windows, so light was not an issue. She had Hannibal the cat for company – Aurelia had insisted on retrieving him from Elira, with whom he'd been left. Yet these things helped only a little. The three chambers: living room, bedroom, and a kitchen area with a small latrine off it, were in effect, a jail.

In the past, Aurelia would hardly have noticed the everyday noises that carried in from the street below. Now, they felt like torture, because they represented a normal world, one that she could never be part of. Children shrieked with pleasure as they played; shopkeepers vied for the attention of passers-by, promising that their bread, their ironmongery, their wine was the best in Syracuse; men greeted soldiers whom they knew, and grilled them about the state of the defences and the disposition of the enemy. Women bemoaned the prices of food, their children's behaviour, their husbands' failure to listen to what was being said. Aurelia had taken to standing by the side of the windows, out of sight, and listening longingly to the carryings on. Hearing soldiers joking with each other made her think of Quintus, who might be only a few miles away, for all the good it did her. What Aurelia found hardest, however, was hearing a baby cry, or a very small child calling for its mother. Her barely healed grief for Publius would be scraped raw yet again, reducing her to a sobbing wreck. Why had she decided to travel to Rhegium? Why had she not stayed in Rome? The fact that Publius might have as easily been carried off by disease there as in Syracuse was of little solace. In a part of her mind, she lived in Rome with a happy, healthy son, and received occasional letters from her brother.

She wished again that the war was over, that she and Hanno could settle down and live a normal life. They didn't talk much about the struggle – what was the point? – but it was clear that he felt the coming campaign would deliver a decisive victory for Carthage and Syracuse. The size of Himilco's army, and his elephants, lent credence to this theory. It felt a touch traitorous to wish for such a result, for Aurelia still felt very much a Roman, but it seemed the only way that they would ever be able to leave the city, the only way that any kind of ordinary existence could be resumed. Yet even that would be transient, she thought wearily. Hanno's oaths would mean a return to Italy, and to Hannibal's army. For her, that signified life in a followers' camp. Hanno asserted that she would be safe there, but after the few days she'd spent in one, Aurelia knew that her existence would be far from easy.

There was another way, one that she didn't even like to admit to. After all that Hanno had done for her – rescuing her from Hippocrates and helping her to bury Publius were just two of the things – to consider leaving him felt like the ultimate form of betrayal. When her loneliness and grief overwhelmed her, however, she couldn't help revisiting the idea: she fantasised about escaping to the Roman camps outside the city, there to find Quintus. After that, she could travel to Rhegium, to find out if her husband Lucius had lived or died. A different guilt scourged her now. What if he had recovered from his injuries? Would he have given her up for dead as easily as she had him? She doubted it. Did that mean that she should have remained loyal to Lucius, instead of betraying him with Hanno? No, Aurelia decided. Her union with him had been serviceable but sterile, and typical of an arranged marriage. There had been none of the fire she felt with Hanno. Publius had been the cement that had held them together. With him gone, there would have been nothing left but grief-laden memories.

Neither could she return to the family farm, because fighting still raged in Campania thanks to Capua's continued support for Hannibal. Quintus would not return to it until the war was over. Her only other option was Rome, and the house that she had shared with Lucius. Picturing that brought home a stark realisation. To go back would merely move what she had here to another place, with the obvious absence of Hanno.

Aurelia sighed. Life had to be accepted as it was, but that didn't mean that she had to remain incarcerated forever. There could be little real harm in venturing beyond her door, surely? The guards from the palace were unlikely to frequent this part of the city. In broad daylight, other men would not accost her. If she didn't speak to anyone, her Roman accent would go unnoticed. Moreover, the baths that Hanno had taken her to once weren't far.

Her mood lifted at once.

Life could go on. Life *would* go on.

With Hanno.

Chapter XX

Withintithin a day of returning safely, the news reached the Roman camps that it *had* been Attalus who had betrayed the plot to open a gate in the city walls. All eighty conspirators had been tortured to death and, in a stark warning from Epicydes, the heads of many had been shot into the no man's land between Syracuse and the Roman fortifications. As far as Quintus had been able to ascertain, Marius' head had not been one of them, but he still dreaded what the Syracusans had done with his friend's body. He longed to end the siege now, and to avenge yet another comrade's death.

He also wanted to reveal Pera's role in Attalus' treachery, but knew it for a fruitless exercise. As if to prove that his concerns were well grounded, Pera had taken to snooping around the maniple's tents, ostensibly checking to see if Quintus was well. His real purpose was revealed one day when he casually dropped Attalus into the conversation. Quintus put on the blankest of faces, and said that there had been so many Syracusan dogs that he'd long since forgotten their names. Pera had seemed satisfied, but from that moment on, Quintus took care not to wander anywhere on his own, especially at night.

The siege dragged on with no signs of any change. The weather grew warm and pleasant, and the grey, cloudy days of winter became a distant memory. As the days passed, the temperatures climbed steadily, and Quintus and his comrades resigned themselves to another baking-hot summer, covered in dust, manning their fortifications outside the city. Inevitably, the maniple's morale dipped. The thought of going on patrol, once something that they would have wanted to avoid, became every man's dream. When Corax overheard Quintus and Urceus talking of this one day, he laughed and told them not to live in hope.

'Just be grateful that we're not stationed to the south of the city, near those damn marshes,' he warned. 'Men are dropping there like flies, from malaria, fevers, dysentery and the like. At least we don't have to worry about such things.'

Corax's words were of scant consolation as Quintus and Urceus paced up and down the ramparts day after day, with nothing to do other than stare at the distant, impregnable walls of Syracuse. It seemed that the monotony would never end.

Two evenings later, things changed. Corax came strolling over to where Quintus and his comrades were sitting outside their tent. There followed the usual salutes, the offers of wine, and some awkward chitchat. Like his comrades, Quintus was wondering what Corax's purpose was. There was typically an ulterior motive to his visits, but it wasn't for hastati to ask.

'Have you heard about the Spartan that some of the naval boys captured today?' asked Corax out of the blue.

Quintus' ears pricked up. 'No, sir.'

'Damippus, his name is. It turns out he was being sent by Epicydes to talk with King Philip of Macedon.' Now Corax had everyone's interest. Hannibal and Philip had been allies for some time; the Macedonian king had attacked Roman colonies in Illyria two years previously. He had been defeated, but his hostility towards the Republic remained undimmed. It wasn't surprising that Epicydes, who like most Syracusans was of Greek descent, would attempt to win Philip's aid.

'I take it that Damippus won't be getting to Macedon any time soon, sir,' said Urceus with a snicker that was echoed by the rest of the contubernium.

'You'd think so, but Epicydes is desperate to ransom him,' Corax replied. 'An envoy was sent out from the walls within hours of Damippus' capture.'

'The consul's not going to give him up, surely, sir?' Urceus asked.

'This is where it gets complicated, hastatus. Sparta is in alliance with the Aetolian Confederacy. Our Senate is angling to weave a similar union, because it always pays to have friends on the Greek coastline, especially if military action has to be taken against Macedon. By ransoming Damippus, we'd have more chance of the Aetolians looking favourably on our overtures of friendship.'

Corax had the hastati in the palm of his hand now, Quintus decided, gazing around the circle of rapt faces. As ordinary soldiers, they never heard information of this type. By including them, Corax deepened their loyalty to him – without them even realising it. Although he could see through his tactics, Quintus felt the same way. Corax was a great commander, and fighter. He led from the front, and always exposed himself to the same dangers as his men. He looked out for them as if they were his wayward children, and in return, thought Quintus fiercely, we love him.

'Why are you telling this, sir?' Urceus voiced the question in everyone's mind.

'You were bitching the other day about being bored.'

Urceus coloured, and Quintus took a sudden interest in the strap of a sandal.

Corax chuckled. 'Relax. This isn't a punishment duty. Marcellus has agreed to talks with the Syracusans about Damippus. The meeting is to take place at the Galeagra tower.'

'The Galeagra, sir? That's opposite our section.' Quintus cringed at Placidus' ability to state the obvious.

But Corax didn't lambast him. 'That's right. Which is perhaps why Marcellus thought it fair that this maniple provides a century to accompany his officers to the negotiation.' The hastati voiced their enthusiastic agreement and Corax smiled. 'It should be straightforward enough, brothers. Unless something disastrous happens, there won't be any fighting. You'll get a chance to see the walls up close without the risk of stones from the enemy catapults smashing in your skulls, and to gauge the mettle of the soldiers who'll be with Epicydes' envoys.'

'We're honoured, sir,' said Quintus. 'When is the meeting to take place?'

'Tomorrow. Just after dawn, before it gets too hot.'

'What other troops will there be, sir?' asked Quintus.

'A century of extraordinarii. You all know what those stuck-up pricks think of themselves, so your gear will have to be parade-ground standard. Anyone's that isn't will have me to answer to.'

Quintus' comrades grumbled under their breaths at the extra work that Corax had handed to them, but they were happy enough. The prospect of seeing the enemy defences close up was exciting, and best of all, thought Quintus, Pera wouldn't be present.

Corax inspected his century when the rising sun was still tingeing the eastern horizon. They had formed up in the square space created by their tents and mule pens, eight men abreast and six deep. The fifteen velites stood off to one side in a small block. Hypothetically, there would have been eighty soldiers in total, but that hadn't been the case as long as Quintus could remember. Four men were in the camp hospital with fevers, or inflamed eyes. Two were recovering from injury and the rest were dead. Replacements would come in time, but there was no knowing when or where. The legions on Sicily weren't exactly a priority to the Senate.

Despite their diminished numbers, they looked good, Quintus conceded. The triple feathers atop their shining helmets moved gently in the dawn breeze. Mail shirts that were normally obscured by rust glistened silver. Vigorous polishing had turned the bronze fittings on belts and straps an alluring gold colour. The hastati seemed to stand more proudly as a result.

Quintus felt a trace of nerves as Corax began his inspection. Being on constant campaign didn't have many consolations, but one was that kit inspection and parade duties were almost non-existent. It had been so long since Quintus had had to prepare his gear for Corax's eagle-eyed scrutiny that he worried he'd forgotten all the details. It appeared that others found themselves in the same predicament. Every few paces, Corax growled his disapproval over a belt that hadn't been sufficiently polished, or a fingerprint that was visible on a shield boss. To Quintus' surprise, though, he didn't come in for any criticism. He muttered his thanks to Urceus. His friend, who also survived Corax's examination, had helped him to get ready.

Corax gave the hastati he'd picked out a short time to right their mistakes; the rest were allowed to stand at ease. When he was happy with the penitents, he marched the century to the area of open ground that lay just inside the camp walls. They arrived moments before the extraordinarii, which was pleasing. Their centurion scowled as Corax greeted him, which increased the hastati's enjoyment. Quintus spotted Sattio, who looked as pissed off as his commander about being second to arrive. Good enough for him, he thought, the dour prick.

Yet his spirits fell as the group of officers who were to undertake the negotiations appeared. It wasn't the two tribunes who concerned him, but Pera. Smug-faced as ever, he was resplendent in a transverse-crested helmet and shining cuirass.

'The whoreson gets everywhere,' Quintus muttered to Urceus.

'He's Marcellus' cousin. Do I need to say more?'

Urceus' attempt to reassure Quintus was partially successful. Nonetheless, he was careful to lower his helmet a little so that it covered more of his forehead, and to aim his gaze at the ground. Pera would know he was here because of Corax's presence, but if he kept himself from view, nothing could go wrong. Could it?

The party set out with the extraordinarii in the lead, as they would be when the army marched. Pera and the tribunes came behind the allied soldiers, along with a number of trumpeters, scribes and slaves. Corax and his hastati were positioned next, and the velites took up the rear.

The party took the safest route, the track that ran along the inside of the Roman fortifications. Only when they were close to the Galeagra tower did they pass through a gate into no man's land. To the credit of the extraordinarii, their pace did not slow, but that didn't stop a frisson of nervousness rippling up and down Quintus' spine as they left the safety of their lines. His comrades' faces were marked with tension, and even Corax seemed on edge. Yet the truce held. No missiles were launched as they drew close to the city walls.

Their destination lay to the east of the Hexapyla and adjacent to the Trogilus harbour, an anchorage that had formerly been used by the Syracusans to unload merchant goods for transport into the city. The area was now under Roman control, but it had fallen into disuse, thanks to the enemy artillery. When the chance arose, Quintus and his comrades were fond of swimming in its shallows – under the cover of darkness.

Leaving the water at their backs, the column made its way towards the Galeagra, a squat, hexagonal affair that guarded the point where the fortress walls met both sea and land. It was unsettling to see defenders lining the parapet in silence, their weapons kept from sight. Yet as Corax muttered, they couldn't show the bastards anything but a brave face. So the hastati marched on, chins jutting, with their shields held high. Knowledge that a truce was in place didn't mean that treachery was out of the question. There were plenty of men whispering prayers. There was nothing wrong with asking the gods for protection that might not be needed; Quintus did the same. Better that than to end up dead.

Nearing the gate, the column came to a halt. The extraordinarii took up a position to the left, nearest the sea, while the hastati stood to their right. The tribunes, with Pera and their entourage in attendance, advanced a short distance before the soldiers. The trumpeter sounded his instrument. It was a mangled version of the 'recall', a derisive set of notes that delivered a peremptory summons to the Syracusans and which amused every Roman present.

The Syracusans must have realised the insulting nature of the trumpet call because there was no response for over an hour. During this time, the tribunes had the trumpeter play twice more, but it made no difference. Although the ramparts remained full of spectators, the gate remained firmly shut until the sun was high in the sky. The legionaries were cooking in their armour, and a couple of men reached for their water skins, but Corax's threats soon put paid to that. Appearances were everything, and so their thirst had to wait.

When the gate did finally open, there was no warning. The tension shot up, but Corax was quick to mutter reassurances, and his men settled. The troops who emerged in a double file were similar to the Syracusan infantry that Quintus had encountered before. Dressed like Greek hoplites, they bore large round shields and long thrusting spears. He counted them as they formed a defensive line. At eighty, a party of officers in muscled cuirasses and Hellenic helmets walked out. They watched the Romans from a spot by the gate as the first section of their troops moved into a mini phalanx some fifty paces from Corax's maniple. A second set of eighty soldiers followed; they formed up opposite the extraordinarii. The Syracusan officers then paced to stand facing their Roman counterparts.

'This feels bloody weird,' said Urceus, glaring at the Syracusans. 'Let's fight these goat-fuckers!'

As he so often did, Corax overheard. 'That's not why we're here,' he called in a low voice. 'We keep a watchful eye on this lot, and that's it, unless one of the tribunes says so. So help me, great Jupiter, if a single man among you as much as scratches his balls without my saying so, I will personally shove a sword in his guts.' He broke formation and marched up and down the front rank, eyeballing every hastatus. Urceus in particular was careful not to meet his gaze. 'Do you hear me?' His tone was low but threatening.

'Yes, sir,' they replied meekly.

A moment later, one of the Syracusan officers approached the tribunes. He was shieldless, and held his hands up to indicate his peaceful intentions. Twenty steps from the Romans, he stopped. After a brief pause, Pera paced out to meet him. They spoke, and each man returned to his superiors. Next, Corax was summoned by the tribunes. He came back wearing a big grin. 'We're to guard the officers, not the sodding extraordinarii.'

A pleased murmur rose from the hastati. This was more honour than they'd expected. It was always a sore point among citizen infantry that a group of allied troops protected the consul. Tradition or no, it rankled. This went a small way to redress the balance.

Corax didn't waste any time. He took the first five ranks of eight men, Quintus and Urceus among them, and had them form in an open square. With the tribunes and Pera safely inside, they marched to meet the Syracusans, who responded by also moving forward with a similar number of men. The tension rose once more. Not a soldier present – on either side – had ever been this close to the enemy without intending to kill them. Who would order his men to stop first? wondered Quintus. They drew close enough to see the strain they all felt mirrored in the Syracusans' faces, and then the sweat beading below the rims of their helmets. Still no order came to halt. Shit, thought Quintus. What will happen if we hit them?

Five paces separated the groups when a command in Greek had the enemy soldiers grind to a stop. It was followed a heartbeat later by a similar order from the senior tribune. The victory, while tiny, gave the hastati an instant feeling of superiority. They sneered over their shields at the Syracusans, who glowered back.

'Open ranks!' cried Corax.

The same instruction was repeated in Greek.

The four Romans came together with a quartet of Syracusans not a dozen paces from where Quintus stood. To his surprise, Kleitos was one of the enemy officers. He looked as arrogant as ever. Like Pera, he appeared to be there to act as an intermediary for his superiors.

Quintus and every other man within earshot – Roman or Syracusan – listened in with all his might as polite greetings were exchanged, in Greek and Latin, and each set of officers introduced themselves. The decision was made to talk in Greek, as the tribunes – and particularly Pera – spoke it better than the Syracusans did Latin. Quintus was pleased; he'd be able to eavesdrop on the entire process. Enquiries were made as to the health of both Epicydes and Marcellus; both parties thanked the other for honouring the truce.

The flowery courtesies ceased at last, but the negotiations did not move fast. Initially, the tribunes denied that they were holding Damippus captive. Even when they had admitted it, their manner seemed to indicate that Marcellus' commands were to spin things out as slowly as possible. The Syracusans responded in kind, acting as if they did not care one way or another whether Damippus was repatriated to them, or whether he ended up crucified. When Corax's eyes were elsewhere, Quintus explained what was going on to Urceus.

The dialogue continued in similar vein. Pera seemed to be playing a larger role than Quintus would have thought, which annoyed him intensely. Pera's reputation would grow from this. He diverted himself by studying the hoplites. As was to be expected, they seemed a solid lot. It wasn't long before his eyes strayed to the Galeagra tower. Its size and position oozed strength and impregnability. One day, it might have to be taken, and an opportunity to study it was rare indeed.

Quintus tried not to think of the enemy artillery. It was best to assume that in any theoretical assault, he and his comrades would reach the wall in one piece. Things would not improve at the base of the tower, however. There they would have to resist withering barrages from the bolt throwers that poked from the gaps in the rampart. Many more men would die. Attacking the gate might seem preferable to climbing a ladder, but there were many paths to Hades. Even if they were under *vineae*, manmade tunnels covered with water-soaked leather panels, while they tried to batter down the gate, the Syracusans could kill them from above.

The damn city would never be taken, Quintus decided angrily. He and his comrades would spend the rest of their miserable lives besieging it, never free to return to Italy. About the only way to leave was to die at the foot of these defences.

His eyes wandered over the tower again. It was so well constructed. Great blocks of limestone had been stacked on top of each other with incredible precision. There wasn't a trace of mortar present in the gaps between the stones. Quintus doubted that he could shove even the very tip of his gladius between them. Rumour from the legionaries stationed to the south of the city had it that the stone had been quarried from a site used to house Athenian soldiers taken prisoner by the Syracusans more than two centuries before. Some said that in 'Dionysus' Ear', a leaf-shaped tunnel where the stonemasons' chisel marks could still be seen, echoes and cries of the Athenians were regularly heard, that their essence had somehow soaked into the stones, giving the walls an invisible layer of protection.

An uneasy feeling settled over Quintus. It's bullshit, he thought, remembering his father, who had been excellent at rubbishing such rumours. 'Unless you can talk to the man who saw stones falling from the sky, or statues moving on their plinths,' Fabricius had been fond of saying, 'do not believe a word you hear.' The wall needed no unearthly aid anyway. Its sheer solidity and height were enough to keep out any attackers. To either side of the Galeagra, it was eight large blocks tall. The tower itself was two courses higher than that.

He blinked.

A hoplite had just walked out of the gate. Raising a hand to his eyes against the sun, he moved to the left of the entrance and stood for a moment, searching for someone. That didn't interest Quintus especially. What did was the fact that the hoplite had placed himself right at the base of the wall, and that he was roughly twice the height of one of the stone blocks. The realisation hit him like a lightning bolt. Far away, and without a man standing before it, the wall appeared much taller than it actually was. 'The damn thing's not as high as it looks!' he hissed.

Urceus gave him an odd look. 'Eh?'

'Look,' ordered Quintus, but the hoplite had moved. Ignoring Urceus' confusion, Quintus craned his head to see where Corax was. His centurion was busy talking to Pera for some reason; Quintus had to bite his lip. He wanted to tell Corax, but it was out of the question at that moment. And if he did it later, there'd be no way of proving his theory. Corax wouldn't go to Marcellus unless he had proof. There was nothing he could do.

They were all out at Galeagra again the next morning, but not the junior tribune. According to the gossip, he had come down with a fever. In his absence, Pera played more of a part than he had during the first meeting with the Syracusans. This was to become the tone of the next two days: the lone tribune and Pera haggling with the enemy officers over the price for Damippus. Progress was slow but steady. One evening, Quintus was utterly incensed to hear Corax complaining to Vitruvius. He'd been in the mule pen to feed the beast belonging to the contubernium when the two centurions appeared. It had been a gut instinct to duck out of sight, and their conversation had proved his intuition right.

'At this rate, the prick will be made an equestrian,' Corax growled. 'I wouldn't mind if Pera had any real ability, but I've yet to see any. He's an arrogant fucking hothead, who happens to have a golden tongue.'

'He's also related to Marcellus,' said Vitruvius wryly. 'That helps.'

'Aye.' Corax spat. 'And if his hare-brained plan comes to ought, we'll never hear the end of how Pera was responsible for the fall of Syracuse.'

'What plan?'

Quintus listened with all of his might.

Corax snorted. 'Apparently Pera has been getting on well with one of the Syracusans, who has a real taste for Gaulish wine. It's in short supply at the moment, for obvious reasons. Pera's been telling the tribune that they should run in a shipload of wine to the Syracusan, using the fishermen. That would be the start, but if he proved amenable, gold would follow. So too would the promise of a position of high authority – once the city has been turned over to our forces.'

'It's audacious, I'll give Pera that. Would it work, though?'

'Even if it doesn't, it keeps Pera's nose in Marcellus' arse crack.'

While he hated to hear of Pera's successes, this was a welcome revelation to Quintus. Corax might side with a fellow centurion against him, but the truth of it was that he detested Pera.

'It might be a little smelly, but it's a good place to be if you want to climb the social ladder,' said Vitruvius with a chuckle.

'You and I aren't built like that, old friend.'

'We're not, thank the gods, but there are plenty of men like Pera. The worst of it is that Marcellus can't see sycophants for what they are.'

'Aye, he just laps up the attention. And Pera . . .' Corax paused for a moment before adding: 'I don't think that there's much he wouldn't do to get where he wants.'

'I hope you're wrong there,' said Vitruvius.

'As do I.'

The centurions' voices diminished as they walked away.

Pera's strategy with the Syracusan officer might come to nothing, thought Quintus, but if it did, his rise to pre-eminence would be assured. He would be posted elsewhere, and Quintus would lose his chance to avenge Marius' death. *That* stuck in his gullet like a splintered chicken bone. At this point, a mad plan hatched in his brain. What if *he* were the one to hand Corax the means to take the city?

Chapter XXI

'You want me to leave my post, climb down into no man's land in the pitch dark and walk to the bottom of the city walls, so that you can *measure* them?' Urceus' voice cracked a little on the second last word.

'Not so loud,' urged Quintus. It was night-time in the Roman camp, and some time since they'd retired to their blankets, but that didn't mean the four others were asleep, or that the men in the neighbouring tents were.

'Do I sound as if I have taken leave of my senses?' Urceus' eyes were pools of black disbelief. 'I grant you that the Syracusans might not hear us, but what if you're wrong about the height of the stones? What if this is all for nothing?'

'I tell you, I'm right!'

Urceus didn't appear to hear. 'And if someone other than Corax discovers that we're gone? We'll be executed! And even if it is Corax who finds out, our safety won't be guaranteed.'

'I know, but—'

Urceus interrupted him angrily. 'The other lads could easily be sentenced to the fustuarium too, for letting us go. Because they'd have to be in on it.' He glared at Quintus.

Quintus took a deep breath. He hadn't expected this level of opposition. Perhaps Urceus was right? Pera was an unmitigated whoreson, but *he* had been stupid to win the horse race. Maybe it was best just to let the centurion's star rise beyond reach. When Pera vanished, he could forget about him.

Then Quintus pictured Marius' face in the final moments on the jetty. He remembered how his friend had stayed to die, so that he could live, and his blood boiled with fresh anger. 'What about Marius?' He hurled the question at Urceus so accusingly that Placidus, who was the next man over, stirred. Quintus no longer cared.

'What's Marius got to do with it?'

It was time to reveal what had happened. If he didn't, his friendship with Marius would have meant nothing. He would let Urceus and, later, his comrades be the judges of what to do. 'I'll tell you,' he said.

By the time Quintus had finished his tale, he was aware that every man in the tent was listening. He wasn't sure if it was Placidus who had woken the rest; it didn't matter. Everyone in the contubernium, the soldiers who had been Marius' friends, knew that the conspiracy in Syracuse might not have been betrayed if Pera had gone to Attalus. More importantly in their minds, Marius might well not have died. 'Now you know why I want to do this,' he said, breathing heavily.

Urceus reached out to grip his shoulder. 'I understand your motivation, but what I don't comprehend is how doing this will avenge Marius. Pera might find out that it was us who measured the stones, but he won't know why we did it.'

Quintus could feel the weight of the others' stares through the darkness. If he didn't pitch his answer in the right way, he might lose them all. Help me, Fortuna, he prayed. 'That's where you're wrong, Jug, because our chance will come when we storm the walls at Galeagra. I'm going to seek out Pera and find a way to kill the cocksucker in the confusion. As he slips into oblivion, the last thing he'll hear is my voice telling him what we did, and why, and that he was never going to get away with leaving me and Marius to die like dogs.'

No immediate response was forthcoming, and Quintus' heart sank. It was natural for his tent mates not to want to risk their lives on such a risky venture. Unease licked the base of his spine as a further thought occurred to him. If but a single one disagreed with what he'd just said, they could denounce him to Corax, or any officer. There would then be only one conclusion.

'Forget it,' he whispered. 'I'll go to Corax. Tell him what I've seen. He can do what he wants with the information.'

'We'll approach Corax *after* we've measured the wall,' said Urceus.

'Aye,' said Placidus.

Stunned, Quintus counted the growls of agreement that followed. There were four – with Urceus, that was everyone left in his diminished contubernium. His heart swelled with emotion, with pride that his comrades would do this. 'Thank you,' he muttered.

By the time that they had reached the walls near Galeagra, Quintus was beginning to think that everything would go off as planned. They had waited until the cavalryman whose duty it was to check on their sentry post had come by and collected their *tessera*, the wooden tablet with the day's password on it. It was almost unheard of for another inspection to take place after that, but to minimise the risk, Quintus and Urceus had waited about an hour before making their move. It was the middle of the night by the time their comrades had lowered them between the projecting wooden spikes and down the ramparts' face to the ground below.

Faces, arms and legs blackened with soot gathered from the fire, and without any arms or armour save a dagger each, they had tiptoed away until they were a good five hundred paces from the Roman fortifications. At this point, another sentry would be unlikely to hear them, but they had moved with caution nonetheless. It would have been foolish to use a torch, but fortune had favoured them with a clear sky, and a sliver of moon to add to the stars' light.

Five score paces from Galeagra, recognisable by its shape and the noise of lapping waves nearby, they had halted. Quintus wasn't afraid to admit that he was scared now. Urceus' stiff posture revealed the same emotion. If they made the slightest sound, the Syracusans would rain a barrage of missiles down on them. There was no telling if the darkness would be any protection. They would have to be as silent as cats creeping up on their prey.

Quintus placed his lips against Urceus' ear. 'Can you see the gate?'

Urceus pointed at a square that was blacker than the rest of the bottom of the wall.

'We need to stand about thirty or forty paces to the right of that.'

Urceus nodded. He motioned for Quintus to go first, that he would follow three steps behind.

A metallic sound carried from the walls, and they froze. Quintus studied the ramparts with intense concentration. After a moment, he saw something moving slowly towards Galeagra – a sentry. Casting his eyes to and fro, he observed no one else atop that section. His mouth was bone dry. This was it. He couldn't back out, or the risks that they'd taken would have been for nothing. Quintus took a step forward. Asking Somnus, the god of sleep, to render the enemy sentries drowsy, he began to walk towards the spot that Urceus had identified.

After ten paces, he paused to look and listen. Not a thing. Quintus' gut instinct told him that the sentry was gossiping with the soldiers in the tower. Ten more steps, and still he saw and heard nothing. At thirty paces it was the same, and at fifty. Quintus' pulse was increasing steadily, but Urceus' presence gave him strength. He forced himself onward, praying that there weren't pits or other traps that he hadn't spotted during the negotiations. When they were thirty paces out, the sentry reappeared on the rampart. Quintus stopped dead, indicated that Urceus do the same. This was when, break over, duty reasserted itself. At such times, it was Quintus' ritual to gaze out from the Roman defences for long moments, until he was satisfied that nothing was awry. The Syracusan wasn't quite as vigilant. Barely ten heartbeats later, he moved on. It didn't take long for him to vanish from sight. Quintus waited, counting silently, until the man had returned. When he had gone again, Quintus beckoned Urceus towards him, bent to his ear once more. 'We have a count of two hundred to get in and out. I'll take twenty off that to be sure. You keep tally as well. Ready?'

Urceus nodded. 'Go,' his lips framed.

They were going to do this, Quintus told himself. Twenty. He slid his feet forward with cool purpose. Twenty-one, twenty-two, twenty-three. All the while, his gaze moved from the ground to the ramparts and back, seeking obstacles that would trip him or make noise, and an unexpected sentry who might see them. A score of paces from the base of the wall, they met the defensive ditch, a 'V' shaped trench as deep as a man standing on another's shoulders. Thirty, thirty-one. They both sat down on the edge. Quintus slid down first, using his heels as brakes. The bottom was lined with spiked branches, but he was able to stand upright and wave Urceus on. Forty-eight, forty-nine.

Quintus looked up the wall, which towered over them now, and his stomach wrenched. In the darkness, it seemed even more insurmountable. Sentries would be able to spy on him too, yet they'd be out of his sight. Don't dwell on that, he thought. Stay focused. Fifty-six, fifty-seven. He squeezed between two sets of branches, snagging his tunic in the process. Urceus came after. There was no need for words about what they had to do next; it had been discussed beforehand. Sixty-four, sixty-five. This was the riskiest part, but Quintus did not pause. If he did, his fear might gain the upper hand. Urceus stood with his back to the wall, as close as possible to the inward face of the ditch, and made a bridge with his hands. Quintus placed his right foot in it and leaped up, placing his other foot on Urceus' left shoulder and gripping his friend's head for balance. When he was steady, he lifted his right sandal up so that he was crouched astride Urceus' shoulders. Seventy-nine, eighty.

Quintus was breathing heavily, from nerves and physical effort. *Calm down.* He inhaled deeply and held it for a count of four before letting the air out through his nostrils. Urceus moved a little beneath him. It was damn hard to carry a man like this, Quintus knew, but it was better this than he jump and miss his grip. He peered at the ditch, the surface of which was made of packed earth. Spiked branches had also been buried here, but some had broken off and not been replaced. Luckily, he was

facing such a spot. Ninety, ninety-one. Gods, but the time was flying by.
A trickle of panic entered his mind. Ninety-three, ninety-four. Raising
his arms, Quintus launched himself up and forward. As he hit the bank,
a protruding stone drove into his tunic, striking him just under the ribcage.
The pain was excruciating, and Quintus had to bite his lip, hard, to stop
himself crying out.

Somehow he remembered to reach up with his hands and grab whatever
came within reach. His left hand found a branch; with his right, he sank
his fingernails into the earth as deep as he could. Thankfully, his feet found
a little purchase below him. There was no way of knowing if his weight
would prove too much for his precarious holds, but he didn't have time to
check. One hundred and two, one hundred and three. Gritting his teeth,
Quintus slid first one sandal up to knee height, and then the other. They
didn't slip, so he pushed up with his thighs, reaching out at the same time
with his right hand and gouging his fingers into the dirt. The branch
creaked a little and his pulse hammered out an even faster rhythm in his
ears. He let go of the wood and scrabbled for a grip with his left hand.
Found it, and thrust up again with his legs.

All of a sudden, he was up on the narrow strip of ground that ran
along the base of the wall. He gave Urceus the thumbs up, but his friend's
response was to mouth 'One hundred and eighteen'. Quintus' exhilaration
faded as fast as it had arrived. He moved to and fro along the wall, looking
upwards to see where the most even blocks had been placed. One hundred
and twenty-eight, one hundred and twenty-nine. Finding one, he stood
close to it and placed a hand on the junction between it and the second
course of blocks. It was almost two cubits in height, he judged. Standing
back a little, Quintus carefully counted up to the battlements. There were
eight slabs. He repeated the exercise, to be sure, reaching the same total.
The wall was fifteen to sixteen cubits in height. One hundred and – he'd
lost count. It was time to go. He was about to sit and repeat what he'd
done to get down the other side, but Urceus' urgent hand gestures stopped
him dead. His friend's fingers wiggled back and forth, telling Quintus

that the sentry had come back sooner than anticipated. Acid roiled in his belly as he waited. For all that he expected a warning cry to ring out, there was no point staring upward. He could not see what Urceus could. After several nauseating moments, Urceus signalled him to move. Quintus slid down, uncaring that the back of his left thigh was gouged open by a sharp rock.

'He's gone into the tower. Only the gods know how long he will be,' whispered Urceus in his ear. 'We should keep moving, or we could be here all night.'

Quintus nodded. This time, he made a bridge so that Urceus could get out of the ditch. With a helping hand from Urceus, he climbed out too. Together they studied the ramparts yet again. There was no sign of the sentry. Grinning at each other like madmen, they began walking back to their own lines. They had succeeded.

When they reached the foot of their own fortifications, Quintus sent out the low whistle that they'd agreed beforehand. Placidus and the others sent the rope snaking down the wall a few heartbeats after. The friends went up it at speed, hand over hand, to the top. The questions started as their feet hit the walkway.

'You did it?' 'No one saw you?' 'How high is the wall?'

'Steady,' replied Quintus, smiling. 'Has anything happened here?'

'There hasn't been a soul about,' said Placidus happily.

'Eight blocks, each about two cubits high,' announced Quintus. 'Our ladders will need to be that long, plus a bit more to account for the ditch.'

'Great news, brothers! All we have to do is find the right night and we can be up there before the molles know what's hit them.' Urceus looked like a small boy who'd been given the key to a shop selling pastries.

Placidus clapped Quintus on the back. 'You're going to tell Corax?'

'Yes. First thing. We just need this damn sentry duty to be over, and we're there.'

'Aye. Back to our positions, then. Your equipment is here, and a couple of damp cloths to clean yourselves off.' Looking pleased, Placidus and the others headed off in both directions.

'We'd best make a good job of this,' whispered Urceus. 'Otherwise it'll be bloody obvious that we were up to something.'

'We can check each other over now, and again when it's getting light,' said Quintus. 'That should do the trick.'

'You're a mad fucker, Crespo, do you know that?' Urceus gave him a rough clout. 'But you're a clever one too. Let's hope that Corax likes our story.'

'He will,' Quintus declared with more confidence than he felt.

Quintus was very relieved when the rest of their watch passed off without incident. The trumpet had barely sounded from the praetorium when he was at the foot of the ladder, urging Urceus and the rest down. 'Get a move on! The sooner Corax hears, the better.'

Urceus stopped with his foot on the first rung. His face changed.

Quintus, who had his back to the camp, knew at once that there was someone behind him. Panicked, his mind went blank. Please, let it be Corax! He floundered for something to say. 'H-he'll want to hear that your twisted ankle is better,' he stuttered at last.

Urceus stiffened to attention, saluted. So did the rest of their comrades.

When Quintus turned, his bowels went to jelly. It was Pera. What business had the bastard here? Quickly, he copied his friends. 'Sir.'

Pera didn't acknowledge any of the salutes. Curling his lip, he sauntered closer. 'So you turned an ankle, did you?'

'Yes, sir,' replied Urceus. 'I slipped off the last few rungs of the ladder about a week ago. My own fault.'

'And Corax will want to know that it's all better, will he?' Pera's voice was honey-sweet.

Urceus looked uncomfortable. 'I don't know about that, sir. My brother here was just taking the piss, sir.'

Pera eyed Quintus as a snake might look at a mouse. 'Is that what you were doing?'

'Something like that, sir.'

Pera lifted an eyebrow. 'I wasn't aware that Corax was such a caring soul. Things must be very different in your maniple to mine.'

'I wouldn't know, sir,' said Quintus humbly. *Great Jupiter, I beg of you – make him leave.*

But Pera stayed right where he was, rocking back and forth a little on the heels of his polished leather boots. 'Finished your sentry duty?'

'Yes, sir.'

'You will be glad to get some wine in your belly, I'd say.'

'That'll be good, sir, yes.' *What's he playing at?*

'You're filthy. Doesn't Corax insist on a certain level of hygiene?' Pera sneered.

Quintus fought to stay calm. He wanted to check himself for patches of soot, but didn't dare. 'Aye, sir. He does.'

'I have to disagree, if that's how you look. Go on, then. Clear off, the lot of you.' Pera walked away.

Quintus let out a long, slow breath. He felt as if he'd just run ten miles in full kit.

Urceus and the rest descended the ladder, their shields slung from their backs. Quintus kept a surreptitious eye on them. Placidus and one of the others had taken half of the rope each; to hide it, they had wound it around their waists, under their mail shirts. He exchanged a relieved look with each of them as they set off towards the maniple's tent lines. To lighten the mood, he said, 'Who's preparing the food today?'

The usual dispute began. It was another well-worn routine. The man whose turn it was would accuse someone else of trying to foist the duty on him. The accusation would be vigorously refuted, so the duty cook would drag a third man into it. The banter didn't end until everyone in the contubernium had been named.

Quintus was busy denying that he should have to make the day's meals when they rounded a corner on to the avenue upon which their unit was stationed. Catching sight of Pera again, he stumbled over what he was about to say, before recovering his poise as best he could. 'Don't be stupid, Placidus,' he said loudly. 'We all know it's your turn to cook.' Then, as if he had just noticed Pera, he saluted. 'Sir.'

'You didn't expect to see me again so soon,' said Pera, falling in alongside them as they drew level.

'No, sir.' Quintus tried to sound nonchalant, but inside, he was panicking.

'Is that ash I can see?' asked Pera. Quintus felt real fear as the centurion wiped his fingertip on the back of Urceus' neck, above his tunic. 'It is. How curious!'

A dull red flush coloured Urceus' entire face. 'Sir,' he said.

His answer sounded stupid, and everyone knew it.

'Halt!'

The tent mates obeyed. None dared look at another, but everyone could feel the fear.

'It was only after I walked away that I thought it odd that you two should be so dirty, while your comrades were not,' mused Pera. He jerked his head at Quintus and Urceus, and at a spot five paces away. 'Fall out. Over here. Helmets off.'

Helpless before Pera's authority, the pair did as they were told.

Pera came as close as a woman might, if she were in a seductive mood. His purpose was a lot less pleasant, however. Lifting the arms and necks of their tunics, he inspected their skin with intense interest. He pulled their ears back to check there, and even brushed at their hair. As a little cloud of soot floated away from his head, Quintus felt sick. He shot a look at Urceus, whose complexion had gone from red to grey.

Pera stepped back. 'It looks to me as if you smeared ash all over your faces and arms so that you wouldn't be seen. Enlighten me. Quickly.'

'Sir, we . . .' Urceus began. He hesitated.

'Yes?' Pera's tone dripped venom.

'Nothing, sir.'

Pera glared at Quintus. 'What have you to say, hastatus?'

As Quintus flailed for something that would sound even remotely feasible, Pera prowled over to his tent mates. A moment later, he crowed with triumph. 'You and you! Fall out. Join your maggot friends.'

Placidus and the other hastatus with the rope joined them, their faces miserable. Pera pounced, lifting their mail shirts one by one. 'Rope! This explains much. You' – here he prodded Placidus in the chest – 'and some of the rest lowered those two whoresons down the wall while it was dark.' An outraged note appeared in his voice. 'What were you up to, you traitors? Selling us out to the Syracusan arse-lovers?'

'No, sir!' Quintus and Urceus protested.

'I bet that *was* it! Or you were planning to desert. There have been rumours of this, but I never thought to see it. Marcellus will be furious! He'll want to make an example of the entire contubernium before the whole army. It'll be the fustuarium, I'd imagine,' Pera gloated. 'Corax will be disciplined too.'

A group of passing principes slowed up when they heard some of what Pera was saying, but a snarled order sent them on their way.

While Pera was occupied, Quintus and Urceus glanced at one another with total dismay. 'Tell him what we did,' mouthed Urceus. 'We're fucked either way.'

Gods above, help us, asked Quintus. Do not let my comrades suffer for my stupidity. On my head be it. When Pera wheeled on him again, he met his gaze. 'We're loyal servants of Rome, sir.'

'Really?' scoffed Pera. 'Explain away what I've found here, then.'

'Urceus and I did go over the wall, sir, yes.'

'I knew it! The crime of deserting your sentry post carries the death penalty, you fool!'

'I know, sir. No one was to find out—'

'Until I came along! Fortuna be thanked that I did, eh?'

Quintus longed to ram his sword so hard into Pera's mouth that it shattered his teeth, but instead he waited until the centurion indicated that he should go on. Trying to be as concise as possible, he told the whole story. A malicious interest lit up Pera's eyes the instant that Quintus mentioned the height of the wall, but he did not interrupt once. When Quintus finished, an eerie calm fell. None of the sweating hastati broke it. They were in enough shit as it was.

'You're sure about the number of blocks?' demanded Pera.

'Yes, sir. I wouldn't miscount them after risking my neck like that.'

The trace of a smile passed across Pera's lips. 'I suppose not.'

Another silence, during which Quintus could see Pera's mind working fast. It was clear that he wanted to take this information to Marcellus and, in the process, take all of the credit. Could he achieve this while also claiming that Quintus and Urceus were traitors? If there were no mention of them measuring the enemy's wall, what would he allege that they had done? Quintus had attended the trial of a veles who had abandoned his sentry post. The accused had been closely cross-examined: discovering the reason for his absence – a trip to his tent to recover a skin of wine – had been an important part of gathering evidence against him. Pera needed to make them convincing scapegoats, or suspicion would fall on him over his incredible 'discovery' of the wall's height at Galeagra.

'Listen to me, you filth,' growled Pera. 'Every one of you deserves to be beaten to death for this, d'you understand?'

'Yes, sir,' the hastati mumbled. In his comrades' faces, Quintus saw only despair. In his heart, however, a trace of hope had appeared. 'Deserves', Pera had said.

'What you did was misguided. Stupid beyond belief. It beats anything that I've seen in all my years in the centurionate.' Pera paused, and let them stew for a dozen heartbeats. 'Yet Rome might benefit from it. I will tell Marcellus about the wall. You miserable lot will never speak of it again, to anyone. If you do, I will not rest until every one of you is sentenced to death by the fustuarium. Do I make myself clear?'

You fucker, thought Quintus even as he spoke the words, 'Yes, sir.'

'Are you sure?' asked Pera, his expression fierce.

'Yes, sir,' they muttered.

'Fine. We have an arrangement, then. Why don't you piss off to your stinking tent and drink some wine? After a sentry duty like that, you deserve it.'

They would live, Quintus reflected bitterly, but in the knowledge that Pera could turn on them in the blink of an eye. True, questions would be asked if he tried to bring their dereliction of duty up in a year, say, but that didn't mean that they wouldn't still end up being sentenced to death. The word of lowly hastati was as nothing compared to a centurion, especially one who was related to Marcellus, and who had delivered the method of taking Syracuse to him.

They couldn't go to Corax now. As before, he wouldn't challenge another centurion in public. Even if he did by some miracle speak out, Quintus and his comrades would be exposed as having deserted their posts. A deep gloom settled over him. Why had he been so stupid?

'Ho, Pera! Are you trying to take over my command?'

In the black depths of despair, a ray of hope. Quintus was overjoyed to see his centurion. Pera, on the other hand, looked mightily pissed off. 'Nothing like that. I just picked this lot up on their scruffy appearance, that's all.'

'They're always filthy, my boys. It's of little concern, as long as they can fight, I say.' Corax sauntered up casually, but his eyes held a dangerous glint. 'You don't agree?'

'No,' replied Pera. 'But I let them off with a warning.'

Corax scrutinised his men's faces. 'It doesn't seem that way to me. They look as if they're about to get on the ferry over the River Styx.'

'You know how it is,' said Pera with a laugh. 'The fear of another officer who isn't one's own and all that.'

'Fair enough.' Corax nodded as Pera made his excuses and began to walk off.

Quintus' shred of hope vanished. Beside him, Urceus let out a tiny but audible groan. Pera had got away with it.

'Pera! You didn't notice this?' called Corax.

Quintus was stunned to see Corax waving the length of rope that had slipped, unseen, from around Placidus' waist to the ground. Pera's face was the picture of shock. 'I— No,' he said. 'I didn't.'

'What in hell's name is this for?' bellowed Corax, not just at Placidus, but at them all.

Quintus knew that he was risking his life anew, but trusting Corax with that was infinitely preferable to leaving it in the keeping of a snake such as Pera. He stepped forward, ignoring Pera's threatening glare. 'We used it to climb down the wall, sir. I've found a spot near Galeagra where the defences are only sixteen cubits high. It's a weak point, sir. Somewhere that an attack could be made, if the right men did it.'

'He's lying!' snarled Pera.

Corax ignored him. 'You had to desert your post to do this,' he said accusingly to Quintus. 'You and—'

'Me, sir.' Urceus stepped forward, his shoulders back. 'The rest of the contubernium had nothing to do with it.'

'I'm sure they didn't,' drawled Corax.

'You're not going to listen to these pieces of scum, are you?' Pera's voice was shrill.

'These *pieces of scum* followed me through the horror that was Cannae. Where were *you* that day?' Corax shot back. Pera spluttered, and Corax smiled – but it was all teeth. 'Ah yes, I'd forgotten. You were posted elsewhere.'

'That's right,' said Pera. 'If I had been there, I would have done my duty like any of you. I'd have happily laid down my life.'

'Happily? I'm sure you would.' Corax's tone gave the lie to his words. 'I will listen to my men. Then you can have your say.'

'As a ranking officer, I should speak first!'

Corax turned his back. Pera's face went puce with rage, but he did not move.

'Tell me everything,' Corax ordered Quintus.

Quintus laid out his idea, from the hoplite he had seen during the negotiations to the details of their night-time mission.

'Why didn't you come to me first off, when you realised how low the wall was?' demanded Corax.

'I didn't think you'd believe me, sir. I wanted to be absolutely sure.' And I wanted to stop Pera, Quintus wanted to add. He held his breath, praying that Corax would understand.

'You swear this to be the truth?'

Quintus sensed how important it was that Corax believed him. 'Yes, sir. On my life.'

Corax glanced at Urceus, Placidus and the rest. 'Is it as Crespo says?'

'It is, sir. May Jupiter, Optimus Maximus, strike me down if I lie,' said Urceus.

The other hastati bobbed their heads and muttered their agreement.

Scowling, Corax studied their faces as he had never done before.

Pera could contain himself no longer. 'They're lying whoresons, all of them! They're planning to go over to the Syracusans. Last night's exercise was just a trial run for when the whole damn contubernium deserts. Marcellus must hear of this!' He made as if to go.

'STAY, PERA.' Corax's voice was parade-ground loud. 'You will not say a word to Marcellus.'

Like a whipped cur, Pera obeyed. When he wheeled, however, his eyes were murderous. 'How will you stop me?'

Corax strode to Pera's side and grabbed his arm. Leaning close, he began to speak in a quiet voice. Quintus strained his ears, but he could only hear snatches of what Corax was saying: 'That damn horse race', 'cheating', 'Enna', 'massacre', 'completely unnecessary'.

At this stage, Pera pulled free of Corax's grasp. 'Fuck you,' he hissed. 'None of that matters to Marcellus. He'll still believe that these whoresons of yours are traitors.'

'If you won't listen to sense . . .' said Corax. He lowered his voice even further, meaning Quintus couldn't catch his exact words.

The colour, and the fight, drained from Pera's face. 'W-what did you say?'

'You fucking heard me. I have witnesses as well. You know who they will be,' Corax growled. 'I can't predict Marcellus' reaction, but I imagine it will be harsh – despite your relationship.'

Pera's jaw clenched and unclenched. 'The price for your silence?'

'Your baseless charges against my soldiers will never be brought up again.'

'And the wall at Galeagra?'

'I will tell Marcellus about that, as if I had noticed it myself during the talks.'

Pera seemed about to protest, and Corax went for the jugular. 'If you don't agree, I will ensure that by nightfall every man in the army knows what has passed between us.'

Quintus had never seen Pera look so deflated. 'Very well.'

'We understand each other then.' Corax glanced at his men as if nothing had happened. 'Salute the centurion!'

Quintus and the other hastati obeyed with alacrity. Pera barely noticed.

'Back to our tent lines,' cried Corax. 'At the double.'

The group marched off, each man still not quite believing what had happened. They had been delivered from the threat of execution, and also from Pera's blackmail. Their plan, which had crumbled to dust before their very eyes, had miraculously succeeded. Quintus had caught the look that Pera shot after Corax as they passed, however. His centurion had a new enemy. Yet Quintus didn't feel *that* concerned. Corax was more than capable of handling himself, of dealing with sewer rats such as Pera. He had just proved it.

Quintus' spirits rose with each passing moment.

From now on, Pera would be less likely to harass him too.

Chapter XXII

'Remind me again why we're doing this,' muttered Hanno.

'Because it will please the goddess – and because it's crazy, of course. That's why you came along, isn't it?' Kleitos laughed quietly.

They were standing in the shadows beneath Syracuse's main southern gate, a grand affair that stood taller than three men and which was guarded on each side by a strong tower. Hanno regarded fifteen of Kleitos' best soldiers, who waited nearby. Between them, they were restraining three deer and a decent-sized boar. Being prey animals, the deer had stopped struggling against the ropes that bound them, but the boar was a different matter altogether. The bindings around his feet, and the fact that he was hanging upside down from a hefty branch borne by four men, did not stop him thrashing to and fro and squealing in anger. Every so often, his efforts would unbalance one of those carrying him, and the whole party would stagger about until they regained control.

'The sentries think this is hilarious,' said Hanno dourly, 'but it'll be a different bloody matter when we're outside the walls. The Romans can't fail to hear the noisy bastard.'

'They'll think it's a demon, come to take their souls,' replied Kleitos with a chuckle. He shifted the long, leather-bound package on his back into a more comfortable position.

Hanno stifled his curiosity. He had asked what it was, but Kleitos, winking, wouldn't tell him. 'Maybe. Or maybe they'll send a patrol to see what's going on.'

'You don't have to come, my friend.'

Stung, Hanno scowled. 'All right, I'll stop complaining. Let's hope that it's worth it, eh?'

'Who are we to argue with the high priestess of Artemis? She has decreed that nothing could please the goddess more than a grand sacrifice at the triple junction of the marshes, the land and the sea. Artemis loves nothing more than transition, you see.' Kleitos eyed the grey-bearded priest who was to accompany them.

'It sounds promising.' Hanno stifled his misgivings. If it wasn't up to him, a foreigner, to question the wisdom of venturing beyond the defences at night with a protesting boar, it wasn't his place either to query where it was done, or the decision to offer up animals that were usually considered sacred to Artemis. If it was so important, why wasn't the priestess here too? Stop it, he thought. Just enjoy the madness. There was no doubt that this crazy enterprise appealed to the risk-taking side of his nature – the one that had once seen him attack a trio of armed bandits with no weapon of his own, in the process saving Aurelia's brother Quintus' life. Where was Quintus now? he wondered. Somewhere out there in the Roman camp, surrounded by comrades. He felt a stab of envy.

Epicydes would be pleased by their enterprise – their successful sacrifice to Artemis, the goddess of the hunt, on the first night of a three-day festival in her honour. It would reveal that his continued defence of Syracuse had divine approval. The city's inhabitants would love the tale – how a daring party of their soldiers had sneaked out and sacrificed to Artemis, right under the Romans' noses. It would raise morale, which had slumped somewhat during the long winter months. And if they failed? At least he'd have Kleitos, a true comrade, by his side. A trace of guilt clutched at him. Aurelia would have hated the very idea of this dangerous mission, so he hadn't told her about it. 'I'm not even going to ask how the animals were trapped and then brought inside the city without the Romans noticing,' he said.

'You should have a good idea, living out by Euryalus. Epicydes sent out the best hunters in Syracuse; they used the tunnels both to leave and to return.'

'Gods, but that was risky. If they had been discovered, the Romans would have taken the damn city.'

'Yet they got away with it.' The smell of wine was thick on Kleitos' breath. 'The goddess was smiling on the hunting party, as she is on us. It is she who has ensured that there are plenty of clouds in the sky.'

I'd rather put my trust in my sword arm, and yours, and those of your men, thought Hanno. He offered up a prayer to Baal Saphon, asking him to watch over them, and to keep the boar quiet, or the Romans deaf to its protests. A knot of worry twisted in his belly, and he begged Artemis' forgiveness that he, a foreigner, should commune with his own deities. I mean no disrespect, Great Huntress, he said silently.

There was a low whistle from above. The guard captain, a solid veteran with a dented helmet, approached. 'That's the all clear. There's been no sign of the Roman whoresons since sundown. Go now, and may the gods protect you.' He lowered his voice so that the priest couldn't hear. 'Give that fucking boar a stab from me.'

'I will,' replied Kleitos, chuckling.

The guard captain gestured at the six of his men who were standing ready by the entrance. They bent their backs and lifted the great wooden locking bar from its supports. Laying it quietly to one side, they pulled open one of the gates. To Hanno's surprise, it made little sound.

'We oiled it specially for you boys,' whispered the captain with a sly grin. 'We'll shut it after you, but we will be ready for your return. Don't forget the signal for us to open up.'

'Two short whistles, then a long one and three short,' said Kleitos.

'That's it. Good luck.'

Kleitos eyed Hanno, who signalled his readiness. The priest drew his cloak closer around his body and nodded.

'Follow me!' Kleitos called in a low voice to his men. It was as if the boar sensed the danger that they were about to expose themselves to. Its shrieking redoubled. Hanno longed to slice its throat from ear to hairy ear, but he stayed his hand. Even if he didn't truly believe in Artemis, it wasn't worth upsetting her. Like many deities, the Huntress was reputed to have a prickly, fickle nature.

With Kleitos, Hanno and the priest in the lead, they stole out on to the causeway that led south, towards the villages around Cape Pachynus, the southeastern tip of Sicily. In peacetime it was a busy thoroughfare, but nowadays nothing touched its gravelled surface except an occasional night-time scout, or a Roman envoy. Well used to the dark by this stage, Hanno peered into the gloom before them. He saw nothing, which wasn't surprising. Because of the marshes, which rolled almost to the bottom of the walls, the enemy fortifications here were further away than they were at other points around the city. Hanno didn't relax even a little. The boar's squealing would easily carry the ten stadia that lay between them and thousands of legionaries. According to Kleitos, it was about a third of that distance to the spot that the priestess had recommended. By the time they'd reached it, the Romans would have had time to respond to the unusual noise.

The boar grunted and lashed its head from side to side, making the men carrying him stagger. 'Stupid fucking beast,' said one of them, throwing a kick at it, but his blow missed. The boar resumed its squealing, alternating the sound with deep grunting. Kleitos laughed again, and Hanno had to smile. Hopefully, the Roman sentries would be terrified by the unearthly racket.

They made good progress along the causeway, which was straight, and wide enough for two wagons to pass abreast. It was a case of moving at speed, thought Hanno. Get in, get the job done, get out. That's all they had to do. His eyes scanned the road before them yet another time. Nothing. Out over the waves to his left, a night bird called. It was answered by another, and then another.

'Here,' said the priest suddenly.

Hanno looked. It was as well that the old man was with them. He would never have spotted the tiny path that led off the causeway towards the sea.

With a great deal of sweating and muttered curses, the deer and boar were manhandled down the gravel bank that formed part of the road's foundation. Kleitos and the priest followed, leaving Hanno and five of the soldiers to keep watch. 'How far away will you be?' he called after them.

'About a hundred paces, apparently,' replied Kleitos.

'I'll put two men on the path then, thirty-odd steps apart. If I hear anything, you'll know about it at once.'

'Very well.'

'Kill the boar first if you can.'

'I'll mention it to the priest.' With that, Kleitos was gone.

'Gather round,' Hanno ordered. His five men obeyed with alacrity. They were experienced soldiers, with well-maintained equipment and weapons. Following Kleitos' orders, all metalwork they wore – helmets, shield rims, armour, greaves – had been smeared with mud to render it less visible. 'Clearly, we don't want to see as much as a Roman's pubic hair out here.'

They smiled, reassuring Hanno. Scared men didn't have a sense of humour.

'If we're going to, though, we'll need to know about it as fast as possible. Who's the fastest runner among you?'

'Me, sir,' said a wiry soldier with a thick black beard.

'And the second?'

The wiry soldier glanced at his companions. 'Him.' He indicated a man with a Gorgon's face on his shield, who grinned.

'Head out along the causeway, both of you. Count out the distance carefully. I want one man five hundred paces from here, and the other at two hundred and fifty.' The lead soldier would be damn close to the Roman siege wall. Hanno waited to see if there'd be any protest, but the pair didn't even flinch. Good, he thought. 'You'll hear some sounds from the enemy line. Sentries talking, moving to and fro – you know. I don't care about any of that, unless you think it's a patrol. If that happens, you run back here like the wind itself. Clear?'

'Yes, sir,' they both replied.

'Off you go.'

They vanished into the blackness while the other two clambered down on to the path. Hanno tried to listen to the progress of the first pair, but the boar's complaints put paid to that. Offer the stupid creature up soon, please, he pleaded silently. Ordinary legionaries might be panicked by the noises, but an officer or a steady veteran would eventually realise what was going on. But there'd be no hurrying the priest. Proper ritual would have to be observed before the sacrifice could take place.

He and the remaining soldier waited in silence. A hundred heartbeats dragged by, then another hundred. Hanno felt sweat trickling down his forehead, but he didn't wipe it away. It was better if the other man remained unaware of his nerves. *Damn it, how long does it take to say the necessary words?*

The boar's shrieking took on a new urgency, and an even greater volume. *Squeal! Squeal! Squeal!*

It stopped.

Hanno found that he could breathe again.

'Let's pray that the goddess likes the offering,' hissed the soldier beside him.

And that they can kill the deer fast, Hanno wanted to add. Instead he said, 'She will.'

With the boar silenced, they could now listen out for the enemy. Hanno had hoped that this would make his task easier, but he twitched at every sound. The soldier seemed more unsettled as well. Time moved even slower than it had before and, to Hanno's consternation, the clouds were clearing overhead. A myriad of stars appeared, improving the visibility beyond measure. By the time another three hundred heartbeats had pounded by, Hanno wanted nothing more than to find out from Kleitos what was taking so long. He stayed put, however, worried that to do so might affect how Artemis took the sacrifices.

Thudding feet on the track pushed everything from his mind. Hanno's worries surged as the two soldiers he'd sent out came charging out of the blackness. They skidded to a halt before him. 'Well?' he demanded.

'They're coming, sir,' said the fastest one, panting. 'I heard a gate creak open and men moving outside. They weren't walking in step, and had no torches.'

'How many?'

'If I had to guess, I'd say more than us, sir. They're moving steadily, but not that fast.'

'How far were you from the Roman fortifications, could you see?'

'Not exactly, sir. Three hundred paces, maybe four?'

Hanno cupped a hand to his lips. '*Pssst!*'

The first man on the path came trotting in. 'Sir?'

'Tell Kleitos that he'd best hurry. We've got company. Potentially lots of it. Move!'

The soldier saluted and hurried off.

'Form a line across the road,' hissed Hanno at the rest.

Four of them were able to block the causeway, but they wouldn't be able to hold it if the enemy came in any strength. It was as if the men with Hanno knew that. He could sense their rising fear as the moments passed without any sign of their messenger, or Kleitos. 'Remember, brothers, that the Romans have no idea what's been happening out here. They will be shitting themselves. We'll let them come within a couple of hundred paces, and then I want you to start screaming, to make a racket that would wake the dead. Pretend that your throat's being cut, or your balls cut off with a blunt knife. Lay down your spears beside you now, and draw swords. Hammer them off your shields when the time comes. Got it?'

'Aye, sir.' 'Good idea, sir.' They liked his suggestion, he could tell.

They were joined by the pair of soldiers from the path soon after. 'The priest has to kill the last deer yet, sir,' one explained. 'Kleitos said they'd come when that was done.'

Clenching his jaw, Hanno settled down to wait a little longer. Perhaps eighty heartbeats had gone by when the unmistakeable sound of men moving along the causeway reached his ears. He leaned towards the man nearest him, the fastest runner. 'Hear that?'

'Yes, sir.'

'Go and take a look. Be careful.'

Without hesitation, the soldier did as he was told.

I must find out his name, thought Hanno. He's a brave one.

There was still no sign of Kleitos or the priest by the time that the lookout came tearing back. 'They're picking up speed, sir. There are thirty or forty of them, right enough.'

A half-century, Hanno decided.

'There's a pair of scouts a short distance in front of them too. They're why I had to come back.'

'How far behind you are they?'

'A hundred and fifty paces, sir, no more.'

Hanno glanced down the path. No Kleitos. He cursed. If the enemy scouts saw them, they would alert the rest. If the Roman commander then ordered a charge, it would smash the Syracusans apart. It'd be sheer luck if any of them survived.

They would have to implement his plan on just the two men in front of the Roman patrol, and before he and his soldiers were seen. Hanno had no idea if it would cause panic among the main body of the enemy, but his options had been reduced to one. Damn it, he thought, where was Kleitos?

'Prepare yourselves,' he whispered. 'I want your shouts to be heard on the bloody mainland. I'll give you the signal by raising my right hand.'

Hanno left it until his nerves could take it no more, until he could smell his men's sweat. He could hear the scrape of sandals off the causeway's surface, and he fancied he could see two shapes creeping towards them. Lifting his hand, he screamed with all his might, an unintelligible roar that hurt his throat. 'AAAAAAAAAAHHHHHHHHHH!'

His five men bellowed, roared and yelled beside him. They clattered their swords off their shields in a staccato rhythm, as maniac blacksmiths might beat a piece of metal.

They kept it up for only the gods knew how long.

At last, Hanno signalled them to halt. Sucking air into their chests, his men fell silent. Hanno listened. For a moment, he heard nothing. Then, the sound of sandal leather slapping off the ground at speed. Men were running – away. Exhilaration filled him, and he glanced at the fastest runner. 'D'you hear that?'

'Aye, sir. They must have imagined that Hades was sitting here on the road with Cerberus by his side!'

'Good job, brothers.' They weren't out of danger yet, thought Hanno. What happened next depended on the mettle of the Roman officer in charge.

The arrival of Kleitos and the rest was most welcome. Hanno scanned his and the priest's faces. 'Did the sacrifices go well?'

'Aye,' replied the priest in a satisfied tone. 'All the beasts died easily, even the boar. Their livers and intestines were unblemished, and the goddess accepted the libation of blood.'

How the priest could have seen enough to determine that the animals' organs were free of disease, Hanno had no idea. And as for the libation – well, it was nigh-on impossible for blood not to pour out of an upturned cup. To say anything, however, would be counterproductive. The soldiers who'd witnessed the offerings seemed delighted. The news that Artemis was pleased would spread through the city like wildfire, and that had to be good.

'The Romans sent out someone to take a look, did they?' asked Kleitos.

'Yes.' Swiftly, Hanno explained what he'd done.

'Ha! The screaming was an excellent idea. No doubt they're running for their wall with brown sticky arses,' said Kleitos. The soldiers guffawed. Even the priest smiled.

'I hope so,' answered Hanno.

'Let's head back. We've finished what we came to do.'

Kleitos' men were still forming up when there was a shout in Latin, not a hundred paces away. 'FORWARD!'

Everyone froze. The Romans couldn't have entirely broken, Hanno realised in alarm. Now, they would have to fight. It was that or flee, which was as quick a path to Hades as any. Roman legionaries were lethal in the pursuit. He glanced at Kleitos. 'We'd best make a stand, eh?'

'I knew this might come in handy,' muttered Kleitos, unslinging the package on his back. He pulled at the leather thongs that bound it tight.

Hanno watched, bemused, as the distinctive shape of a carnyx, a Gaulish vertical trumpet, was revealed. 'Where in all the gods' names did you get that?'

'There's an old merchant from Gaul with a premises near my barracks. Before the siege, he used to import wine from his homeland. These days, he deals in whatever's hard to obtain in the city. I buy cheese and wine from him. This normally hangs on his wall.'

Hanno remembered Trasimene, and the fog, and how the hideous booming of hundreds of carnyxes had sent panic tearing through the Romans. Hope rose in his chest. It might do so again now. 'Can you play it?' he asked.

'Let's see. I had one go, which wasn't to the Gaul's liking, although it was loud enough.' Kleitos stepped forward and raised the carnyx to his lips.

'AT THE DOUBLE!' roared the voice in Latin. Hobnails crunched off the surface of the road. The jingle of mail became audible. Hanno gestured urgently at his friend.

Parr-parr. Kleitos coughed a little, and replaced it against his mouth. *Boooooooooo. Parr-parr. Parr-parr-parr. Parr-parr-parr. Zzzeyrrp. Boooooooooo.*

'Shout! Scream, as if we are a hundred men!' hissed Hanno at the soldiers.

They took his meaning at once, bellowing at the tops of their voices, and clattering their blades off their shields. Fifteen of them made far more noise than five had. Spurred on, Kleitos blew and blew until it seemed the tongue might fly out of the beast's mouth at the top of the carnyx.

Parr-parr-parr. Parr-parr-parr. Zzzeyrrp. Booooooooo. His efforts were like a strangled version of the noise made by the instruments that Hanno had heard before. For all that, they were deafening. What they would sound like when coming out of the pitch-black night, he had no idea. With any luck, they would be bowel-churningly frightening.

Parr-parr-parr. Parr-parr-parr. Zzzeyrrp. Booooooooo. Parr-parr-parr. Parr-parr-parr. Zzzeyrrp. Booooooooo.

Hanno peered into the gloom, preparing for the arrival of a large number of Roman legionaries. He waited, heart thumping in his chest. And waited. Around him, the men continued to shout and roar, but Hanno could sense that they too were increasingly uneasy.

At last Kleitos had to stop to draw breath. He lowered the carnyx, looked at Hanno. 'Well? Are the stinking dogs coming? Or have they run?' He wiped his brow and lifted the instrument again. *Parr-parr-parr. Parr-parr-parr. Zzzeyrrp. Booooooooo.*

Hanno's stomach knotted. He knew what Kleitos meant. Someone had to advance to see if their enemies had fled, risking instant death if the legionaries had not been scared off. Fuck it, he thought. With a white-knuckle grip on his sword, he slid his feet forward. Step by sweating step, he moved towards the Roman fortifications. Five paces. Ten. Fifteen, and then twenty. Behind him, Kleitos blew as if his life depended on it. His soldiers' clamour went on unabated. The combination made a horrendous din, but Hanno would have preferred to stay close to it rather than to walk away, into the mouth of death.

At fifty paces, he stopped. There was something large lying on the road. Hanno crept closer, ready for a trap. Finding a scutum, he laughed out loud. Two steps away, he saw a pilum. 'They ran,' he said. 'They bloody ran!' Fear gone, he strode forward another fifty paces along the causeway. There wasn't a Roman in sight. One more scutum, and a few pila, but no flesh-and-blood legionaries.

Parr-parr-parr. Parr-parr-parr. Zzzeyrrp. Booooooooo. Kleitos' efforts on the carnyx continued, but they were faltering somewhat.

Hanno grinned. He should return with the good news before Kleitos collapsed. He trotted back. The news made Kleitos laugh so hard that he had a coughing fit. 'It's almost a shame that the wine is being given out for nothing at the moment,' he said, recovering. 'I wouldn't have had to open my purse for a day or two.'

'Longer than that,' Hanno observed, wiping tears of amusement from his own eyes. 'To think of taking the carnyx was pure genius.'

'It wasn't a bad idea, eh?'

'Truly, the gods are on our side this night,' added the priest with a pleased look.

Hanno bowed his head in respect. It did indeed seem as if the divine powers had given their approval. Thank you, Great Huntress. Thank you, Baal Saphon. With your help, we can smash Marcellus' legions when Himilco arrives, and end the war on Sicily.

Upon Kleitos' order, they began a quick march back to Syracuse, making no effort to be quiet. It was unlikely that the legionaries would be rallied, but as Kleitos said to Hanno, it would be a shame to suffer any casualties because they had dawdled too long. 'Let our suffering be in the form of pounding heads and cold sweats from the wine we drank tonight,' he declared.

'I think I'll join you in the pursuit of that,' said Hanno happily. After what had just happened, the hangover would be worth it.

Chapter XXIII

Quintus and Urceus were in the same spot below Galeagra as they had been on their spying mission a week before. This time, it was with an altogether different purpose. Corax was with them; so too was the entire maniple. Five other maniples of hastati were manoeuvring into position behind: almost a thousand soldiers all told. Pera's unit was among them. Ten ladders that had been constructed secretly were with Corax's troops. Marcellus *had* believed Corax, thought Quintus triumphantly. Marcellus had questioned him for two hours and more, Corax had told Quintus later, but he had accepted his story. As if to show the gods' favour, a newly arrived Syracusan deserter had mentioned the forth-coming festival of Artemis, which would last for three days. To placate the city's restless inhabitants, who were angered by the growing shortage of food, Epicydes had let it be known that unlimited wine would be available, gratis, during the entire festival.

It had been clever of Marcellus to delay their attack until the second night of festivities, Quintus decided. Everyone who had abstained on the first night would want to catch up with what they had missed out on. The ones with sore heads would be adopting the hair-of-the-dog approach. And the ones who didn't drink? Well, there were few people indeed who could refuse free wine. If there had ever been a good opportunity to attack Syracuse, this was it. It was all thanks to him. Marcellus didn't know that, but Corax did. He'd even taken Quintus aside and thanked him afterwards.

'If this works, I'll personally find enough wine for you and the rest to get pissed for a week,' he'd also said.

'I will hold you to that, sir,' Quintus had replied, laughing.

Quintus didn't feel quite so humorous now. He was crouched before the defensive ditch, weighed down by his equipment, and by the knowledge that when Corax gave the signal, he would be the first to move to the base of the wall. The men behind him – Urceus and his other tent mates, and after them the remainder of the maniple – were carrying the twenty-cubit-long ladders. Once they had reached him and they had listened out for enemy activity, it would be Quintus who went up the first ladder. Urceus and his comrades would follow him, and then Corax and the rest.

Corax had set them this task. 'It was your observation that made this possible.' He'd chuckled wryly. 'But you lot weren't ever going to get away with such a dereliction of duty. Abandoning one's sentry post is inexcusable, whatever the reason. If you survive the attack, however, I'll forget what happened – this once.'

That was fair enough, thought Quintus. His bladder twinged; irritated, he did his best to ignore it, and his churning guts. It was as if he hadn't emptied his bladder and bowels before they left the camp. He had, twice. Everyone had been at it: packing out the latrine trenches and making overloud jokes. I'll forget about it when the fighting starts, he told himself, trying not to imagine what would happen if he never got that far. If a Syracusan sentry heard him climbing the ladder—

Corax materialised out of the blackness and put his face close to Quintus'. 'Ready?' he mouthed.

Quintus nodded.

Corax pointed at the wall. 'Go,' he meant.

With a final look at the ramparts, Quintus set about getting down into the ditch. The process was nerve-racking. He felt as if a warning cry would issue from above at any moment, or that a massive rock would be dropped on his head. Maybe the lunatic with the carnyx, he who had so terrified a patrol on the south side of the city the night before, would even appear. Nothing of the sort happened, but that didn't make Quintus feel any better. With gritted teeth, he and Urceus took the first ladder from Placidus' hands. When more men had joined them in the ditch, they passed it over the bundles of sharp-ended branches. Quintus took a moment then to listen for sentries. Apart from some singing a little way off, he heard nothing. Without further ado, they lifted the ladder up and laid it against the wall. Despite their best efforts, there was a soft noise on impact. They froze, but no challenge rang out.

Quintus burned to ascend at once, but their orders were not to begin the assault until at least five of the ladders were in place. They just had to stand there, hearts pumping, as the rest of their maniple copied what they had done. Eventually, it was done. Hastati packed the ditch like fish in a pool. Scores of others were visible at the edge of the trench, waiting their turn. Pera was out there somewhere too. Gods grant that he comes within reach of my blade later, thought Quintus bitterly. He was determined to utilise the chaos granted by the sack of a city to take his revenge. Urceus agreed with him. If the chance came, they would kill Pera.

'Fortuna be with you,' whispered Corax in Quintus' ear. 'Go.'

Quintus hated climbing ladders in full kit. In the darkness, it was even harder than he expected. What it would have been like with his shield as well, he could only imagine. With every step, his scabbard threatened to betray him by knocking against the wood of the ladder. Through trial and error, he worked out that by tucking his sword hilt into his armpit and keeping his upper arm clamped against his body, he could minimise the gladius' movement. With luck, Urceus and the men behind him would work the same thing out.

Up, up, keep going up. Dry-mouthed, sweating, stomach churning, Quintus counted the rungs as a way of getting through the terrifying experience. The tactic didn't stop images of the soldiers who'd been flung to their deaths during the first assault on the city from filling his mind. When his head popped over the rampart, he almost cursed out loud with surprise. A glance to the left, to the right. Exultation filled him. There was no one in sight. Fifty paces to Quintus' left, Galeagra loomed. He could hear nothing from within. Stay in there, sleeping off your wine, he prayed, throwing a leg over the top of the wall and easing himself on to the stone walkway beyond. That done, he leaned out and beckoned to Urceus, who was already halfway up.

Before long, there were five of them atop the defences. Then it was ten. Corax appeared with the next set of men; on his orders, they waited until thirty of them had gathered. 'Remember, stealth is everything still. We kill everyone in the tower, so that it remains in our hands, but our main objective is the Hexapyla.' Leaving ten soldiers to guard the ladders – yet more hastati were climbing – the centurion ordered the rest to draw their swords and led them towards Galeagra. For the first time, Quintus began to feel naked. The troops they'd be facing would have shields; he and his comrades did not. *Fuck it, stop worrying.* They'll all be asleep, he told himself.

But the first man wasn't. They came upon him right by the door into Galeagra. Yawning, rubbing his head, clearly drunk, he didn't see them. With his cock in his one hand, he pissed out over the top of the wall. Corax darted forward before anyone else, grabbing the man around the mouth with his left hand and sawing through his throat with the gladius in his right. Black blood showered down into the ditch below as the man struggled. His heels drummed a hypnotic rhythm on the walkway, and then he went limp, like a sacrificed beast at the altar.

Corax lowered him down with care. When he straightened, he pointed to Quintus, and to the door, which was ajar.

Quintus moved before fear froze his muscles. The strip of light cast on the paving meant there were lights burning inside. With infinite caution, he peered around the jamb. His eyes took a moment to readjust. He took in the slumped shape of a man propped up against the outer wall of the room within. There was a trapdoor to the chambers below, and that was it. 'One soldier,' he mouthed at Corax. The centurion motioned him in.

Around the doorframe. In, sliding his feet over the timber floor, sword raised. His victim didn't stir, even when Quintus stood right over him. His eyes opened wide with shock, however, as Quintus' blade thrust deep into his chest cavity via the point where shoulder met neck. Quintus shoved his left hand over the man's mouth to keep him silent and ripped out his sword. As blood showered everywhere, they stared at one another in the brief, bizarre exchange that Quintus hated – and loved so well. The Syracusan was dead a few heartbeats later. Quintus propped him against the wall and went to get Corax and the rest.

It didn't take long to seize control of the rest of Galeagra. Its entire garrison was asleep; discarded jars and beakers of wine lay in every chamber. Level by level, the hastati stole down the ladders and slew the occupants, most of whom were in their beds. Corax summoned the rest of his men from the ramparts and then liaised with another centurion. The decision was taken to move at once for the Hexapyla with two maniples. The rest of the hastati, who were still climbing the ladders, could follow on with all speed. With that, Corax led them out of the Galeagra and on to a narrow way that led along the inside of the wall. It was lined with two- and three-storeyed brick houses that faced on to the defences, but not a soul was to be seen. Despite the almost complete darkness, and the danger that they were in, Quintus was beginning to enjoy himself. There was an insane delight to be taken in their mission. They were but two maniples. If the alarm were raised, thousands of Syracusan defenders would rise from their beds, drunk or not, and annihilate them. If it weren't, the rewards would be immeasurable.

They moved as fast as was possible, cursing under their breaths at the uneven paving and the rubbish strewn everywhere. Scrawny cats eyed the group with suspicious eyes. An occasional cur stood chewing on the scraps dropped by drunken revellers or thrown from the windows above.

The massive stone towers that formed the Hexapyla had just come into sight, profiled against the starlit sky, when they came across a postern gate. Its bolts were fastened with padlocks, but that didn't stop Corax grinning and summoning the other centurion. After a brief conferral, Corax's maniple continued on for the Hexapyla while the second unit waited by the gate. They were to wait for a count of five hundred – enough time for Corax's hastati to gain a foothold in the towers – before breaking the gate down with axes.

It would have taken Hercules himself to stop Quintus and his comrades from reaching the ramparts over the Hexapyla gate. The momentousness of what they were doing had really sunk in now. The tower's garrison, some hundred soldiers, was as deeply asleep as that at the Galeagra had been. They died without waking in their beds, on the floors where they had fallen down drunk, and in the latrines, where several had collapsed. Inevitably, a couple of men were roused by the muffled sounds; they cried out as they died, but the noise made no difference to the final outcome. Groups of hastati were moving through all the other rooms, thrusting, hacking, stabbing. By the time that Quintus and his comrades stood atop the massive gate, the light of the rising sun revealed them to be spattered with blood from head to foot. From below, they could hear other soldiers heaving back the great bolts that sealed the portal. Soon after, a hastatus arrived to tell them that the postern gate was also in Roman hands.

'We've done it,' said Urceus, chuckling like a maniac. 'We've fucking done it.'

'Almost. We find Pera next,' Quintus added in a whisper.

They would do this together, without involving Placidus or the rest. No blame could be laid on their tent mates if they'd been with the maniple for the entire duration of the attack. Corax might notice that the pair were gone, but he wouldn't be able to do a thing until they returned. Quintus already had a story concocted about being swept away from the unit in a fight and not being able to find it again in the confusion.

Corax appeared from the gate below. 'It's open, but I want no over-confidence. The army isn't inside yet.' There was a trumpet in his hands. 'This is Roman. It must have been taken after our first assault. Crespo, can you sound it?'

Quintus' heart sang. This was another acknowledgement of what he'd done. 'I'll do my best, sir.' He raised the instrument to his lips, took a deep breath, and blew with all his might. The discordant noise that emerged had a smiling Corax and Urceus stick their fingers in their ears. Quintus sounded it again and again, shredding the night air with his cacophony until he felt breathless.

Still chuckling, Corax cupped a hand to the side of his head and leaned out over the rampart. 'Listen.'

First, Quintus heard the shouts of officers. Then, the familiar *tramp*, *tramp*, *tramp* of thousands of sandals hitting the ground in unison. Marcellus' legions, which had been assembling under the cover of darkness for this moment, were answering his summons. 'Syracuse is ours, sir,' he said proudly.

'I don't owe you that wine just yet, Crespo,' warned Corax. 'But I'd say it could be yours by the day's end if the gods continue to smile on us as they have done this night. Our orders now are to take Epipolae, the area to the west of here, first. We're to be ready to face enemy attacks from every direction. The most likely responses will come from the east or southeast, towards Achradina and Ortygia. That's where our intelligence tells us that Epicydes is. He won't want to let his city fall without a fight.'

'Let them come, sir,' said Urceus fiercely.

Corax looked pleased. 'It's time to send the fear of Hades into the hearts of everyone inside the walls. Make as much noise as you can from this point. We'll head south, to the limits of Epipolae. Assemble with the rest of the men, outside.' He was gone even as they replied.

'Now's our moment,' hissed Quintus.

Urceus lifted his gladius, which was red from tip to hilt. 'Aye. It's time to avenge Marius.'

Aurelia rolled over and sleepily reached out a hand to where Hanno should have been. Her fingers met only cold blankets. Waking, she remembered. This was the second night running that he hadn't been there. She still wasn't used to Publius' absence, which meant that she missed Hanno's warmth in the bed even more. Yet she couldn't deny him the pleasure of a couple of big drinking sessions. What he and Kleitos had done the previous evening was already the stuff of legend. The story of how they had daringly sacrificed to Artemis outside the walls, before putting to flight a large Roman patrol, had swept through the city as if borne by the wind itself.

It might have been so different if the legionaries hadn't been panicked by Kleitos' carnyx, but Aurelia had refrained from mentioning that. Such a huge boost to everyone's morale had been worth it, for the long months of siege had taken their toll. Even Hanno, who like her had had the freedom of a period in Akragas, had grown tired of it all. She was heartily sick of it; of the shortages of foodstuffs and essentials such as lamp oil; of the refugees who, having fled the Roman legions as they closed in, were packing the city until it bulged at the seams; of the soldiers who felt that it was their god-given right to harass every able-bodied woman they saw. An image of Pox Face came to mind, and Aurelia sighed. So far there had been no instances like that – she didn't go out very often, and wore a hooded cloak when she did – but any hope of getting back to sleep had just vanished.

Aurelia looked down to the foot of the bed, where the cat was still curled up, asleep. Bless him, she thought. She fed him some scraps from her plate when Hanno wasn't about, but meat was far too scarce a commodity to give to a pet cat. If it weren't for the young boys in the neighbouring apartments who hunted rats for sport, Hannibal would have had precious little to eat. With a little luck, they'd deliver one or two later. The small silver coin that Aurelia gave them once a week meant that they tended not to forget. It was fortunate that the boys also liked feeding the cat, because it meant that Aurelia didn't have to handle the dead rodents. She had insisted it was done in one of the nearby alleys.

After a little while, she rose and got dressed. Sunlight was starting to creep through the gaps in the shutter slats, which meant that it was nearly time to begin the day. If she went to the bakery now, there was more chance of getting some bread. It was nicer hot from the oven too. The fishermen would have returned from their night's activities, Aurelia realised with a flash of excitement. Fish was one of the few commodities in abundant supply, and Hanno might appreciate a plate of fried tuna or mackerel later. It was worth walking several streets to the fishmonger's to check what he had in. While she was there, she could look in the market for some vegetables.

A sharp pang of grief struck home. It still felt odd to consider going out without Publius. I miss you every day, little one, she thought. May the gods look after you in Elysium. I will join you there one day. When he'd died, she had wanted to follow him daily, but her love for Hanno had changed that. There was only one life, and it had to be lived, not ended prematurely. She'd see Publius again when her time came. Before that, she hoped to have children with Hanno. Not now, for that would be insane, but when the peace that she longed for arrived. Until then, she would continue to take the herbs sold by certain midwives.

A boy shouted on the street, and she smiled. It was the red-haired, sturdy leader of the rat-catchers. Hanno had said that – red hair aside – the boy reminded him of himself when he was young. The idea of having a miniature version of Hanno to look after warmed Aurelia's heart. Gathering up her wicker basket and purse, she prepared to go out.

Tan-tara. Tan-tara-tara. The sound repeated, over and over. *Tan-tara. Tan-tara-tara. Tan-tara. Tan-tara-tara.*

The sound dragged Hanno up from the depths of unconsciousness. That's a trumpet, he thought dully. A fucking trumpet. Whoever's blowing it needs the thing shoved up his arse. That would soon shut him up.

Other men stirred, shouted irritably. 'Piss off!' 'We're not on duty.' 'It's a festival day, you idiot!'

To Hanno's frustration, the trumpeter remained unaware of their discontent. The noise went on and on, until he was awake enough to take in his surroundings. He was lying on a dirty floor, partially under a table. Kleitos sprawled beside him, oblivious. Between them was a half-full jug of wine, miraculously unspilled. They were still in Poseidon's Trident, he realised. He reached out with a foot and kicked Kleitos.

'*Urrrrr*,' Kleitos groaned. 'Gods, my head hurts.'

'Mine too,' said Hanno, trying to find enough moisture in his tacky mouth to spit. Failing, he leaned up on an elbow and took a swallow of wine. Its acid taste made him choke. He forced it down anyway, and took a second mouthful. 'The hair of the dog that bit us,' he muttered, offering it to Kleitos. 'Want some?'

Tan-tara. Tan-tara-tara.

Kleitos' face, which had been slack and exhausted-looking, changed. He stared at Hanno, mouth agape. 'Has that been going for long?'

'A little bit. Why?'

'Greeks don't use trumpets.' Kleitos lunged upwards, using the table to help himself stand. 'UP! UP, YOU FUCKING MAGGOTS! THE ROMANS ARE INSIDE THE CITY! UP! UP!'

There was instant uproar.

The nausea that had been threatening Hanno's stomach grew a lot worse. He swallowed it down and stood with an effort. 'How? How can they have got in?'

'You tell me!' yelled Kleitos. Wild-eyed, he darted about, coming up a moment later with his sword and baldric. 'It'll have been a traitor,' he said with a bitter laugh. 'That's always how cities get taken, isn't it?'

'I suppose.' Hanno found his own weapon further under the table; his helmet was there too. At least they had come to the inn without going home to change. He and Kleitos were still in their armour. 'Where was the trumpet sounding from?'

'Who fucking knows? Let's get outside and find out.'

Hanno studied the men around them, who were from a mixture of units and clearly of varying quality. Some looked to be veterans, but the majority were young men who could have only been pressed into service when the siege began. Their panicked faces told him plenty.

'You! You. You, and you!' Kleitos yelled. The four soldiers he'd pointed at – veterans – responded, which was something, thought Hanno. They shuffled closer. 'Sir?' asked one.

'Grab whatever weapons you came with and meet us outside,' barked Kleitos. 'Quickly!'

'Sir.' They began rooting around on the floor amid the broken cups, spilled wine and vomit.

Outside, chaos ruled. The trumpet's blaring had stopped, but there were frantic-looking people running hither and thither. Soldiers wandered by in twos and threes, many of them still drunk. A half-dressed officer barked orders from a first-floor window; the troops ignored him. Conflicting reports filled the air: the Romans had smashed through several gates; they had already butchered half the garrison; Epicydes had been assassinated; a fleet of enemy triremes had sailed into the Great Harbour. A woman carrying a screaming baby stumbled by, calling in panic for an older child who was lost. A madman with long, filthy locks and a piercing stare announced that the world was ending. Shopkeepers who had been opening their premises moments before slammed shut their doors.

Hanno fought to stay calm. Despite his combat experience, he'd never been in a situation like this. Aurelia, he thought, Aurelia. The fact that she was Roman would mean nothing to legionaries crazed with bloodlust. May the gods protect her. 'What should we do?'

Kleitos' response was to seize a passing soldier by the arm. The man wheeled on him, his hand going for his sword, but he relaxed, realising Kleitos was an officer. 'Sir?'

'What in Hades' name is going on?' Kleitos demanded.

'The word is that a party of Romans scaled the wall at the Galeagra tower, sir. They killed the garrison and moved on to the Hexapyla. I don't know, but I assume that the trumpet's call was to let the bastards outside know that one or more gates have been opened.' The soldier flinched, as if expecting to be punished for uttering such calamitous news.

'My thanks,' said Kleitos. 'Trying to find your unit?'

'Yes, sir.'

'Good. On your way, and may the gods help us all.'

With a quick salute, the soldier ran off. A moment later, the four veterans emerged from the inn, bleary-faced but with weapons in their hands. 'Ready, sir,' the lead one said to Kleitos.

'Good.' Kleitos glanced at Hanno. 'My men – and yours – are up near the Hexapyla. It's going to be fucking carnage there. If that soldier was right, our troops will already be dead.'

'They might not be,' retorted Hanno. 'I think we have two choices: wait to see what Epicydes' response will be, risking that it'll all be over by the time we reach the Hexapyla with enough force, or to head up there now, which could be akin to tossing ourselves into the crater at the top of Mount Etna.'

'Damned if we do, and damned if we don't,' Kleitos snarled. 'Those motherless, cocksucking Roman bastards!'

He's not sure what to do, thought Hanno, and every moment we lose is worth ten where it's needed. 'We make for the Hexapyla,' he declared. 'My money says that Epicydes is yet scratching his arse.'

Kleitos shook his head. 'Aye. That's the best plan.'

'Which direction?' asked Hanno, who still barely knew how to find his way to the inn from where he lived, let alone find the Hexapyla.

Kleitos pointed to their right, where the press was thickest. 'That way.'

'I know the back streets around here, sir,' volunteered one of the veterans. 'They'll be far quicker.'

'You lead,' ordered Kleitos. 'Move as fast as you can. Every damn moment is vital.'

'Aye, sir.' The veteran led off at a brisk pace; Kleitos followed; after him came Hanno and the rest.

Hanno's churning stomach told him it wouldn't be long until it rejected the wine he'd just drunk, but that was the least of his worries. The city could well have been already lost. They'd arrive at the Hexapyla and be slain by the Romans, dying for nothing. Meanwhile, Aurelia was alone and defenceless in their rooms. Hanno's limbs nearly betrayed him then, so strong was his desire to run towards Euryalus. I am Hannibal's man, he repeated to himself. I was sent here to help Syracuse fight

Rome. That is my duty, and it comes before everything else. Everything. As they ran on, Hanno wished that the bitter taste in his mouth was because of the wine.

It had nothing to do with it.

Aurelia.

According to the soldier who was leading them, it was a little over twenty stadia to the Hexapyla gate. Under normal circumstances, Hanno would have expected to make the journey quite fast. Today was very different. Although they made good time in the tiny alleys and narrow paths between houses, they were hampered by tides of people on each occasion that they emerged on to larger thoroughfares. If it hadn't been for the fact that they were armed, and purposeful, they would have made little progress. It didn't take Kleitos long to order that they should give one verbal warning for passers-by to step out of their path before using their fists or the flat of their blades to achieve the desired result.

If the suburbs of Achradina and Tyche had been crowded, then the streets beyond their inner walls were packed like salted fish in a barrel. The shocked and hungover guards had opened the gates and were just letting the tide of refugees enter. It was good to know, Hanno supposed, that Achradina and Tyche remained in Syracusan hands, yet if every inhabitant of Epipolae entered, their supplies would not last long. They managed to squeeze through the gates, against the flow. On the other side, the crowd coming towards them made it impossible to move at anything more than a snail's pace. Scared-looking men shouted and cursed to no avail. A red-cheeked priest demanded that he be let through before anyone else. Babies and small children wailed, and their harassed mothers tried to calm them. A pair of donkeys brayed their unhappiness.

'It will be too late by the time we get there, damn it,' said Kleitos, scowling.

Behind his blinding headache, Hanno was thinking the same thing. Wherever the Romans were, on the other hand, people would be running. The enemy would be moving fast, like rainwater from a storm that forms new trails through dusty ground. Swathes of the city would have fallen before Epicydes managed to marshal enough troops together. His men wouldn't have much spine for a fight either, thanks to the vast amounts of wine that had been consumed for the two nights prior. Bitterness took Hanno. What difference to the outcome could they, six soldiers, make? What difference could he make? The resounding answer to both questions was 'none'. Whereas if he reached Aurelia, he might be able to get her out, before the Romans reached the quarter near Euryalus. To where, he had no idea, but anything was better than her just waiting, terrified, for him. 'Kleitos,' he said.

His friend glanced at him. 'Go.'

Hanno stared in shock.

'You don't have to prove your loyalty to me,' said Kleitos in a low voice. 'Your sword isn't going to change what happens to the city today, but it might save Aurelia's life.'

'I—'

'If I'd had the chance, I would have done the same in Enna, for my woman. Go, Hanno, and may your gods watch over you.' Kleitos reached out a hand. 'I'll see you in Achradina, later.'

They shook. 'Will Achradina hold, do you think?' asked Hanno.

'I damn well hope so. If it doesn't, all of Syracuse will fall today. I don't even want to think about that.'

'No.' Hanno had been thinking of using the tunnels near the Euryalus fort, but doing that would still leave them within the Roman fortifications. In reality, it also meant deserting. Despite his desperation to save Aurelia, Hanno couldn't do that. He came to a decision. In Achradina, he could fight on. They would have access to Ortygia, and ships. If it came to it, escaping by sea would be easier, perhaps. 'Very well. We'll make for there. Thank you, Kleitos. Zeus Soter protect you.'

'We'll need his help. Do you know which way to go?'

'Aye. I recognise this square.' Hanno didn't know what else to say. It was likely that he and Kleitos would never meet again. Their eyes met, reflected the same intense feeling. 'Farewell.' Breaking the gaze, he ducked off into an alleyway to his left.

He lost all sense of time during the journey that followed. Sometimes he walked, sometimes ran. He shoved and pushed, squeezed through narrow gaps that left scrapes on his bronze armour. It wasn't long before he had to stop and throw up. Sadly, it did not relieve his nausea, and made his headache far worse. On another occasion, he would have felt sorry for himself. Now he ignored it, and soldiered on. He crawled on his hands and knees to get past a wagon that was blocking a narrow street. A short while after, frustrated by a neighbourhood that was entirely at a standstill, he pounded up the stairs of an apartment block and clambered on to its roof. The view he was afforded sent cold sweat slicking down his back. Thick plumes of black smoke were rising from every part of Epipolae. There was no mistaking the sound of screams either, or the ring of arms. The Romans had not been contained, nor could they be any longer. Cursing, he turned away.

The red clay tiles of the roof made treacherous footing. More than once, he came close to falling. The short distance between buildings proved an advantage, however, allowing him to jump from one to the next. In this fashion, he made it around the area of blocked streets. When the time came to climb down from his lofty position, Hanno gave an elderly woman the shock of her life by dropping on to the landing outside her open door. He smiled and raised his open hands to show that he meant her no harm, and clattered down the stairs. There was no point saying anything to the crone. It was safer for her to remain where she was than to risk the insanity on the streets. He found it far harder to ignore the pleas of the attractive young mother with two children, who begged him to help her reach safety. 'I can't, I'm sorry,' said Hanno without looking at her. 'Take us with you, then,' she pleaded. 'I can see you're a good man. We'll be no trouble, I swear it.' With guilt tearing at him, and the hammers of hell beating at his temples, he muttered an excuse and left her sobbing in his wake.

Thankfully, the crowds and the panic eased a little as Hanno drew further away from the centre of the city. People were still flocking towards Achradina and Tyche, but there was room to move on the streets. This development accentuated his worries rather than easing them. What if Aurelia had already left their rooms? There would be no hope of finding her. He broke into a sprint, covering the last five stadia in less time than it had taken him to travel the first one. At the house, he had to take a moment to dry retch and wipe away the sweat that coated his entire face. Gods, but he wished that he hadn't drunk so much the night before.

It was with a wave of relief that he heard her moving within as he pounded on the door with a balled fist. 'Aurelia! It's Hanno.'

There was a heartbeat's pause. 'Hanno?'

'Yes. I'm here.'

The bolt slid back. She opened the door and regarded him, red-eyed, before throwing herself into his arms. 'Oh, Hanno! I've been so scared. The screaming on the street has been terrifying. People are saying that the legionaries will kill us all.'

'That won't happen,' he lied.

'I knew you would come.'

Thank the gods she didn't know how nearly he had not, he thought guiltily, holding her tight. At least they were together. What he wouldn't have given, though, for Mutt and his Libyans to be at his side as well.

Chapter XXIV

A couple of hours after their search for Pera had begun, Quintus had been forced to accede that the gods had had no intention of helping them. Their quest had been hampered by the utter chaos that reigned in the city. It had been fine at first, all the way back to the Galeagra, where they had hoped he might still be. There had been no sign of Pera, however, nor of anyone in his unit. The hastati who were holding the position by that stage didn't even know his name. 'Forget about your commanding officer,' one had advised, assuming that that was whom Pera was. 'He'll find you later. Until then, do what you want!' The soldier's comrades had laughed cruelly, and Quintus' mind had filled with dark images of Enna.

By now, the garrison had been roused from its slumbers, yet there was no organised resistance. Small groups of enemy soldiers appeared here and there, but it was clear that most were too drunk or incapacitated to fight, or had stumbled outside without fully arming themselves. Their officers were missing, or they were intimidated by the number of legionaries swarming through the city. Again and again, Quintus saw a single charge put the enemy to flight. Every time that happened, the panic spread even faster. It didn't help the defenders' cause that hundreds, even thousands of terrified civilians were trying to flee the carnage. Quintus grew used to seeing Syracusan troops cutting down unarmed residents in an effort to escape.

They had to halt their search for a time when an optio in charge of half a century of principes ordered them to help clear a wide thoroughfare of enemy forces. When that was done, it was easy enough to slip away again into the mayhem. Odd images stuck in Quintus' mind as they sought Pera. In a market square, they found legionaries gorging themselves on the wine that they'd taken from a warehouse. Some were already drunk, and were bathing in the central fountain, naked apart from their baldrics and sheathed swords. They saw hens running hither and thither in an alleyway, trying to escape the clutches of a pair of laughing velites. With their arms full of fresh loaves and pastries, legionaries trampled uncaring over the gutted body of a baker. Five horses, mounts for the enemy cavalry, galloped wildly down a street, sending Romans and Syracusans alike diving for cover.

Most of what Quintus saw was far worse, however, and the horror was impossible to ignore. In the middle of one lane was the corpse of a child – a boy, a girl, Quintus couldn't tell – without a head. In another, an old man sprawled over the body of a woman of the same age, attempting even in death to protect her. Both had been stabbed so many times that their garments were saturated with blood. A pregnant woman tried to give birth where she lay, her grievous wounds ensuring that she would die before her labour ever ended. A tiny baby in swaddling clothes mewled its distress from the arms of its dead mother. The air reverberated with shouted orders, war cries and the clash of arms. Mixed with these were screams of fear and shrill voices calling on gods and goddesses, asking for their help, their intervention – anything to stop the slaughter – or seeking family members lost in the confusion. Another sound was also constant: the terrible screeches of women who were being raped. Quintus blocked it out as best he could.

At some stage in the morning, the noise of fighting grew deafening. It didn't take long for the friends to find out why. Epicydes had sallied forth from Ortygia with his forces. All Roman soldiers were to advance to the edge of Epipolae, there to put themselves at the disposal of the officers present.

It was Urceus who called a halt to their search. 'Face it, Crespo. We're never going to find him. There hasn't been hide nor hair of the cocksucker. I don't like it any more than you do, but it's time to find Corax and our brothers. If we don't, some whoreson of an officer is going to accuse us of shirking our duty. We've pushed our luck too often on that score.'

Quintus scowled. Much as he didn't want to admit it, his friend was right. 'Very well.'

It wasn't difficult to know which way to go. Every Roman soldier in sight was heading south, or southeast. Officers chivvied them along with encouraging shouts, but the streets were so full that the pace was slow. The two friends had little option but to trudge along with the multitude, and after a while, Quintus grew sick of it. Spotting an alley that ran at right angles to the thoroughfare that they were on, he nudged Urceus. 'Let's try that. What have we to lose? We can always retrace our steps, or cut down on to another street that might be less crowded.'

Grumbling under his breath, Urceus followed Quintus. Ten steps in, he stopped dead. 'This is human shit underfoot. Filthy Syracusan arse-lovers.'

'Keep going. There isn't any where I'm standing,' lied Quintus. By the time that they emerged at the far end of the alleyway, he couldn't stop chuckling.

'You bastard. I'll get you back for this,' warned Urceus, doing his best to wipe the excrement off his sandals.

'You can try,' retorted Quintus, enjoying the moment's light relief.

Jinking down alleys whenever they could, they made reasonable progress. The noise of metal hitting metal, and men's screams, drew nearer. Quintus felt his stomach clench, the way it always did before he went into battle. He eyed Urceus, who was licking his lips. 'It won't take long, eh? With so many of us inside the city walls, the Syracusans won't have much stomach for a fight.'

'Let's hope so.' It seemed that Urceus wasn't looking forward to it either, because his gaze slid sideways. 'Look! A wine shop. The door's open too. Why don't we have a swift drink? Just one. It'll knock the edges off us.'

'Aye. Why not? The battle can wait a while longer,' Quintus replied. The wine might blank out some of the appalling things he'd just seen.

But what they saw inside drove all thoughts of wine from their minds.

A man lay slumped against the counter, his head on his chest. One hand was cupped protectively over his belly. Blood oozed between his fingers, coated his mail, stained his pteryges scarlet. A glistening red trail on the floor reached to his feet, marking his path from the spot where he had been stabbed.

Corax.

Quintus' gaze shot around the room, but he saw no one. Spitting curses, he raced to Corax's side. Urceus was one step behind him. They knelt, glancing at each other in fear. 'Is he dead?' whispered Urceus.

Quintus reached out and touched Corax's cheek. It was cold, but not deathly so. With great care, he tipped the centurion's head back. There was a low clang as Corax's helmet touched the wall. He moaned, and his eyelids flickered. Quintus and Urceus exchanged another look, hopeful this time.

'Sir?' murmured Quintus. 'Can you hear me?'

Corax let out another moan. 'Should have . . . should have known . . .'

'It's me, Crespo, sir. Jug's here too.'

One corner of Corax's lips pulled upwards. 'Crespo. Jug . . .' A moment later, he opened his eyes. 'Take my helmet off. It feels as if it's made of lead.'

Quintus hurriedly undid the chinstrap and lifted the helmet off Corax's head. Underneath, the centurion's felt liner was drenched in sweat.

'That's better,' muttered Corax.

'Let me take a look at your stomach, sir,' offered Quintus, his hands reaching for Corax's belt buckle.

'Leave it.' A trace of the familiar iron had reappeared in Corax's voice. 'I'm done.'

This time the look Quintus and Urceus shared was despairing. 'Are you thirsty, sir?' Quintus asked.

'No.' Corax managed a little chuckle. 'It's ironic to die in a wine shop without even getting to taste what it has to offer. Ah, Crespo, you were right. I should have known.'

Black fear slithered around Quintus' stomach, but he dared not vocalise it. 'I don't understand, sir.'

'That Pera was a murderous dog.'

An incandescent rage darkened Quintus' vision. He heard Urceus' voice asking, 'Pera did this to you, sir? Not some Syracusans?'

'Pera. It was Pera. He lured me in here with a simple ruse, promising the finest vintage he had ever tasted. Like a fool, I sent my men away, told them I'd find them later.' Corax coughed. There was fluid on his breath. 'He stuck me the moment we were on our own. I never had a chance.'

Quintus wanted to find Pera and slice him to pieces, but he knew in his gut that the centurion was long gone. 'Why did he do it, sir?'

'Because . . . because of the hold I have over him. He's scared that Marcellus will find out he's a mollis.'

The friends gasped in unison, in shock. Love of another man was outlawed in the army.

Pera must also have hated that Corax had defended him, Quintus decided. Guilt scourged him.

'I never imagined that another centurion would kill me . . .' Corax's voice died away.

Quintus thought for a moment that Corax had gone. Hot tears ran down his face. Urceus was in a similar state. 'He was the best damn centurion in the whole Roman army,' he whispered.

Corax took a shuddering breath, visibly rallied himself. 'You're good men, both of you. Promise that you'll get Pera for this. I'd hate to go thinking that he got away with it.'

'I'll kill Pera if it's the last thing I do, sir,' swore Quintus.

'Same here, sir,' said Urceus fervently.

Satisfied, Corax closed his eyes. A moment later, he shivered. 'I'm cold.'

Quintus could see nothing in the room that they could use as a blanket, but by the time his gaze had returned to Corax, it was too late. The centurion had stopped breathing. His eyes had opened again, and had a glassy look to them. Quintus checked for a pulse, but there was none. He bent to Corax's lips, to let his soul leave his body.

'He bled out.' Urceus' voice was tight with emotion. 'Bled out, like a stuck pig.'

'That fucking whoreson Pera will pay for this,' said Quintus. 'Even if I have to hunt him for the rest of my life.'

'You won't be alone.'

Both of them wept for a time. There was no shame in it. They had been through so much together, and Corax had always been there to lead them. He had been a permanent feature in their lives, like a great sea wall upon which the waves endlessly break. No matter how bad the situation, they had been able to depend on Corax. The disasters at Trasimene, Cannae and, more recently, Syracuse, had not shaken his resolve. And now he was gone, just like that. Murdered by one of his own. It was so damn pointless, thought Quintus bitterly. Pera would die for what he had done.

When they had reined in their anger and grief a little, they laid Corax out on the floor of an empty storeroom with his hands folded on his chest.

'Let's hope that none of our lot touch him,' said Quintus, knowing that some soldiers wouldn't think twice about taking something as fine as Corax's sword.

'With a bit of luck, they'll be more interested in the wine. No Syracusans will come in either. They're all too damn scared. Corax will rest here until we can come back for him.'

Quintus nodded sadly. 'Aye. We need to find the rest of the maniple. Tell them what happened.'

'The gods help Pera when we tell the lads. They will want to tear him limb from limb.'

'We might get lucky and come across him somewhere. I'll offer up a prize bull to Fortuna if we kill him today,' swore Quintus.

'Make that two bulls. And if we don't find him, well, some Syracusans will do instead.' Urceus laughed unpleasantly.

Quintus recognised the same ugly feeling in himself. He wasn't interested in slaying unarmed civilians, but if there were enemy soldiers to lay
in the mud, that was a different matter. It wouldn't bring back Corax, but
it *would* release some of his overpowering rage. In a savage way, harking
back to ancient times, it could be considered a sacrifice in the centurion's
honour. After that, Quintus wanted wine. More wine than he had ever
drunk in his life.

Then, if Pera wasn't already dead, he, Urceus and those who wanted
to be involved could begin laying their plans. It was a matter that they, the
ordinary soldiers, would have to solve for themselves, for there was no
way of proving what Pera had done. The knowledge that his comrades
would want to help did little to ease Quintus' pain, which pressed like a
heavy weight on his chest. But it gave him a focus, for which he was
grateful. Without it, he would have been lost. Keep breathing, he thought.
Keep walking. Do as Corax would have wished. Stay alive.

At first, Hanno and Aurelia had made good progress. His plan was to
follow the southern city wall as it snaked its way along a ridge from the
Euryalus fortress towards the sea. After perhaps fifteen stadia, they would
have to negotiate the slope down into the walled suburb of Neapolis, where
he hoped to find refuge. If it had fallen, however, Achradina and its strong
defences were not far away. The idea had seemed excellent, but to Hanno's
rising frustration, he had not been the only person to have it.

Within three stadia, the narrow, unpaved street that ran along in the
shadow of the high wall became clogged with humanity. Entire families
– grandparents, mothers, fathers and terrified-looking children – walked
together, the adults carrying their most prized possessions on their backs.
Dogs – their family pets – ran up and down between the groupings, sniffing
noses and barking incessantly. One optimist had decided to take his fattening
pig with him, on a lead. It snorted and grunted its unhappiness at being in
such a crowd. Hanno laughed when, after not long at all, it decided that
it had had enough and charged off up an alley, leaving its cursing owner

with nothing more than a length of rope. Shopkeepers and craftsmen laboured along, bent under the weight of goods, tools and, from the chinking sound, bags of money. There were even a couple of merchants with over-loaded ox-drawn carts, which almost blocked the street.

'They're fools,' he complained to Aurelia. 'At times like this, what's important is your own skin. But none of them can see it!'

'You're a soldier, Hanno. You intuitively know what to do in situations like this. These people don't.'

'It'll be the death of them,' declared Hanno more harshly than he might have if they hadn't been in such danger. If he hadn't forbidden Aurelia to look for Elira, hadn't insisted that she leave her cat behind. 'We'll never reach safety at this rate.'

'Where are you taking us?' asked Aurelia as they ducked into a lane so narrow that a fat man would have to walk sideways in it.

'I've no idea. It doesn't matter, really, as long as it's away from where we were.' Hanno could picture the slaughter that would happen if – when – the legionaries arrived. 'We need another street that runs southeast, towards Neapolis and Achradina.'

Her answering smile wasn't convincing, but Hanno didn't have the time to reassure her. Never had time been more of the essence.

It didn't take long to find a thoroughfare that led where they wanted, but it was even more crowded than the street by the wall. Against his better judgement, but gambling that there would be fewer people about, Hanno led them further north, closer to the city centre – and the Romans. His ploy worked for a while. They made their way through an abandoned market surrounded by shops and temples, and into an affluent residential area full of apartment blocks that rose three and four storeys high. Most of the residents had already fled; only the stubborn, old and criminal remained. A number of the latter eyed Aurelia with lustful eyes. At first, Hanno's drawn sword and fierce demeanour were enough to intimidate such lowlifes, but when five ganged up together, their courage suddenly soared. It vanished as fast when two of their number were choking to death on their own blood. Hanno left the shocked survivors to their own devices, shoving Aurelia away. 'They're cowards. Once we're out of sight, we'll be safe.' From those ones, perhaps, his worried side retorted. What about the thousands of Romans?

They saw no legionaries for some time, however, and Hanno began to hope that they might reach Achradina, their new objective. What he hadn't gambled on was getting lost. Smoke from burning buildings filled the sky, preventing him from using the sun as a guide. He wasn't familiar with many of the streets off the main avenues and had been using the noise of fighting as an approximate pointer to keep them heading in an easterly direction. Too late, he realised his error. Battles were raging in whole swathes of Syracuse. Nor had all the defenders fled. When they stumbled upon a group of Syracusan troops under the command of a determined-looking officer, Hanno was forced to join them. It was only the arrival of large numbers of Romans at the other end of the street that gave him and Aurelia the opportunity to run. Curses followed the pair as they charged down an alley. Hanno took the rear, in case they were pursued. After fifty paces, the lane gave on to a triangular-shaped area lined by shops and with a central fountain. Aurelia halted abruptly. Hanno peered over her shoulder and cursed. It was full of legionaries. Some were ransacking the businesses, while others were busy with several wailing women and girls whom they'd captured. The bodies of those they'd already slain – a couple of middle-aged men and a boy – lay like bloody, discarded puppets on the ground.

Shouts and the sound of fighting came from behind them. They couldn't go back, or forward. 'What should we do?' whispered Aurelia.

'Stay where we are,' replied Hanno grimly.

'And if we're seen?'

'I'll protect you.' It sounded as stupid as Hanno had thought it would. He wasn't Achilles, and she knew it too.

'I don't want to be taken alive.'

'It won't come to that.'

'I know how this might go, Hanno. Promise that you'll kill me if you have to.'

He flinched before her steady gaze. He wanted to rant and rail at the gods, but instead offered up a silent prayer to Tanit, the mother goddess so revered by Carthaginians.

Protect us, please. Do not ask me to slay the woman I love.

She didn't press him further, and they settled down to wait until it was safe either to retreat or to proceed. It felt like Hades on earth, with the screams of women and men's laughter assaulting their ears from one side, and the din of soldiers killing each other doing the same from the other. There was no way to avoid hearing any of it: each of them had to keep watch on an end of the alley.

Hanno had hoped that things might grow a little better when the fighting to their rear died down. What he hadn't gambled upon was for the Syracusans to have gained the upper hand *and* that the officer would remember where they'd gone. The first he knew of it was when three Syracusan soldiers entered the far end of the alley. They spotted him and Aurelia at once. With eager cries, they broke into a run.

Hanno's stomach turned a neat loop. *We are fucked.* If he fought the men, the Romans in the street beyond would hear. If they exited the alley, they'd be seen. Which fate was worse?

'I've been looking. There's a shop around the corner,' hissed Aurelia. 'I don't think there's anyone inside.'

'Go, then!' replied Hanno. The trio of Syracusans were thirty paces away.

'Wait. There's a legionary facing our way.' Aurelia's calm stunned him, but he obeyed.

Six heartbeats later – it felt like six hundred – she tapped his arm. Crouched down, they sloped out into the open with Aurelia in the lead. Hanno didn't look beyond the door of the shop, which was ajar. It would become obvious if they were seen. No shouts filled their ears, however, as they slipped inside and pushed the door to. It seemed to be an apothecary's – the air was thick with the smell of aromatic herbs and more exotic substances. Two large mortars and pestles occupied a prominent space on the counter, and the shelves on the walls were lined with pots and small glass jars. Hanno scanned the room, but there was no locking bar visible for the door. Heart racing, he leaned against it and pressed his ear to the timbers. Aurelia watched him, her face taut with fear.

'Where have they gone?' shouted a man in Greek.

'Shut your mouth,' growled a second voice.

'Why?'

'Ho, Julius, you'd better finish quick!' roared a man in Latin. 'We've got company. It's some Syracusan whoresons, come to save their womenfolk.'

'Shit! Go back!' cried the first Greek speaker, and Hanno exulted.

Confusion reigned outside as the Syracusans fled, and the legionaries grabbed their weapons and followed. When the sound of men charging into the alley had died away, Hanno risked a look outside. All of the legionaries appeared to have gone, apart from one man, whose backside could be seen pumping up and down between a woman's legs.

Sprinting forward, Hanno stabbed him in the back. Then, heaving the legionary off his sobbing victim, he cut his throat for good measure. The woman – girl – stared up at Hanno, mouth agape with terror, her face and breasts a mass of bruises. 'Run,' Hanno ordered, heaving the corpse to one side. 'Find somewhere to hide.'

Aurelia made to help the woman up, but he pulled her back. 'She's only a child!' Aurelia protested.

His grip on her arm tightened. 'We *can't* help. It's asking enough of the gods that *we* should survive. What's happening now is just the start, believe me. By nightfall, things will be infinitely worse.'

Her gaze dropped to the girl, who hadn't stirred from where she lay. 'Save yourself, please. Before they come back.'

The girl turned her face away.

Aurelia snatched up a bloodied gladius and thrust it, hilt first, at her.

'Take this. You can use it on them, or yourself.' As the girl took it, Aurelia regarded Hanno, her eyes full of tears. 'I'm ready.'

Praying that their run of bad luck had ended, Hanno made for the small street opposite.

For a short time, they saw no soldiers – of either side. At a crossroads two hundred paces further on, Hanno dared to hope. There was a human hand painted on a wall, the forefinger pointing down one of the four streets. Underneath it, he read the Greek word 'ACHRADINA'. Signs were rare in cities, so he had extra reason to feel grateful. 'This way.'

They had gone perhaps fifty paces before a quartet of legionaries stepped out of a cheesemonger's. Each man bore a round of cheese under one arm. They whooped at the sight of Hanno and Aurelia, and swaggered towards them.

'Go back,' whispered Hanno frantically, but his heart sank as he turned. Alerted by the noise of their fellows, another three Romans were clattering down the front steps of a house that they must have been ransacking. Their path to the crossroads was blocked, and there were no alleys in sight. He hammered on one door and then another, but they had been barred from within.

'I'll tell them I'm Roman,' said Aurelia. 'That you're not to be harmed.'

'They won't listen to a word you say. Look at them, they're like wild animals.' Placing Aurelia behind him, Hanno moved to stand against the wall of a shop. At the last moment, he saw a Syracusan shield lying in the dirt nearby. Gripping that, he felt a little better. With luck, he could take a few of them before he was overwhelmed or slain.

'Give me your dagger,' Aurelia said. 'I can fight too, when they get close enough.'

There was so much Hanno wanted to say. How glad he was that they had met, how much he had enjoyed their time together. How it had been his dream to take her to Carthage in peacetime, where they could have started a family together. Without a word, he tugged the blade from its sheath and passed it to her.

As the first leering legionaries closed in, Hanno saw two more appear further down the street. They paused, as if unsure whether to get involved, and then marched towards them with grim purpose. Hanno's despair nearly overcame him. Seven to one had been bad odds, but it hadn't been out of the realms of possibility that he and Aurelia could have escaped.

Against nine enemies they had no chance.

Chapter XXV

Quintus and Urceus wandered aimlessly through the streets, joining in on occasion with the brutal fights against the few Syracusan soldiers who were prepared to resist. For the most part, though, the grief-stricken pair kept searching for Pera. However unlikely it was that they would find him in the violence-riven city, neither man could give up, for they could not put Corax from their minds. For more than four years, he had been their leader, their guardian, their father-figure. To lose him was bad enough, but to lose him to murder – by Pera – made it an outrage of the most terrible kind.

There was no sign of their quarry, but they did not let up. Pera was somewhere in Syracuse. While the fighting went on, there was every chance of slaying him unnoticed, and if the word of the legionaries whom they encountered could be relied on, they were gradually nearing Achradina and Tyche. Pera was likelier to be there than elsewhere, they decided. Mollis and treacherous whoreson he might be, but he'd do his duty.

Their advance was halted by a set of burning houses. Thick smoke billowed into the sky and flames licked up the sides of the wooden buildings. From there, it spread on to their roofs, threatening the edifices to either side. Shrieks could be heard within. As they paused, a woman threw herself from a second-floor window, landing with a terrible crack on the cobbles below. She did not move again, but laughing legionaries gathered to watch as a man – her husband? – appeared in the window with a small child in his arms. By mutual, silent consent, Quintus and Urceus turned and headed the other way.

Neither spoke for some time. Surrounded by such horror, there was nothing to say.

'Look,' said Urceus.

Quintus looked. Fifty paces in front, two small groups of legionaries were closing in on a pair of figures with their backs against a shop front. 'We can't stop them,' he said with a sigh.

'We have to pass by, though, or go back past the burning houses.'

'I can't watch children jumping to their deaths,' snapped Quintus, images from Enna filling his mind once more. 'Keep going.'

They walked on. Within a few heartbeats, the fight had begun. Only two of the legionaries could attack their victims at a time. The others stood back and issued loud opinions on what to do. As Quintus and Urceus approached, one – a hastatus – fell screaming with a deep wound in his belly. Shouting oaths, another legionary took his place. His lack of caution was disastrous. The cornered man – a Syracusan officer from what Quintus could see – used his large shield to punch first at one legionary and then the other. As both men stepped back in reflex, the officer stabbed the cursing one in the throat. Blood sheeted the air as he ripped his blade free. The legionary dropped to the ground like a stone tossed in a well.

'He's not bad,' said Urceus admiringly. 'He's fighting like that because he has a woman with him. See?'

Quintus didn't want to look, didn't want to see yet another woman's face distorted by terror. All the same, his attention was locked on the deadly struggle being enacted before them. It was inevitable that his gaze would fall on the officer's companion. What he saw didn't register at first. He blinked and looked again. A band of iron closed around his heart. 'Aurelia?' he whispered. 'It can't be. It can't be.'

Urceus caught the urgency in his tone. 'What is it?'

Quintus drew nearer, his heart pounding out a disturbing, irregular rhythm. At twenty paces, he could see that it *was* his sister. Their years of separation had not changed her. What she was doing in Syracuse, and with an enemy officer, Quintus had no damn idea, but it was Aurelia. In his excitement, he paid her companion no heed. He grabbed Urceus' shoulder. 'Do you trust me?'

Urceus gave him a surprised look. 'With my life, you know that.'

'Believe me now, brother, when I tell you that that woman is my sister. I have no inkling why she's here, but it's her.'

Urceus' jaw slowly hardened. 'You're certain?'

'Certain enough that I'm going to wade in here against our own, and try to save her.'

Urceus swore long and hard. While he did, another legionary went down, his guts sliced apart. The rest had had enough. Bellowing like maddened bulls, they advanced together.

Quintus didn't wait for Urceus' response. He ran forward, sword and shield at the ready. 'Leave her be! She's Roman! Roman!'

A number of things happened at once. Aurelia screamed, 'Brother?' Two legionaries looked around, and saw Quintus. 'Who gives a fuck what she is?' roared one. 'After what her friend has done, she'll get what's coming to—' His words became an inarticulate scream as Aurelia's protector thrust him through the side.

'Drop your weapons and walk away,' roared Quintus. There were still three uninjured legionaries. He didn't mind about himself, but if they concentrated their attack on Aurelia and her protector, she could easily be killed.

'I'm with you, brother.'

Urceus was by his side. Quintus felt a surge of relief. Now the odds were even. The legionaries faltered, and Aurelia's protector drove his blade into one's calf. The man fell, screaming, and he finished him off with a powerful thrust to his middle.

'She's a Roman, you say?' asked one of the two remaining legionaries. He backed away to the side. 'She's all yours.'

'Fuck off then,' snarled Urceus.

'C'mon, brother,' said the first legionary.

'Aye.' Avoiding eye contact, the second man shuffled away.

'You can't let them live,' said Aurelia's protector. 'They'll tell someone that you aided the enemy.'

Utter shock bathed Quintus as he recognised the voice. The fighting and the man's helmet and stubbly beard had prevented him from realising before. '*Hanno?*'

Hanno shook his head and laughed; then he stepped forward. 'By all the gods, Quintus, I didn't expect to see you here.'

'You *know* this sheep-fucker?' the first legionary screeched at Quintus.

Savagely, Quintus' instincts took over. If word reached any officer about what he had just done, he'd be executed. So would Urceus. It was their lives against those of the two soldiers, and *that* was no choice at all. Spinning on his heel, he drove at the legionary with his scutum. Catching the man off guard, Quintus punched him in the belly with its iron boss. The *oooofff* as the air left the legionary's lungs was followed by a high-pitched scream as Quintus' gladius rammed over the top of his mail shirt and deep into the base of his neck. The shock in the man's eyes pierced Quintus to the quick. *It was you or me.*

When he turned back, Hanno had finished off the last legionary.

Time stood still. Chest heaving, Hanno stared at Quintus. Quintus' disbelieving eyes moved from Aurelia to Hanno and back, and back again. Urceus stood by, looking totally confused. It was Aurelia who broke the ice. She threw herself at Quintus, sobbing. 'Brother! I never thought to see you again.'

He dropped his shield and pulled her close. 'Aurelia. By all the gods, it's good to see you.'

She pulled away after a long moment, smiling through her tears. 'Thank you for saving us.'

'Us,' he repeated, wondering if he wasn't hallucinating. Again his eyes moved to Hanno, who hadn't moved. Hanno inclined his head, neither friendly nor unfriendly. 'My thanks, Quintus. Things were going badly until you and your friend came along.'

'You know *both* of them?' cried Urceus.

'I do.' Urceus could also see Aurelia and Hanno, so he hadn't gone insane. The situation was so ridiculous, so bizarre, that Quintus began to laugh.

After a moment, so too did Hanno. And Aurelia.

Urceus coughed. 'This reunion is *lovely*, but we can't stay here. Not with him' – he pointed at Hanno – 'being one of the enemy and all.'

'Any Syracusans who see us aren't going to be friendly either,' added Hanno.

Quintus found that everyone was looking at him. *Shit*. 'Where were you going?' he asked Aurelia – and Hanno.

'To Achradina. Hopefully, it will be holding out,' said Hanno. Aurelia murmured in agreement.

'Come with me,' Quintus replied, staring at his sister. 'I'll keep you safe.'

'I'm with Hanno,' she replied, chin jutting. 'Where he goes, I go.'

Quintus tried to digest the meaning of that, and could come up with but one conclusion. The world had gone mad, he thought. Not only were his sister and Hanno here in Syracuse, but they were companions. Lovers even. Anger flared in his belly. 'I could force you to accompany me.'

'You could try,' growled Hanno.

Quintus glared at Hanno, who glared back. Urceus glared at both of them. A couple of moments went by.

The noise of tramping feet from the north brought the peril of their situation into sharp focus. 'Make your mind up,' said Urceus to Quintus. 'Or we'll all be in the shit.'

Quintus gave up trying to understand. Saving his sister came before everything else. 'Back this way,' he said. 'Follow me.'

It seemed that they had done it, thought Hanno, peering at the main gate into Achradina. Incredibly, it was not shut. Epicydes had sallied forth from here at some stage in an attempt to save the city. He hadn't come back – there was widespread fighting yet going on in the streets that led up to Epipolae – but he'd clearly ordered that the gate remain open until his return. Hours had passed since Quintus' intervention had saved their lives. The sun had sunk behind the houses, and the sky was turning orange-red. It was as if the gods were recognising the oceans of blood that had been shed that day.

There had been little chance for conversation as they had hurried from house to alley, and alley to house, avoiding all open spaces. Despite this, Quintus and Aurelia had bent their heads together at every opportunity. They were at it now. Hanno was glad, for time was short and they would have much to tell each other. For his part, it was beyond strange to see Quintus again. It was also a relief to find that there was no hatred in his heart for his former friend. In other times, they would have remained friends, Hanno knew.

A wave of noise from behind them – frantic voices, the ring of weapons – announced an escalation in the struggle for the rest of Syracuse. 'We had best not linger,' said Hanno to Aurelia. 'Once that gate shuts, it won't be opening for a while.'

She nodded.

Quintus looked stricken. 'You're certain about going?'

It was Aurelia's turn to be sad. *Publius died because I came here*, she thought. 'Yes, brother. My destiny is with Hanno, come what may.'

'Very well.' Quintus pulled her into a fierce embrace. 'I doubt that we will meet again in this life,' he said, releasing her.

'I hope that you are wrong. One day, when this is over, we shall see each other once more.'

'Let it be so. The gods keep you safe, sister.'

'And you, brother.'

Hanno found Quintus' gaze upon him. 'Look after her.'

'You know I will.'

'Even after so long, I do.' Quintus took a deep breath and then held out his hand.

After the slightest hesitation, Hanno accepted the grip. They shook. 'My thanks for stepping in. I'm in your debt.'

Quintus inclined his head in recognition. 'Protect Aurelia, and I'll consider us even.'

'Very well. Stay alive if you can.'

'You do the same.'

There was time for one last embrace between Quintus and Aurelia, and they parted.

Aurelia looked back several times as they walked away, but Hanno didn't. When she muttered a prayer for Elira, he felt a trace of guilt and added his own. It had been the right decision not to search for her, however. They had only reached safety because of Quintus. Relief filled him as they approached the gate into Achradina. The walls were lined with hundreds of soldiers. The batteries of catapults were manned and ready. Despite the disaster that had befallen much of the city, this part wasn't going to be taken today. He felt sure of it. Nor was the struggle for Syracuse over. Himilco's army would arrive any day, and the tables could be turned on the Romans. Soon he would be able to send Hannibal news to that effect.

Until then, he and Aurelia were alive. So too was Quintus.

That last piece of information warmed Hanno's heart.

The sadness in the pit of Quintus' stomach swelled as Aurelia and Hanno were lost to sight. It was tempered with relief that his sister was safe.

'You all right?' asked Urceus.

'I'm fine.'

'Are you sure? It's fucking mad to find your sister in the middle of this insanity, let alone with a Carthaginian whom you know.'

'You're not wrong. If you weren't here, I'd think it was all a dream.'

'Or a nightmare.' Urceus shook his head. 'I still can't believe you stuck one of our lads.'

Quintus dragged his eyes from the gate into Achradina. 'I had to, Jug. Otherwise it would have been the fustuarium for us both.'

'Not if you'd killed him – your sister's companion. Hanno.'

Quintus felt some guilt for his actions – but only a little. 'Hanno used to be a friend of mine, and I'd never seen the damn legionary before in my life. You would have done the same.'

'Maybe I would.' Urceus spat. 'But I never want to have to make such a decision.'

'Nor do I, again.'

'Pera, now, he's a different matter.'

Quintus' grief at Corax's death resurged, along with his hatred for Pera. 'We'll find the cocksucker, I know it.'

'Aye. We will, and take the rest of Syracuse, in whichever order. I don't care. And when the city falls, Sicily will follow suit, mark my words. Maybe then the Senate will let us go home.'

Quintus pulled a crooked smile. There *was* much to be thankful for. *We* – me and Urceus, he thought – did this. *We* were responsible for breaking the siege. The victory that had followed was an incredible one. More successes would follow in its wake. Eventually Rome would *have* to acknowledge the efforts of Marcellus' legions. Corax's murder and the shocking news from Aurelia about their mother had not yet really sunk in, but he had saved his sister from a terrible death. That had lifted his spirits from the depths, as did the fact she appeared to be happy. In these turbulent times, that meant a great deal.

He looked towards the high walls of Achradina. For the short term at least, they would protect his sister and his friend. His friend, thought Quintus again. For, like Urceus, that's what Hanno was. He let out a long, slow breath.

The gods only knew what tomorrow would bring, but for today, all four of them were alive.

That was what counted.

Epilogue

Much of Syracuse fell to the Romans on that bloody day in 212 BC, including the entire Epipolae district. When the commander of the mighty Euryalus fort heard that the suburbs of Neapolis and Tyche had surrendered, he gave up his bastion without a blow being struck. This meant that all of the western city had been lost. While the areas of Achradina and Ortygia continued to hold out under the command of Epicydes, the respite Hanno and Aurelia had sought proved to be brief. The arrival of Hippocrates with Himilco and his army did not provide the much-hoped-for relief of the siege. Nor did the strengthening of the Carthaginian fleet in the Great Harbour. There was some inconsequential skirmishing, during which the Romans reinforced their positions in the city, and renewed their blockade of Achradina and Ortygia. Quintus, Urceus and their comrades took an active role in this, but Pera continued to elude them.

The autumn brought with it outbreaks of plague. Both sides suffered, within and without the city, but the Carthaginian camps' situation on marshy land to the south, and their poor sanitation, ensured that they lost far more men. Among the tens of thousands who died were Himilco and Hippocrates. Despite this huge setback, the remaining Syracusan forces advanced once more on the city to try and break the Roman siege. They were encouraged by news of a large Carthaginian fleet off the southern coast. However, a violent storm and a robust response by Marcellus, who sailed to meet the enemy head-on, ensured that the reinforcements broke away from their course and made for the Italian city of Tarentum, which had recently fallen to Hannibal.

When the Syracusans heard of their abandonment by the Carthaginian fleet, they tried to seek terms from Marcellus. It wasn't surprising that the Roman deserters within their ranks, of whom there were many, were unhappy with this development. A wave of tit-for-tat killings resulted, and the balance of power between those who wanted to continue fighting and those who wanted to surrender changed more than once. Increasingly dismayed by the levels of distrust and barbarity, Hanno prepared to flee with Aurelia.

Marcellus' opportunity to seize complete control came after he'd made secret overtures to one of the commanders of Achradina, a disgruntled Iberian mercenary called Moericus. Soon after they'd come to an agreement, the Romans launched a simultaneous dawn attack on Ortygia and Achradina. Quintus and Urceus eagerly played their part in this. When Moericus and his soldiers joined the Romans as agreed, the remaining defenders on Ortygia were soon overrun. Wishing to preserve the riches of the royal treasury for himself, Marcellus had his troops withdraw from Ortygia for a time. This allowed the Roman deserters, and also Hanno and Aurelia, to escape. A terrible fate awaited the last defenders in Achradina. When they opened their gates, wishing only to surrender, Marcellus' soldiers launched a savage assault on the suburb that left few people living. Famously, Archimedes was one of the casualties, slain by a legionary who interrupted him as he drew a geometric design in the dirt. Outraged, Marcellus executed or banished the culprit, and had Archimedes buried in his family tomb.

After more than five centuries of independence, Syracuse had fallen to an invader. Reputedly the largest and most beautiful of Greek cities, it had been stripped bare during the siege. Although the inhabitants of several suburbs had suffered grievously, the rest had escaped relatively lightly according to the standards of the time. Normally, when a city was taken by force, every male inhabitant was killed and all women and children were sold as slaves.

Despite all that had happened, there were some who still wished to

Author's Note

When the opportunity to write a set of novels about the Second Punic War (218–201 BC) came my way, I jumped at the chance. I have been fascinated by the time period for many years. The word 'epic' is overused today, but I feel that its use is justified when referring to this incredible seventeen-year struggle. Life in Europe today would be very different indeed if the scales had tipped but a fraction in the opposite direction to the way they did on a number of occasions. The Carthaginians were quite unlike the Romans, and not in all the bad ways 'history' would have us believe. They were intrepid explorers and inveterate traders, shrewd businessmen and brave soldiers. Where Rome's interests so often lay in conquest by war, theirs lay more in assuming power through the control of commerce and natural resources. It may be a small point, but my use of the word 'Carthaginian' rather than the Latin 'Punic' when referring to their language is quite deliberate. The Carthaginians would not have used the term.

Many readers will know the broad brushstrokes of Hannibal's war with Rome; others will know less; a very few will be voracious readers of the ancient authors Livy and Polybius, the main sources for this period. For the record, I have done my best to stick to the historical details that have survived. In places, however, I have either changed events slightly to fit in with the story's development, or invented things. Such is the novelist's remit, as well as his/her curse. I apologise now for any errors that I may have made.

The term 'Italy' was in use in the third century BC as a geographical expression; it encompassed the entire peninsula south of Cisalpine Gaul. The term did not become a political one until Polybius' time (mid second century BC). I decided to use it anyway. It simplified matters, and avoided constant reference to the different parts of the Republic: Rome, Campania, Latium, Lucania, etc.

A reasonable amount of information survives about the Roman army of the third century BC, but when writing about it, one often has to make assumptions and logical leaps of faith. The same applies to the Carthaginian and the Syracusan armies. We have some details about Roman funerals – I used them to the best of my ability in this book. Another obstacle course that I had to negotiate concerned Carthaginian names. Not many have survived the test of time, and most of those that have are unpronounceable, or sound awful. Hillesbaal and Ithobaal don't exactly roll off the tongue. I *had* to use Muttumbaal, however. There's a modern ring to the nickname 'Mutt'! There were a number of important historical characters called Hanno, but I desperately needed a good name for my hero, so he took precedence.

The prologue of the novel begins soon after the second title in the series, *Hannibal: Fields of Blood*, ended. Maharbal's prophetic warning to Hannibal is recorded. Rome's response to Hannibal's envoys, soon after, gives us an indication of their people's determination, even in the depths of defeat. When the Carthaginian embassy reached Rome, they were refused entry to the city and told that the Republic would never treat with an enemy still on Roman or allied soil. Furthermore, ransom for the high-ranking prisoners held by Hannibal was denied, condemning eight thousand unfortunates to execution or a life enslaved. Rome's harsh stances towards its own continued: the legionaries who had survived Cannae were shipped in disgrace to Sicily, and banned from returning to Italy for the rest of their lives.

The main action of this novel doesn't start until 213 BC, when much of the conflict was taking place on Sicily. I had the privilege of visiting the island in March 2013, when I took in as many of the plentiful historical sites as I could. Sicily is the most remarkable place, and what can be found there equals anything on the Italian mainland. The history of conquest on Sicily stretches back nearly three thousand years. It was colonised by Greeks, which explains why the inhabitants of Syracuse and other towns spoke that tongue, and also by Carthaginians. This explains my use of Greek-spelt words, such as the River 'Anapos', rather than River 'Anapus', which is the Romanised version. The city of Akragas was not renamed Agrigento until it fell to the Romans, after the end of this novel.

By the fourth century BC, Carthage had vanquished the western third of the island. Conflict continued throughout much of the rest of Sicily, but Syracuse remained fiercely independent. During the First Punic War (264–241 BC), Syracuse's dictator Hiero took the side of the Roman Republic. He remained a loyal ally of Rome until his death, even sending soldiers to Italy to fight against Hannibal. The city's defences were renowned in ancient times; at the time of the Second Punic War, its walls were more than twenty miles in length. Archimedes really did invent various lethal engines of war, including the 'iron claw' that I described; the awesome fortifications at the still-standing Euryalus fort (Castello Eurialo) are also reputed to have been designed by him. The wheel with leather buckets that was used to raise water from a well is a fictional addition to his inventions, but such a device has been found in London and dated to Roman times, so it's not impossible that a genius like Archimedes could have built one.

If visiting Syracuse, try to see Dionysus' Ear, the site of a quarry that has been dated to the time of the city's construction. The marks of the stonemasons' chisels can be seen within it. Nearby, there is a vast altar upon which more than two hundred bulls were sacrificed around the time of the Second Punic War. Arethusa's spring, mentioned in ancient documents, is still pumping out fresh water right at the sea's edge on Ortygia, the island that forms part of central Syracuse. There you can see the only papyrus to grow in Europe.

Hippocrates, Epicydes, Marcellus, Pulcher, Pinarius and Damippus were all genuine historical characters. So too was Attalus, the man who betrayed the conspiracy to open the city's gates to the Romans. It's extraordinary that Hippocrates' and Epicydes' success in winning over the Syracusan troops near Leontini was down to the fact that the first soldiers they met were Cretan mercenary archers. They had met the brothers when they were being held as captives by Hannibal after the battle of Lake Trasimene. Hannibal's policy of freeing all non-Roman prisoners paid off in that one respect, if nowhere else. The dramatic events of the first Roman attack on Syracuse, including the 'sambucae', is attested, as is the magnitude of their defeat.

The ambush by Marcellus on Hippocrates' patrol occurred; so too did Hippocrates' flight to Akragas. The horrific events at Enna happened, in the manner that I have described. It was unusual for the Romans to admit later that the massacre might have better been avoided. Incredibly, the means of taking Syracuse came about thanks to an observant but unknown Roman soldier, who noted the height of the stone blocks at the Galeagra tower. As I described, Marcellus waited until the second night of a festival to Artemis before launching a night-time attack.

There is no direct evidence for the use of whistles in battle by Roman officers. Trumpets and other instruments were used to relay commands. Yet whistles have been found in sites all over the Empire, including in the proximity of the legionary fortress at Regensburg in Germany. In my mind, it's not too much of a jump from that to have them in the hands of centurions during a battle, as they were used by army officers in wars up until recent times.

We have the film *Ben Hur* to thank for the inaccurate depiction of drummers on warships setting the speed for the rowers. In real life, flautists or singers were used. My attempt to produce words that sounded like the Gauls' carnyxes came about after listening repeatedly to John Kenny, a modern musician, playing a modern replica of this vertical trumpet. It sounds terrifying. Listen here: http://www.youtube.com/ watch?v=NYM0xB5Jrc0.

While the graffiti I described on the wall of a tavern is made up, its style and content very much reflects that found in Pompeii and other places. Take a look at the back of some toilet doors in motorway service stations in the UK and you'll see that little has changed in two thousand years! Having my characters use the terms 'brothers' and 'boys' is quite deliberate and accurate. Roman soldiers referred to each other as *'fratres'* and a letter written by a Centurian in Britain mentioned his 'boys'.

After the loss of Syracuse to the Romans, the struggle in Sicily continued around the city of Akragas, on the southern coast. When that city fell in 210 BC, those who could fled to Carthage and beyond, and the fighting on Sicily ended. The war was far from over, however. In Iberia, the Scipios fought a bitter contest against various Carthaginian generals, and in Italy, Hannibal continued his attempts to defeat the Republic. The next volume of the series will take place in Iberia, and continue to follow the stories of Hanno, Quintus and Aurelia. I hope that you feel the need to find out what happens to them next. Before I write that tale, however, I intend to travel to Germania. In 9 AD, the Romans lost three legions in the forests there. They fell victim to a magnificently executed ambush by the local tribes. The shocking and unexpected loss had major consequences on the Empire's policy of expansion. *Eagles at War* will be the first part of a trilogy, and it will be released in the UK in early 2015.

A bibliography of the textbooks I used while writing *Clouds of War* would run to several pages, so I will mention only the most important, in alphabetical order by author: *The Punic Wars* by Nigel Bagnall; *Life and Leisure in Ancient Rome* by J. P. Balsdon; *The Punic Wars* by Brian Caven; *The Tyrants of Syracuse* by Jeff Champion; *Greece and Rome at War* by Peter Connolly; *Hannibal* by Theodore A. Dodge; *The Fall of Carthage* and *Cannae*, both by Adrian Goldsworthy; *Armies of the Macedonian and Punic Wars* by Duncan Head; *Hannibal's War* by J. F. Lazenby; *Atlas of the Greek World* by Peter Levi; *The War with Hannibal* by Livy; *Carthage Must Be Destroyed* by Richard Miles; *Daily Life in Carthage (at the Time of Hannibal)* by G. C. Picard; *The Life and Death of Carthage* by G. C. & C. Picard; *Roman Politics 220–150 BC* by H. H. Scullard, *Carthage and the Carthaginians* by Reginald B. Smith and *Warfare in the Classical World* by John Warry. My job is made easier because of Osprey Publishing and its numerous excellent volumes, Oxford University Press and its outstanding *Oxford Classical Dictionary*, and *Ancient Warfare* magazine (buy it!), which has frequent articles on the time. Thanks, as always, to the members of www.romanarmy.com, whose rapid answers to my odd questions are often of great use. I owe Christian Cameron, the superlative historical fiction author, a big 'thank you' and a few beers for help with a number of questions about ancient Greeks. For those of you who spotted Corax's ritual of snapping his sword in and out of his scabbard before battle – yes, it's a homage to Ballista, the hero of Harry Sidebottom's great *Warrior of Rome* novels. Thanks to him, and to the other members of the #JAFRA[1] 'Romani', the unofficial group of Roman (and Viking) authors, for being my colleagues and more importantly, my friends. That's you, Anthony (Tony) Riches, Russell Whitfield, Giles Kristian, Doug Jackson, Robert Fabbri, Henry Venmore-Rowland and Nick Brown. If you haven't read all of their books, you need to!

Here I need to mention the 'Romani' walk that I did in April/May 2013, along the line of Hadrian's Wall. I did it in the full kit of a Second Punic War hastatus, including hobnailed boots. It was for fun, for charity, and because three other madmen agreed to accompany me: the afore-mentioned Tony Riches and Russ Whitfield, and Dr Mike Bishop, esteemed archaeologist, author and expert on Hadrian's Wall. If you're interested in seeing photos of the walk, take a look at my Facebook pages. If you'd like to listen to a podcast of it, head to Mike's blog at: http://perlineamvalli.wordpress.com/2013/06/04/podcastella/. But I digress. I mentioned the walk for another reason. To help raise money, I was

---

1 JAFRA stands for Just Another F— Roman Author. We can 'thank' Angus 'the Hood' Donald for that soubriquet . . .

auctioning signed books, signed first editions etc. Then, for whatever reason, I decided to auction a minor character in this book. Whoever bid the largest amount would get to 'star' in *Clouds of War*. The character auction went so well, topping out at over £300, that I decided to do it with a second minor character. So when you read about Quintus' comrades Mattheus and Gaius Marius, know that they are named for, and roughly based on, a Mr Matthew Craig and a Mr Ryan Yates respectively. Together these great guys donated over £600 to charity. Thank you, Matthew and Ryan, and my apologies for killing you both! Thanks also to Robin Carter, Paul Warren and Ray Brown, for digging deep into your pockets, and helping out, on many occasions. There are a host of other generous people out there who donated or helped in various ways: they're too numerous to list, but thank you all, very much. Watch out for the Romani Walk 2014, in Italy!

I owe gratitude too to a legion of people at my publishers, Random House. There's Selina Walker, my wonderful editor, whose eagle eye keeps my work on the straight and narrow; Katherine Murphy, my expert managing editor; Kiwi extraordinaire Aslan Byrne, who gets my novels into every possible UK outlet; Jen Doyle, who devises wonderfully inventive marketing; Richard Ogle, who designs my amazing new-look jackets; Amelia Harvell, ingenious procurer of all kinds of publicity; Caroline Sloan and Nathaniel Alcaraz-Stapleton, who persuade so many foreign editors to buy my books; David Parrish, who makes sure that bookshops abroad do so too. My sincere thanks to you all. Your hard work is very much appreciated.

So many other people must be named: Charlie Viney, my agent, deserves my thanks and gratitude as always. I'm appreciative of Richenda Todd, my copy editor, whose incisive input improves my novels; Claire Wheller, my first class physio, who stops my body from falling to bits after spending too long at my PC; Arthur O'Connor, an old friend, who also supplies excellent criticism of and improvements to my stories. Massive thanks also to you, my loyal readers. It's you who keep me in a job, for which I am

Glossary

acetum: vinegar, the most common disinfectant used by the Romans. Vinegar is excellent at killing bacteria, and its widespread use in western medicine continued from ancient times until late in the nineteenth century.

Aesculapius: son of Apollo, the god of health and the protector of doctors. Revered by the Greeks, Carthaginians and Romans.

Aetolian Confederacy: a federal league between the peoples of west-central Greece. In the third century BC, this confederacy was quite powerful. In 212 or 211, the Aetolians became allies of Rome against Philip of Macedon.

agora: the central meeting area in a Greek city.

Alps: In Latin, these mountains are called *Alpes*. Not used in the novel (unlike the Latin names for other geographical features) as it looks 'strange' to modern eyes.

amphora (pl. *amphorae*): a large, two-handled clay vessel with a narrow neck used to store wine, olive oil and other produce.

Aphrodite: a Greek goddess associated with human sexuality and reproduction.

Apulia: a region of southeast Italy roughly equating to modern-day Puglia.

Artemis: an important Greek goddess associated with many things, including hunting and the rites of passage from childhood to adulthood and parenthood for both women and men.

Asklepios: the Greek spelling of Aesculapius (see above).

Athena: the Greek goddess of war.

atrium: the large chamber immediately beyond the entrance hall in a Roman house. Frequently built on a grand scale, this was the social and devotional centre of the home.

Attic helmet: a helmet type originating in Greece, which was also widely used elsewhere in the ancient world.

Baal Hammon: the pre-eminent god at the time of the founding of Carthage. He was the protector of the city, the fertilising sun, the provider of wealth and the guarantor of success and happiness. The Tophet, or the sacred area where Baal Hammon was worshipped, is the site where the bones of children and babies have been found, giving rise to the controversial and unpleasant topic of child sacrifice. For those who are interested, there is an excellent discussion of the issue in Richard Miles' textbook, *Carthage Must Be Destroyed*. The term 'Baal' means 'Master' or 'Lord', and was used before the name of various gods.

Baal Saphon: the Carthaginian god of war.

ballista (pl. *ballistae*): a two-armed Roman catapult that looked like a crossbow on a stand, and which fired either bolts or stones with great accuracy and force.

Boeotian helmet: a broad-brimmed helmet worn by Greek and Roman cavalrymen during the Second Punic War.

bouleuterion: the building in a Greek city where the *boule*, or ruling council, met.

Bruttium: the modern-day Calabrian peninsula.

caldarium: an intensely hot room in Roman bath complexes. Used like a modern-day sauna, most also had a hot plunge pool. The *caldarium* was heated by hot air which flowed through hollow bricks in the walls and under the raised floor. The source of the piped heat was the *hypocaustum*, a furnace constantly kept hot by slaves.

Campania: a fertile region of west central Italy.

Cannae: modern-day Canne della Battaglia, a site about 12 kilometres/7.5 miles west of the town of Barletta, in Apulia. It was the site of Hannibal's incredible victory over the Romans in August 216 BC.

Capua: modern-day Santa Maria Capua Vetere, near Naples, in Campania. In the third century BC, it was the second largest city in Italy and had not long been under the control of Rome.

carnyx (pl. carnyxes): a bronze trumpet, which was held vertically and topped by a bell shaped in the form of an animal, usually a boar. Used by many Celtic peoples, it was ubiquitous in Gaul, and provided a fearsome sound alone or in unison with other instruments. It was often depicted on Roman coins, to denote victories over various tribes. See also the Author's Note.

Carthage: modern-day Tunis. It was reputedly founded in 814 BC, although the earliest archaeological finds date from about sixty years later.

cenacula (pl. *cenaculae*): the miserable multi-storey flats in which ordinary Romans lived. Cramped, poorly lit, heated only by braziers, and often dangerously constructed, the *cenaculae* had no running water or sanitation. Access to the flats was via staircases built on the outside of the building.

centurion (in Latin, *centurio*): one of the disciplined career officers who formed the backbone of the Roman army. See also entry for maniple.

Cerberus: the monstrous three-headed hound that guarded the entrance to Hades.

Ceres: the Roman goddess of agriculture, grain crops and fertility.

chiton: the standard wool or linen tunic worn by Greek men.

Cisalpine Gaul: the northern area of modern-day Italy, comprising the Po plain and its mountain borders from the Alps to the Apennines. In the third century BC, it was not part of the Republic.

consul: one of two annually elected chief magistrates, appointed by the people and ratified by the Senate. Effective rulers of Rome for twelve months, they were in charge of civil and military matters and led the

Republic's armies into war. If in the field together, each man took charge of the army on alternate days. In other circumstances, each could countermand the other; both were supposed to heed the wishes of the Senate. No man was supposed to serve as consul more than once, although in practice this was not the case.

contubernium (pl. *contubernia*): a group of eight legionaries who shared a tent and who cooked and ate together.

corona muralis: a prestigious silver or gold award given to the first soldier to gain entry into a town under siege. Such awards were denied to the exiled legionaries on Sicily, hence my fictitious description of Marcellus' recognition of his men.

crucifixion: contrary to popular belief, the Romans did not invent this awful form of execution; in fact, the Carthaginians may well have done so. The practice is first recorded during the Punic wars.

cubit: an ancient unit of measurement, used by the Egyptians and Romans, among others. Depending on the civilisation, it measured between 44 and 45 cm, or 17 to 18 in.

Demeter: the Greek goddess of corn (grain, not maize), and the mother of Persephone. Together, they were the patron goddesses of Sicily. She was revered in Italy as Ceres.

didrachm: a Greek silver coin, worth two drachmas, which was one of the main coins on third century BC Sicily, and in Italy. Strangely, the Romans did not mint coins of their own design until later on. The *denarius*, which was to become the main coin of the Republic, was introduced around 211 BC.

Dionysos: the twice-born son of Zeus (see below) and Semele, daughter of the founder of Thebes. Recognised as man and animal, young and old, male and effeminate, he was one of the most versatile and indefinable of all Greek gods. Essentially, he was the god of wine and intoxication but was also associated with ritual madness, *mania*, and an afterlife blessed by his joys. Named Bacchus by the Romans, his cults were secretive, violent and strange.

drachm: a silver Greek coin. See entry for *didrachm* above.

equestrian: a Roman nobleman, ranked just below the class of senator. In the third century BC, men such as these provided the regular cavalry for the Roman army.

Eros: the Greek god of love.

Etruria: a region of central Italy, north of Rome and the homeland of the Etruscans, a people who had dominated much of north-central Italy before the rise of Rome.

extraordinarii (sing. *extraordinarius*): the pick of the Roman allied troops, a mixed force of infantry and cavalry placed at the immediate disposal of the consul. See also entry for *socii*.

falcata sword: a lethal, slightly curved weapon with a sharp point used by Hannibal's light Iberian infantry. It was single-edged for the first half to two-thirds of its blade, but the remainder was double-edged. The hilt curved protectively around the hand and back towards the blade; it was often made in the shape of a horse's head. To see an example of one, take a look at the cover of the UK paperback of *Hannibal: Enemy of Rome*. That's my sword!

flute girls: one of the numerous terms used by the ancient Greek writer Aristotle to describe prostitutes.

Fortuna: the Roman goddess of luck and good fortune. Like all deities, she was notoriously fickle.

fugitivus: a runaway slave. The Roman practice of branding the letter 'F' (for *fugitivus*) on the forehead of such unfortunates is documented; so is the wearing of permanent neck chains, which had directions on how to return the slave to his or her owner.

fustuarium: the punishment meted out to soldiers who had fallen asleep on sentry duty, or been convicted of stealing, lying, attempting to evade duty by self-inflicted wounds, or committing the same crime three times. The guilty party was beaten or stoned to death by his comrades.

Gaul: essentially, modern-day France. Gaulish warriors were renowned fighters, and many thousands of them fought in Hannibal's army.

gladius (pl. *gladii*): little information remains about the 'Spanish' sword of the Republican army, the *gladius hispaniensis*, with its waisted blade. It is not clear when it was adopted by the Romans, but it was probably after encountering the weapon during the First Punic War, when it was used by Celtiberian troops fighting for Carthage. The shaped hilt was made of bone and protected by a pommel and guard of wood. The *gladius* was worn on the right, except by centurions and other senior officers, who wore it on the left. It is quite easy to draw with the right hand, and was probably positioned in this manner to avoid entanglement with the *scutum* while being unsheathed.

Gorgon: in Greek, 'Gorgo', a mythical monster whose gaze turned people to stone. Her head was often depicted on Greek warriors' shields.

gugga: In Plautus' comedy, *Poenulus*, one of the Roman characters refers to a Carthaginian trader as a 'gugga'. This insult can be translated as 'little rat'.

Hades: to Greeks and Romans, this was the underworld – hell. The god of the underworld was also called Hades.

hastati (sing. *hastatus*): experienced young soldiers who formed the first ranks in Roman battle lines of the third century BC. They wore mail shirts, or bronze breast- and back plates, crested helmets, a single greave, and carried *scuta*. They were armed with two *pila*, one light and one heavy, and a *gladius hispaniensis*.

Herakles (to Romans, Hercules): the greatest of Greek heroes, who completed twelve monumentally difficult labours.

hetairai (sing. *hetaira*): in ancient Greek, literally 'female companions'. They were courtesans, or high-class prostitutes.

himation: an extremely large piece of wool, often embroidered. It was worn by wealthy Greek men as their main garment.

Iberia: the modern-day Iberian Peninsula, encompassing Spain and Portugal.

Illyrian: someone from Illyricum (or Illyria): the Roman name for the lands that lay across the Adriatic Sea from Italy, including parts of modern-day Slovenia, Croatia, Bosnia, Serbia and Montenegro.

Isis, Bark of: the Navigium Isidis, or Bark of Isis, was a festival held in honour of the Egyptian goddess Isis. It was celebrated on 5 March, and marked the beginning of the Roman sailing season – in other words, when it was 'safe' or propitious to begin a voyage.

Jupiter: often referred to as Optimus Maximus – 'Greatest and Best'. The most powerful of the Roman gods, he was responsible for weather, especially storms. His Greek equivalent was Zeus.

kopis (pl. *kopides*): a heavy Greek slashing sword with a forward curving blade. It was normally carried in a leather-covered sheath and suspended from a baldric. Many ancient peoples used the *kopis*, from the Greeks to the Etruscans and Persians.

kleptai (sing. *kleptes*): ancient Greek for thieves, or brigands. The word 'kleptomaniac' derives from it.

krater: a large vase used to mix wine and water in ancient Greece.

lararium: a shrine found in Roman homes, where the household gods were worshipped.

Lenaia: a Greek festival to Dionysos. Greek cities had their own calendars of festivals; we have no idea of that used by the Syracusans, so I have used a celebration attested to the Athenians.

Libyans: soldiers from Carthage's African territories. They were heavy infantry, and played important parts in many of Hannibal's famous victories.

Macedon: also known as Macedonia, a region linking the Greek peninsula and the Balkans. It was the birthplace of Alexander the Great, and at the time of the Second Punic War, it was still an independent kingdom, hostile to Rome.

maniple: the main tactical unit of the Roman army in the third century BC. There were thirty maniples in a legion, and a total of about

4,200 men. Each maniple was commanded by two centurions, one more senior than the other. There were three classes of infantry in each legion (*hastati*, *principes* and *triarii*) as well as skirmishers, or *velites* (see individual entries). Maniples of *hastati* and *principes* were composed of two centuries of sixty legionaries; forty *velites* were also attached to each unit. A maniple of *triarii*, however, was smaller. It was composed of two centuries of thirty men each, and forty *velites*.

Mars: the Roman god of war.

Melqart: a Carthaginian god associated with the sea, and with Herakles (see above). He was also the god most favoured by the Barca family.

mollis (pl. *molles*): Latin word, meaning 'soft' or 'gentle'. It's my usage to make it a term of abuse for a homosexual.

Neptune (in Latin, Neptunus): the Roman god of the sea. I've used the more modern word, as it's far easier on the ear.

obol (in Greek, *obolos*): a silver coin; six of them made a drachm.

optiones (sing. *optio*): the officers who ranked immediately below centurions; an *optio* was the second-in-command of a century.

Oscans: ancient inhabitants of much of southern Italy, most especially Campania.

Palikoi: twin gods sacred to a lake in the Sicilian interior. Traces of their sanctuary are still extant.

Persephone: Greek goddess, wife of Hades and queen of the underworld. Together with her mother Demeter (see above), she was a patron goddess of Sicily.

phalanx: the traditional tactical unit of ancient Greek armies and, it is thought, of the Libyan spearmen who fought for Carthage.

phalera (pl. *phalerae*): a sculpted disc-like decoration for bravery which was worn on a chest harness over a Roman soldier's armour. Phalerae were commonly made of bronze, but could be made of more precious metals as well.

Phoenicians: a seafaring, merchant people who lived mostly on the coastline of modern-day Lebanon. They were the founders of Carthage.

pilum (pl. *pila*): the Roman javelin. It consisted of a wooden shaft approximately 1.2 m (4 ft) long, joined to a thin iron shank approximately 0.6 m (2 ft) long, and was topped by a small pyramidal point. The javelin was heavy and, when launched, all of its weight was concentrated behind the head, giving it tremendous penetrative force. It could strike through a shield to injure the man carrying it, or lodge in the shield, rendering it impossible to use. The range of the *pilum* was about 30 m (100 ft), although the effective range was probably about half this distance.

poppy juice: the drug morphine. Made from the flowers of the opium plant, its use has been documented from at least 1,000 BC.

Poseidon: the Greek god of the sea.

Priapus: the Roman god of gardens and fields, a symbol of fertility. Often pictured with a huge erect penis.

principes (sing. *princeps*): these soldiers – described as family men in their prime – formed the second rank of the Roman battle line in the third century BC. They were similar to the *hastati*, and as such were armed and dressed in much the same manner. The *triarii* were the oldest, most experienced soldiers, and formed the third rank of the battle line. These men were often held back until the most desperate of situations in a battle. The fantastic Roman expression 'Matters have come down to the *triarii*' makes this clear. They wore bronze crested helmets, mail shirts and a greave on their leading (left) legs. They each carried a *scutum*, and were armed with a *gladius hispaniensis* and a long, thrusting spear. See also entry for maniple.

pteryges: also spelt *pteruges*. This was a double layer of stiffened linen strips that protected the waist and groin of the wearer. It either came attached to a cuirass of the same material, or as a detachable piece of equipment to be used below a bronze breastplate. Although *pteryges* were designed by the Greeks, many nations used them, including the Romans and Carthaginians.

quinquereme: the principal Carthaginian fighting vessel in the third century BC; it was also used extensively by the Romans. They were of similar size to triremes, but possessed many more rowers. Controversy over the exact number of oarsmen in these ships, and the positions they occupied, has raged for decades. It is fairly well accepted nowadays, however, that the quinquereme had three sets of oars on each side. The vessel was rowed from three levels with two men on each oar of the upper banks, and one man per oar of the lower bank. See also entry for trireme.

Samnites: the people of a confederated area in the central southern Apennines. Samnium fought three wars against Rome in the fourth and third centuries BC, losing the final one. Understandably, the Samnites did not rest easily under Roman rule. They backed both Pyrrhus of Epirus and Hannibal in their wars against the Republic.

Saturnalia: a seven-day festival held in mid-December, and one of the most important celebrations in the Roman calendar.

scutarii (sing. *scutarius*): heavy Iberian infantry, Celtiberians who carried round shields, or ones very similar to those of the Roman legionaries. Richer individuals may have had mail shirts; others may have worn leather cuirasses. Many *scutarii* wore greaves. Their bronze helmets were very similar to the Gallic Montefortino style, a type also used by Roman soldiers. They were armed with straight-edged swords that were slightly shorter than the Gaulish equivalent, and known for their excellent quality.

scutum (pl. *scuta*): an elongated oval Roman army shield, about 1.2 m (4 ft) tall and 0.75 m (2 ft 6 in) wide. It was made from two or three layers of wood, the pieces laid at right angles to each other; it was then covered with linen or canvas, and leather. The *scutum* was heavy, weighing between 6 and 10 kg (13–22 lbs). A large metal boss decorated its centre, with the horizontal grip placed behind this. Decorative designs were often painted on the front, and a leather cover was used to protect the shield when not in use, e.g. while marching. Some of the Iberian and Gaulish warriors used very similar shields.

Senate: a body of three hundred senators who were prominent Roman noblemen of the highest rank. The Senate met in central Rome, and its function was to advise the magistrates – the consuls, praetors, quaestors, etc. – on domestic and foreign policy, religion and finance.

Seres: the Roman name for the Chinese people.

socii: allies of Rome. By the time of the Punic wars, all the non-Roman peoples of Italy had been forced into military alliances with Rome. In theory, these peoples were still independent, but in practice they were subjects, who were obliged to send quotas of troops to fight for the Republic whenever it was demanded.

stade (pl. *stadia*): a Greek word. It was the distance of the original foot race in the ancient Olympic games of 776 BC, and was approximately 192 m (630 ft) in length. The word stadium derives from it.

strigil: a small, curved iron tool used to clean the skin after bathing. First perfumed oil was rubbed in, and then the strigil was used to scrape off the combination of sweat, dirt and oil.

Styx, River: the river of the underworld, Hades.

tablinum: the office or reception area beyond the *atrium*. The *tablinum* usually opened on to an enclosed colonnaded garden.

Tanit: along with Baal Hammon, the pre-eminent deity in Carthage. She was regarded as a mother goddess, and as the patroness and protector of the city.

tessera: see entry for *tesserarius*.

tesserarius (pl. *tesserarii*): one of the junior officers in a century, whose duties included commanding the guard. The name originates from the *tessera* tablet on which was written the password for the day.

Thracian: someone who originated from Thrace, a region spanning parts of modern-day Bulgaria, Romania, northern Greece and south-western Turkey. It was inhabited by more than forty warlike tribes.

Trasimene: the modern-day Lago Trasimeno, in north-central Italy, close to Perugia and Siena.

Trebia: the River Trebbia.

tribune: senior staff officer within a legion; also one of ten political positions in Rome, where they served as 'tribunes of the people', defending the rights of the plebeians. The tribunes could also veto measures taken by the Senate or consuls, except in times of war. To assault a tribune was a crime of the highest order.

trireme: the classic ancient warship, which was powered by a single sail and three banks of oars. Each oar was rowed by one man, who on Roman ships was freeborn, not a slave. Exceptionally manoeuvrable, and capable of up to 8 knots under sail or for short bursts when rowed, the trireme also had a bronze ram at the prow. This was used to damage or even sink enemy ships. Small catapults were mounted on the deck. Each trireme was crewed by up to 30 men and had around 200 rowers; it could carry up to 60 infantry, giving it a very large crew in proportion to its size. This limited the triremes' range, so they were mainly used as troop transports and to protect coastlines.

velites (sing. *veles*): Roman light skirmishers of the third century BC who were recruited from the poorest social class. They were young men whose only protection was a small, round shield and, in some cases, a simple bronze helmet. They carried a sword, but their primary weapons were 1.2-m (4-ft) javelins. They also wore wolf-skin headdresses of some kind. It's unclear if the *velites* had any officers.

Via Appia: the main road from Rome to Brundisium (modern-day Brindisi) in the far south of Italy.

Victumulae: an ancient town in the vicinity of modern-day Piacenza in northern Italy. Its exact location is unknown.

Vulcan (in Latin, Vulcanus): a Roman god of destructive fire, who was often worshipped to prevent – fire!

Zeus: the main divinity in the Greek pantheon, and god of the weather. The word 'Soter' means 'saviour', and was added to many Greek gods' names by ancient peoples. I have the wonderful author Christian Cameron to thank for the word!